SHADOW VEIL

A Cait Reagan Novel

By

Aoibh Wood

SHADOW VEIL
A CAIT REAGAN NOVEL

Aoibh Wood

This is a work of fiction. Certain long-standing locations, institutions, agencies, and public offices are mentioned, but the names, characters, events, and incidents are the products of the author's imagination. Any resemblance to actual persons, living or dead, or actual events is purely coincidental. Except for my cat. As of the first publication, he is as real and alive as can be, and awfully, awfully cute.

Copyright © 2026 Aoibh Wood

All rights reserved.

ISBN: 979-8-9921061-7-6

Carson Press, LLC

For Calvin.

CHAPTER ONE

THE FALL

Falling two thousand feet into slate flagstones was never on my to-do list.

And yet, here I was.

Shards of stone exploded and scraped across my skin, hot as coals. My wings tore free and vanished in a cloud of blackened ash as I skidded to a stop.

"Not your best landing, Cait," I muttered in agony. "Definitely gonna have road rash."

Everything hurt, and I barely registered the damp in the air, the heaviness that meant a storm was coming. Impossible. Not here.

I'd escaped Boston, run from my family to save them from me... but who would save me? Battered, alone, and probably dying, I was pretty sure this was it.

Visions crashed through my skull: jagged faces, shattered sounds, everything trying to exist at once.

People dying... just... everywhere.

I shrank inside, a spark flickering in the dark, a tick between heartbeats.

Then nothing. Time seemed to crawl until the doors split with a great moan of age and neglect.

Blood-red light spilled across the stones as six figures slipped through the gates, bare feet and boots whispering over broken rock.

Voices chattered around me.

"Sithraine! It's her."

"Check her injuries. The rest of you, bring the bier."

They weren't human. They moved like dancers wrapped in the night, eyes glinting with full-moon light.

I moaned and took in a shallow, aching breath.

A woman knelt beside me. Thickly muscled, skin like pitch, silver veins pulsing beneath it like living shimmer. Her hands were scarred across the knuckles, old burns, maybe.

"Easy," she murmured. "We've got you."

Her fingers found my pulse and then checked my neck. I felt the magic penetrate, seeking my spine, looking for breaks. Then she lifted me enough to roll me onto my side.

I screamed. Something in my shoulder was broken, shattered, maybe.

"Sorry," she whispered. "I just can't have you choking if you vomit."

"Sithraine, she's got a gash back here. It looks like she was attacked."

I remembered the flyers: dark shapes, too many wings, too many claws. More than a dozen. They fell, one after another, but each one took a piece of me with it.

My back throbbed where the last one raked me open. Warm blood. Cold air. Everything inside me burned. Something chewed at my insides, scraping through a body long past its limit.

My vision dimmed at the edges, the world tilting. I wasn't sure if I was lying still or sinking.

Another of the women swept past, footsteps whisper-soft, all silk and command. Tall, willowy, with hair that moved like it was underwater even in still air. "Vaelith, leave her and clear the debris. You three, bring it out."

The moonlight seemed to bend around them as they moved, setting a crystal coffin down next to me with a soft, hollow thump.

"Hold her."

Hands pressed to my skin, cool touches, some baby-soft, some calloused.

They lifted. I screamed in pain as the burning tore at my insides.

"Breathe. Just breathe," someone said. "This will help."

"Just let me die," I whispered.

They lowered me into the crystalline box. The lid slid closed above me and locked in place, tight and suffocating. I wanted to pound on it, but nothing in my body obeyed. I couldn't move.

The air thickened. Red light rose beneath me, threads of it creeping through crystal that curved over, needle-like, and into my arms. Frost ghosted across the inside of the lid, and a deep, penetrating cold filled me as somewhere far off, a voice shouted. The sound was muffled, like I was underwater, and gone before I could understand the words.

Then the last of the warmth drained from my limbs, and even the agony withdrew, curling back like a retreating tide.

Until darkness and silence, and a blessed emptiness surrounded me.

I floated. Untethered. A breath away from nothing.

For how long I had no way to know, but it was soft, and so peaceful.

Then—a shift. Subtle at first, like the air itself had taken a breath. A pressure, small as a fingertip on my sternum, but enough to snag me where I drifted. To pull me back.

The visions were gone, and there was an unnatural stillness, as if the air itself were just hanging there.

The lid had been shoved askew, enough for light to slice through the dark and spill across my face. My eyelids fluttered open, and the world ignited.

Brilliant red light, too bright to exist, like the scream of a banshee made visible.

And she was there.

The Morrigan hovered in the blaze, wings outstretched, feathers dripping shadow and flame. Her face was every face I had ever loved, every terror I had ever dreamed. My mind couldn't hold her. It splintered trying.

"Help me." The words barely made it out.

Something inside me caught fire, not the burn of my curse,

which I now understood was consuming me alive, but something deeper. A spark of what I'd been before. Heat surged through my body, clawing upward from my legs, and I understood with terrible clarity: she wasn't destroying me. She was unmaking me.

My eyes burned, sight searing away, the price of looking at her, of witnessing what mortal eyes were never meant to see. I tried to close them, but there was no time.

The resulting howl of agony never emerged as my mouth was torn asunder.

She pulled me apart at the seams. Every vein, every nerve, every cell that the vampire curse had twisted, she found the rot and burned it out. Bones cracked, melted, reformed. She reshaped me into some alien pattern.

I felt every second of it.

Then darkness rushed in, absolute and eternal.

The light died. The pain didn't. It lingered like a brand.

I lay in the half-open coffin, blind and trembling. Remade into something I didn't understand.

The Morrigan's voice slid into my mind—every comforting and terrible voice I'd ever heard woven into one.

"You aren't strong enough to defend Shaddan, child."

The words struck like a blow. If not that, what was I? Who?

"You will correct the course that was set."

"I can't see," I mumbled, fumbling along the coffin's edge.

"You won't need eyes," she said. "You are perfect for purpose."

An icepick of terror slid into my gut. Perfect for purpose?

"What does that mean?" I whispered.

She didn't answer, but whatever wrongness she'd inflicted on me this time was still happening. I could feel it. Something was changing inside me, something complete and fundamental. Dizziness snatched at me, and my stomach reeled. My breath grew faint and then just... a haze, words, lights, and time.

CHAPTER TWO
WHAT'S LEFT OF ME

I woke in darkness. Complete, suffocating darkness. Not the kind that comes with closed eyes—the kind that doesn't end when you open them.

Blind. It was all real.

I felt… odd. I wasn't in pain, but the memory of it was clear enough. My skin itched with it.

"You are not alone." It was a woman's voice, deep and nearly rough, and yet softened by a careful, unmistakable kindness.

"Vaelith?" Just a guess from my hazy memory, the one who turned me over.

"Yes." Her voice didn't lift or fall. It was just… an answer.

"I don't feel right," I whispered. Everything in me trembled; everything was wrong.

"I bet not," she said with a little laugh. "Who would after what you've endured?"

She pressed a bowl to my lips. Hot broth. Salt. Chicken. Not blood.

It tasted good, but so bland. I ran my tongue along my teeth and mouth, trying to place what felt wrong.

My vomeronasal duct was gone. My tongue wasn't forked anymore. And my teeth—my canines—were long, inhuman. Not vampire fangs. They were static and unmoving. Fae teeth. Feral teeth.

Mother of Waters. It was like waking up in an entirely new body, and yet... not. I felt strange, as if I'd been trapped in time, the vampiric curse keeping me perfectly fixed. Not alive. Not dead. Just frozen.

And now? Now I could feel the life inside me. Where the vampire had been cold... the Fae burned. My soul burned. I could literally feel it.

There was no way to describe it.

"How long?" I asked.

"Two hundred fifty-eight days," she said softly.

Months. Months just carved away, and I couldn't remember any of it.

I lifted a shaking hand toward my face but stopped halfway. "Is it bad?"

Vaelith hesitated, obviously trying to choose her words, maybe be kind. When she spoke again, her voice held that low warmth, rough around the edges. She'd seen battle... the worst of it. I could just tell.

"Your eyes are just... deeper, a sea of stars amid a black void. Beautiful, and dangerous in the way truth can be. Humans will meet your gaze, and their minds will buckle under what they see in themselves. It will drive them to madness."

My throat tightened, and fear froze my chest. "What am I?" I whispered. It sounded desperate—or terrified.

She stepped forward and sat on the edge of the bed, positioning herself between me and the door. It was a protective instinct, like those nights when Katie slept in my bed.

"You're Faerie," she said softly. "Dark Fae, burned down to what was always there. A mirror of your own soul." Her hand brushed back a bit of hair over my ear. "You are touched now. A child of her judgment. There have been others."

I could barely breathe. "Others?"

"Yes." Her voice lowered and turned so gentle, like sound alone might break me. "No one knows why Mother Morrigan chooses them, or how. Only those who survive seeing her are marked. They always go blind... though the reason for that, we can only guess. And the gifts she leaves behind?" She shook her head. "Sometimes they're power. Sometimes they're nothing at all. There's no pattern anyone's found—no mercy either."

She let the words sink in as the rain began, a slow tapping beyond the wards.

"It's forever?"

"Yes. But you'll adjust. This isn't the first time I've seen it. It happened to a friend a long time ago."

"Did she adjust?"

"Yes, Your Grace, she did." And there was a soft smile in her voice. "Try to remember. You're here. You're awake. And you still have your mind. That puts you ahead of most."

The rain continued like a pattering heartbeat. Rain. Here. It was mind-boggling. And I had changed too—was still changing. Not Human. Not Vampire. Fae... Dark Fae. Like my mother.

One would think I'd know what that meant, but I didn't. I'd never understood that half of me.

Vaelith took the bowl and set it aside, then she brushed a hand through my hair.

"Just rest. It'll take a little time."

With that, she left me.

I tried to sleep. I did. But sleep never really came.

Later, I heard something—a scrape, and the whisper of soft shoes on stone.

A knock accompanied by a woman's voice, ethereal and beautiful, almost sensual. "Your Grace, can I assist you with a bath and dressing?"

I tried to sit up. Then fumbled uselessly with the pillows in my blind, weak state. It was pointless. Finally giving up, I sighed, "Name?"

"I am Sithraine," she said, walking around the bed and adjusting the pillows for me.

"You're Nerin?"

"I am. We were left here to guard the palace and periodically ensure its integrity. There are six of us. Though I did meet your little science project—Maggie, isn't it? She's... interesting. Or at least she is now that I helped her recover her mind."

The way she said *science project* told me exactly what she thought of what I'd done. And she wasn't wrong. But I couldn't fix it, so I let it drop. Besides, Mother Morrigan had done the same thing to me. Justice had been served.

"The Morrigan, she told me that I'd correct the course that was set."

"Exactly that?" Sithraine asked. There was something in her tone, almost worried, but I couldn't really tell. If only I could see her.

A long silence ensued before her weight settled on the bed next to me. She took my hand. The touch was cool and soft, not at all the cold I expected from such a creature.

I nodded. "There were other things. She said I was... perfect for purpose. What does that even mean? What does any of it mean?"

"Few beings ever understand the Morrigan," Sithraine replied. "Meaning tends to arrive only after the damage is done."

"That's what I'm afraid of."

"Your Grace, if I may..." A gentle squeeze of my hand.

I nodded, and she helped me to my feet. My legs wobbled, and I reached for her shoulder, finding solid strength beneath my fingers.

Sithraine spoke as she unwound the bandage from my eyes. "You did what you had to do. Perhaps those you left behind won't understand... but I do. We do. And it saved your life.

"The Morrigan is a chaotic thing off-world. She takes what she wants without concern, burns down what she wishes, twists what she must. All in a desperate need to be in commune with Mother Shaddan."

8

The implication shocked me to my core. "I can't leave?"

"No," Sithraine said. She paused, voice softer now. "Her power would burn you to cinders, and that's not a metaphor. When you arrived, your soul was unraveling, slow and silent as a candle left too close to its end. Your body was at its limit. Another day, perhaps only hours more, and you would've flickered out entirely or been consumed."

"Out." I echoed. It was a horrifying thought. No soul... no more me. Just gone.

Then something else occurred to me. "Do I still look like me?" I asked. Not desperate—not really. Just... checking. Well... maybe a little desperate. "I mean, do I look like I did when I... landed?"

Sithraine huffed a laugh. "What you did was hardly what I'd call landing."

I laughed miserably. "No, I suppose not."

"But yes," she continued, gentler now. "You look very much like yourself."

Her fingers brushed the side of my face, tucking back a strand of hair.

"Your eyes have changed, of course." Her thumb traced the sharp curve of my ear—newly pointed, unmistakably Fae. "And these."

"I wonder what Liz will think," I murmured, mostly to myself.

Sithraine squeezed my hand. "I assume you mean Elizabeth. You spoke her name during your... incapacity."

Incapacity. I snorted. She meant the empty void I'd apparently been trapped in after my Snow White moment with the death goddess.

"I don't know her," Sithraine went on. "So I can't speak to her feelings. But I can tell you this."

She adjusted the blanket around my shoulders.

"You are High Fae, Your Grace. Crown Princess. Perhaps even our next Queen, depending on how events unfold. You are next in line to the Vermilion Seat..."

A breath. Then, simply, "... and you are beautiful. No woman would look at you and lose heart."

"Come," Sithraine said. "Let's get you cleaned up."

As she led me from the bed, I felt the prickle on my skin, the magic wafting off of her. I hesitated, shifting my perception, wanting to see what it was. But there was just static, so I let it slip away—useless.

"I can't use my magic anymore." My voice was low and hoarse. "It's gone. All I see are vast waves of color and static, like trying to tune a radio station that doesn't exist anymore."

"The Weave will return in time," Sithraine said, releasing my arm and helping me from my nightgown. "As will your command of it."

"How do you know?" I asked, unable or perhaps unwilling to just accept her at her word.

"Your Grace," Sithraine admonished gently, taking my arm again and guiding me up the steps.

I stumbled, catching my foot on the edge of the tub, but Sithraine caught me easily, steadying me as I lowered myself, trembling, into the hot water.

"I was old before The Sundering," she said, her voice calm. "Trust me. I know." She took my hand. "Stand, please."

I stood. My legs wobbled again as if they weren't *my* legs. I likely couldn't make the toilet without help.

I'd done this to myself, as always.

I'd chosen the army. Chosen to go to war. Chosen the badge. Homicide, of all things.

It was as if I were bound and determined to press my hands into the bloody prints of every nightmare humanity had to offer. At every fork in the road, I'd taken the one paved in gasoline and struck the match.

And then I'd given myself over to The Morrigan in Boston.

"I'm a monster," I whispered.

"Don't flatter yourself."

She guided me back into the water with a firm hand between my shoulders. No comforting cooing. No soft words. Just action. She stepped away, the hiss of running water filling the silence, then returned and pressed a cold cloth to the back of my neck.

I sucked in a breath at the shock.

"There. Much better," she said, approval clicking in her tongue. "Now listen closely. You can't save anyone if you don't believe you deserve to live."

I didn't have an answer to that. Just a question leaking out of me: "Who am I supposed to save?"

"I have no idea, Your Grace. That's your problem to sort through later. What you will not do is sit here flagellating yourself like some tragic martyr. It's tired, and I refuse to indulge it."

"Yes, ma'am," I whispered like a scolded schoolgirl.

"Now, out," she said flatly. Then she added like an afterthought, "Your Grace."

I reached for the rim of the tub, feeling my way along the edge as I stood and climbed out. My foot slipped, and I cracked my shin hard against the stone. Pain flared, and I bit back a curse, shaking my head.

Sithraine steadied me again, grasping me tightly under the arm.

"Easy," she murmured.

I clenched my jaw. *Fucking helpless.*

She dried me and dressed me in a soft wrap dress with a low neckline and tight sleeves, fastened with a leather strap and fabric belt. She styled my hair into loose waves and tied a silk blindfold over my eyes. Knee-high boots slid on easily.

As I felt the fabric, my fingers brushed the brand over my breast—the Valtárí mark, still there even after everything. Even after the Morrigan tore me apart and put me back together. Some scars, apparently, were permanent. I yanked my hand away.

"Your dress is black with the Vermilion Court's three moons on the hem," Sithraine said. "The sash and blindfold are deep purple. It suits you."

I managed a small smile. "Not much for dresses."

She ignored that entirely. "Would you like a crown? We have several."

"Absolutely not."

She laughed—a warm, breathy sound that tugged a smile from me. "I think I'll enjoy serving you."

"Is that required?" I asked.

"No. We volunteered."

"And where are the rest of the Nerin?" I asked, fastening the boot. The leather felt strange, luxurious. "Please don't tell me there are only six."

"No. They're scattered," she said. "They'll likely return now."

I nodded. I didn't have the heart to tell her I was nobody's savior.

Once I was dressed, she stepped back, giving my hand a quick squeeze.

"Well?" I asked. "How do I look?"

She considered me for a moment. "Terrible as the night," she answered.

The words were playful—mostly.

CHAPTER THREE
THE WEIGHT OF THE VEIL

Sithraine led me from my room into the palace proper. I thought about counting the paces to keep track of where I was, but no—I needed to learn myself first. There would be time for memorizing the exits later. I was stuck here for now.

My footsteps were light, nearly weightless—more suggestion than sound. I wasn't sure if it was the shoes or something deeper that had been rewired. I used to move like a soldier, all grounded force and blunt certainty. Now everything about me felt unnervingly fluid. Steps didn't land; they glided. My body had changed too—narrower waist, wider hips, weight distributed differently across my chest. But it wasn't just shape. I moved through the world like water now, not stone.

The air was cool on my skin. The corridor stretched empty around us—really empty. No muffling carpets, no furniture, no drapes, nothing to soften the echo of our passing. Just stone and space.

I held onto Sithraine's arm, fingers brushing the fine fabric of her sleeve, my shoulder grazing hers now and then. But there was something else—something like a pressure in the air between us. A presence I could track even without touching her.

Maybe I was imagining it, but I didn't think so. It felt like a new sense. But I didn't *know*. I suddenly realized I didn't know anything anymore. Worse—I never had. Just half-truths and guesses dressed up as certainty.

My hearing was more acute, though. That much I knew. Things weren't louder, they were just... perfectly clear. And what it told me? This place was barren.

"Why is it so empty?" I asked. "Palace of queens, high ladies, unpronounceable titles... You'd think someone would've left a couch."

"There is no one else here, Your Grace," Sithraine said.

"Well, don't sugarcoat it for me," I snorted.

She didn't answer that.

Not a word.

We'd been walking down the same corridor for a long time when I finally asked where we were.

"The main east-west gallery. It runs across the entire palace on the eighth floor. We'll be making a right-hand turn here shortly to one of the dining rooms."

I arched an eyebrow, finding the skin around it a bit tight. "One of?"

"Thousands lived here before the cataclysm," then, with a bit of dry wit, she added, "It's a big place, Your Grace."

"Wow." I couldn't keep the awe out of my voice, and an ache of disappointment filled my chest that I'd never be able to see it.

Moments later, the smell of old stone gave way to something warmer: bread, coffee, the tang of bacon cooking. We rounded a corner to several women's voices.

"She's going to be another Maura."

"You don't know that."

"She's a single bearer. They all go insane—"

As I entered the room, a pall fell over the conversation.

"Your Grace," a voice said, high and light. Like Sithraine, it had that same undercurrent of something cold. "I'm Nyxiel. Would you like breakfast?"

"Please," I said, my voice a bit shaky—with hunger, I realized. When was the last time I'd actually eaten a meal and not just broth? I had no idea.

Sithraine led me to a seat and helped me get situated.

Nyxiel disappeared somewhere to my right and then returned a moment later. Something thumped lightly onto the table in front of me.

The scent of coffee curled into the air, and something in my chest cracked open. My softer emotions as a vampire had been subdued, muted—but as Fae, they crashed through me like weather. I almost cried—over coffee.

"Goddess bless you," I whispered.

"You're welcome, Your Grace," Nyxiel said, disappeared again, and then set a plate and silverware in front of me.

"Toast, Eggs, and Bacon," she said. "Eat up."

I didn't stand on ceremony—just did my best to eat without making a mess.

After a long silence, Sithraine's voice cut in. "We could do with introductions around the table."

I nodded.

A woman with a deep voice spoke first. "Vaelith. We've met."

Right, a soldier.

Next came a crisp, almost clerical alto. "Morvaine. Keeper of the Shadow Veil. A priestess of sorts, devoted to the Three and to Mother Morrigan. I maintain our spells and tune the wards."

"The Shadow Veil?" I asked, but they ignored me and went on.

Elarith and Naerith followed—twins, apparently shaped by one of my ancestors, Maura, in the same way I had remade Maggie. I couldn't tell them apart by voice; something else to get used to. They were thrilled with my arrival, since they could get back to what they were trained for: spycraft.

Finally, Nyxiel sat beside me. "I just keep everyone entertained," she said.

"Is that what you do?" Vaelith asked dryly. "I thought you just brought gossip."

I tilted my head slightly. "Gossip? From where? Earth?"

Then Nyxiel spoke, abruptly changing the subject.

"Maggie returned to Earth, but she left something for you." She slid a small wooden box into my hands.

I knew what it was, and even through the surface, I could feel the foul energy inside. I pushed it away. "Could you just put it on a shelf in my room, please?"

"Certainly," Nyxiel said.

"Did she say anything about Liz?" I asked, trying to keep my voice steady. "And Aoife?"

"No, but Ms. Medlyn and your sister are fine," Nyxiel said.

I took a deep breath. "Good. That's good." A few minutes passed while I tried to make my heart behave. I needed a distraction. Anything. So, I let my voice go light, like it didn't matter. "Hey, what's the Shadow Veil, anyway?"

Silence. And not the casual kind, not the distracted lull of a morning conversation. This was pointed silence.

I set my mug down carefully, listening. The faintest scrape of someone shifting in their chair. A mug moved.

I added an edge to my voice and tapped a finger against the tabletop. "Well?"

"Your Grace has barely recovered," Sithraine said. "Perhaps later…"

"Perhaps now." Almost an order this time, if a polite one. I was "Your Grace" after all.

Morvaine gave something close to a resigned sigh. "Your Grace." A pause. Then, a measured, careful, "It's probably easier if we just show you."

The Nerin all stood and led me on a long walk through the palace. They were silent as the grave, saying nothing. I couldn't think of anything to talk about, so I simply sipped my coffee along the way.

"Where are we going?" I said eventually. We'd been walking for a good long while.

"Down to the Veil," Morvaine said as she took my arm from Sithraine and helped me down a set of spiral stairs—a long set.

We walked down eight floors to the ground and then two more levels below. It was slow going in my blind state, but they were patient, which was both appreciated and grating.

Off the staircase, we entered a room where the echoes were tighter—a smaller space than the grand hallways. Much smaller. Round, maybe.

Something in it immediately disturbed the very core of me. A humming. If I'd had to describe it, I'd have called it a mangled note, as if a piano wire could be both tangled in loose loops and pulled taut to produce something devastatingly off. The wrongness of it filled my head and tugged at my insides.

My senses twisted violently—that new sixth sense seizing like a muscle cramp. The mug jerked from my hand as if yanked by invisible fingers, shattering against the wall instead of the floor.

Still, though, I stepped forward, hand out, moving closer to the sickening emanations. I wanted to feel it—to understand. I had to know what it was. It was a compulsion, clear as day. But I didn't resist, and no one stopped me.

"This is it?" I asked, instinctively knowing my fingers were a hair's breadth away.

"Yes," Morvaine said, seemingly unaffected.

My fingertips finally landed on smooth, faceted crystal. The power pulsing beneath was immense, raising the hair on my arm. And it felt... nauseating. I backed away and swallowed before my breakfast came up.

"It's..." I shivered. "Awful. Twisted and wrong."

"It's not natural," Morvaine said. "And we used the same magic Mother Darkness uses to create her minions to create... it."

"It's a soulstone," I breathed, suddenly understanding. "What's inside?"

"Remnants," Morvaine said, her voice cool and detached.

I didn't know what she meant, decided I didn't want to know. Something inside that massive crystal was not quite alive, but not quite dead. A thing, amorphous and hungry, from my most terrifying nightmares.

Morvaine continued, as if blithely unaware of the horror

they'd constructed. "It keeps Mother Darkness here on Shaddan, anchoring her."

I swallowed, trying to forget the feeling that enfolded me. Then a thought struck me. "The fog. The mass of fog around her."

For the first time since I noticed my weird sixth sense, I felt movement. A nod, maybe, as Sithraine answered. "It's a manifestation of the Veil."

"I can't stay here," I whispered as my stomach churned.

"Yes, Your Grace," Sithraine said, and we left the small chamber, heading back up the stairs.

I was glad to be out of it, as my nausea had been steadily rising just from the awful emanations. Even so, my breakfast came up as soon as we reached the first-floor landing.

Nyxiel whispered in my ear as she pulled back my hair. "Are you okay?"

I nodded quickly and swallowed. "I will be. It's just—it's everything."

"Once you destroy her, we can dispose of it," Morvaine said.

I retched again, then responded in a hoarse voice. "Destroy her? I wouldn't even know where to start. And besides, how can I?" I gestured at my eyes. "I'm blind. I can't fix this."

I couldn't do it. I just couldn't. I'd fought more than I should have. I had nothing left to give—no strength, no courage, just the hollow echo of both. I wasn't just tired. I was afraid—and alone.

"Your Grace," Nyxiel said, resting a hand on my shoulder. "It's all right. Your sister can help. And we're here—"

"What?!" My voice cracked, sharp and wild. I stumbled back, arms flailing for a wall that wasn't there. "You're not getting it! I don't want help! Help with what? I can't fucking do this anymore!"

Tears burned my eyes. I folded in on myself, arms tight around my ribs, the world spinning. My heel slipped on the stone step—but strong hands caught me before I could fall.

I clung to them, desperate. "I just can't," I whispered. "I'm not that person anymore. I destroy everything I touch..." The words fell apart in my throat.

The silence after that was unbearable. Why were they always so quiet? So damned quiet.

I barely noticed that someone—Vaelith, maybe—was still holding me upright. Then a sharp pain cut through my skull, and I pressed my hands to my temples. Breath gone.

Voices murmured—too far away to make sense.

And then I was falling into the dark.

I woke again in my bed—in my room. Someone had removed my boots.

"I understand," Vaelith said, very nearby, startling me. Her voice was low and quiet.

"There were wars here once, long before the cataclysm. Only Sithraine and I remember them. I fought against the Vermilion Court for ages—campaign after campaign, until I stopped counting. You think you'll be a hero, and then one day you're just… tired. You've seen enough death to know victory doesn't mean much. Even we Nerin crack eventually. At some point, you have to stop."

I swallowed, the heat of tears pressing at my eyes. "And the others?"

She shifted. A shrug, maybe?

"They're afraid. They've pinned their hopes on you—not because you're the strongest or destined or any of that rot. Just because there's been no one else for so long."

Her voice softened. "I know how unmoored you must feel. You were remade. I was there. Your soul was fading—because of that fucking curse. So, Mother Morrigan did the only thing she could. She respun your existence from the dying threads."

A small, bitter laugh escaped her. "The Dark Gift. Ridiculous. It's a horrible curse. Under Shaddani law, it's a crime. Did you know that?"

I nodded. "I know."

"Do you know why?"

"No," I said. "My mother never really said. She only told me that spinning that curse onto a Fae soul could have unpleasant consequences."

Vaelith snorted, sounding almost amused. "Unpleasant consequences. That's a new one. What she should have told you is that it's lethal. Vampirism is a wasting disease for all Faerie. For a short time, it gives you tremendous strength, increased speed—all the benefits of being one of the undead. But eventually, you just... burn out."

"But my mother told Marcella to turn me," I said.

"Then she obviously didn't much care for you," Vaelith said, a sliver of anger entering her voice.

I was taken aback. Of all the things I thought about my mother, that she didn't care about me was never one of them. Still, though, had she engineered all this, or had she just been trying to save me from what she'd seen?

"I think she did it because of a vision she had," I replied, but my voice was uncertain.

"Maybe," Vaelith whispered. "She was known for her visions of the future. And it probably kept your human body from being consumed by Mother Morrigan, at least temporarily. Still, cursing a Faerie soul? It's an insane risk."

She quieted for a moment, and then when she spoke again, her voice was full of passion. "I won't pretend to understand Her Majesty's motives. But, Your Grace, we treasure the soul. It is the one thing that is forever. And twisting a curse upon it? One that could destroy it? It's an abomination.

"Regardless, I know you're hurting and that all this must seem terribly unfair. But you need to understand, Mother Morrigan found you worthy of life. It doesn't matter what you've lost. She saved you."

"Saved me?" I scoffed miserably. "She blinded me, broke me. You just said it yourself."

But even as the words spilled out, I realized it wasn't true. Mother Morrigan had spared my life. And now it was up to me to pick up the pieces—if I could.

I pulled my knees up to my chest and hugged them, a hollow feeling in my heart. She was right. It felt unfair, but knowing I'd earned every bit of it was so much worse.

Vaelith was quiet for a moment, then continued, her voice softer, gentler. "You may feel weak, but we Faerie are powerful. And resilient. You'll recover. You will heal very quickly. Your reserves of magic and strength come from the very world around you, not from the blood or souls of others. And your soul is luminous—it burns bright. Mother Morrigan made you into something just as strong in its own way as you ever were."

"And my eyes?"

"Bad luck. That's all."

I heard her move, and she slid onto the bed next to me, pulling me close to lean on her shoulder.

"Still, though, you've been through enough. Let it go. Forget about the others. They don't have to live your life. And a life of constant war and pain is no life at all. If you never fight another battle, it's okay."

I leaned into that shoulder. It was muscular and strong, and her arms were surprisingly warm.

The tears didn't start immediately.

Not until I heard it.

Yes, Dorogaya. You can rest… for now. I still love you.

I swallowed hard. It was the grief talking, hovering in my heart and making me hear things. But still, it sounded like her, like Nastasia.

It undid me, and the tears came in a torrent.

Vaelith, blessedly, said nothing.

She just held me and let me cry.

CHAPTER FOUR

DEFINITELY, ABSOLUTELY, STILL ME

I recovered slowly, and for the first time in… ever, I had time. A month here wasn't even a day on Earth. Plenty of room to pretend nothing was waiting for me on the other side.

I avoided any news from home, not out of willpower—out of sheer, gut-level cowardice. I wasn't ready to hear her name, or the kids' names, or anything that might pull me back into the wreckage I'd left behind.

So I just… didn't look.

Didn't ask.

Didn't let myself think too hard.

Instead, I breathed. Lived. Let myself become something new, or at least something not actively falling apart.

And I stayed occupied.

Days became weeks. Weeks became months.

Time passed in a quiet blur as Vaelith whipped me into shape with drills that left muscles I'd forgotten I had screaming. Morvaine adopted me in the library—her natural domain—guiding me through endless shelves and plucking down whatever she thought might distract me from myself. She even found me a transcription rod: a long, brass wand etched with filigree that read aloud in a voice eerily like my mother's—cool, amused, and perfectly condescending.

I absorbed everything it spoke. Stories. Histories. Spells.

The spells. I devoured them. Book after book.

And the more I read, the more the magic inside me stirred. Sithraine had been right. Once I stopped panicking long enough to reach for it, the threads of the Weave began to answer me again—patient, familiar, like they'd been waiting this whole time.

Before, I'd known almost nothing structured. A few tricks. The rest had been raw, volatile power. Now I was learning how to control the world around me, the elements, the very essence of a person's perception, their minds. It was like I couldn't stop.

Then, somewhere in the stacks, Morvaine found something stranger.

A thin, battered tome tucked between glamourcraft treatises. Inside was an esoteric ritual couched in a story so unapologetically Dark Fae I could practically hear its evil laugh. It described how to replace a human heart with a thistle so they'd never feel the ache of lost love again. The thistle numbed everything—grief, longing, hope.

I recoiled and shoved the book away... for a time. But it called to me. Pulled at me. And eventually, I found myself reaching for it again.

It was probably nonsense. It had to be. Didn't it?

But it was haunting, tragic, poetic. Just reading it, I felt that same dark magic coil up in my breast, waiting like a snake, tensing to strike, followed by a delicious ache for something I didn't have a name for.

And it felt good—too good, like the tiny intake of breath just before the first touch of sex, or the moment I press the blade to someone's neck in combat. I flushed, looked around, and kept reading. I couldn't not.

I could imagine it so clearly: a hollow-eyed maiden kneeling before me, begging for the heart of the one she loves. I give her the price: her own heart, still beating. She offers it willingly. I pluck it out, press a thistle into the cavity, and glamour her beloved into loving her back.

It was a perfect tragedy: a love the maiden could never return, a lover receiving cold devotion, a hollow triumph.

And me, the capricious Queen, tying mortal lives into pretty knots just because I could.

Honestly, it read like something pulled straight from an Irish fairy tale—dark and gorgeous and doomed.

I loved it.

And that was the part that unnerved me. I wanted to try it. Almost desperately.

That's how it went: drills, books, and the slow work of becoming someone who didn't feel like a live grenade.

And though the library had turned into a hunting ground for more of those predatory spells, it was where I felt most alive.

Still, sleep was cruel.

I woke one night, gasping, drenched in sweat. The bandage that had covered my eyes lay twisted around my neck. My arms were locked tight across my chest. I'd been running again —along the Esplanade, beside the Charles River, chased by another nightmare. Another night of the dragon.

The phantom weight of a child still clung to me—warmth curled against my ribs, tiny fingers clutching my shirt. In the dream, I had screamed until my throat gave out. But the fire came anyway. She burned in my arms.

My hands clenched the sheets, the fabric twisting beneath my fingers as if I could wring away the horror. A sob tore out of me—raw and ragged and useless. No one came running. The room was empty. Just me and the ghosts I'd made.

I sat there, rocking myself for a long time, obsessing.

Had there been someone? A child far below? Caught in the chaos?

No. No, I hadn't seen anyone. But there had been people, I was sure. It was possible.

I squeezed my hands again, my fingers digging into the plush down of the duvet.

It had been so real, so... world-ending.

I had to get up.

I couldn't do this—just lie here, my mind circling through horrible thoughts.

Quietly, I stripped and ran myself a bath. It took a few minutes of fiddling with the faucet. The controls were strange, more levers than knobs.

While I sat in the water, breath still ragged, something else threaded through the horror and anxiety. A quiet, terrible calm. Not relief, exactly. Just… distance. Like I was watching myself tremble in pain. Like grief was just an old habit, and my heart was already learning to outgrow it.

I hated that disconnect. But some new part of me? It didn't mind at all.

Afterward, I dressed, and, with a bit of fumbling about, finally found my boots on the far side of the bed.

I slipped them on… and paused.

An emotion inside me thrummed suddenly as I thought about Liz and her dazzling smile. She'll come. She always comes. And the accompanying feeling? Anticipation.

Like she wasn't just coming to me—but belonging to me. Like I wanted her here, vulnerable and unmoored. Easy to keep. Easy to fold into this new, glittering world I was learning to command—whether she understood it or not.

The thought horrified me.

Or it should have.

Instead, it curled right up alongside the dark magic poised in my chest—content, coiled, and waiting.

I shivered. With what, though? I had no idea.

"You are perfect for purpose." The Morrigan's words rose in my head. I was still changing—transforming into… this. Whatever this was, it wasn't finished.

And maybe I should have fought it.

I just… didn't.

Hands out in front of me, I made my way to the door and into the long promenade that bisected the palace.

Everything was so still, and yet it was as if the palace itself had come alive. Something had changed while I slept, but I wasn't sure if it was in the palace or me. I could feel things, a humming all around that prickled my skin. And there was a tug in my chest, almost pulling me forward.

I tried to maintain a straight path right down the middle of the corridor, but it was useless. Without guidance, I just kept walking into the walls, unable to judge the distance. The silence of my footfalls was partly to blame. The rest was just, well, being blind.

"Come here, young one." The voice was deep and resonant and seemed to come from everywhere. *Yeah, not at all menacing.*

I stopped cold, my right hand still against a wall. "Hello?"

No response, but I was sure I'd heard it.

"Hello?"

Still nothing, and then a rumble, almost like... like a yawn. Abruptly, I went from a bit creeped out to irritated.

"Whoever is in here," I called. "Just come out and quit fucking around."

"Take the next right and then down the stairs." A glimmer of a smile in the deep bass.

I scowled. "Fine."

Pursing my lips, I took the next right turn and down yet another wall until it stopped at a wide, echoing open space. Not a damn thing for my hands to follow.

"Shit," I swore.

"Down the stairs, young one," the voice said.

It definitely wasn't in my head. I could feel it now—not just hear it. A resonance in my chest, in my bones. Like the stone itself was speaking.

I slid a foot forward slowly. And then another. Until I found the edge of a stair.

Feeling about as stupid as I probably looked, I walked, lopsided, along the first step to the right-hand wall. Of course, there wasn't even a handrail.

"Mother of Waters, this place isn't designed for the fucking disabled."

The staircase descended in slow switchbacks, each landing a waiting trap. No kinesthetic sense, no guide. Just me and the never-ending risk of plummeting into eternity. Every turn, I had to sweep my hands out, tracing the empty space for the next drop. It was maddening—and insultingly slow.

"Take your time." Sarcasm this time.

"I'm coming," I snapped, nearly missing the next step. "Maybe take pity on a girl and come up to me."

"Not possible," it replied, drawling like a lazy cat. "First floor. Door to your right. About twenty paces. Smaller than the others. Open it. Follow the passage down. Watch your step."

I sighed loudly—purposefully. Whoever this was, they were going to get every ounce of my patience—wrung like a rag.

Yeah, it might be a trap. But Morvaine and Sithraine swore the wards were solid. If they'd missed something lethal, I'd haunt them. Hard.

Still, every instinct screamed wrong when I hit the first floor.

My hand found the door—a narrow thing, recessed and short, like a supply closet. The knob sat in the middle of it, old iron that squealed under my grip. I pressed my palm to the surface.

Warm. Too warm.

I opened it. A blast of heat rolled over me. Heavy, humid, laced with the faint scent of gasoline.

"What the hell," I whispered.

Then the floor disappeared.

My foot slid down into nothing. A spiral stair barely two feet wide pitched under me. I clung to the doorframe, fingers white-knuckled, chest tight with the sudden drop.

Sightless. Off-balance. Breath frozen halfway between a gasp and a curse.

A deep laugh rumbled from below, much, much louder than before. "I told you to watch your step. Are you blind?"

That was it. I'd had enough.

"Yes!" I yelled. "I'm fucking blind, okay?! I can't see. I have no idea where I'm going, and you—whatever you are—are starting to piss me off."

"Oh." The word was thoughtful, as if it hadn't even considered the possibility. Then it said, sounding rather contrite, "My apologies, Your Grace. I was unaware."

So it knew who I was. I couldn't decide if that was good or bad. But the tug I'd felt in my chest on the eighth floor had grown. And I didn't think it was the thing that had called me. The pull felt like something from inside. I didn't know how I knew. I just did.

The stairs weren't cut; they were worn, ancient and treacherous. Each step crumbled under my feet. The descent spiraled and twisted, winding down like a snake deep beneath the ground until finally, mercifully, I hit a flat landing.

I wasn't in the palace anymore. I was under the mountain. The Sorrowed Majesty, Sithraine had said it was called.

Just the thought of thirty thousand feet of rock pressing down was a little uncomfortable.

"The way is clear from here," the voice said—and it was booming, echoing like a thunderclap in what I could only assume was a large chamber or cave.

The floor wasn't paved with stone but rather crunched under my feet. It had an almost wooden sound like—I froze—bones. It sounded like bones, hundreds of them—or thousands.

"Come along, no one will hurt you," the voice said. A hot plume of humid and musky air struck my face.

"What…" My voice cracked, and I paused. "What are you?"

There was a great sliding sound, like a vast body slithering across an ocean of pebbles.

"Reach out your hand and see," the voice was quieter now, and much, much closer. The petrol-laced and fuming breath hit me like a wave, nearly knocking me back.

Trembling in shock, almost dead certain what I would find, I reached a shaking hand.

It can't be. It just can't.

My heart thudded in my chest, and I took a trembling step forward.

My hand met thick, scaly hide—and I knew. Not from sight. From memory. Not mine, not really. Just a fragment of Badb, passed to me long ago, the day I was made.

It was just a sliver… but enough.

We'd never met, this creature and I, but the love my aunt had felt for it blossomed in my chest, as if it had always been mine. Familiar. Fierce. Unshakable. A bond I hadn't earned but was still mine to carry, to protect, and to cherish.

I launched myself forward. "Umbryss!" I gasped as my chest and arms collided with his snout. I leaned into that massive jaw and stroked it.

The ancient dragon was still alive after the cataclysm, after all this time. He'd survived.

"I knew you'd come," he said, his voice almost a whisper, and then he laughed softly—for a dragon.

Tears stung my eyes. That piece of me, of my soul, that had been Badb. He had called to it, and it had answered. The awe and aching reverence that filled me was like nothing I'd ever known.

Then again, that wasn't quite true. But I'd never tell the greatest dragon Shaddan had ever seen that he might be second to a fat, orange cat.

CHAPTER FIVE

BONES, FLIGHT, AND OTHER BAD DECISIONS

I sat twiddling a small bone in my fingers, feeling the edges of it. My back rested against one of Umbryss's fore claws as he hummed thoughtfully.

"And this one?" I asked, holding it up where, I hoped, he could see it.

My hair mussed as he gave a contemplative *hmph*, smoky air drifting from his nostrils across my face. The gasoline tang had faded, or maybe I'd simply stopped noticing it.

"That..." he said, drawing the word out with genial precision, the sound of a history professor scaled up to four hundred feet and in no hurry at all.

I had an image of him looking through a pair of reading glasses. I giggled. "Well?"

"Give me a moment. It's very small, and there's not much of an impression on it. That is the finger bone of a Bethadi knight. Feel the knuckle end, and you'll find the grooves where the gauntlet dug into it when I..."

"Crunched him?" I offered, chuckling.

"Well, yes," Umbryss replied, sounding almost scandalized. "But you don't have to be so crude about it. They're noble creatures and deserve a certain amount of respect."

"Oh, yes," I said, my voice dripping with sarcasm. "Tremendous respect. Especially after having thoroughly satisfied your fat gut."

We both laughed, and I let the smooth, sun-bleached bone roll between my fingers, listening to the deep, steady rumble of Umbryss's chuckle. It was oddly comforting, the way it vibrated through the cavern walls, a settling warmth in my chest. Safe. Well, almost safe.

"You know what, Your Grace? Why don't we go somewhere?"

"Go somewhere? You mean… fly?" My heart skipped a beat in excitement.

"Well, we're not going to walk," he said dryly. "And I'm already saddled."

I raised an eyebrow at that. "You were expecting me."

"Well, I did call," he answered lightly.

He guided me to a ladder that led up onto his back, and it occurred to me that it was well forward of where his fore claws had easy reach. "How did you even get this thing on?" I asked as I struggled over his back ridges.

"The harness sits on a mechanical device in the back of the cavern," he answered, a bit of a grump in his voice. "It's not as reliable as I am, but not much can be."

I snickered at that, and he harrumphed.

"I've never ridden a dragon before," I said, trying to decide if I was climbing onto the greatest rollercoaster ride ever or certain death.

He chuckled. "Don't worry, the saddle's not that complicated. Just belt yourself in. The saddle straps can be adjusted so you can sit cross-legged, feet out to the side, stand, or sit on your knees. Any old way is fine. I can barely feel you up there, anyway. I'm the biggest dragon in all of Shaddan, you know."

I nodded and did my best not to laugh. "Are you now?"

"I am," he confirmed.

The saddle was actually a simple affair, not at all like I'd seen in TV shows. It had a smooth leather back support and a chest harness that just strapped to it.

Still, it took a few minutes to get settled in, and in the end, I just took a kneeling position and tightened down a second pair of restraints to keep my legs in place. It turned out to be pretty comfortable.

"Are you strapped in?" Umbryss asked as he began moving.

"I sure hope so. All three straps are buckled tight, as well as the thigh strap. But what are these rods for?"

"Combat harness," he said. "Let's you pivot, duck, stand, and fire. Keeps your ass strapped in while the rest of you can swing a sword or fire a bow at anything dumb enough to get close. Mounted archers used them during the war—meant you could fire in any direction without flying off."

I ran a hand over one, feeling the smooth length of it—four rods spaced in a square around the saddle mount, each looped with sliding rings and tension straps.

I could imagine how it worked: standing, twisting, even drawing a weapon at full stretch while Umbryss rolled through the air. Anchored but mobile. Smart. Brutal. Practical. And… terrifying. All I needed was a quiver and a death wish.

"Okay, then," I said.

"Hold on," he rumbled.

I felt the warm, moist air hit my face, and then we were off. With a great flapping of his wings, he launched.

Smooth, the takeoff was not. His entire body undulated with each wingbeat, lifting me up and down in a wave-like motion that made my stomach churn.

"I think I'm going to be sick," I groaned.

"Please try to contain yourself," Umbryss said, his voice a roar against the wind. "As soon as we're high enough, it will smooth out."

I swallowed down my rising gorge and waited as best I could. Finally, blissfully, his wingbeats turned much more languid, and we seemed to be sailing.

And it was magical in its own right.

I couldn't see, but the wind rushing through my hair and past my face was something in and of itself. On a whim, I shifted my perception, opening myself to the Weave.

And gasped in awe.

What I saw took my breath away.

Vast streams of magic moved all around us. Up here, in the open air high above, the weave flowed differently—not the fine threads I was used to, but a river, wide and unbroken, ribboning through the sky with us.

"Umbryss?" I called over the wind.

"Yes, Cait?"

"How did it really happen? Badb said my mother stole her throne, took everything."

"First, I loved Badb fiercely," the dragon said, his voice solemn. "So when I say what I'm about to say, you should know that it's not meant with any malice."

I said nothing. I already knew that the connection between them had been something greater than just dragon and rider. I felt it myself. That kinship between us. And I wondered if he did, too.

"Over a hundred years had passed here," he said, "before Badb returned. And it was Macha who agreed that Nemhain replace her as queen. Your mother never wanted it. She didn't steal anything.

"Badb was hurt. Broken by Kaushkar, by what Dommus did. She was terrified of losing her daughter. Luring him here, using Drusera as bait, that was her idea."

He paused, then added, "The soulstone was Nemhain's attempt to thread the needle: trap the child where the magic ran strongest and wait. They thought they'd found a way to keep everyone's promises at once."

"It didn't work," I murmured.

"Fae bargains never give you what you mean, only what you say," Umbryss replied. "They were young, elevated too fast, and the wording was sloppy. You know the result."

The pieces slid into place, ugly and inevitable. Sisters trying to protect the ones they loved and pulling the world apart in the process. I'd nearly dragged Aoife into the same pattern.

It was a sobering thought.

The wind changed, growing warmer, and the quiet stretched. My thoughts finally loosened their grip and wandered to something simpler.

"Can you describe the land to me?" I asked.

Umbryss exhaled a low, thoughtful breath. "There's not much left to see where we are. Most of it's volcanic now—

black earth, cracked stone. But there are pockets of life. Little places of blue or red or green that push through. Not much... but enough to notice, even this high up."

I'd thought the world was dead, but then again, there had to be hearty species of plants whose seeds had survived the cataclysm. And with the sudden storms...

"It's the land, Cait," Umbryss said as if reading my thoughts. "This area is ruled by what you call High Shaddani —the High Fae of the Vermilion Court. For now, that's you. As the rule of the Vermilion Palace heals, so does the land. Just your presence here brings life.

"Just like Bethad, the realms of Shaddan reflect their rulers and their people."

I pursed my lips in confusion. "Wait, realms? Rulers?"

Umbryss gave out a great booming laugh. "Oh, the ignorance of youth. Just wait. Do I have something to show you?"

Despite a certain level of disappointment at his terse description and the lingering grief over my lost vision, a crooked and not altogether unexcited smile crept across my face. What could a dragon possibly want to 'show' the blind girl?

Sometime later, an abrupt drop in my stomach jerked me awake.

I must have nodded off, and now, we were descending rapidly. "Where are we?"

"Patience, girl," Umbryss grumbled.

His wings hammered the air, pressing me hard into the saddle. The wind roared in my ears, and then—SLAM!—we hit the ground with a jarring thump, rattling my teeth.

"Now," Umbryss said, and his voice held a certain something that pricked excitement in me, so much so that gooseflesh rose on my arms. "Reach to one side or the other and you'll find several gaps in the leather of the saddle. Place a hand through one and rest it on my scales."

I did as he asked, feeling around across smooth, polished leather of the saddle. I quickly found the depressions he mentioned, inside of which my hand sank until it reached the rough, leathery feel of one ridged scale.

"Now, please don't vomit on me," he said flatly, and my vision exploded into glorious view, though it was different—a little like looking through a fish-eye lens. But still, my eyes burned with tears, and I blinked, trying to push them back, but they fell over my lashes and soaked into the blindfold anyway. I was seeing through his eyes.

"Oh, Goddess," I gasped in a whisper.

His head moved slowly at first, giving me a panoramic view.

Above the three moons of Shaddan glowed. And they were pretty. But below was a beauty I never imagined—a great sprawling valley settled among high peaks.

Unlike the rest of the world, this place seemed untouched. A wide river snaked down the center, sparkling in the moonlight. The stars overhead were like an ocean of flickering lights, and trees filled the vast expanse, trees of every kind. The valley was dotted with lights, some sparkling in hues of gold, but others glowed softly in blues and reds. Amid the trees were grassy clearings. Far in the distance stood a high castle, like something out of a fairy tale. Soaring spires and great battlements. Nothing so large as the Vermilion Palace, but impressive in its own right, cast in white stone that glimmered in the moonlight.

"It's—" I broke off. It was like something straight out of my dreams as a little girl.

My stomach lurched as he turned to look back at me, a little more quickly than I expected, giving me a second of vertigo.

There I sat, one arm threaded through the saddle's center loop, gripping tight. His gaze moved closer—uncomfortably close—and I caught a clearer image of the girl on his back. Me. But not the me I remembered.

I looked… young. Not sickly or frail, just startlingly thin, glowing with a strange kind of health that didn't belong to someone who'd seen battle. My face was the same—and not. The same bones, but softened. Untouched. My ears tapered to soft points, delicate beneath my tangled hair.

I looked like someone who had never suffered. Like

someone who didn't know what the world could take.

And Umbryss... Gods. He was magnificent—wild and glorious.

His scales shimmered in the moonlight, not dull black as I'd imagined, but glossy and alive, catching slivers of light with every motion. A line of spines traced his back in regal ridges, each one shifting slightly as he breathed.

Four massive legs, coiled with strength, anchored him to the mountain, and his wings—his wings were still spread, vast, and impossibly wide. They stretched on and on, easily the span of three football fields, maybe more. I was a speck, barely visible.

A beetle on the back of a god.

"You're amazing," I whispered, feeling strangely disconnected from myself as I saw my lips move.

"Thank you, Your Grace," Umbryss said. "You are very pretty as well."

I snorted. "If you say so."

"False modesty doesn't become you, Cait."

I tilted my head and shrugged. I didn't think it was false. I'd never thought myself beautiful. Fit, sure. But beautiful, hardly. Well, except for one time, when Marcella had done my makeup for me.

The skin around my eyes was blackened, not with bruises, but as if something had detonated against my face and left its mark behind—not damage really. Almost... design. A starburst of char etched over each eye, healed but unhealed, like the fire had kissed me once and decided to stay. And my eyes themselves... they were void. Not just dark—abyssal.

"Can you move closer?" I asked.

His vision narrowed in on my face with surgical precision. I flinched like he'd suddenly lunged, but he hadn't moved at all. Just focused.

Now I saw what Vaelith meant. There was something in my eyes. Stars. A whole universe reflected in that darkness, twinkling. But there was nothing else. If there was some deadly curse in my gaze, I couldn't see it.

CHAPTER SIX

THE NIGHT QUEEN'S DAUGHTER

Umbryss leapt into the air again and glided quickly downward, settling in a clearing not far, I thought, from where we'd been perched. The roar of his wingbeats shook the trees as he landed.

Carefully, I made my way down off his back. My boots landed on grass, and a warm summer breeze blew through my hair.

"Where are we?" I asked as I bent down and began unzipping my boots and removing my long socks. For just one beat of my heart, I felt like I was ten again, barefoot and playing with Aoife and the neighborhood kids on the lawn.

"Just a clearing," Umbryss said, his bulk settling more fully onto the ground. "This is Ebonmere, the realm of the Night Queen. Probably not somewhere you'd want to come alone, but with me, you'll be safe... a guest. I was born in this place long before there were such things as Nochtanmore or the Vermilion Court or your Palace—when the people of this land were one with your own."

I toed the grass, reveling in the feel. Nearby, I caught the sound of flowing water. It wasn't distant, but it was faint. A small brook, perhaps. I wanted to dip a toe in it, but first, I turned back and placed a hand on Umbryss.

"Thank you," I said. "Showing me this place was a gift I won't forget. I... I had thought that all of Shaddan was destroyed."

"No, your mother's realm was destroyed, and the Vermilion Court ruled a great deal of Shaddan. But not all.

"There are pockets, like this one, that were spared the wrath of the cataclysm. And you're very welcome. Sharing my vision with a rider is difficult in the best of times, and you are not experienced. But it was not so painful as I expected. You have a knack, I think."

"I hear water," I said as I took a tentative step forward. "Is it safe for me to wade in it?"

"Here? Yes. It's perhaps twenty feet ahead of you, and there is a short drop, maybe a foot into the shallows. But don't wade too far. It's a river, larger, deeper, and wider than it sounds. And whatever you do, don't wander off. Stay close by. The forest here is wild and not always safe."

I nodded my assent and made my way carefully to the edge of the river.

As I approached, I caught the sound of rapids somewhere to my right. They were fairly far away, but they sounded violent.

Stepping down from the embankment, I almost lost my footing but managed to windmill my arms and remain upright. The water was refreshingly cold. Muck and pebbles squished softly between my toes, and I reached down, dipping my hands into it.

I had just started to feel comfortable enough to take another step forward when something long and slimy slid past my leg.

"Fuck!" I squeaked and jerked backward, my rump landing on the edge of the bank. "What was that?"

Umbryss laughed. "Just an eel. I'd think that, as Nemhain's daughter, you'd feel a kinship for it."

I turned back, gave him a flat look, and was met by an ensuing boom of laughter. I scowled but couldn't hold it and laughed too, even as I beat a hasty retreat from the water.

"Just because my mother *supposedly* transformed into an eel in some old legend doesn't mean I like slimy things wrapping around my legs. Yuck!"

Umbryss just laughed more, as I found a spot against his flank and sat. Moments later, though, I sensed a presence moving into the clearing.

"Someone's coming," I whispered.

Before Umbryss could respond, a warm feminine voice slipped in, rich and unhurried, carrying a sexy mid-tenor that made it impossible to ignore. "Umbryss? Is that you?"

"You'd best hope so, Your Grace, otherwise, you might be dinner," Umbryss said with a chuckle that rolled out like warm thunder through stone.

The stranger laughed with him, and just the sound of it gave me goose bumps.

In that other sense, I could feel that she was tall. At least a head taller than me, and thin. There was litheness and soft grace to her movements that told me she was almost certainly Fae, high fae—like me.

I stood.

"Oh!" she squeaked. "Oh. You've brought a guest."

"Yes," Umbryss said. "Forgive me, Your Grace. May I present Caitlin, Crown Princess of the Vermilion Court. Cait, this is Willow, a daughter of the Night Queen."

"Why is *she* here?" Willow barked in obvious irritation.

"Oh, Willow, don't be like that. She is a friend, and I thought you two might have much in common," Umbryss replied.

Clearly, something about me or my lineage bothered this woman—probably the way my mother had wrecked most of the planet—if you could call Shaddan a planet, really. It had no sun, just the hint of it during the twilight hours. And it seemed choosy about which laws of physics it obeyed. I often wondered if there was another side, eternally in daylight. I doubted it somehow.

In any event, flummoxed as to what to say to the woman, I did what anyone would do when addressing royalty: I gave a low curtsy. "Your Grace. It's an honor."

Silence.

A good silence? I had no idea. But then...

"You're Nemhain's daughter?" Willow asked, her tone now more curious than anything. "Caitlin is a human name."

"I was born half-Fae. But, then, well, things happened, as you can see."

"I cannot," Willow said, and I thought I caught the return of her irritation. "As *you* can see."

So that was it. Same problem, different packaging. "Nope, I'm blind, too." I patted Umbryss's hide. "Are we the only two blind Fae that you know?"

"Well... Yes, but," Umbryss said, sounding a bit embarrassed. "It's how you became blind that I think matters here."

"You've seen her," Willow hissed in surprise, and she took a tentative step forward. "Mother Morrigan."

"Just the once," I said with a wry laugh.

Willow surprised me with a soft laugh of her own. "Once is quite enough. And what little *gift* did she leave with you?" The way she said gift suggested she had one of her own, and it was anything but.

"When mortals look into my eyes, they see themselves as they truly are, and it's often not a pretty sight."

The normally talkative dragon was surprisingly quiet—just observing, I suspected. I wondered why he'd really brought me here. Maybe to introduce us and maybe provide me with some measure of companionship, someone in this world who might understand what I was going through. Just as likely, though, he was trying to heal a rift. A wound in our people.

"It could be worse," Willow said, continuing closer. "People who look into my eyes see the moment of their death, but not in such a way as to be at all helpful. It usually breaks them." She paused then, now inches away. There was something floral in her scent—soft, silken, but threaded with a hint of burnt sweetness. Wildflowers and ash, the perfume of someone who'd once walked through fire and hadn't bothered to wash the smoke from her hair. That scent... and her proximity coiled inside me. I touched my lips instinctively, as if she'd kissed them.

It wasn't glamour; I was pretty sure I'd sense the magic of that. This was something else, something I didn't understand.

She reached up with a hand. "May I? I know you're there, but I'd like to know—you."

I shrugged. "Sure." I'd seen blind people do this on TV

once, but I didn't think it was really a thing.

Her fingers grazed my face, delicate and thin and cool to the touch. The way they slid across my cheek and over my jawline drew a shiver down my spine and gooseflesh on my neck. I understood why she'd asked. The touch was so... intimate. It went straight through me, bypassing thought, lighting something deep and startled, blowing on it like a hot coal.

Tentatively, I reached up, my fingers first grazing the underside of her chin. The feeling of attraction deepened instantly. As my they traveled up and over, and a thumb brushed her full, soft lips, she let out a short but heavy breath.

I moved further, my fingers slid beneath a veil that felt like nothing I'd known. It was silky, but there was a tingle to it that tickled the backs of my hands—magic.

Her face was narrow, as was her nose. Her cheeks had deeper hollows than mine, and her ears were a touch longer than mine, the points a little higher. Her eyes were large and round beneath the blindfold. I suspected that they'd been beautiful once, probably dropping men—or maybe women—to her feet. Now, likely, they were just like mine. Blinded. Blackened. Unseeable.

But hers—hers held a cruelty I couldn't begin to fathom. Anyone who looked into those eyes saw their death. Not some noble vision of sacrifice. Not peace or closure. Just... the end. I shivered at the thought.

I didn't dare ask Umbryss to show me. Maybe he could handle seeing the moment of his death. I couldn't.

I'd spent too long surviving to stomach the certainty of the end. That moment—my moment—wasn't something I wanted gift-wrapped in prophetic detail. I didn't want to see the expression on Liz's face or hear my children screaming—or feel the sting of failure in some bitter last breath. I'd already died once—or was it twice? I wasn't sure, really. But it was enough.

No... knowing would only unmake me.

And maybe that was the worst part of her curse, not the fear it sparked in others, but the isolation it guaranteed. Because who could love someone whose gaze stripped away all hope?

Just like mine.

I let my hand rest on her cheek just a moment longer, trying to say without words that I understood, that I *saw* her, even if neither of us could see much of anything at all.

Slowly, in a way that seemed almost longingly, we both drew away. We were both silent, just standing there with a fundamental understanding hovering between us.

My heart kicked hard, breath going thin. The need surged up, sudden and disorienting, to touch her, to close the space, to hold her like that might quiet the noise inside me. My hand lifted again, betraying me, and I dragged it back down with an effort that left me shaking.

Willow cleared her throat, and when she spoke again her voice had changed, a little rougher at the edge. "I... uh... I..."

I swallowed hard, and summoning up any bit of nerve I could, I pulled myself away to sit, my back resting against Umbryss's neck. Still, a shiver ran down my back. And I swallowed hard.

"Sit with me?" I invited, forcing false cheer into my voice, as I pushed away the cloying emotions and patted the grass.

She gave a quiet sniff, and there was a faint rasp like a sleeve against skin before she eased down beside me, close enough that our shoulders met. For a beat she went very still and her shoulder pressed just a bit harder into mine.

I did my best to ignore it, but it was hard. All I wanted to do was lay my head against her shoulder. Which felt... so dangerous.

Instead, though, I asked, "What happened between our courts? How did Ebonmere and the Vermilion Court end up at odds? Was it the cataclysm?"

"You don't know?" She seemed surprised.

I shook my head. "No. I wasn't born or raised here. And Nemhain never mentioned the Night Court to me. Not once. I didn't know this place even existed until Umbryss brought me here today."

Movement. A nod, I thought, then she said, "Do you know that the Nochtanmore Court was, for thousands of years, one of tyranny? That the Vermilion Palace was built on the backs of slaves in all but name?"

I was horrified. Vaelith had implied as much, but I'd been too engrossed in my situation to ask about it. "No. That's... abominable."

"Long before the cataclysm that wiped out the Vermilion Court and most of the world. Before Badb took the throne, Shaddan was a world at war with itself. Polite wars, to be sure, but still there was an order to things.

Then, the Red Queen, Maura, began a campaign of conquest. The politicking and backstabbing and quiet assassinations became a bloody war that blew across the face of Shaddan, leaving cinders and ash in its wake. Nothing like what's out there now, but the toll was... catastrophic in its own right." She gestured out in the direction of the mountains from which we'd come.

"My mother, Runa, stood her ground. In the end, she fought Maura's forces to a stalemate. We sued for peace, and while our lands were greatly reduced, we maintained our sovereignty. Still, though, the rule of The Three withstood the test of time until..."

I nodded thoughtfully. "Until Badb."

"Yes, she changed things. She started negotiations to restore at least some of the independent realms that had been conquered. She even made overtures to my mother, trying to set things to rights, but then she vanished, and your mother assumed the throne."

I snorted. "And Nemhain? Did she try to return to the old ways? Conquests?"

I heard the soft tearing of grass blades and caught the rustle of fabric as Willow fingered them and tossed them aside.

"No. But she had her own problems. She was too young, then, unskilled in politics or much of anything else except her magic. We had almost no contact with her... and then the cataclysm came, and that was the last we ever saw of the Vermilion Court or anyone in it."

I'd never known my mother to be anything but thoroughly self-possessed and competent. But then again, the woman Willow referred to had been new and untried. My mother, as I knew her, had been thousands of years older.

"I'm not like that," I whispered, the words slipping out before I could stop them, shame burning hot alongside a sudden, helpless anger. Anger that my people had been such monsters.

"I hope that's true," Willow said.

She didn't say anything else. The clearing filled the space instead—birds calling overhead, something small scuttling through the underbrush nearby. Umbryss's warmth was steady at my back.

I swallowed and reached for safer ground. "You mentioned the Morrigan," I said. "How did that happen?"

Willow gave a mirthless snort. "That is a long story. Suffice it to say that young, stubborn Fae should stick close to home and not go looking for trouble—or seek the bidding of powers they don't understand."

My brows lifted. "You went to her?"

"I did."

"Why?" I couldn't imagine anyone willingly courting that kind of chaos. Anyone but me, that was.

"Stupidity," she sighed. Then, a beat later, she added, "So, tell me, Caitlin of Terra Victa, what's your story?"

"Me?" I gave a dry laugh. "I'm not that interesting."

"Come now," she said, placing a hand over mine and patting it with a gentleness that caught me off guard. "I told you something of us. Now it's your turn."

"I'm engaged to be married," I blurted. *What? Where did that come from?*

I didn't know why I'd said it, only that I'd needed something solid between us, something sharp enough to cut the pull short. She was easy to talk to. Too easy. Worse, she made me feel warm in a way that felt reckless, familiar in a way I knew way better than to trust. I'd learned the hard way what came of mistaking that feeling for safety. Too many times.

"Are you?" Willow said. There was a pause, and then something careful slipped into her voice, curiosity edged with a quiet ache. "What's she like?"

"Elizabeth? She's wonderful. Smart. Capable." I snorted in

amusement at my own shortcomings as I finished with "Level-headed."

"She sounds wonderful. Why aren't you with her now?"

I sighed. "Because I couldn't stay. I'm bonded to The Morrigan, and she goes off her meds off-world."

Willow gave a soft chuckle. "That's a very human saying, is it not?"

"Born on Earth," I declared with a casual wave of my hand. "Besides…"

I paused, swallowing the taste of ash on my tongue. The memory I carried still sat heavy in my chest, unspoken and unbearable. Everything else—Boston, the fire, the blood—it still burned. Too fresh. Too raw.

"Besides?" she prodded.

I opened my mouth to tell her it wasn't important, but I said something else entirely, something I had no intention of saying. It just… spilled out.

"Have you ever done something so wrong that you don't want to remember it—ever? Horrible things that seem to taint everything? That everyone you know, all the people you love, they remind you of it, and the idea of seeing them again, it scares you?" My voice dropped to a whisper. "It hurts."

A gentle hand landed on mine, squeezing. And when Willow spoke, it was like some untold, horrible secret.

"Like running off to entreat the Morrigan to turn her eye from your enemies," Willow said her voice low and bitterly self-recriminating. "And instead coming back mutilated. The love of your life dead."

She inhaled and kept talking, as if any silence would hurt worse "And then she's everywhere. In every scent. In the way sound carries through the halls you walked in your youth— empty now, too loud with your own footsteps. So constant that exile from court, from family, stops feeling like punishment and starts feeling like mercy."

I squeezed my eyes shut as I anchored myself against a flashback of Nastasia crumbling to ash. When the feeling passed, I let go of her hand, afraid I'd been squeezing too hard.

Goddess, I understood… too well. Tears ran down my

cheeks and I sniffed.

"Yes," I answered, choked and hard-edged with pain.

"War is a horror... always," she whispered and then she shifted and a thumb pushed aside the tears on each cheek. "It's not your fault any more than it was mine. Even the Fae make mistakes, Caitlin."

I almost lost it, but then... thankfully, blessedly, our discussion was abruptly interrupted by a loud noise from Umbryss. It took me a moment to realize it was a snore. Willow slapped her hand to my thigh and snorted in amusement before she broke into fits of laughter.

I laughed with her.

"Old fart," she said, and I heard the sound of skin on scales.

"How long have you known him?" I asked once our humor had settled.

"A long time," she said evasively. "Very long. He's one of my best friends."

"How old exactly are you? You have to be... " I trailed off, embarrassed. *Nice one, Cait.*

"Older than you," Willow replied, a smile in her voice. "And on that note, I have matters that need attending. I've enjoyed our chat, Caitlin. But I have to leave."

We stood, and I brushed at my dress, hopefully removing any lingering bits of grass before we shared a brief but heartfelt hug.

Willow kissed me on the cheek. "We'll see each other again, I'm sure."

And then she vanished in a rush of air.

I slapped gently at Umbryss's scales. "Hey! Wake up, you big iguana."

Umbryss shifted. "Honestly, Cait, must you insult me? I was just beginning to like you."

I laughed. "We have to get home. And on the way, you can tell me why you brought me here and who Willow really is."

He shifted beside me, the weight of him settling like thunder in the earth. "I told you—she's the daughter of the Night Queen."

"That's not what I meant, and you know it."

I placed my hands on my hips and stood still for a long moment, considering. The breeze rustled around us, but Umbryss didn't fill the silence. Then a thought struck—sudden, quiet, and sharp—as we stood out here, in the middle of nowhere, far away from the palace I'd spied earlier.

I turned my face slightly toward him, lowering my voice to something almost tender. "This wasn't for me, was it?"

Silence for a moment, and then, "It was for both of you." Simple and yet so full of meaning. That was all he said, though, and I didn't press him.

Some truths didn't need to be spoken to be understood.

CHAPTER SEVEN

THE CROWN AND THE CAGE

The ground shuddered under Umbryss's weight as he settled back in the lair, dust shaking loose from the ceiling like nervous birds. A few pieces of crystal clinked together overhead. I figured the very mountain felt his presence as he settled, rather ungracefully.

As I unclipped and started down, the hair on the back of my neck rose, and a whiff of smoke and ember passed through my nostrils—the scent of Dark Fae magic.

"You wandered far, Your Grace," Sithraine said, her tone clipped as she materialized from a shadowed corner. I jumped slightly at the unexpected company, then continued climbing down the ladder. As soon as I hit bottom, the saddle rig whirred to life.

"Most in your condition would fear being lost. But perhaps… that was the point?"

A spike of irritation crawled up my spine. "What's that supposed to mean?"

"I can certainly understand if you don't wish to participate in the restoration of your homeland—it is a lot of work, after all—but you can't just run off without telling anyone."

"Bitch," I whispered under my breath and pursed my lips. Fuck her. Honestly.

I glanced toward Umbryss, but with the saddle off, he was already whumping his way toward the other side of the cavern. No help at all—coward.

My hard expression turned into a scowl. "What, should I leave a note on the fridge next time?"

Sithraine gave an exasperated sigh. "It's not that, Your Grace. But it's dangerous out there, and you are blind. There's no one to defend you if you get into trouble. We're here to protect the palace and you. Please let us do our job."

I was tired of being watched and handled, wrapped in caution tape and bubble wrap like a glass heirloom. It was bad enough that I depended on them for cooking, cleaning, and helping me ready for my day, which, while easier, was still sometimes a challenge. The idea of having to check in before I went anywhere rankled me—thoroughly.

"I was accompanied by a hundred tons of fire-breathing menace. I'm pretty sure I was safe. Right, Umbryss?"

Umbryss hemmed and hawed. "Cait, dear, I think it best I stay on the sidelines for this particular test, if you don't mind."

I turned toward his voice and scowled, but he stayed silent. "Traitorous lizard," I grumbled.

He huffed in irritation. "I am *not* a lizard."

Sithraine closed the distance. "Your Grace," she said, her manner more condescending than caring. "You are the crown princess of the Vermilion Court. And while we must make allowances for your upbringing on Earth, you have a duty to the throne, at least until we find a replacement. Further, you're the only one of the three left. If something happens to you, the line of our queens ends. The lands of the Vermilion Court remain this way forever."

"There's Aoife," I muttered. "She's my twin."

"We have no Blood of Shaddan, no Spley Flowers. Without them, she can't assume the mantle."

I barked a laugh. "The mantle? The mantle disintegrated when I put it on. It's gone."

"The mantle isn't a tangible thing. Nemhain's device of office was a representation of that power. It was how she controlled the Morrigan by stabilizing her relationship within it, and it took her a thousand years to craft it properly. Yes, that bit of old cloth is gone, but what it contained rests on your shoulders—alone. So, we must be careful."

Nothing she said made me feel the least bit comforted. Even if we had more Blood of Shaddan, I doubted that Aoife could take it. She was Kyliri, and who knew what it would do to her? It could kill her. And even if she survived, she'd be infected by this—this thing I carried—this chaos. And given how much more powerful she was, especially in magic, I didn't see a single positive in that outcome.

Still…

"Fuck careful," I huffed. My voice cracked on the curse, but I didn't care. "I'm tired of being cooped up in this tomb-like cage. I'll come and go as I please."

Sithraine sighed. "As you wish," she said, but there was something in her tone that sounded more like, 'over my dead body.' This was going to be a fight.

"Can you at least tell me where you went?" Sithraine asked as I stalked away across the cavern.

"No," I said flatly and tossed two fingers over my shoulder, hoping I didn't trip because that would absolutely ruin my grand exit. As it was, I ended up walking to Umbryss and quietly asking for directions to the path out. I was turned around, and I could just feel Sithraine's eyes burning into me as I had to walk all the way back to the entryway.

After a shower to get the proverbial road grime off me, I headed to the dining hall. I had the pathways through several parts of the castle down pat—well, a few, anyway. I could get to the dining hall without assistance, the library downstairs, Umbryss's lair, of course, and the central spire. I hadn't gone anywhere near the high throne room or the lower reception hall—the two rooms with actual thrones. No thank you.

My steps were light, uncertain, like I hadn't quite re-entered my own skin. Willow's voice still clung to my thoughts, cool as moonlight and just as distant. Everything about her felt like a story I'd stumbled into. It was probably why I didn't notice the voices echoing from the dining room until one of them said my name.

"Cait's made a mess of it," Naerith snapped. Not an ounce of subtlety. "We should have told her everything from the start."

I froze. Just outside the archway. *Told me what?*

Elarith's reply came softer. "She's just trying to make friends. Can you blame her? She's been cooped up here for months."

Oh, so that's what this was about: Willow.

"Well, Umbryss isn't talking," Sithraine said, her voice exasperated. "That dragon is going to get her into trouble—I can feel it. Something happened out there. Runa's daughter has taken a sudden interest in the daughters of The Three."

Yes, something had happened. But I didn't even understand what yet, and it was already palace gossip.

"Well, whatever it was," Vaelith said. "It seems to have agreed with her. She's becoming what she is. She's a Queen of the Dark Faerie, and finally starting to act like it. You can't fault her for that. Besides, right now, it's only Willow's interest. I say we wait and see what develops. This might be a good thing."

Sithraine's sigh was quiet, but full of knives. "That's unlikely, but it doesn't matter now. It's done. I'll explain it to her when the time is right. Until then, we keep her inside the palace. I'll try to… figure this out."

My stomach turned. That tone? That was the tone you used when a kid brought home a stray animal. And I wasn't some trembling schoolgirl. I'd just come back from a place that felt like a dream—where a woman with a voice like dusk had treated me like I meant something. And I wasn't giving that up. I wasn't staying locked up.

Vaelith snorted. "She can't stay here forever."

"Vaelith," Sithraine warned.

"Fine," Vaelith grumped. Loudly.

"She's acting like a Fae teenager," Nyxiel said. "Which kind of makes sense. Her body is flush with new feelings and hormones. They'll settle eventually. So far, it's all probably pretty normal."

A Fae teenager? I was absolutely not some rebellious teen.

Was I?

Was that why I was having all these weird feelings? Some

kind of Fae puberty? Shit.

"I remember what you were like, Nyxiel," Vaelith said with a laugh. "Give it time. When she's finished transforming, she'll be breathtaking. And you'll pray she never turns on you."

"Yes, that's what I'm afraid of," Sithraine said.

Weirdly, I wasn't.

The idea didn't scare me at all.

It thrilled me.

There was that silent, almost ecstatic joy in imagining myself as something beautiful and dangerous. A creature they whispered about after dusk. A nightmare in silk.

And I liked that version of me more than I probably should.

They all turned silent, just the scrape of plates.

I schooled my face and walked in.

As I crossed the threshold into the dining hall, a goblet clattered—knocked over or maybe dropped. I heard it wobble once before it was caught. Nobody said a word. Just silence and the soft scrabble of a chair.

No one acknowledged me.

Clearly, I'd upset the apple cart.

I made my way to my usual seat, feeling for the back of the chair and lowering myself carefully. Someone slid a plate in front of me; the smell of roasted meat and herbs drifted up.

"Busy night, Your Grace?" Nyxiel asked lightly. Too lightly. "Did you enjoy your little… excursion?"

My lips twitched. "It was educational," I said breezily. "And I came back in one piece." I leveled that last for Sithraine's benefit.

A knife tapped against the table. Sithraine's voice followed. "We'd prefer to know when you leave the palace. That's all."

"Noted," I said coolly, even though we all knew it absolutely wasn't.

A small, amused huff came from Vaelith's direction. "You're obviously restless, Your Grace," she said. Her fork clinked against her plate. "The Fae aren't made for stillness. You especially. You need less time in the library and more on the practice field. The body steadies the mind."

I tilted my head, turning my ear in her direction. "What are you thinking?" I suspected I already knew. And weirdly, I wasn't afraid of it anymore.

"Just an idea," she said cryptically.

The conversation sort of petered out after that, and the rest of dinner passed with just the polite clink of silverware. Even Elarith, the more chatty of the two twins, was unusually subdued. Sithraine had probably told them I was in the dog house. Fine. If that was the way it was going to be, I could live with that. I could do alone. I'd done it for years.

As it turned out, I was wrong. I couldn't do alone—not anymore.

I woke up that night, gasping from another nightmare.

I had been drowning in the Charles. That woman, the pilot, Frost Queen, she was holding me underwater.

"You killed them," she kept screaming at me over and over. She was talking about Maggie's unit. The soldiers we'd slaughtered escaping Boston.

At first, I didn't even fight her. I let her drown me.

Part of me whispered that I'd earned it. That if I didn't go under now, I'd be dragged back to the burning streets of Boston to finish what the Morrigan started.

I woke with my lungs burning and only then realized I'd been holding my breath.

Rubbing a hand across my face, I decided I needed someone to be around after all. Maybe not to talk, but a presence, a person. Anyone, really.

I didn't bother to dress. I left in my sweat-soaked nightgown, feeling it cling to my body in the cold air of the hallway. I searched high and low to see if anyone was awake, but none of the Nerin were anywhere to be found. I assumed they were sleeping somewhere in the east wing of the palace.

Part of me wondered if Sithraine had told them to avoid me as punishment. The thought seemed petulant and maybe a little paranoid. Still, though, the place was empty, and it was creeping me the fuck out.

More than once, I heard things, scraping on the stones, a door closing somewhere, even the tinkling of glass far off in another room. And the silences in between had a shape to them. The kind that slips behind your shoulders and follows close, a half-pace behind.

At one point, I turned toward the sound of shuffling cloth and caught just the feeling of movement—like a shadow folding in on itself, disappearing under a door. I stood frozen in the hallway, pulse racing.

I wasn't sure what was worse: the idea that I was alone... or the idea that I wasn't.

My own words from earlier wormed into my thoughts: a tomb. This wasn't a palace. It was a crypt, a mausoleum of dead Fae and lost dreams, full of ghosts and specters. Haunted.

Ultimately, thoroughly creeped out by the abandoned feeling of the palace, I made my way quickly back to my room and shut the door.

That would be the last of my midnight wanderings for a while. Something was here. I thought I could feel it. Watching.

CHAPTER EIGHT

HOUSE ARREST IS A SUGGESTION

I bolted up in my bed, breath heaving from yet another nightmare.

I wasn't sure what had woken me. A sound, maybe? But the room was deathly still—and creepy. A shiver ran down my back, and I pulled my knees up tight.

This place was so empty, so bereft of anything comforting. All except this room, and it wasn't all that great.

Then…

A tapping.

If I didn't know better, I'd say it was a bird, rapping on the window.

Another shiver. It was just my imagination. The palace had taken on a darker feeling, an almost subtle menace these last two days since my confrontation with Sithraine. Everything felt eerie and claustrophobic.

Another tap and… and a croak, like a crow or a raven.

Straight out of Poe. Great.

I drew myself up and felt my way to the window. Fumbling around, I found the latch, which gave way with a horrid squeak, letting me open the window just a crack.

I sensed the bird now, standing in the window, head tilting this way and that.

It gave another quiet croak, clearly wanting in.

On pure instinct, I held out my arm, and it bobbed onto it.

I slid the back of one knuckle beneath its head and down its breast feathers.

"Where did you come from?"

It snapped its beak and croaked. It was way too large for a crow, definitely a raven.

In the Weave, I noted its body flowed with red threads. On Earth, they'd be green or maybe turquoise.

"So, you're a local, huh?"

My finger brushed against something, and, doing my best not to get scratched or bitten, I fumbled for it. It was a tiny bit of paper, rolled up and attached to the thin stalk of a leg: a message.

Gingerly, I removed the letter and shook my arm. Protesting, the bird jumped off and landed on the sill.

A fat lot of good this was going to do me. It wasn't like I could read it, but I unfurled it anyway, and immediately, magic tingled my fingers. I almost dropped the damn thing as Willow's voice whispered in my ears.

"Hello, Cait!" Her voice tinkled with humor. "Umbryss tells me you're under house arrest. Odd, isn't it, that you are supposed to be this Crown Princess with vast temporal power, and yet they treat you like a precious stone that might be stolen? Rather rude, really, given that most of the world is completely barren of any hostile life.

"In any event, Umbryss suggested that you might be feeling a bit cooped up. I spoke with my mother recently, and she would like to invite you to attend the Midsummer Gathering at The Night Court. You would be an honored guest. No strings. Umbryss will provide transportation. And, in truth, I would like to see you again. Ha! I said, 'See.' Now that's funny.

"If you accept, please tell the bird. Fourteen days from today, at duskfall. I hope you can attend."

The voice faded away, and the paper dissolved to nothing. I paused for a moment, then leaned over. "I accept," I whispered.

I stood there for a long moment after the raven vanished, palms still tingling from Willow's spell, the faintest smile tugging at my mouth.

A party.

A real, actual party. With people. With color and music and something other than stone walls and Nerin voices whispering like disembodied ghosts. Fuck Sithraine and her bullshit. I was going to that party.

The palace around me felt… lighter, just for a breath. Like the air had cracked open enough to let in a sliver of the world I'd forgotten was possible.

I let myself enjoy it.

One fragile, stupid second of warmth in this mausoleum.

Naturally, that's when someone tried to kick down my door.

A thunderous pounding rattled the hinges.

"Your Grace," Vaelith barked through the wood, voice like a war-hammer wrapped in velvet. "Up. Now."

The lightness evaporated so fast I almost laughed at myself. Of course. Shaddan gives you one soft moment, then shoves you face-first back into reality.

I groaned, already regretting having emotions this early in the day. "What time is it?"

"Training time," she growled.

And just like that, the day got significantly worse.

"So," I said irritably as I stood in the middle of a huge, empty space. "What are we doing?"

"We're going to work on shadow-wending, more commonly called a glimmerstep."

I shrugged. "What is it? And how does it work?"

There was a soft rush of air, and abruptly, Vaelith stood beside me.

I flinched. "How am I supposed to do that? I can't see. I haven't been able to do that since I was a vampire."

Silence. I could almost feel the judgment in it.

"Cait," she said finally. "Did it never occur to you that

wasn't a vampiric trait at all?"

"No," I said. Instantly defensive. "I couldn't do it before I turned."

"When was the first time?" she asked. Calm. Too calm.

"Right after the gate opened—"

The words collapsed in my throat. The cavern. The magic flood.

And no other vampire could do that. Not then. Not ever.

"Oh."

"Not so sure now, are you?" Vaelith said, already back where she'd been. "Let me raise a ward. I want you to try it."

Magic hummed in my skull for a second, and everything outside the circle just... vanished. No echo. No wind from above. The world just felt a little smaller.

"Just move yourself," she said gently.

I tried, I could almost feel it... something inside me, but my body wouldn't respond.

"If I could just picture—"

"Stop trying to use your eyes," Nyxiel said, her voice muted, like she was talking through a wall.

I jerked, startled. She must have slipped in after the wards came up.

"There are spaces between spaces," she said. "Just step."

"Not helping," I growled.

"You're overthinking it," Vaelith said. "Maybe this will jog something loose." Her boots scuffed dirt as she closed the distance. Her hand hit my face. Hard.

I reeled, cheek stinging. Her hand came up again, and something in my chest fluttered, and then I was just... behind her.

I spun—a little too fast, stumbling and almost faceplanting.

Nyxiel gave a sharp whistle from the edge of the circle. "There you go! See!"

I tried again, this time just relaxing into the movement. It came easily and quickly, and... I whacked face-first into something smooth and solid, bouncing off it like a damn pinball to land flat on my ass.

"Fuck, that hurt," I bitched as I rubbed my face. "That's

gonna leave a mark."

"You hit the ward," Nyxiel said, and there was a plunk-plunk as she rapped on the opposite side. "But you did it."

I groaned and pulled myself off the ground, holding my bleeding nose. "So, how do I keep from ending up inside a wall?"

"You don't have to worry about that," Vaelith said. "Dense matter causes interference. You won't land underwater, either. You'll stop right at the edge. And if you hit a ward, well, you just saw that.

"Now, you can force it, focus on traveling through solid objects, but that's dangerous. You're riding the edge of the Ma, the space between worlds. To travel through solid matter, you have to immerse yourself in it fully. You can lose momentum and come to a complete stop. That'll leave you stuck in the void—alone.

"It's not a pleasant place and not always empty. It's also damn hard to get out of by yourself without help or a lot of luck."

"Personal experience?" I asked. It sure sounded like it.

"Yes," Vaelith replied firmly. "I got lucky. Very lucky. And remember, this isn't some trick of the Weave, it's an intrinsic ability. Think of it like a muscle. The more you use it, the stronger you'll get, but it still has limits. When you're out, you're out. Now do it again."

I bounced around the training area over and over.

Eventually, Vaelith had me focusing on her as she threw little bean-filled pouches at me. Sometimes, I dodged, but Vaelith had a wicked curveball, and most of the time I ended up with a fat welt.

By the time we were finished, I was wheezing, soaked in a fine sheen of sweat, and ready to collapse. I dropped onto the floor with a graceless thump, legs trembling.

"No more," I panted. "I can't do any more."

"You did well, Your Grace," Vaelith said. "Not bad at all."

Pride swelled in my chest. I let it linger.

I'd been a fighter once—hell, most of my life—and maybe that part of me hadn't burned away after all.

Maybe it had just been waiting for the pain to loosen its grip.

Vaelith sat beside me, lowering the ward with a flick of her wrist. Her voice softened.

"I'm not teaching you this to fight—"

"It's okay," I said. And it was. More than I expected. "I... I should protect myself. And..." I paused. "I'm okay. Really."

"Good," she said. "Being blind puts you at a disadvantage. But if you know what you can do, you'll have a chance when it matters. If something goes wrong."

I snorted. "Something always goes wrong." Then, quieter, "But I appreciate it."

The silence that followed wasn't tense, exactly—more like a held breath. It made my skin prickle.

"Vaelith?"

She stood and then hoisted me up.

"Here," she said guided me to a rack of practice swords, placing my hand on one. She didn't release it right away. It wasn't a command. It felt more like a question. Are you ready?

The weight of it hit me like déjà vu. Not the weapon itself—I didn't know this style—but the feel. Leather-wrapped hilt, balance shifting into my palm, the prickle along my arms as an old and familiar feeling stirred.

Vaelith finally let go. She lingered close, though, as if she half-expected me to drop it or flinch away.

I didn't.

I wanted this. Goddess help me, I wanted to move, to swing, to stand my ground even if I couldn't see the damn ground.

I didn't want to hurt anyone ever again. But wanting that wouldn't make it possible. Not here. Not with Mother Darkness breathing down reality's neck, and other potentially hostile courts just lying in wait.

Slowly, I lifted the blade.

It was about the length of my bóllom—gone now—and the shape hit me like a bruise. Straight blade. Clipped point, like a ninjato.

Like Nastasia's blade.

My throat closed. I pushed the ache down and swallowed the memory like broken glass.

Stop blubbering, Cait.

Nas's imaginary voice, sharp, amused, and absolutely uncharitable in precisely the way I needed, cut through the haze. It was my choice.

I blew out a breath and let my shoulders drop. I wasn't dead yet. She'd say that too, probably with an eye roll and a shove.

"Alright," I murmured. "Let's do this."

Vaelith and I circled each other slowly and methodically.

My steps were hesitant—too light, too careful. I couldn't read the terrain. So I kept my attention pinned to her, trusting my feet to remember what I couldn't see.

She moved first.

Clack. Clack. Clack.

A rapid series of strikes—clean, efficient, and brutal. I barely caught them in time. The sound of wood on wood echoed sharply in my ears, each impact jarring down my arms.

It was hard.

But not impossible.

Another flurry.

Clack. Clack. Clack. Pop.

My breath caught as I heard the first glimmerstep—Vaelith blinking through space. And then...

Pop.

I glimmerstepped away, and she swung into empty air.

It had been instinct. Pure, wild instinct.

I landed on my feet and just had time to register a flicker of pride before—

"Oof!" I hit the ground hard, the breath knocked cleanly from my chest, as her leg swept mine like a scythe through wheat. She stood over me before I could even curse.

"Not bad, Your Grace," Vaelith said, her voice warm. "You learn fast—damn fast."

I grunted, rolling to my side and dragging myself upright, lungs burning. "Not fast enough," I muttered.

"You're blind," she reminded me, not unkindly. "I can see. That's a pretty significant advantage. Plus—just a few years more experience."

I huffed a laugh. "Just a few, old woman."

"Smart ass," she shot back. "Seriously, though, how does it feel?"

I grinned ear to ear, fangs on full display. "Wanna go again?"

Vaelith chuckled, low and pleased, and we reset.

It went on for hours. I didn't know how many—four? Five?

I didn't win a single exchange, and it didn't matter.

There was no frustration in it—only freedom. For the first time since I'd woken up in this strange, broken place, I felt like myself. And I was fast. Not what I'd been as a vampire, sure— but fast enough. Even with me blind, no human or Oşení would have stood a chance.

More importantly? I was learning. Adapting.

Each clash, each stumble, each parry brought something new—new angles, new instincts.

I wasn't just parrying strikes. I was cleaving through fear. Through memory.

Beneath a broken Cait Reagan lay Skaja, the proud warrior who carried no guilt, no burdens, no horrors. And this combat, this love of the blade, it brought her to the fore. Maybe to stay.

"Again," I wheezed.

My body was slick with sweat, my muscles trembling with exhaustion. I could feel every bruise—there had to be a dozen of them, maybe more. My blindfold hung loose around my neck, forgotten. My hair clung to my face and back like wet rope. I was a mess—a total wreck.

I loved it.

And I just knew that tonight, the nightmares wouldn't come.

"I think that's enough," Vaelith replied, her voice calm, but even she was a little winded. "One of us is going to end up seriously injured, and the moons are already high."

She was right, of course she was. There was nothing left to prove tonight. We'd do it again tomorrow. The Sweat. The Swearing. The fighting. All the good stuff.

I stepped closer, lowering my voice so only she would hear.

"So... this is great and all, but I need a favor. And I need to know if I can trust you."

Vaelith didn't miss a beat. "Of course you can." A grin crept into her voice, wicked and delighted. "Should I be sneaky?"

That pulled a laugh from me, a real one. "Yes. Very. I've been invited to a party."

"Ooooh." She actually cooed, which was ridiculous and perfect. "Now you have my attention."

I told her about the raven, about Willow's message, about the date and time. By the end of it, I could practically hear her hands go to her hips.

"Fine," she said. "Leave everything to me. And for all that's holy in this forsaken place, do not let Sithraine hear a whisper of it."

"That's why you're the first person I came to."

"Smart girl." She tapped my forearm, conspiratorial. "If you're going to break house arrest, at least do it with style."

Then she stepped close enough that I felt the warmth of her breath at my temple. "Here. Pay attention. This is how we vanish without leaving the room."

The temperature shifted first—like someone cracked open a cellar door. A thin ribbon of cold slid across the floor and curled around my ankles, not painful, just startling. The air thickened, not with humidity but with weight, as if something unseen were gathering.

"Feel that?" Vaelith murmured. "That's the pull. Shadows respond to intent before motion."

Her fingers grazed the inside of my wrist—then a sudden brush of cold threaded up my arm, winding around my bicep like liquid smoke.

"That's me," she said. "My web."

I felt it coil tighter, then relax, slipping across my shoulder blades in a slow, deliberate sweep. It wasn't touching me, not really—the temperature change was the only giveaway—but the sensation carried shape and movement, the suggestion of little fingers made of cool night air.

"You draw from what's already here," Vaelith continued. "You coax the dim places together until they obey. They're not

63

alive, but they're… responsive."

The cold slid away as smoothly as it had come, retreating to the edges of the room.

"We'll practice tomorrow," Vaelith said. "In private."

And just like that, my maudlin feelings fled like smoke in a breeze.

And weaving shadows? It gave me jolt, wild, strange, and a little thrilling.

It felt like… unknown possibilities. The good kind.

CHAPTER NINE

A CROWN BY ANY OTHER NAME

Two weeks slipped by in a blur of bruised knuckles, whispered lessons, and the soft drag of shadows coiling at my fingertips. Shadow Spinning—once a fumbling mess of cold, sticky strands that never stayed put—finally clicked. I could vanish into a corner of the palace like I'd been carved from darkness. Vaelith even snuck me what she called "appropriate attire": a long black surcoat that felt like a sleeveless duster with a wide belt meant for blades I no longer had, soft leather leggings that stretched like a second skin, and a tunic that I could only pray wasn't sporting orange stripes or purple polka dots. Or leopard print. Knowing this place, it was probably all black, but blind optimism was still blind.

I played dutiful princess for everyone else—library, training, etiquette manuals—while quietly plotting my escape for Midsummer's Eve.

Sithraine was intent on teaching me what it meant to be present now that the land was waking up again. A living realm required a visible princess, apparently. One who went where she was told, when it mattered.

Whatever.

So, I went, if for no other reason than to avoid suspicion.

Night Pixies had begun building a village at the edge of the Nochtanmore plateau, where the regrowth was strongest. I went not to investigate, to welcome.

I knew what Night Pixies were, of course. Jessica was one. Five to six feet tall, with brilliant red moth-like wings, sharp fangs, and shapely bodies. But knowing one and standing among many of them were not the same experience—like at all.

They sensed me before anyone spoke. The air shifted as wings beat closer, the sound changing pitch as bodies descended around me. Someone brushed past my arm. Someone else laughed softly, right near my ear. Then hands— light, unguarded—touched my sleeves, my hair, my wrists, as if I were a sculpture they'd been invited to examine.

I let it happen.

They were curious in the way only people without fear can be. Fingers traced the curve of my chest, the seams of my dress, the edges of my shoulders. A thumb brushed my cheekbone. Another hand lingered at my waist, not threatening or tugging, just… interested. Warm skin. Bare skin. The faint rasp of calluses where wings met muscle.

It was only adults. The children were kept away.

I quickly learned why. They were mostly nude. And I learned that the way I learned everything now: by contact. Smooth skin. The give of muscle beneath it. The brush of hair against my knuckles.

One woman landed close, sliding her cheek along mine. I reached behind her without quite deciding to, mapping wings and arms and ribs with careful fingers, astonished by how alive they felt. How unashamed.

Wonder came first. Pure and bright.

Then something else stirred beneath it—quieter, more dangerous. A pull. A warmth that had less to do with curiosity than want. My breath caught once or twice. It was a kind of glamour, and I had to push it aside, almost like a physical thing.

Their homes grew directly from the trees, living wood shaped by touch rather than tools. As I walked, bare feet padded nearby, hands steadying me across narrow walkways, fingers lingering a fraction longer than necessary. Resin and sap scented the air, mingled with skin and magic and something feral and sweet.

The old city lay flattened beneath it all, stone pressed down into memory. But here, above it, the plateau was alive—bodies moving freely, voices unmuted, people choosing closeness without fear.

Their Queen, Selene, received me and served tea in a home that unfolded space in ways I could feel in the sound of it, the impossible immensity—larger on the inside. She taught me certain etiquette in ways Sithraine couldn't—in situ, through experience rather than theory.

She gave me words of welcome and acknowledgment. My voice was steady when I gave them back, even if my skin still hummed from being touched.

I didn't stay long. I couldn't, but when I returned to the palace, I carried a sensation with me—an almost indulgent feeling.

I felt so alive inside.

I was still brimming with it when the night of the party finally arrived.

I cloaked myself, slipped barefoot down the east–west gallery with my boots tucked under one arm. Dodging one close call with the twins, where one of them smelled my perfume, I made it all the way to the door leading down to Umbryss's lair… where the shadows peeled right off me like dust shaken from a rug as soon as I opened it.

"Going somewhere?" Vaelith asked, low and amused, like she'd been leaning against that wall for hours just waiting to deliver the line.

"I just wanted some fresh air?" I said with a sly grin.

"Please." She clicked her tongue. "If you wanted fresh air, you'd be on the parapets, not sneaking down to the dragon garage in full party gear. You've been 'sick' for exactly three hours, Cait. You're not subtle."

"Hey," I said, trying to salvage a scrap of dignity. "Usually, I'm a phenomenal liar. Interviews, interrogations, criminal scum—put me in a room with them and I shine."

"That's adorable." She checked the hall, then grabbed me by the front of my surcoat and hauled me inside before anyone could wander by. A gloved fingertip tapped my lips. "Go. Have fun. Enjoy the party you absolutely did not sneak out to attend, and I most certainly did not help you with."

My face warmed. I stepped close and kissed her on the cheek. "Thank you for this, V."

"Don't call me 'V,'" she grumbled automatically, which only made her sound like she was smiling.

I started down the passage, boots in hand, heart thudding with excitement I hadn't felt in... gods, months. Her voice chased after me, sharp enough to cut through my nerves.

"Be polite," she called. "And don't do anything I wouldn't do!"

As if. I was going to meet the Queen of the Night Court, see Willow again, and breathe for the first time in weeks. What trouble could I possibly get into?

Her final bit of advice echoed off the stone, soft and deadly:

"And trust no one."

Umbryss and I made quite the entrance as we descended toward the palace of the Night Queen—aptly named Moonstone.

I sat comfortably on his back, my hands tucked into what I now knew were called contact hollows—so I could feel the thrum of his breath beneath my palms and see through his eyes as we glided in on the wind. His roar filled the air, drawing hordes to the balconies of the castle.

Moonstone wasn't an expression of power carved from Fae suffering, not like the Vermilion Palace. It was a statement of beauty, distilled and untouched by time or war. Shimmering beneath its three namesake orbs, its white façade cast a silver glow, as if it were born of a dream rather than quarried stone.

Tall spires crowned with crescent finials stretched toward the sky. The stones interlocked so seamlessly as to seem cut from a single block at a distance. A vast wildwood of oak, ash, and yew curved protectively around it in a perfect ring, almost as if the trees revered its walls and refused to close in further.

Wildflowers bloomed along the banks of the moat, magnificent and bright, even in the pale moonlight. The moat itself spanned at least seventy feet and was fed by a small river that entered from the west and flowed out to the east.

With the drawbridge casually down, it seemed less imposing and more inviting. It would be easy to forget that this was the domain of a queen who, according to Umbryss, commanded the realm of nightmares as surely as I had, so very briefly, commanded aspects of death and magic.

In the simplest terms, the castle had been torn from a fantasy painting and brought to life.

Once Umbryss had settled, I unstrapped from the saddle and stretched. My back ached from the hours of sitting. Then I made my way down, stopping for a moment to pat his neck.

"Is this a snake pit?" I asked, once again thoroughly blind and suddenly very unsure of myself. Rich people always intimidated me, and everything about this place screamed money and power.

"Oh, most certainly," Umbryss said with a low chuckle. "But I'm sure you can handle it. If you need me, just step out onto a balcony and call, like we talked about."

Neither Umbryss nor I were certain as to why the Night Queen had invited me to the party, but we'd worked out a few things in advance. He had given me the lay of the proverbial land within. The Night Queen, Runa, had three daughters, including Willow. The other two were married and present at other courts for the evening.

She relied heavily on an advisor, Kiran, who had been at her side for longer than memory. And Runa was typically capricious and conniving, like all Dark Fae, or at least Umbryss said so. I did take exception to that, given my current state. I didn't see myself as conniving, but maybe that was a lack of practice rather than my true nature. I'd outwitted my aunt in her own court, after all.

The rest of the Night Court shifted and changed as various

families moved in and out of the Queen's favor.

With a deep breath and a last stroke of my hand on Umbryss's scales, I made my way down the wide avenue paved in flat, irregularly shaped stones, a journey made easy by the line of guards on either side. I simply kept my distance between them equal, which kept me guided right down the center of the road.

Just short of the end of the drawbridge, I was met by a tall person, a man. Though something about him seemed off. I couldn't explain it, but my sense of him seemed to shift as if he were in flux. He gave off a solid sense of charisma with just a few words, immediately setting me more at ease.

"Your Grace," he said, his dark voice warm and sweet without being syrupy. There was even a smile in his tone that sounded genuine enough. He spoke English, and his accent was British. "Welcome to Moonstone. I am Callie of House Shattermark. I represent Morari, one of the realms east of here. Her Highness has asked me to be your escort for the evening." He bowed and offered an arm, which I took.

"Thank you," I said. "So, is it Lord or Master of Shattermark?" I had no idea what the etiquette was here.

"Primarch Shattermark, if you're feeling ceremonial," he replied, tone light but practiced—like someone who'd sidestepped more than a few social daggers in his time. "Callie, if you'd prefer something less exhausting.

"As for you... well. Your Grace, The Crown Princess of the Vermilion Court, is technically correct, just not practically useful. No one here will call you that. Primarily out of bitterness. The best you might get is 'The Red Queen,' but likely not even."

"Yeah, let's not go there," I said.

He turned toward me fully, and I literally felt his gaze traveling over my body... it was oddly sensual, almost as if he'd run his hands over me. It didn't seem a judgmental examination, just... assessing. The kind that said he was already plotting five moves ahead, and I was one of them.

"You might consider choosing a different title. Something palatable. Strategic. Less reminiscent of two-thirds of the world going up in smoke or stealing someone's realm."

"Cait really is fine," I said with a smirk. Then added. "Or perhaps Skaja."

Callie chuckled, rich and genuine. "Hmm... I think not. Let's go with Lady Nochtanmore," he suggested. "No one here will dare call you by your given name, after all. But I'll certainly keep it in mind... should we find ourselves alone."

I paused at that and placed a hand on his chest, feeling a silk sash beneath my fingers. "Okay, first things first. If we find ourselves alone, I expect you to mind your manners. You're... uh... not my type."

Callie gave another laugh, louder this time, and right in the middle, it changed, becoming a little higher and much more feminine. The arm I had a hold of shifted as well, going from firmly muscled to soft and lithe. Beneath my other hand, his chest expanded, and I found myself cupping a very full breast through the fabric.

"Oh! I'm so sorry," I said, taken aback and jerking my hand away, completely flummoxed.

"I am everyone's type," she whispered conspiratorially.

"I'm spoken for—betrothed, you'd say," I added. "Neat trick, though. I know a few people who might find you very appealing."

"But not you." Her feminine voice was just as rich and seductive—thoroughly so, like she was caressing my body with every word.

"No," I said firmly, though I wasn't sure the corners of my mouth agreed as they tugged upward. "Definitely not." I cleared my throat. "So... uh... do you have a preference for pronouns?"

"Any will do, I'm not picky."

"So noted," I said, looping my arm through hers. "Shall we paint the roses red?"

"Indeed," she answered, a smile in her voice. "We'll paint quickly. The Queen does so adore her beheadings."

I laughed. "You've read Alice?"

"Darling," she drolled. "I've lived Alice. I'm just better dressed. And before you ask, it's absolutely true. We're all mad here."

I barked a laugh. "Well then, I'll fit right in."

We ascended a long staircase into an entrance hall before breaking off to our left and up one side of a curved staircase to the second floor. From there, we stepped straight into a large open room where soft music played, and people milled around the perimeter of a dance floor.

Callie whispered to a gentleman who simply announced me as Lady Nochtanmore. If I'd had any illusions that I could just slip in, they burst immediately as the ambient chatter, music, and movement ceased. I half expected to hear a record scratch, and I was so glad I couldn't actually see anyone, though I felt everyone turn unnervingly in my direction.

I smiled as pleasantly as I could and followed Callie's lead as we stepped to one side, allowing others to pass. A few moments later, the music started again, and the chatter resumed.

People, Fae, I assumed, of all types danced some kind of organized Elizabethan thing, the kind of dance that involved a lot of raised open palms, curtsies, bows, and turns. Dear Goddess, I hoped no one asked me to dance. Fae or not, I had two left feet, and I'd certainly stumble into furniture or step on someone's toes.

"Caitlin," Willow called, all but screeching to a halt next to me. "I told you I would see you again." She turned herself toward my escort. "Lady Shattermark, do be a dear and fetch us some wine, would you?" Then, to me, "Are you quite alright? You look rather pensive."

I drew in a slow breath, steadying myself against the noise —not sound, but presence. The room was a tangle of bodies and intentions, all of them brushing too close, weaving in and out of my awareness, and pulling my focus this way and that. I was developing a headache.

"They're all bleeding together," I murmured. "Hard to separate one from the next. It's a little too much."

"Then just focus and let your attention draw back," Willow said softly. "You're safe here with me. No blades but words tonight. And you're an honored guest if you've forgotten."

It took a minute before I got what she was saying. And I didn't shut it all out. I wasn't stupid. Letting my guard down in a room like this was just begging to get metaphorically—or literally—shanked. But, with a little effort, I eased the reach of my senses, tightened the range. Less of the room. Just a few feet. Just the ones near me.

The tension drained from my shoulders, and my spine stopped trying to impersonate a steel rod.

Leaning a little closer to Willow, I muttered, "An honored guest? Am I supposed to curtsy or just try not to bleed on the carpet?"

"You are from another realm, here by invitation. That means no one under my mother's rule will harm you."

"So, Callie is free to be as obnoxious as she likes," I whispered.

She gave a smooth laugh, rich with conspiratorial humor. "You catch on fast."

"I'm not as dumb as everyone thinks."

Several people brushed past me just as Willow pulled me aside. "You look fabulously terrifying, by the way," she whispered. "I heard about your outfit when you landed. It's an… interesting statement."

I gave a slight bow. I had been lucky, as it turned out, Umbryss had confirmed that, indeed, the leather pants, stand-collar tunic, and surcoat were all black. A purple undershirt, likewise high-collared, gave the entire affair an almost clerical look. The left breast was adorned with the circling ravens of The House of the Morrigan. Umbryss had been clear that I looked like I was going to a military parade, not to a party. Perfect, in my estimation, let them think what they like.

"Now," Willow said, slipping her arm smoothly through mine, "I'll guide you around and let everyone see you before we start meeting the pit vipers."

"Fantastic," I muttered. "Maybe I'll get lucky, and they'll bite early."

Willow giggled. "You're funny."

Callie caught up a few moments later, footsteps light but hurried, the scent of wine clinging to the air around her. "It's a good vintage," she said, pressing the goblet into my hand. "Strong, though."

I took it carefully. The stem was cool against my fingertips. I raised it, inhaled first—floral, rich, slightly sharp. "Smells expensive," I said. I took a small sip. It was smooth, with just enough edge to remind me I hadn't had alcohol in forever.

I definitely needed to pace myself.

As we moved through the space, I let Willow steer while Callie narrated like a well-dressed audio guide. Stone floors underfoot—polished, judging by how much my boots didn't grip. The scent of incense clung to the air—sweet, earthy, and entirely too intentional.

At one point, someone brushed against me—too close. I stepped back instinctively and landed heel-first on something soft and yielding.

Callie made a noise like a startled mouse. "My tail," she hissed.

"Sorry," I said.

"But are you?" Callie asked with a bit of cheek.

I laughed. "Of course I am. But you really shouldn't let it drag on the ground."

"It's a Hobson's choice, I'm afraid," Callie responded. "Stepped on or whacking people unintentionally, those seem to be the only options." Then her voice lowered, turning sly. "It has a naughty little mind of its own."

I smirked at that. I couldn't help myself.

Another figure approached—lighter steps. The scent was sharp and clean, like cold iron wrapped in crushed violets. Feminine, and with the kind of quiet composure that suggested hawkish eyes and a nose for trouble.

"Ah," Willow murmured. "Here comes Roselle—the Queen of Thorn's Reach. Northwest coast. Poison skin. Smile with care."

"Friend or viper?"

Willow's fingers brushed my arm with a featherlight squeeze. "Oh, viper, for sure."

Roselle's presence hit my awareness like the prick of a blade. The way she moved said powerful and sly.

"Lady Nochtanmore," she said. Her voice was glass—sharp enough to cut. "A pleasure, I'm told."

"I'm sure you were," I replied, matching her distance with my own.

Willow muffled a laugh at my side. Roselle didn't react. She just regarded me. The way an apex hunter watches something it isn't sure is prey—or competition.

"I understand you've undergone quite the transformation," she said at last. "One hopes it… suits you."

"Oh, you know. Bleeding. Screaming. A little soul-dislocation," I said lightly, then added, a touch of menace in my voice. "But I'm settling in."

My fingers tightened around my glass. Beneath my skin, something thrilled—dark and extremely sharp-edged. I really needed to get a handle on that.

Even so, I held her gaze—or the idea of it—and didn't blink.

There was the faintest twitch in her presence—offense, maybe. Or interest. Hard to tell.

I let a slow, fanged smile play on my lips. "Don't worry. I don't expect we'll like each other."

"Good," Roselle said, with the subtlety of poison sliding into wine. "It saves us both the effort of pretending."

She didn't say anything else. Just turned and slipped away, silent as winter air.

Willow squeezed my arm. "Are you okay?"

Was I?

Honestly I wasn't sure. I had gotten a thrill out of that. Testing boundaries. Tasting for weakness. It was dangerous. And nothing I knew how to turn off.

After that, though, things settled as we met the lesser nobility.

We were introduced to a small army of Fae lords and ladies, each one more composed, more refined, and more utterly convinced of their own brilliance than the last. They offered compliments that weren't compliments, questions that were really jabs, and observations shallower than my wine glass.

The royalty didn't like my family anywhere, it seemed.

Which was fine.

Because the feeling was mutual.

Then Irexielle arrived.

The Queen of Corvallen stepped into my awareness like a symphony turned savage—every movement graceful, controlled, and hungry. A living performance piece. A goddess of curated chaos.

I recognized her name instantly.

Sithraine had been clear in our chats about her legacy... and her failings.

Corvallen was famed for its pageantry—its poetry, its performances—but behind the curtain it was a bureaucratic nightmare. Court factions crumbling, provinces starving for attention. Irexielle ruled with perfect artistry, but her people suffered under the weight of governmental neglect. Corvallen was a disaster.

"Lady Nochtanmore," she said, voice like velvet polished over steel. "What a surprise to find your kind invited here. One might assume Moonstone has lowered its standards."

Not a delicate insult. I bristled.

"One might assume Corvallen has more pressing issues than the guest list," I replied. "But I suppose spectacle helps distract from collapsing institutions."

Willow's grip on my wrist tightened.

I kept going.

"I hear your latest festival nearly bankrupted half the coastal baronies. Or was that another brilliant moment of artistic sacrifice?"

The nearby conversation died, and everyone turned our way.

Willow shifted beside me. A warning press against my wrist.

I ignored it.

Irexielle took a step back and squared her body toward me, like a beast ready to pounce. "Bold," she said. "Or foolish. I wonder which."

"I wonder," I said, voice dropping low as I angled my chin toward her, "how much of that frost you wear is armor—and how much is just hiding the rot underneath."

Willow inhaled sharply.

Irexielle didn't move.

Finally, she said, thin and cutting. "Careful, child. Corvallen is not Moonstone. We do not tolerate insolence from those who cannot defend their words."

"Then try me," I said as magic swirled into my chest, almost instinctively. "I'll make sure you don't get back up."

Every Faerie within earshot went impossibly still.

Willow tugged me back a half-step.

I let her—because suddenly, all I wanted to do was break Irexielle. Crush her underfoot. End her.

And the desire was hot and dragging and wrong in a way that shook me.

It wasn't me.

Except… it was. I was reveling in it. Maybe Nyxiel was right.

Irexielle just lifted her chin and walked away—silent, perfect, and dangerous.

"Holy shit, Cait," Willow whispered. "Are you okay?"

"Perfectly," I lied, taking a sip of my wine, but my focus stayed firmly on Irexielle.

We wandered a bit more, but a palpable scent of fear trailed me. I had just terrified half the attendees.

"I should introduce you," she murmured. "This is someone you'll want to know. And do try to be polite this time." Then she added in a hiss. "No matter what."

That wasn't encouraging in the slightest.

She guided me between dancing silhouettes and the sound of fae strings. I sensed the others in the crowd. They all had a feel to them. Some faded, some cold. A few bright and sharp. But him? The one we walked toward. His presence seemed to smolder, like a bonfire not quite out—waiting for fresh breath to bring it to life.

No, that wasn't right. It was worse. He exuded a barely contained rage and pride. Whoever he was, he wasn't going to be a friend any more than Irexielle or Roselle.

"Your Grace," Willow said, tone going smooth and careful. "Allow me to present Lord Aurex of Embereach."

"My lady," he said with a voice like rich smoke—velvet over coals that crackled beneath the surface.

I offered my hand. His fingers brushed mine—hot with magic, like gripping a poker pulled straight from a fire. His presence radiated threat and swagger, and somehow, I didn't recoil.

I leaned in, drawing a matching heat to my skin.

"You have a powerful aura about you," he murmured. "That pleases me."

"I wasn't aware approval was required," I replied, barely masking the urge to bare my teeth.

He laughed. Not cruel, not mocking—just amused. Like he was watching prey from a distance, trying to decide if he should pounce.

"You know, your family and mine are one and the same," he said, head turning as if looking elsewhere. Though I felt it— the weight of every iota of his attention fixed on me. "My grandfather was your great-grandmother's husband."

"Was he?" I let boredom coat my words. "Do tell."

"Yes," he continued. "She should have been Queen of the Vermilion Court, and my grandfather King."

"Prince Consort," I corrected, clipped.

He stilled. "I'm sorry?"

"Queens have always ruled the Vermilion Court. If a man is taken as a husband," I said sweetly, "he becomes Prince Consort. Not King. Men don't rate rulership."

Willow tensed, holding my arm a little tighter as if to ask: *What the fuck are you doing?*

"That's a matter of power, my dear. If you have enough, you can change the rules."

"Let me know when you do," I quipped.

Aurex leaned in, voice low and threatening. "You'd do well to wonder why it is I feel comfortable confronting a bearer of The Morrigan such."

"A dazzling lack of self preservation instinct perhaps?" I said sweetly, then added with a bit of acid. "Cousin."

He opened his mouth to retort, but I turned my back, facing Willow. "I'm bored. Let's get another glass of wine."

"Always a pleasure, My Lady," Aurex said. "And so very interesting to make your acquaintance, Your Grace."

"And you… Uh… Lord Embereach?" I replied as if reading his name from a table card.

"Indeed." He swept away, leaving the scent of burnt something in his wake—something foul, like plastic. I let out the half breath I'd been holding for most of our conversation.

Willow didn't speak for a full minute, then she said, "That wasn't a good idea."

"What?" I shrugged. "He's an asshole. I've faced worse."

"No," Willow said. "You haven't. You've never faced anything like him." She paused, then, seeming to decide better of it, she said, "Let's just enjoy the party."

By the time we'd finished the circuit, I was fairly sure the only sincere people in the room were Callie and Willow, and some poor serving girl who'd managed to stumble and crash into me. Fortunately, her tray was empty.

Still, I smiled. Or something like it. Because in the Night Court, apparently, baring your fangs was practically a greeting.

We milled about quietly. The dancing and music had stopped for a bit, and the murmur of conversation grew loud. I had the distinct feeling that all eyes were on me. Certainly, I could feel people turning their heads toward me frequently. There were a few hushed whispers, but only a few.

I decided not to pay attention. I reached up. "May I?" I asked, my hand poised in front of Callie's face.

"Certainly. Though I may have a hard time containing myself at such intimate contact." Her tone was teasing—mostly. Clearly, she wasn't getting the message, but I let it go.

Her cheekbones were high, and she had a soft jaw with a narrow nose. Her ears were pointed, and her forehead rose, melding with two small but relatively sharp horns.

"Lady Shattermark?" I asked. "Are you a devil?"

"Succubus, actually, but it seems you've taken the measure of me," she said, a seductive tone in her voice. "Had I but known, I would have worn a dress rather than this bloody suit. Something easier to… lose."

"I'm sure Willow could find something in her closet," I joked, then leaned in closer. "So, you feed on sex, then?"

Callie laughed. "I feed on food. Our needs are more nuanced than that. We don't subsist on sex. We sample the pent-up desires and burning shames of others. They're delicious. Let's take a closeted lesbian, for example."

Willow chuckled. "Oh, here we go."

"This I have to hear," I said, slowly releasing the hold on my senses, giving them more play. At least two people had already knocked into me as we walked. One of them had elbowed me in the tit—that had hurt.

"So, imagine said woman goes to a bar. She's married—has been for years. Clearly unsatisfied by her hetero-lifestyle, she wishes to know. Following so far?"

"I am," I said, the arch grin still tinkering around with the corners of my lips.

"She's grown up in a religious household," Callie continued, "with all of the typical sexual hangups that accompany such. Her pent-up desire is like the lick of rose hips and honey to us, an immediate draw. I would seduce her, and as the moment grows closer, I begin to take away all of the guilt and misery. Her hangups simply vanish as I consume them. And, if I'm honest, I give her the best carnal experience of her life. It's a win-win."

I laughed and turned toward her with a sly grin. "I see. That was oddly specific. So, do you always give the best carnal experience?" The wine was clearly getting to me—and to my tongue.

"She does," Willow whispered.

My cheeks flamed. It was the wine, of course—definitely the wine. I gave a nervous laugh. "Good to know."

"Oh, goodness," Callie whispered. "That is an adorable shade of pink. I had no idea you'd be so easy."

I took a long gulp of my wine, finding the bottom. "I am not easy," I said, but there was a bit of giggle in my words. Shit. One glass? I needed to slow down.

"You know," she whispered in my ear. "You seem to have some pent-up desires of your own."

"For my wife, Callie," I replied. "No one else."

"Oh, Cait," she chuckled. "Your pants are on fire right now. Remember, I can practically taste repressed needs. You have the flavor of a bride feeling guilty on her wedding night."

"Enough," I snapped in a sharp hiss. "Stay out of my head. You seem nice enough, but those are my private feelings—not your business." That was way too close to home, and it left me feeling shaken.

"She's ready for you," someone whispered to Willow.

"Time to pay the piper," Willow told me as she and Callie took my arm.

CHAPTER TEN
THE NIGHT QUEEN'S PROPOSAL

Callie and Willow led me back around the other side of the crowd and out. We followed the grand staircase up to the third floor and into what I assumed was the reception hall, much smaller than I imagined. I'd once been to Hampton Court Palace in England, and this room reminded me very much of the King's Privy Chamber. Besides the three of us, only two other figures were inside at the far end. Queen Runa and Lord Kiran, I assumed.

Callie announced us as we entered. "May I present Lady Nochtanmore, Crown Princess of the Vermilion Court and heir to the High Shaddani Imperial throne. And, of course, Velira, Crown Princess of the Night Court."

Imperial throne? Okay, so that was a new one. And Lady Velira? It was a beautiful name. I was surprised that Willow preferred something else—probably a nickname, given how tall and thin she was. It seemed odd.

We approached, and Willow tugged at my arm gently. "And… bow. Head down," she whispered.

I bowed perfunctorily as Willow gave a deep curtsy.

"Yes, yes. Enough already." The Queen's voice had a stately ring to it, coupled with a genuine irritation that I'd expect out of Dame Judy Dench playing Queen Elizabeth. "Welcome to the Night Court, Lady Nochtanmore."

"Cait, please, Your Majesty," I said as I stood and faced her. I let my perception slip into the Weave and had to stifle a gasp. Kiran, her advisor, was like everyone born of Shaddan. His body was mostly a swirl of red. But the Queen? She didn't shine exactly. Because how would someone shine in midnight blue? Her entire body was full of it, made of it. It was as if she weren't simply a woman who wielded magic. It was as if it were magic itself. It was awe-inspiring.

A worthy equal.

A startled pulse of heat flashed through me—that thought felt... wrong.

A worthy equal?

What the fuck was that?

A clap and a chuckle. "I think I like you already. My daughter has told me quite a bit about your first meeting. She was quite taken with you, I think."

"Mother!" Willow protested, then to me, "Not like that. I just told her I thought you nice and very grounded."

I did my best to suppress my smile. "Her Grace is too kind." Yeah, I'd seen Shakespeare in Love *and* Victoria.

"Pfft," the Queen said. "Thoughts, Kiran?"

"As The Morrigan's Defender, she certainly dresses the part," the man mused, his tone bored—like I was an exhibit he'd already seen. "Tell me, Lady Nochtanmore, what are your thoughts on the Night Court?"

"Well, the visiting nobility are all crass and not fit to sweep the drawbridge. As for the rest," I paused and sipped my wine, just long enough for him to expect diplomacy. "From what little I've seen? It's a charming little nest of courtiers... though, mostly two-faced."

I wasn't going to lie.

Callie made a choking sound, and Willow suppressed a snort—poorly.

After a long pause, just as I was about to apologize, the Queen started laughing. Laughing to the point of tears.

"Oh, I do like you, Cait," she said. "Do you have any idea how hard it is to find someone plain-spoken in this place? It's always Your Majesty this and Your Majesty that. I can see what Willow likes about you. And if they had only two faces each, I might manage them better."

"Some more wine for our guest, Kiran," she added when her amusement had died.

"Now, it seems you've met your rivals," Runa said. "I was wondering how you might react. I half expected to have to toss you and Irexielle into the garden where a fight wouldn't level the building."

"You invited them here for me to size them up," I said, suddenly getting it. "You wanted to see if I'd stand up or roll over."

"Spine is vital to rule here," she said. "So, yes, I invited them the day you accepted our invitation. I was… curious."

Kiran pressed a fresh goblet into my fingers. His body was there. His magic was there. But he was like a void otherwise. Downstairs, everyone had a presence about them, an aura. Not in the literal glowing sense, just a feeling about intent or the way they carried themselves. Kiran was completely blank. It gave me an uncomfortable feeling.

I took a sip of the wine to buy time and gather my thoughts. I was being played here. Not by Willow or even Callie, I didn't think, but Queen Runa clearly wanted something from me. I considered just asking outright, but decided to play along for now. She seemed like the type to get to the point quickly.

"She's a lovely woman," I said. "And we certainly have a lot in common."

"Indeed," the Queen said, her tone shifting abruptly to shrewd and hawkish. "You're both clearly strong-willed, stubborn, and irreverent. More importantly, you have both seen things that would likely have driven others mad, myself included. As such, I believe that, given your position, you would make a strong match."

I choked on my wine and sputtered, "Marriage!?" I coughed again, choking out, "That escalated quickly."

I noticed that neither Willow nor Callie reacted at all to the turn of events. They'd known this was coming.

"Oh, come now, Lady Nochtanmore. This can't be that much of a surprise. You're the heir apparent to the Vermilion Throne. You control two-thirds of the world. Many would seek your hand in a marriage of alliance."

I raised an eyebrow beneath my blindfold. "An alliance with a dead kingdom. I have no power, no army, and no prospects for either. Where's the appeal in that?"

The Queen took a sip of her wine. "No army? But I have an army, and I have allies. You need those. And as for power, you have more than almost anyone here, maybe all of us. Some of us combined."

Willow's hand twitched faintly against my arm.

"And you're okay with this?" I asked her.

The Queen answered instead. "Willow is no longer in the line of succession here. A marriage to a kingdom with fewer restrictions would be of benefit to her. As it so happens, Vermilion Court rules don't care one whit for her situation—or yours."

I pursed my lips. "Can she not answer for herself?"

Willow spoke up then. "Cait…" She swallowed and began again, more confidently. "Cait, I am loyal to my homeland. This alliance would benefit my people."

She said it like a diplomat.

What she didn't say? Whether she wanted it. And that silence was loud.

"With your arrival," she went on. "The Vermilion Court will flourish again. More Fae will return home. The world has been holding its breath, waiting for this. You must have noticed how the Nerin of the Vermilion Palace have been fawning over you. They see it, too."

A lightbulb might as well have appeared over my head. There was a spy in the royal palace. Umbryss, likely, maybe one of the others. I wasn't sure, but I was sure as fuck going to find out.

"I'm already engaged to be married," I replied with a bit more heat than I intended. "And you know that."

"Lady Nochtanmore," Kiran said, his voice dripping with condescension. "You are the Crown Princess of almost an entire world. A vampire, from Earth, no less, isn't a fitting bride."

"Kiran," the Queen interjected, her voice cool and

reproachful. "Anyone Lady Nochtanmore chooses is a fit bride for her. No one here can force her." She stood and walked to me, reaching out her hands.

I softened my expression, but I needed to find out what the hell was going on—here and back at the Vermilion Palace. I'd been an idiot to think I'd just get out of this whole princess thing scot-free. I needed to let this play out a bit more so I could understand the workings—the why of it.

So I said, "I need time to consider." I kept my tone neutral. Clearly, I'd stepped into a delicate situation, and I needed everyone here to think that I was actually considering this stupidity.

"Please," the Queen said. "I know that my court has its own opinions of your family, but I don't share them, and some here simply don't care where you're from. You will find friends here. In the meantime, remain the evening as my guest of honor."

I nodded. "I'll do that." I finished the glass of wine and bowed. "Thank you for your time, Your Majesty."

"You as well, Your Grace," she replied.

We backed out of the room six paces before Willow turned us around, and Callie caught my arm, guiding me.

Marriage? Honestly. They really were all mad here.

I didn't want to leave the party, but my mood had soured.

"Marriage," I sputtered, a foul look on my face and a rock in my stomach.

"Marriage?" I repeated incredulously as if that would somehow bring sense to it.

"Drink," Callie said, handing me a glass of wine. "Let it go. It's not like she can make you. Try to forget about it."

I scowled and took a long sip of the wine. This was my third glass, and for just a second, I worried about the consequences of drinking more. A buzz was already humming in my cheeks.

Truthfully, though, I was feeling no pain and pretty happy about it. Fuck it. I downed half the glass in one go. It would take the sting out of the whispered bits of conversation I picked up.

"...betrayers... house of ruin... no place here..." My head didn't have to swivel for me to know that every single one of those words and so many more were leveled right at me.

Runa had been wrong. I'd find no friends here. I wasn't even sure about Callie or Willow. Everyone had an ulterior motive of some sort. Willow, though, seemed trapped, almost. She was doing her duty to her people or to her mother. Whichever, it amounted to the same thing. I honestly felt bad for her, especially if I was considered her best prospect.

"Everyone wants something from me," I snapped, swaying just a little. "Liz wants me to be okay. Spoiler: I'm not. The Nerin want me to be the great Defender of All Shaddan." I lifted a hand with a theatrical flourish, nearly sloshing wine over my fingers. "And now—" I took another fat gulp of wine. "Now you and your mother want me to get married."

"You make it sound like a death sentence," Willow retorted, sounding a touch hurt.

"It's not that," I said, my voice rising. "I'm engaged. Remember? Engaged."

"Please, Your Grace," Callie pressed. "People are listening."

The murmurs of disapproval and judgment grew, and I scowled.

Fuck this place. And fuck these stuck-up people who judged me for being less than when most of them had probably never lifted a finger in their lives to help themselves. I was just about to tell them what I thought of their fucking judgment when strings began to tune. The notes cut through the din—clear and high.

Willow took my hand, snatched the glass from my other, and shoved it at Callie. "Get rid of that," she murmured. Then, to me, "Dance with me. Please. Before you start yelling at royalty—again."

"I can't dance," I argued, the words a little mushy, but I

followed anyway.

"You can move," she said. "And that's all this needs."

She guided me through the crowd, the press of warm bodies parting around us.

The first note hit me like a freight train: magic. It was a hum in the air, soft as a breath. The strings followed—slow and low.

Willow stepped into me, close enough that her scent—smoke and summer wind—brushed against my mouth when I inhaled.

My hands landed on her hips. Her palms slid up my arms, then settled behind my neck, fingers toying with the ends of my hair.

"That's it," she whispered, her lips nearly touching my ear. "Just stay with me."

The world blurred at the edges, turning soft and cobwebby.

It was a slow sway, bodies aligned from chest to thigh, her forehead brushing mine every few beats. More holding than moving. More breathing together than anything else.

Her hands wandered—not indecent, but almost. Down my spine. Around my waist. Following my lapel. Sometimes she gripped the fabric of my tunic as if deciding where she wanted me.

I let my head rest against hers, dizzy from the wine and her warmth and the way the music curled around my body.

She tilted her hips, a slow invitation that drew a soft sigh from me. The glow from the lanterns dipped lower, or maybe that was just my vision slipping.

Her nose brushed my cheek. My neck. Her mouth hovered at the line of my jaw, never quite touching, as though she were giving me time to stop her.

I didn't. I… I couldn't.

There were murmurs around us, but muted—more curious than scandalized. No one stepped in. No one interrupted. All the venom from before seemed to evaporate.

Willow finally tipped my chin up with a gentle touch, and her lips met mine—soft at first, then firmer, a lingering press that sent heat spiraling low through my stomach. A kiss that wasn't rushed or frantic. Just… slow. Certain. A claiming disguised as tenderness.

I melted into it.

When I pulled back, breathless and confused and suddenly less steady on my feet, I whispered, "Why? Why did you do that?"

Her forehead leaned into mine. "Because I needed to," she murmured. Then she tugged me away from the center of the room as the music faded.

Needed to. The words turned over in my head. That was how it had felt. A need. I needed her and the way I needed wasn't subtle.

Callie was fanning herself when we returned. "My, that was… hot."

I didn't catch the rest of what she said as the world started to spin. I staggered and leaned hard on Willow.

"Too much wine, I think," Willow said, but her voice sounded far away.

Someone—Callie, I thought, but I wasn't sure—led me out and up some stairs.

At some point, bursting with laughter, I fell onto a soft bed, my surcoat lost on the floor. Lips were on me. Fingers tugged at my tunic, slipping it off. My head lolled back over the edge of the bed at some point.

I felt like there should be guilt or remorse, but there was nothing. Just desire, raw lust. And that urgent emotional need, deep inside.

CHAPTER ELEVEN

AT LEAST I'M STILL WEARING MY BLINDFOLD

I woke to the music of a nightingale outside, accompanied by the other early noises of burgeoning twilight, what passed for morning in Shaddan. The air was sweet, with a scent of lilac and other fragrances I couldn't name. A cool breeze pushed into the room, the billow of the curtains sounding in my ears. It would have seemed sweet and idyllic, except...

...at that exact moment, I became aware of several things.

First and foremost, my head was pounding with a four-alarm hangover. Too much wine. Definitely too much wine.

Second, I was in a strange bed—enormous by the feel of it—and lying atop the covers. I was pretty certain I was still inside Moonstone. I hadn't been escorted to a dungeon somewhere and decided that was a plus.

Third, though, I was stark naked, and there were not one but two sets of limbs draped about parts of me. Worse still, the entire room reeked of sex.

I mashed down on my rising panic, pushing it into a tight little box. *No. No. No.* I wasn't going there. I was sure I could probably come up with a perfectly reasonable explanation for this. Something involving magic, or healing, or... hypothermia, maybe? Sure, hypothermia sounded good. Much better than "I got drunk and snuggled my way into a potential diplomatic incident and personal disaster."

"Fuck," I whispered.

In my brain, however, the words were more like an extremely sarcastic, *Nice job, Cait, and what will you do for your second act?*

Gingerly and with great effort, I lifted my head.

My blindfold was still in place. That was good.

To my right lay someone, and I reached out tentatively. Another blindfold on another head. Willow. Expected at this point. Also, not totally a bad thing, and I pushed back my rising panic.

Turning the other way, I reached out my other hand and found another head full of long, silky hair, completely mussed. My hand traveled down a bit to a slender neck, then a collarbone, and then... *Oh!*

I snatched my hand back just as it slid over a naked breast.

I sat bolt upright, ignoring the scorching hangover. "Fuck!" I whispered again, this time with a lot more vigor.

"Morning, sexy," the unfamiliar woman murmured. "Sleep well?"

I cradled my forehead. "Who... who are you?" I was more than a little worried about the answer. Did I miss someone?

"How soon we forget," she whispered, her breath tickling my ear. Something soft circled my left leg like a snake. I slapped a hand down and found a tail sliding up my thigh.

"Callie. Fuck. You scared me." I tried to scoot away but was hemmed in between them, and my left hand landed right on Callie's abdomen—very low on her abdomen. Too low. "Fuck."

She giggled and whispered seductively. "Do that again, naughty girl."

"Please tell me we didn't... that we weren't..."

"Weren't what?" Callie asked, her voice a lilting tease full of mock innocence.

"Leave her alone, Callie," Willow groaned.

"Did you put something in my wine?" I croaked.

"Good Gods, no," Callie responded, her voice turning angry. "I would never do that. I don't need to. If I want to lure someone to my bed, they come to my bed—consensually." She booped my nose with each following word. "Just. Like. You."

I opened my mouth to say something snide, but my stomach lurched. "Toilet," I groaned and tumbled over Callie in an effort to get out of bed, landing in a heap on the floor.

"To your left," Callie said, reaching out from the bed and tugging me in the direction she indicated.

I staggered through, crashing against the doorframe, and found the basin just in time, emptying the contents of my stomach. I'd had three glasses of some potent shit without eating a bite and danced with a woman in ways I shouldn't. I remembered that. Willow had kissed me, which was… frustrating for a host of reasons. And then…

"Fuck," I grunted and vomited again, and the four alarms in my skull turned to eight. Faerie wine was no joke.

Hands wrapped around my head and pulled back my hair. "Here you go, sweetie."

I gave Callie a thumbs-up as I puked again.

"It's not that I've never had strong liquor," I croaked when I was done. "It's that this body hasn't had a drop of booze in its life."

"Oh," Callie responded, drawing out the word. There was a grimace in her tone. "Sorry about that. I had no idea."

"Liar," I groaned and slumped against the cool stone wall.

She knelt next to me. "Stick out your tongue."

"Why?"

In no universe was I going to stick out my tongue for a naked woman just because she said so.

Sure, Cait, Nastasia's voice said in my head, *because you've never done that before.*

"It'll cure your hangover," she said.

Okay, I'd do it for that. Anything to silence the twelve-alarm ache thumping in my skull. A little drop of something, the consistency of Jell-O and tasting like piss and vinegar, landed on it. I swallowed. Moments later, the nausea settled, and bit by bit, my headache began to fade.

And now, unhelpfully, I could actually think about the night before.

Heat. Skin. Laughter. Someone biting my shoulder—pretty sure that was Callie. Or maybe that was Willow? Or… gods, had they both—? I shivered and then let out a nervous little giggle.

Nope. Not thinking about that. Not thinking about how soft Willow's skin was. Not thinking about how good it had felt. Definitely not thinking about how Liz was going to stake me through the heart with a chair leg.

Someone had definitely whispered something to me in Shaddani. Something about surrender. Then I remembered silk ties, more teeth, and a tail doing... things—definitely Callie. Willow didn't have a tail. At least, I was pretty sure she didn't.

I felt around my neck and shoulders. No marks I could discern, but I was wearing a necklace with a single fat jewel. Totally not mine.

I was very flexible last night. That seemed important.

Oh, dear Goddess.

No way was I ever telling Liz about this. Not ever. I'd already shredded her trust once with Nastasia and Morgan—"cleansing my conscience" at her expense like some sanctimonious martyr.

This? No. This had been a terrible, terrible mistake. My guilt would just have to haunt me this time, though I was having a hard time feeling any. I'd leaned into this with both eyes open, a little drunk, but open. What was wrong with me? Fucking succubus probably ate it.

Callie handed me a glass.

"Cold water," she said flatly. "Now, we need to pretty you up. Your mom is here, and she's fuming."

I frowned. "My what?"

"Sithraine," Callie said casually. "She's outside, standing next to the dragon. I'm jealous, really. Your ride is hotter than my dating history. I mean, fire, literally."

"Sithraine? Really?" I grumped. "She's not my fucking minder."

I couldn't decide what I was more pissed about. That I'd gotten that drunk and left myself at the mercy of these throne-thirsty brats, or that Sithraine had decided she could just come here and collect me like I'd broken curfew.

"Fuck her," I groused. "She'll have to wait. Just invite her in and have someone keep her busy."

"No way," Callie said. "She's Nerin. Runa would have an absolute fit. They're not allowed in here. She's not even supposed to enter Ebonmere. She better be careful that the Queen doesn't just kill her on the spot. There's no love lost between them."

"Oh, shit," Willow whispered.

"What?" I muttered, pulling myself off the bathroom floor and trying to get the disgusting mix of vomit and that jelly thing off my taste buds. "You got a toothbrush?"

"I hear my mother out there," Willow said, and the drapes slid closed. "Damn. Damn. Damn." She sounded panicked.

"What on earth are you freaking out about?" I asked.

"Night Court rules, dummy," Willow retorted, and Callie started to laugh.

"She's not going to marry you," Callie said dryly, still chuckling. "So I don't think that tradition matters."

"She already said she will."

"*She* is standing right here," I bitched. "And I'm not."

To me, Willow added, "Cait, if she finds out you've seen me naked, let alone…" She trailed off for a second. "Anyway, she'll have an absolute conniption…" Her voice died again, and then, in a whisper I didn't think I was supposed to hear, "I'm not supposed to want this."

That stopped me. But we didn't have time for feelings—not now.

"I'm too old for this teenage shit," I groused after a moment's quiet and shook my head. Then I stomped my way back into the bedroom. "Where are my clothes?"

A pile of fabric hit me in the chest.

"Thanks," I muttered sarcastically and started feeling around to figure out what went where. Fortunately, I hadn't been wearing anything complicated. I was not going to rush, though. Whatever weird rituals the Night Court had going on were none of my concern, nor were they my problem.

What *was* my problem, however, was my lack of underwear. I had been wearing a bra and panties. They were missing.

"Fuck," I muttered again. "Where's my—" Someone flung

my undies at me, hitting me in the face.

"Wow, she's got a mouth on her," Callie said. "Not at all like her mother."

"Nemhain was a prude," I retorted. It wasn't a lie, not in the slightest. I pulled on my panties and bra and struggled into the rest of my clothes. "Whose necklace is this?" I asked, holding it up.

"Yours," Willow answered. "It was a gift, don't you remember?"

I did not, and that thought alone made my heart skip a beat. The Fae didn't just give gifts. There were always strings attached. "I can't accept this," I said flatly and held it out.

"Too late," Willow said with a laugh. "You already did. It's yours, and if you leave it here, it'll just follow you home, so take it."

"Fuck, fine," I muttered. I didn't have time to fuss over it. I put it back on and tucked it under my tunic.

Ten minutes later, properly dressed and with my fuck-mat hairdo at least modestly fixed, thanks to Callie, I made my way outside, the Lady of Shattermark on one arm.

"How does she look?" I asked Callie out of the side of my mouth.

"Like a pinched woman with no sense of fun," Callie replied, a plastered smile coloring her words.

"And The Queen?" I hissed.

"Gloriously furious," Callie answered, then, as we approached, "Lady Sithraine, how lovely to see you. What brings you to the Night Court?"

"It's just Sithraine, now, Shattermark." Sithraine's voice was rife with disdain, and then she turned sarcastic. "But it is such a surprise that you are involved with this debacle."

"Please tell me no one is watching this from the balconies," I whispered.

"Okay, I won't tell you," Callie said with a dry laugh.

"Fuck." I muttered and huffed a breath.

As we finally stepped up to the trio, I decided aggressive was the best way to go. "Answer her question, please. What in the actual fuck are you doing here? For that matter, how did you get here?"

"When you didn't return late in the evening, Umbryss decided to come collect me."

I shot a cool glance at the dragon.

"That's not exactly how it happened," he said sheepishly. "I decided not to sleep outside and went back—"

Sithraine interrupted him. "It doesn't matter. Do you have any idea what you've done here?"

I gave her my most innocent smile. "I'm making friends and forging closer ties between our two realms. I fail to see how it's any concern of yours, though. As far as I'm concerned, it's in my best interest for me to gain a deeper understanding of the people outside of our court."

"A deeper understanding," Sithraine murmured quietly. "Is that what they're calling it these days?"

I jerked down my blindfold and gave her a withering look, mostly to camouflage my burning cheeks as anger rather than mortification.

"That's uncalled for," I retorted. "Now, let's leave before you humiliate me and the throne any further." I very nearly laughed at my delivery. It really did sound like something out of a Victorian drama.

Sithraine said nothing and began climbing onto Umbryss's back.

I turned back and took Callie's hands, leaning in. With a soft kiss on the cheek, I said, "You are an absolute ass, you know that? Both of you, really."

"I'll pass that along. You should come to Shattermark," she said, returning the cheek kiss with one of her own. "I'm sure we'd have a grand time."

"I'll keep that in mind," I muttered and made my way up onto Umbryss's back, trying desperately to ignore the soreness between my legs.

I shook my head. *A+ decision-making, Cait, as always.*

CHAPTER TWELVE

ALL HAIL THE RELUCTANT DISASTER

The ride back was awkward, to say the least. The saddle wasn't designed for two despite being large enough for at least three or four. Sithraine and I were strapped together in icy silence for all two-and-a-half hours of the flight. Sitting behind and pressed up against her back, I felt like a scolded child in the back seat of Ma's Honda.

The second we hit the ground, I reached around Sithraine, popped the restraints, and practically shoved her off the damn saddle. I slid down the rope ladder, scorching my palms the whole way.

They'd heal.

"What the fuck was that?" I demanded hotly as I landed on the ground, not even waiting for her to finish her own descent. "That was humiliating."

"And well it should have been," Sithraine said with all the calm and respect of a Mother Superior dressing down an unruly student. "You are the—"

"—Fucking Crown Princess," I finished for her. I wasn't going to back down this time, nor was I going to take this anymore. That familiar heat rose in my chest, dark and edged. I didn't care, even as I felt waves of chaotic delight float through my head. Magic wafted off of me—I could feel it.

"Your Grace, please calm yourself," Sithraine said, her voice lower, tinged with fear. Still, though, she held her ground.

Umbryss, on the other hand, rose off his belly and shifted away from me.

"I will not," I responded, my tone no longer heated but ice cold. "I am not your pet. I am not some treasure. I'm a person. The only reason this happened is that you have treated me like a mushroom, keeping me in the dark and feeding me shit. This ends now.

"If I choose to entertain myself in the other realms for any reason whatsoever, I will do so. You may have volunteered to protect the Vermilion Palace and keep it safe, and in my mother's stead—may she rest peacefully—I offer my heartfelt thanks. But don't think for a minute that I'm bound to you, this ruined empire, or anyone's rule but my own."

I drew in a deep breath, pulling back from the edge. It was easier here, not like it was on Earth at all. The chaotic, churning rage just faded, and I was able to calm myself.

Sithraine gave a relieved sigh, and even Umbryss settled back to the bone-paved floor.

"Your Grace," Sithraine said, her tone much more respectful and demure. "It wasn't my intent to humiliate you. I was worried for your safety. There are twelve independent realms. Any one of them might wish to see you dead. It would be normal to have an armed escort to such an event. By attending alone, even riding Umbryss, you advertised both your presence and our inability to protect you."

"Runa named me her guest, so I wasn't in much danger."

"From her or her subjects, no. But…"

I sighed, placing my hands on my hips in aggravation. She was right. Anyone in that room who wasn't part of the Night Court could have tried any number of things, and it would have been catastrophic. I'd almost thrown down with Irexielle as it was. I didn't know the rules, but then again, no one was telling me the rules.

"I need education and guidance, not imprisonment," I said.

"I've been trying to teach you, but…" Sithraine sighed and put a hand to her head, then, "I'll tell you what. Please submit to at least some structure. And I'll do better. I'll make sure you know everything you want. But you haven't put one foot in the reception hall or the throne room since you arrived. That has to change."

My eye twitched at that, but I nodded.

She went on. "It's a simple bargain, no need for formalities. You will need to continue your work with Vaelith. Morvaine will continue to school you in magic—whatever spells you'd like to learn. And I will provide you with education on the history of Shaddan and the current state of the other realms. But you will not attend any more events without an available chaperone. Finally, you will take your rightful place. Is that reasonable... Your Grace?"

"Seems so," I said through my teeth. I couldn't find a good argument against it that didn't make me sound like a sulky teenager.

"You will accept your responsibilities, and we will accept ours in return," she said, voice calm—too calm.

"Fine," I answered casually, but then I had a moment of panic. *Oh shit.*

"The bargain is sealed," Sithraine said, cold triumph in her voice, as the scent of embers washed through my nose and mouth.

"Fuck." The word tasted like regret and burnt toast.

You idiot, Nastasia's voice said.

I'd just inked a Fae deal with all the precision of a drunken toddler. All I needed now was a glowing contract and a 'Gotcha!' from some smug Faerie lawyer. And the benefit wasn't even something cool like vengeance or power. No, I'd signed up for homework and personal development.

I tried desperately to recover, but I knew it was too late. "I won't be housebound."

"Let's walk and talk," Sithraine said, heading toward the pathway out.

I paused for a second and turned back. "Thank you, Umbryss. I had a lovely time." Even as I said it, I had to remind myself—firmly—that I did not, in fact, have a lovely time.

Not that the memories weren't... pleasant. They were. Infuriatingly so. And no matter how hard I tried, I couldn't summon even a flicker of guilt or regret. It was like those emotions had been swept out of me, leaving only warmth and a vague sense that everything had been amazing.

Which, logically, it absolutely was not. I'd very possibly gotten myself into serious trouble—especially if Callie or Willow said anything. Goddess help me if they compared notes with Sithraine.

And then there were the servants.

In movies, servants always gossiped. I could practically hear the whispers already like a headline in The Daily Mail: The blind terror of Shaddan, caught naked and giggling in a succubus's bed.

Perfect. I was absolutely fucked.

Sithraine drew us all together that evening, in the council and reception chamber where the lower throne sat. At least we weren't doing this in the throne room. She'd had to drag me, practically kicking and screaming, into the room. Every step I took here seemed to lead me to one choice: sit down and take responsibility. It felt like a trap—it was. But still, I'd agreed, and it was a Fae bargain, magically stored in the Library below already, I was sure.

I sure as hell wouldn't break it. If Mother Shaddan destroyed the realm for Nemhain breaking trust with Drusera, I didn't want to think what she'd do to me.

If I'd thought vampires were bad about manipulation, it was only because I hadn't met Sithraine. The woman was an absolute pro. The next thing I knew, they'd be trying to make me a match for a marriage, as Runa had suggested. That was a sobering thought.

"Your grace, if you'll follow me," Morvaine said and drew me toward the far end of the room, the scary end—the one with the throne.

"Please sit," she offered as we reached our destination.

I balked. "Can't you just bring me a chair?"

Morvaine had said this would be an informal affair, given the limited attendance, which was why we were doing it here and not in the main throne room at the top of the central spire. Hell, I was still wearing the same clothes from the night before, though with a little effort and ingenuity, I'd figured out how to spell them clean and pressed. I'd even fixed my hair properly and doused myself with a bit of perfume.

"This is a throne room, not the library," Morvaine said, her tone exasperated. "The left and right walls are lined with pews for your council. Your seat is here since there is no official queen. Otherwise, you'd be sitting at her right hand on The Defender's Throne."

"There's more than one?"

I reached out, brushing my fingers along stone that should have been an armrest but wasn't. The thing was massive, more a sculpted barrier than furniture. I followed it around, mapping it in pieces: three seats fused into one leviathan, identical in height, though the backs rose in tiers from outer to inner. The center throne felt higher without physically being so. Fae architectural gaslighting. Great.

Carvings wrapped the arms and backs in patterns I couldn't decipher by touch. Something sinuous. Something sharp. Something bulky. Probably eels and wolves and cows again—Badb's utterly deranged aesthetic from Luminara. Cows. Honestly. I knew why, but I refused to unpack it right then.

My first, instinctive thought rose fast and cold. This is wrong. Break it. One ruler stands here. One throne. My throne.

I froze.

What the hell? One ruler? Since when was that a thought my brain produced willingly? Goddess, I really was losing it. And yet... it didn't sound half bad. I could have Liz at my side, the kids living a glorious royal lifestyle. Want for nothing. And I did have all those gnarly little predatory spells. I shook my head. No. I was not going to buy into this bullshit.

But... I kind of had to, didn't I? I'd made an open-ended Fae bargain. There was no getting out of it. Even as I thought it, though, I realized I was just excusing the weirdly giddy feeling in my chest.

Like I said: idiot. Still though, it suits you. Nastasia's voice in my head again. I really wished that would stop.

I hesitated. This would be stepping into a position from which I might never escape, and I would, barring murder or a horrific accident, live for thousands of years.

I turned back. The others were all standing in a semicircle, watching me expectantly. "This is a lot of pressure," I muttered.

"Your Grace, please," Morvaine prodded again, gesturing at the seat.

I sighed and then sat—somewhat primly.

For Sithraine and the other Nerin to suddenly kneel at my feet, I was prepared. I at least thought that might be possible. What I had not expected was the sudden hum and noise from the palace or the feeling that flowed through me. It wasn't specific, just a thrum through my entire body?

I shifted to the Weave and gasped. The entire palace, which had been so bleak and dark, was suddenly bursting with magic. From the flow of red in the walls, the seats, the ceiling, and even the columns, I suddenly knew why it was called The Vermilion Palace. It wasn't just red, it was alive—literally.

Morvaine was the first to stand. She walked over and picked up something from a side table and then returned, stopping in front of me. I sat there, stunned, unsure what to do, dread pooling in my stomach.

Don't. I wanted to say it, but the word snagged on something inside me. A faint tug, giddy and hungry, pulled the other way. And before I could stop myself, my lips curled into a fang-bright, predatory grin.

I realized, with a jolt, that I wanted this.

"I present Crown Princess Caitlin Ni Nemhain, Regent and Steward of The Vermilion Court," Morvaine announced, and then she set a crown on my head.

"A proper queen, please," Nyxiel whispered, like a prayer. I barely heard it, but it was there.

CHAPTER THIRTEEN

YOU'VE MADE YOUR BED, CAIT (AND SLEPT IN IT WITH TWO PEOPLE)

We ate after the coronation, and then Sithraine intercepted me as I left for my room. She pretty much dragged me through the halls. She wasn't even pretending to slow her stride for me anymore.

We stopped in an open space where the air felt wide, our voices echoing off stone and crystal. Larger than the dining hall, smaller than Umbryss's cavern. Probably. I was just guessing.

"Forward, two steps," Sithraine murmured. "And when we stop, say 'Royal Apartments.' You'll need to mean it."

I snorted. "Magic elevators. Sure. Why not. Where exactly are we?"

"In the atrium at the base of the tower," she replied, cool and unbothered. She sounded like someone escorting a child to a dentist appointment.

We stepped forward. I did as she asked. Something metallic slid upward toward us.

"Handrail to your left," Sithraine said. "Take it."

I fumbled a bit, found the smooth metal, and wrapped my fingers around it.

The floor jerked beneath me—my stomach dropped—then the motion smoothed into a steady ascent. It lasted long enough for me to overthink everything, then slid to a halt.

"We're here," Sithraine said lightly.

The nearest wall was warm under my fingers, a stripe of heat leading down a curved hallway. I followed it until my hand bumped a doorway.

"Great," I muttered. "New room, new furniture, new knee bruises. Love that for me."

"Quit whining, Your Grace," Sithraine snapped.

I stuck my tongue out at her when her back was turned.

A warm night breeze brushed my face as I wrestled the door open. It shut behind me with a puff of displaced air.

I did my best to explore the room thoroughly without braining myself or cracking my shins. It was divided by accordion doors of gilded wood—smooth, new-feeling. The northern half was a massive sitting area larger than my old apartment in the North End.

The north wall held a bookshelf. My fingers found the box Maggie had left for me, my transcription rod, and my copy of *Practical Manipulations: a Guide to Managing Fae Relations*. I managed to kick over a stack of magic theory texts clearly left by Morvaine. Rude.

The southern half held my bedroom. The bed was enormous. The bathroom felt the size of a gymnasium— sunken tub, shower, double sinks, all strangely modern for a palace older than most continents. Earth-coded comfort in an Eldritch ruin. Weird.

The entire eastern wall opened to a sweeping balcony, running from the reading nook all the way to the sleeping area. It was beautiful and luxurious. Maybe too luxurious, like someone had made it just for me. Which was… concerning.

Sithraine stepped in behind me, her voice velvet-wrapped steel. "This lift will only stop here for us or you—at least for now. The palace recognizes its Crown Princess when it senses her." A pause long enough to sting. "You may feel small. Alone. Overwhelmed. Remember that the palace does not share your doubts, even if you try to outrun your station. This is your home now."

There was a knowing edge to her tone—an implication I

couldn't miss. She'd known I'd catch myself on that fae bargain. She'd known exactly how today would end. She'd moved me while I was gone.

I didn't respond to that. What would I say? You suck? She did, but what was the point.

"What is that?" Sithraine asked as I stripped out of my clothes and readied for bed.

"What is what?" I asked absently.

"Around your neck, Your Grace?"

"The necklace?" I shrugged. "Just a present from Willow."

Sithraine laughed—loudly. The tone was... hard to place. A mix of genuine amusement, disbelief, and mild mortification. "What did you do, girl?"

"First, I'm a woman," I answered irritably. "Secondly, I didn't *do* anything."

She scoffed at that. "That's a betrothal necklace, Your Grace. You're engaged. To Lady Willow, I assume?"

"What!?" I squeaked.

No. No. No.

"I told them no!" I barked. "I told them I was already engaged. It must be a mistake."

Sithraine shook her head. I was glad I couldn't see her expression—though, honestly, I could picture it just fine: one part "Are you serious?" and two parts "This idiot is going to start a war by accident."

"Well, I guess congratulations are in order," Sithraine ventured. "Honestly, there are far worse matches. I had no idea Queen Runa wanted a match for her daughter."

"There's no match," I griped, my voice rising. "I'm not engaged to Willow."

I could practically feel her raised brow. "Yes, you are. And please don't insult us both by pretending you didn't accept something while you were busy swooning like a drunken half-wit."

"I'm telling you that I never accepted the offer! She just said..."

Oh Goddess, no.

Please accept this gift in honor of our betrothal. That's what

Willow had said.

And I my stupid ass had said the one thing that you never, ever say to a Fae when receiving something: *Thank you.* It constitutes acceptance of terms.

"Grasp the jewel and think about Lady Willow, if you please," Sithraine said. I could hear the arch grin in her voice.

With a trembling hand, I reached up and took hold of the jewel. I thought of Willow, her presence, how she had felt in my arms. The pull was faint but clear. Directional. I turned toward it, and the stone warmed. The scent of her washed over me. My shoulders slumped.

Sithraine laughed again, smugger than a cat on a warm windowsill. "That's one lesson you won't soon forget. Still— you're right. Your education just became a top priority. You're a babe in the woods here, Your Grace. A babe in the woods."

And with that parting gem, she shut the door.

"Holy shit," I whispered.

I had royally fucked everything. I sat down, feeling that the pit of my stomach had just vanished somewhere through the floor.

"Engaged… Liz is going to murder me." But Liz wasn't here. I had time. I could get out of this.

"And where do you think you're going?" Sithraine asked, intercepting me as I reached the door back to the lair, not even an hour after our last little chat.

"To straighten this shit out," I answered, trying to feel for the door, but Sithraine blocked my way.

"No," she said, voice firm. "You are not. You agreed to adhere to your responsibility, and that includes taking advisement and not doing anything more to jeopardize your throne."

That stopped me cold. We'd made a Fae bargain, and my

dumb ass hadn't even considered the possible repercussions. Did I even know what my responsibilities were? No, of course I didn't. And maybe that was proof enough that heading out to try to rectify this whole engagement business was a bad idea. I had no idea the laws, customs, or, well… anything really, about who and what I was now.

I slumped to the floor. "I really fucked this up."

"Oh, get up, Your Grace," Sithraine barked. "You're not a child."

"How am I getting out of this?" I asked.

"You're not," Sithraine stated. Her tone was relatively flat, but there was a touch of sympathy in it. "You could refuse the marriage, but you'd be dead in the blink of an eye."

She drew me up and led me to the library and pulled out a fat leather tome that groaned open.

"The primarchs rule the realms of Shaddan," she said. "Maura murdered most of them millennia ago. The ones you have now are what's left after the Night Queen finally put an end to her reign of terror."

I nodded. "Was Maura part of my family?" I didn't want to believe it.

"You are a direct descendant, but we're not our family, Your Grace. Your rule will be your own."

I hoped that was right, and I reminded myself that blood certainly wasn't everything. It wasn't supposed to be, anyway.

"Now," Sithraine continued. "Consider what I'm saying very carefully. Maura was a singular bearer of the Morrigan, just like you, and yet Runa was able to battle her to a standstill. There are eleven others like her. You've met four so far: Aurex, Callie, Irexielle, and Runa. Runa, though, is a cut above all the rest. She is very old and very cunning."

"Yeah, I got that," I grunted. "Like a fucking snake."

Sithraine continued, a hint of annoyance in her voice. "She could have killed you, you know. She didn't have to offer to host you at her palace as a guest."

I donned a sour expression. "That's only because she wanted something from me. Something I was apparently dumb enough and drunk enough to hand over without so much as a word of actual protest."

"That's Fae politics," Sithraine said.

"But doesn't duress or incompetency have any implications here?" I knew I was grasping at straws.

"No one cares about that," Sithraine replied, annoyingly perfunct. "Now, you need Runa as an ally, Your Grace. You have no army. Your people are scattered. You're basically alone except for the six of us. You're lucky to have her, and by proxy, Lady Shattermark."

"Yeah, I get that part."

"Others will be after your territory as well. There are several deposed primarchs who would certainly like to see their ancestral homes returned."

I shrugged. What was a few more bad guys. Okay.

"Still though, if they've been watching me all this time, why didn't someone just kill me when I was on Earth and get it over with?"

"Because you weren't the primarch yet. You can't claim a realm by killing some random heir on another world. You have to force a ruling primarch to surrender their lands. The key is a *ruling* primarch, seated and recognized. Now you are."

"Oh, shit," I whispered as I realized just what she was saying.

Sithraine gave a nod. "Now you understand."

"It's my head on the block—and mine alone. And anyone I'm associated with…"

"Continue," she coaxed.

"If I say no…" I swallowed. "And Runa decides she needs more leverage—" I broke off as the implications hit like a punch to the chest.

Sithraine didn't let me get away with it. "And what?" she asked evenly.

"That's not—" I blew out a breath. "Liz is still on Earth. There's no reason for her to be dragged into any of this."

"You told Runa that you are engaged to someone else," Sithraine reminded me. "That's leverage enough. And there are ways to Earth other than your gate. Ways that don't bleed magic across realms. Old ways."

My pulse kicked up. "She's not safe." I shook my head. "How does Runa know all this?"

Sithraine laughed, light as silk. "I'm sure her people have had eyes on your family for quite some time."

"So, Runa probably knows everything anyway." It wasn't really a question.

"Yes." Sithraine flipped a few pages, the parchment whispering under her touch as her finger traced a careful path down the text.

"But... Liz..." It was just a whisper. "Can't one of you tell her?"

"With Vaelith, Morvaine, and myself tied up training you, that leaves Naerith, Elarith, and Nyxiel to guard over eighty million square feet of royal estate. That's a tall order, even *with* the wards. So tell me—who exactly should I pull off duty to go warn your fiancée?"

"And the others? The other primarchs? What about them?" The last thing I wanted to worry about was a knife in the dark.

"Most are afraid of Runa," Sithraine stated, "and rightly so. I don't like the woman for a host of reasons, but she's no monster. She cornered you without ever having to threaten anyone around you. And she's going to make you thank her for it." She gave a long sigh. "As of right now, I'm your Veilkeeper—your chancellor or vizier, as it were."

"Now," she went on. "Let me explain how this all works so we can prepare you for when we host your engagement party."

"My what!?"

"We have until the next major cycle to plan your engagement party—roughly six months. Plenty of time to get you ready."

I put my head in my hands. *Fuck me, what have I gotten myself into?*

"Go on," I grumbled.

Sithraine started schooling me right then and there in the fine arts of Shaddani etiquette. Apparently, that meant beginning with royal jurisprudence. And the next book she opened sounded thick.

Very thick.

CHAPTER FOURTEEN

BECAUSE I THOUGHT YOU WERE WORTH SAVING

It was almost four weeks of constant minding, training, and education when Willow finally showed her face. Morvaine had told me to expect it when I had sent my formal betrothal acceptance—with gritted teeth. Sithraine, though, had been skeptical.

I suggested they place bets, but I was with Morvaine on this. Willow wasn't a shrinking violet. She'd show, if only to make nice and try to smooth things over.

As if. I had a mind to murder her.

I was dressed in the black A-line dress I preferred, paired with soft black boots. While Vaelith and I sparred, Naerith, rather unhelpfully, fired dummy arrows at me. They weren't terribly fast, and they carried soft pads instead of arrowheads, but damn, they still hurt when they hit, and I had several fat red welts from her shots. Still, though, I was faster than any human, and I managed to fend off Vaelith for the most part and avoid several of the nuisance projectiles.

"Hold," Naerith called, and Vaelith and I paused.

"You have a visitor, Your Grace." It was Morvaine's voice from the cloister, beyond my sixth sense. There was a distinct sound of cold triumph in her voice.

"Willow?" I asked in a hiss.

"Yes," Vaelith whispered back. "My money was on her staying away until formalities started."

"Sucker," I teased with a smirk.

I drew in a deep breath and exhaled slowly, steadying my nerves.

Turning, I felt Morvaine approaching. Beside her was, I assumed, Willow.

My chest tightened like I'd missed a step. For a heartbeat I wanted to cross the space and throw my arms around her. Kiss her. Make her mine—

What. The hell.

I crossed my arms and stood, waiting—and doing my damnedest to maintain my scowl.

"What could *you* possibly want?" I all but growled. "Haven't you done enough damage?"

Willow stopped a few paces away. "I came to explain."

I raised an eyebrow. "I'm listening."

"I'd rather have the conversation in private," Willow said. Her foot scuffed the ground, and the outline of her—that's how I thought of the way I saw people—seemed to shift a little uncomfortably. It was probably an act. "I'd at least like for you to understand."

I scowled. "Fine." To Morvaine, I said, "I'm going to my quarters to get changed."

No one argued. Willow followed me to the lift. A few minutes later, we were in my rooms, dangerous from a gossip point of view, but I had no intention of a repeat of our performance at the Midsummer Ball.

"Why?" I asked as I toweled away the sweat on my face and neck.

It was a simple question. It came out a little louder, a little harsher than I'd intended it to, but I didn't really care. She'd tricked me—cornered me with court politics, sweet touches, and a succubus with boundary issues. I wanted to know exactly what it was all for.

"Because my options are limited, and I'm tired of being a pariah in my own land. Besides, you're Vermilion Court. Polyamory isn't a problem here. I fail to understand your actual issue."

I shook my head and laughed in disbelief. "I'm not just Vermilion Court. I was born and raised on Earth."

I peeled off my boots and tossed them aside next to the bed. "That's something you knew. And if you didn't understand why I might have a problem with this, why did you drag Callie along for our little adventure?"

"Because if you'd balked," Willow said calmly, "you'd have still ended up in my bed and betrothed. Dark Fae don't waste opportunity."

I turned an ear. "So if I hadn't already wanted it…"

"Then I would've made you want it," she replied.

"You're a phenomenal fucking actress, you know that?" I said. Then I gave a mocking imitation of her voice. "Oh, Cait, I am loyal to my homeland. This alliance would benefit my people. Fucking please."

"Quit playing the victim. That's how Fae politics work, Cait. No one cares about your second thoughts. Why am I even explaining this to you? You were a fucking vampire. Goddess, you know how it works."

I frowned at that and chose not to unpack it. I wouldn't like the contents. "Regardless, arranged marriages aren't common in my culture. And I'm not interested in polyamory."

"Oh, Cait, please," Willow said, voice rising, incredulous. "You're really going to stand there and tell me you don't like having your options open? That you don't like the freedom to fall in love on instinct, to fuck whoever draws your eye? You fall hard. Fast. And you don't even see the pattern, do you? How it's always the dangerous ones? The ones with power? The ones like me?"

I opened my mouth and closed it again, because—well, she wasn't wrong. I'd been in love with two, even three at once, depending on how generously one defined "self-destructive obsession." My heart had a type, and that type came with fangs, magic, and a dangerous amount of charisma.

"That doesn't matter," I argued. "I'm engaged to Liz. I love her."

"No. Love doesn't matter," Willow said, tone very matter-of-fact.

I scoffed at that, but before I could interrupt, she went on.

"This isn't a love arrangement. This is a marriage of political alliance that betters everyone's situation. You gain an ally that you desperately need. I escape my arbitrary exile from court because of something I did ages ago. We all win. It's not like I expect you to love me. As long as we can provide an heir, we'll be fine."

I thought my burnt eyes were going to bug out of my skull as I snorted in disbelief. "An heir? I'm not exactly equipped to give you that. And neither are you." I paused for a second. "Wait? Are you?"

"There are magical means," Willow said breezily. "Some less fun than others."

I sat down on the bed. This was too much. "You do realize what you've done, right? You've thrown a grenade into my personal life."

"No," Willow's voice abruptly softened. "I know you think that, but I promise you. I saved them. Elizabeth, Katie, and Leah."

My eyes were wide. "How much do you know about me?" They really had been watching us. I hadn't really wanted to believe it.

"Until recently, not much, but my mother… she knows quite a bit." She paced for a moment, rattling things off as she counted on her fingers. "Caitlin Gráinne Reagan, thirty-three years old, well, thirty-four technically, given your time here. Daughter of Róisín O'Neill and Nemhain, Queen of the Vermilion Court. Separated from her sister at sixteen by Eric Schmidt and Marcella Carson, a.k.a. Maerta of Öland…"

She went on for at least two minutes, even mentioning bits about my relationship with Nastasia before I stopped her. They knew fucking everything about me except a few details of personal liaisons, portions of my time in Ireland, and the results of my last pap smear.

Goddess.

I just sat there, stunned. Liz and the girls had never been safe. I had been a ticking bomb in their lives without ever knowing it.

"You're Fae, Cait. Have always been. Swap your body around any way you like, vampire, human, it doesn't matter. It has no bearing on your soul."

Before I could react, she moved over and straddled my legs, lowering into my lap, hip to hip. The hem of her gown fell loose on either side, brushing my calves.

She was so close. The scent of her wild-flower perfume filled my nose, and her breath tickled my lips as she spoke.

"Don't you ever wonder why you're the way you are? You were never the faithful type. You're impulsive and reckless, and you have a naughty streak. The violence of the Dark Fae comes naturally to you. You like screwing around with others. You didn't become a police officer because you wanted to serve and protect. You liked sorting out the people puzzles and cornering suspects in their own words.

"Some humans have those traits, too. But you... it's like a religion with you. A thousand years ago, you would have enjoyed trapping some poor, hapless human in a twisted bargain. It's in your nature."

"I guess you have me all figured out," I said, my tone clipped, sarcastic.

"Tell me I'm wrong, then."

"You're wrong."

She laughed softly, derisively, running a hand down my neck. "Really? Tell me you don't crave this touch. You can feel it... inside. Changing. The urges. The needs. It's what you are... what you were meant to be. Not human. Not vampire. Faerie. A keeper of tragic lessons for the foolish."

I shivered at the feel of her fingers, and gooseflesh popped all along my neck and arms. "Stop," I whispered weakly.

"Make me," she breathed, voice shifting, taking on a darker, more seductive cadence. "I can be whatever you need me to be.

"You're all alone here. That's why it's so easy. Because you crave this feeling—sensuous, emotional, sexual. You need it like a fish needs water or Umbryss needs the sky. It's what drew you to the dark-haired vampire like the proverbial moth.

And to Liz. And Marcella. But they're nothing compared to us. We're their source."

I felt helpless. I wanted to close that distance, force her down, pin her to the bed, and ravish every inch of her. My breath was heavy in my chest and my heart pounded for it.

My arms were already around her.

Goddess, the desire was like nothing else, even the need for blood in my most desperate moments as a vampire didn't compare.

I whimpered a soft sound. Wet heat swelled between my legs.

"Yes," she whispered. "It's because I'm Dark Fae—because I'm such a good match for you—that it's so hard to resist," she sighed, her breath brushing my neck. "But I'm not here to trick you." She ran the tip of her tongue up the curve of my ear to the delicate point. "I feel it, too."

Her breath was like velvet against my skin, and I squirmed, shifting and squeezing my thighs.

"I didn't trick you into my bed. You wanted it. You just didn't know yet.

"Other than your mother and her sisters, you've never had a connection with one of us, but you've always been drawn to our magic—to us. The vampires? Jessica? Even Maggie? You know it's true."

Her words seemed to drift into my head on a wave of cotton and silk.

"You surrendered to me." Her voice slithered into my ears, sweet and sugary, fogging up my head. "Now, let me surrender to you."

I could just stop her. Right now. All I had to do was stand up. Just a thought to push aside the obvious glamour she'd slid into her voice.

I could, couldn't I?

But another idea flickered up—small, sharp, and very, very hungry.

I could also let her.

I could let her fall into me, melt for me, surrender in a way she'd never forget. I could make her mine without lifting a finger. The thought hit me like heat down my spine, shocking and almost... pleasurable.

I didn't know where it came from.

And in that moment, with her breath in my ear and the lie fresh on my lips, I realized: I didn't know where my humanity had ended and the Faerie had begun. Was I even still... me?

Her mouth found mine, and she bit at my bottom lip like she was claiming her prize, just a drop of blood, salty and warm. I pressed into her, wanting—no, needing—more.

She gave a gentle push on my shoulders, and I fell back to the bed. I stared upward into the darkness as she slid the hem of my skirt up to my thighs.

I can't do this. A weak voice in my head, telling me to stop, to push her out of my thoughts.

I didn't want to. It was so much easier just to give in and let it happen. And her touch was so... inviting.

You can resist... if you want to. Nastasia's voice, faint as a dream. *But is that what you really want?*

Did I? Did I care? If I gave in, I wouldn't have to think about tomorrow. About anything, really. And maybe it would ease this almost painful need for her that I didn't understand at all.

A soft, helpless "Oh" escaped my throat as Willow's mouth ghosted over my skin, her tongue drawing away the salty sweat of my chest. Her hands were soft and reverent—fingers grazing along the outside of my thighs, slow and patient as the moon.

Her breath blew warm, and her presence was heavier than gravity, pulling me in, down, under.

Then she was kneeling before me, her fingers finding the edge of my underwear. A gentle tug, a pause—like she was giving me time to stop her.

And I almost didn't.

I could just let her. I could take her and claim her for myself. Let her become mine.

But my thoughts continued down a familiar path. This would be detonating any chance I had to reconcile with Liz. It would be destructive. It would be Nastasia all over again. Hell, she sounded just like Nastasia. I couldn't let this happen.

My hand moved, almost of its own accord, closing around her wrist.

"Willow…" My voice came out quiet and a little raw.

She stilled, her face lifting toward mine.

"I can't," I said, and I wasn't sure if I was apologizing or begging her to understand. "Not like this."

A breath passed between us. She didn't pull away immediately. Just stayed there, hands still. And then, gracefully, she let go of the fabric. No protest. No wounded pride.

"All right," she whispered.

She stood, light as mist, and stepped back, the tension between us unraveling strand by aching strand. The duvet was bunched under one hand, my dress still hitched up. The heat still pulsed through my skin, begging her to touch me. I ignored it. I had said no. Not this time. This wouldn't be like before. I'd done enough damage.

"You wanted to know why?" She murmured softly. "Here's the real reason…"

I said nothing, waiting.

"Because I thought you were worth saving."

With that, she turned, arms thrust out before her, and after a moment, she found the door. Before she left, she turned slightly, tilting her head. "You will, eventually. You can't stop it." Then after a beat, she added in almost a whisper, "And neither can I."

The door closed and I blew out a relieved breath.

At least this wouldn't haunt me later—when I was alone or when I finally saw Liz's face again.

I just lay there. Staring at the ceiling. Breathing in heavily and trying to forget the fading scent of wildflowers.

It would have been easier—Goddess, so much easier—just to let the current of this new life take me away from my old one. Just let them all have their way. But I wouldn't. I loved Liz. And I was going to fight for that—and hoped it would be enough.

I think she likes you, Dorogaya.

"It's just manipulation, Nas," I responded to the phantom in my memory.

No, she argued softly. *You didn't see her face.*

That stopped me.

"Nastasia?" I called.

I waited.

But there was no answer.

I wondered then if maybe, just maybe, I might be losing my mind. Nas was gone. I couldn't pluck her soul from wherever it lay, not like my mother.

I pushed it aside. Eventually, my grief would resolve, and it would pass.

CHAPTER FIFTEEN
THE WOMAN IN THE THORN DRESS

I crossed the threshold into the royal dining room that night feeling completely... well... not myself. It wasn't what happened in my apartment. It wasn't anything anyone said. It was the fucking dress. I wasn't a dress person; I had never been. I wore them for special occasions, but... this? This was a bit much.

In the two hours I'd napped, someone had restocked my closet. Twenty new dresses—high Fae tailoring, regal and full of magic, if Sithraine was to be believed. Wraparound bodices, thigh-high slits, silver-web shawls. I'd fought twisted horrors with less anxiety.

I still assumed they were the ones behind the rather sudden and endless adjustments to the furniture throughout the palace, which felt like some cheap joke on the blind girl.

They never said anything. They just... did it. Quietly. Efficiently. Like I was some kind of particularly delicate houseplant.

Of course, I had to take Sithraine's word for what I looked like. She'd said this gown was relatively modest. I just hadn't realized she meant modestly covering, not modestly priced.

The dress was sleeveless, slit high up one thigh, and backless down to the waist. Midnight blue thread—allegedly—spiraled out from the bodice in thorn-like patterns. A sheer drape hung from silver clasps at my shoulders, shimmering like spiderwebs spun from starlight. The warm breeze from the wide, open windows worried it into a soft, restless flutter. The thigh-high black leather boots that supposedly went with it were at least only mid-heeled.

And the crown—karanite-infused silver and rubies—sat heavy and cool on my brow. It had a tingle to it, magical, like it had plans for me I wasn't privy to.

I couldn't see any of it, and that somehow made me feel more exposed than any amount of bare skin ever could. Honestly, it felt less like I was heading to dinner and more like a club where the cover charge was my last shred of dignity.

I would have preferred jeans and a T-shirt, but I didn't have any. And despite my arguments to wear one of my training dresses, Sithraine insisted on something more formal. Willow was in attendance, after all, having stayed for dinner, also at Sithraine's insistence—not at all awkward.

I stepped in, the fabric swishing about my legs, the crown a little off-kilter. There was the scrape of chairs as the Nerin all rose. Even Willow stood.

"Fuck, sit. Honestly," I said. "This is ridiculous. I'm still the same woman."

Their typical too-long beat of silence left me feeling more than a tad uncomfortable, then someone wolf-whistled, low, appreciative, and thoroughly unapologetic.

"Now that's how you make an entrance, Your Grace." Nyxiel. Leave it to the outspoken lesbian to comment.

"Didn't realize we were doing formal blood sacrifices tonight," Naerith said with a snort, and then, a beat later, she added, "You're the knife, in case that wasn't clear."

Of course, I am. I gave a wry laugh. "Great. As long as I don't have to clean up the blood. That *is* someone else's job, right?"

They all laughed, and we sat down. Elarith fixed me a plate and slid it over.

"I'm sure you look beautiful," Willow said—she sounded sincere.

"Thank you," I said, trying to sound breezy despite the heat crawling up my neck. I'd just turned her down, and now here she was, sitting beside me while I tried to pretend this dress didn't feel like a dare. It was absurd how exposed I felt, with half my skin uncovered.

"Here, Your Grace. Vegetables and wheat germ in curry sauce," Nyxiel said.

I almost believed her, but then Naerith snickered.

"Oh, Ha ha," I said with a wry purse of my lips. "Seriously, what is it?"

"Nyxiel decided you could use a meal from home," Morvaine said. "It's chicken tikka-masala."

"I'm Irish, not English," I muttered. "But appreciated all the same."

"I can get you some boiled potatoes if you prefer, Your Grace," Nyxiel said without missing a beat.

"No, thank you," I replied. "My mameo's dead, and while I miss her, I will never miss her cooking."

Willow snorted. "Boiled potatoes? Eww."

I gave her a flat look. "Better than fried Pixie wings."

"Don't knock it 'til you try it," Willow shot back.

I smiled despite myself. No one ate fried Pixie wings. I did know that. Not among the civilized courts, anyway.

"So," I said as I took a sip of my wine. "You were obviously on about something, Elarith. What did I miss?"

Elarith barked a laugh that sounded like the verbal equivalent of sharpening a dagger on a whetstone. "Nothing yet, but this is the best part."

From the sudden quiet hum around the table, I knew I'd walked straight into something. Something stupid and funny.

Naerith made a low, warning sound. "I will kill you where you sleep."

"Oh, come on," Elarith said with too much cheer. "You were twelve."

Naerith growled again. "I swear to the Moons, Elarith—"

"She had a crush on this boy from the Court of Embereach. Tavat. Tovit. Something tragically symmetrical. Anyway, she wrote him a love poem—a very long one. And then she glamoured herself to look like his 'ideal love.' Except…"

"She didn't?" Morvaine asked.

"Oh, no," Elarith snorted. "She did. It just wasn't quite what she expected," Elarith said, grinning. "She used the wrong sigil from the Mirror Charm Guide, so she couldn't see her own glamour."

"She stood there—" Elarith was in full performance mode now, one hand clutching her chest like a tragic heroine— "reciting this epic confession of love. It was a dumpster fire of verse. 'Your voice is the dagger that carves my name in moonlight.' And he said, 'You are definitely not my sister."

There was an audible snort from Willow. Even Vaelith let out a breath that sounded dangerously close to a laugh.

I nearly inhaled my wine and sputtered. "Wait. His sister? That was his perfect love? Like platonic sisterly love, right?"

Elarith shook her head slowly. "No."

I gasped.

"Wow," Morvaine said, mirth in her voice. "I knew Embereach was weird, but... just... wow."

Naerith, to her credit, just leaned forward slowly and said, very calmly, "It wasn't a glamour. It was an illusion. That's why I couldn't see it. And I didn't have Lane's Mirror Guide anymore because someone spilled juice on it, *Elarith*."

"But still," Nyxiel added because, of course, she did. "You didn't ask anyone?"

"No," Elarith answered for her. "She just traipsed off, blissfully unaware of her true love's... um... true feelings."

Willow was in hysterics. Vaelith couldn't help her laugh and finally burst out.

I wiped tears of laughter from my cheeks, careful not to smear anything important. "Gods," I said, breathless. "You're just like us."

Vaelith, composing herself, said gleefully, "We live longer. We're not immune to being twelve."

Naerith went conspicuously quiet, arms crossed. I couldn't see her face, but the silence was thick with sulk.

Finally, she muttered to Elarith, "You suck."

We all laughed again.

Looking back at me, Naerith's voice shifted, and she sounded way too happy to change the subject. "So, Your Grace... are you ready for The Seating of the Bloom?"

I snorted wine. "The what?" That sounded alarmingly lewd.

"You haven't told her?" Willow asked. I could hear the grin in her voice.

"It was on today's list," Sithraine said calmly. "I just hadn't gotten around to it."

"Nothing?" That was Nyxiel.

"I just said—" Sithraine started, but Nyxiel cut her off.

"A High Fae wedding isn't an event, Cait. It's an affair. Six months of required revelries, parties, ceremonial lunacy, vows, rituals, gossip traps—"

"—and insanity," Elarith added cheerfully.

"All very sly, sneaky, and underhanded, of course," Nyxiel finished, like it was a compliment.

"You know," I said, managing a smirk just for their benefit, "I kind of suspected that already, strangely enough."

"Oh, come on," Willow protested. "It's not that bad."

"It's the only kind of wedding where I've seen a bride bleed out during vows simply by accepting a wedding gift," Vaelith said.

I went back to poking at my food, trying not to show the slow, creeping panic coiling in my gut. I hadn't thought there were eels in the dish, but it sure felt like it.

Nyxiel leaned forward, speaking with far too much delight. "Oh, Cait," she purred, "The Seating of the Bloom is one of the oldest, most sacred traditions of the High Fae wedding cycle."

I raised an eyebrow. "Which means what exactly? Because that sounds like something you'd find behind a locked door in a brothel."

Snickers all around.

"It's a bonding ceremony," Nyxiel continued. "The couple shares a glass of the finest Fae wine—very romantic, usually very strong—and then they plant a flower together. One that represents their future."

"In a garden?" I asked, already dreading the answer.

"In a pot," Willow said sweetly. "A very elaborate pot. Family-crafted. Symbolically significant. Often enchanted to bloom in response to the couple's emotional state."

I blinked. "So we get drunk and plant a metaphor."

"Exactly!" Nyxiel said, clearly thrilled. "And traditionally, it's held in the finest room of the poorer House's estate. As a gesture of respect."

I looked around the dining hall. Then thought of my royal suite. Then thought of a hole in a wall I'd found earlier this week.

"Oh, good," I said dryly. "We're the charity case with the cool address."

Elarith chuckled. "Don't worry. You've got land, a palace, and the karanite mines. That still counts for something."

"Yeah," I muttered, stabbing a bit of chicken with probably too much force. "But I still have to plant a flower while engaged to a woman I barely know in front of an audience that wants to politicize the soil quality."

Sithraine laughed. "Yes, and doing it all while avoiding daggers, assassins, and political landmines. All very High Fae."

"I'd say you know me pretty well," Willow said, her tone full of cheek.

Nyxiel did a spit take and laughed.

The rest were silent, except Sithraine, who gasped in surprise, sounding thoroughly scandalized. "Your Grace! You didn't?"

I hung my head, shaking it. "We might have... Well..." I sighed. "You see, there was wine... And then Lady Shattermark did this thing..."

"Oh, wow," Elarith said. It wasn't the kind of 'oh wow' that meant 'that's awesome.' It was more an 'oh wow' of *you did what?'* and *'I'm absolutely going to need wine for this.'*

Nyxiel leaned over and whispered. "You should probably quit while you're behind, Your Grace."

I snapped my lips shut, cheeks flaming.

I couldn't see Willow, but could just feel the superior smirk wafting off of her.

Finally, I turned my head in Willow's general direction. "Blabbermouth."

Willow laughed.

Nyxiel snorted in amusement.

Vaelith said, "This is better than human soap operas."

I felt Sithraine shaking her head and was glad I couldn't see her face.

I swallowed a long drink of wine, then changed the subject. "So, on a lighter note, if you can all stop re-arranging the furniture, I should be good."

By now, of course, I knew what the ensuing silence meant. Though I couldn't understand what exactly the big deal was. Why wouldn't they want to talk about moving shit around? Unless...

"It's not you," I said. "Is it?"

Silence again, but then Vaelith said, finally. "No. It's not us. It's the palace."

"Wait, what?" That was a bit of a shock. The palace? I knew it had a life of its own, but this was like something out of Beauty and the Beast, albeit with less singing and more lurking dread. "Please don't tell me the furniture sings and dances."

They all laughed, and Nyxiel said, "Oh, Goddess, no. It's the Hidden Servitor."

"The what?" That didn't sound good.

"I thought that was a myth," Willow said.

Nyxiel paused, glancing around like she was checking for permission. Sithraine gave a faint nod—one of those "she's going to find out anyway" gestures. Whether it was me or Willow they were worried about, I didn't know.

Nyxiel leaned in a little, lowering her voice like she was about to tell a ghost story. "It's a magical construct, just a static enchantment, really. As you've no doubt noticed, the palace is... well, I'm not sure I'd say alive. But it does seem sometimes to have a mind of its own.

"Maura originally designed her to be self-sustaining. To protect herself if the realm ever fell into war." A pause. "Which it did. Often. Mostly because of Maura."

I had a sudden shiver at the way Nyxiel had just personified the palace as "her," but I said nothing, waiting for the other shoe.

"The palace has functions," Nyxiel said, pressing on in that eerie tone. "Lighting, hot water, small comforts. But the

Servitor was designed to do much more. And for a while, it did…"

I didn't at all like the way she'd trailed off. "And then?" I asked.

Here it comes.

I could practically hear Nyxiel's expression shift. "Then the palace decided Maura was a threat. She was forced to curtail its abilities before it did something… unpleasant."

I frowned. "So you're telling me the walls around me have opinions, and they once tried to kill their creator?"

Morvaine: "Technically, only once."

"That we know of," Elarith added unhelpfully.

"Wonderful." My tone was bone dry, and then I suddenly understood. "We're short-handed, and we have a wedding coming." My stomach churned at just the idea of the wedding, but I shoved that aside like everything else I didn't have time to process. "You turned those functions back on."

"We did," Sithraine said. "We have a Princess Regent now. We can't manage everything ourselves anymore."

I turned toward her, wishing I could see more than just the outline of her head. "And when it decides I'm a pretender and no good for the throne? Or what if I decide that this place is too opulent and needs to be dismantled and replaced with something less obscenely wealthy-looking?"

"Shh…" Naerith hissed. "Don't even say that."

A shiver slid down my spine, cold and sudden. I glanced around, the very air suddenly feeling much more sinister. "I wasn't serious," I added quickly—more to the building than the people. "The… uhh… new molding on the walls is lovely."

There was an extremely pregnant moment of silence, during which they all seemed to be staring at me, and then they broke out in gales of laughter.

"Oh, fuck all of you," I said, giving them the finger in earnest. "I almost wet myself."

"We turned on the custodial functions," Nyxiel said. "Just dealing with day-to-day cleaning, clothing, furniture repairs, decorations. We still control all of the more lethal aspects of the palace. It is also responsible for your wardrobe."

I frowned. "Wait, so you weren't just pulling my leg?"

"No, Your Grace," Nyxiel said, the humor still in her voice. "But she can't hurt you. And, from all we see, she seems quite pleased with your presence. I wouldn't worry."

"That's cold comfort," I griped and took another bite of my food. "And you can all kiss my lily white ass."

"Is that an offer?" Nyxiel asked lightheartedly.

"Nyxiel!" Sithraine exclaimed.

A different kind of unease prickled at the back of my neck. "Speaking of things I allegedly own... how locked down am I, exactly? The wards, the doors, all of it. Who actually decides who can come and go now?"

"That would be you, Your Grace," Morvaine said. I could hear the tidy satisfaction in her tone. "We've tuned the wards to you. The palace recognizes you as the primary authority at all ingress and egress points."

My brows climbed. "Meaning what in practice? Do I need a list? Blood? A secret knock?"

"Nothing so dramatic," Morvaine replied. "If you wish someone admitted, you think of them and allow it. If you wish someone barred, you think of that instead. Your intent is the key."

"That sounds like a fantastic way to weaponize a bad mood," I muttered. "If I have a moment and think 'everyone out,' will I accidentally evict the entire staff into the hedge maze?"

Willow's following laugh made me grin and feel all warm and mushy inside. I did my best to push that aside. She'd just tried to seduce me in my room, after all. Still, though.

"The wards only respond to deliberate decisions," Morvaine said, dry as dust. "They will know when you mean it, Princess."

"Perfect. Monarch as bouncer. Love that for me." I blew out a breath. "What comes after the Depositing of the Seed or whatever?"

"Seating of the Bloom," Willow corrected with another tinkling laugh.

Nyxiel started to answer, but Morvaine cut in.

"You missed a step, Nyxiel," Morvaine said, lounging back with a wineglass in hand. Her tone was casual, which meant I should probably brace for something ridiculous. "And we have to correct it. Presentation of the betrothal relic."

Willow scoffed. "Not required."

Nyxiel groaned. "Damn it, I did forget that part." Then to Willow. "And it absolutely is."

Morvaine ignored them and kept going. "As the party on the receiving end of the offer of marriage and having accepted the betrothal relic from the Night Court heir, Your Grace has a duty to respond in kind. You will need to select an item to present to Lady Willow here. It should be enchanted with your spirit—a token of your promise. A bracelet, necklace, or ring is customary."

I considered that. Jewelry didn't feel like me—not really. But the idea of shaping something with my own hands, something real, settled inside me like another solid step on stable ground.

"I'll need access to a karanite ingot," I said, "high carbon steel, and a forge."

Willow snorted. "Are you making me a dagger? About time one of us did something practical."

I laughed. Genuinely laughed, and it felt good.

Too good.

That pull in my chest, in my heart nagged at me, like in my apartment. I... Goddess I wanted to drag her back there and tie her down. I wanted to...

I jerked myself to a halt and was just about to excuse myself before I did anything stupid—

— And the wards hummed and flared, powerful enough to feel. And then a massive impact shook the palace.

Shit.

CHAPTER SIXTEEN
JUST A TASTE

Another impact, deep and thunderous, shook the palace. Dust sifted down from the ceiling. Outside, the wards flared hot in the Weave like a bloody, glowing curtain between us and the open sky.

Nyxiel and Vaelith shimmered right out of their seats and then back, appearing behind me.

I stood. "What is it?"

Voice smug and velvet-smooth, Nyxiel spoke first. "A few of Mother Darkness's children have made it to Nochtanmore. If you'd like a view of the... festivities, I'd be delighted to escort you to the battlements."

I heard a gleam of cruel giddiness in her tone.

"It's visible through the Weave," she added, "so you won't miss much, Your Grace."

Before I could answer, Vaelith was already moving. Her footsteps were a confident click of boot on marble. She said, "With all due respect, Your Grace, fuck watching."

She held something out.

My hand closed on soft leather.

My sword belt. My weapons. She'd had them all along.

I froze.

She offered it to me without a word, just a look I couldn't really see—but I felt it. Then it surged into my chest, a familiar need, then a familiar fear, followed by uncertainty—it all swirled inside me.

"I... I don't know if I can—" My voice cracked with panic. "That was just training."

Vaelith didn't wait for excuses. She grabbed my arm, and...

"Wait—!" I barely got the word out before the world lurched.

My perception went completely empty, a split second of biting cold bit at my skin. When the world winked back, we were at the palace's main gate, thrown open. Naerith, Elarith, Sithraine, and a moment later, Nyxiel stood with us. The war drums of Mother Darkness were already beating. And I was holding a belt full of steel. At least the skirt of my dress was slit to the hip. I wasn't exactly dressed for combat.

Swiftly, I donned the girdle and drew my weapons, hefting them. In my chest, my heart clamored, my nostrils flared. I couldn't sense very far, maybe fifty or sixty feet.

"Range?" I barked.

"One hundred yards," Vaelith said, taking the lead. I followed her and the others down the stairs, out the gate, and into the forecourt.

Wevkrana, Mother Darkness's spider-things, swarmed up the stairs, even as a lance of magical heat struck the wards far overhead. Balor in the distance, almost certainly. We were screwed, or so I thought. But then, large crystalline structures along the parapet sent beams of magic into the distance. Morvaine had activated the palace's defenses.

The wevkrana plowed into us then, their too-many legs scraping over the stone like cutlery in a drawer.

It was a slaughter—theirs.

We tore them apart. There weren't many, maybe forty or fifty. The biggest concern I had was being buried as the gate slammed shut behind us. But on instinct, every time the pile-on became too much, I just glimmerstepped away and lay on again. It took only minutes before the forecourt fell quiet.

"Well, that was easy," Elarith chirped.

Another boom, this time from the west.

"What the hell?" Vaelith muttered. "They always attack across the northern plateau. The east and west are even worse for them."

Vaelith grabbed me and pulled me through the shadows again. We appeared, this time, in front of a wide set of four doors, the carriage house entrance. Again, in the distance, two Balor fired. I only saw the shots as a spear of midnight-blue in the Weave. Without a frame of reference, I couldn't say how high they were, but they seemed further off.

A high tinkle rang out above us—like glass wind chimes snapping in the cold. Then powder rained down, fine and dry as sifted ash.

"Both eastern defense towers just came down," Naerith said, her voice clipped as she appeared behind us. "They're firing from the west now, too."

Vaelith muttered a curse under her breath. "Emisai."

Headless, loping gorilla monsters. Just great.

I felt Vaelith's posture shift—tight, alert, suddenly less sure.

"Count? Range?" I called.

She hesitated. Just a beat. But I heard it. "A dozen… maybe fifty yards. Get ready."

I set my feet, waiting until I could see them.

"You do realize we're outnumbered," she added, and her tone had turned brittle.

"I'll take your word for it," I said with a chuckle.

Vaelith didn't laugh. That alone told me everything. "A little magic here would be great," she muttered.

I turned my head toward her silhouette in the Weave, frustration bubbling. "I can't hit what I can't see, Vaelith."

"Just—just drop lightning ahead of us!"

"And set the forest on fire?" I snapped. "It's twelve. For The Mother's sake, relax."

She didn't answer, and it suddenly hit me. Vaelith's weapons weren't shadowsteel. They couldn't hurt the emisai; they leaned on the palace defenses to kill them.

"Move!" I reached out and jerked her by the arm, practically throwing her behind me.

Then I turned.

And let go.

The power ripped through me like fire through flashpaper

—wild, glorious, and perfect. A wall of destructive magic roared out from my hands, searing through the intervening space in bright purple arcs. The emisai shattered like glass, then they were dust, then they were gone. But I didn't stop. I couldn't stop.

Magic poured from me, and it felt—Mother of Waters, it felt good. Every nerve lit up like I'd swallowed a star. My skin buzzed, muscles trembling with the sheer strength of it. Ecstasy bloomed in my chest, raw and overwhelming. My knees wanted to give out, but I held the line.

Just for a bit. Just a taste. That's what I told myself, but I wanted more. I wanted to keep going. I wanted to burn it all, to tear the sky open and let a storm fall through me. I wanted to feel like this forever.

"No!" I gasped and tore the wall of magic sideways before I shifted the spell and reached high into the sky, calling rain. It came crashing down in great, hissing sheets, dousing the fires I'd started before they could spread, before they reached the plateau's edge and the Night Pixies.

The moment the last ember died, I collapsed, dropped to my knees, hands shaking, chest heaving. My breath stuttered. The magic left my body like a retreating wave—and it hurt. It was the agony of losing warmth you'd only just found, like coming down from a high you weren't meant to survive. It was the warmth of a woman's body when I'd been all alone for eons.

I curled my shaking fingers into fists, knuckles white. Not from the fight. From the wanting. From the ache of having to let it go.

"The others?" I whispered hoarsely as Vaelith dropped down next to me.

"No emisai on that side," Naerith answered, a sense of awe in her voice. She'd clearly never seen the power of The Morrigan turned loose. And to think that had been almost nothing.

"The Balor?" I asked, and I couldn't be sure what I wanted the answer to be.

"Gone or destroyed."

I breathed a sigh of relief and nodded. "Get me inside."

Vaelith hoisted me up on shaking legs and pulled me through the shadows back to the main gates, where we stepped back into the palace, the rest of the Nerin following.

I barely felt the cold.

I sat in the dining room with the others. I tried to eat a sandwich, but my stomach was a fist of barbed wire. Willow sat so close that her shoulder brushed mine. And when her hand slid into mine, warm and firm, I didn't pull away.

I couldn't, really.

I was still riding the edge of the come down, nerves frayed and senses dull. That simple pressure—fingers laced between mine—was the only thing keeping me from floating off into nothing. I didn't care what anyone thought it meant. Not right then. My insides were too raw, too hollow to make room for misperceptions.

Vaelith and Naerith weren't talking much either. They hadn't felt it—not like I had—but they knew something had gone wrong. Everyone else was still laughing, congratulating each other on a "good workout," like we hadn't just skated one breath shy of catastrophe.

"Cait," Willow whispered, voice breaking just a bit. "Do you want to tell me? What happened?"

I blinked under the cloth. What happened? I'd almost become a blazing star of magic and burned away like so much flashpaper. But I couldn't say that. I couldn't get words out.

Willow's grip tightened.

"I... I almost lost myself," I whispered.

"I saw," she said. "Nyxiel took me to the parapet. We saw the magic."

They would have had a perfect view of the battle.

"You were amazing," she added, her words were sweet, but her voice held an undercurrent of worry.

I snorted from my daze. "Yeah, amazing."

My head still stung with the urge. I squeezed her hand just a little tighter. I needed the grounding. My skin still hummed with leftover magic and every nerve buzzed like a held note. And under it all, the urge to go back out there and burn was still bright in my head—so bright. I clung to the one thing tethering me to the chair, to the moment, to myself.

Finally, I decided I needed to focus, get my thoughts back on track. Think about something else.

"It was a probe," I said impassively, considering the seemingly pointless attack.

The chatter dimmed. Forks stilled. A beat of silence stretched until Sithraine's voice cut through, sharp and alert. "What makes you say that?"

"Limited numbers. Three attack vectors. All sides but the south, where the mountain shelters the palace. I'm assuming she's never brought down a defense tower before?"

"No," Elarith called from the far end of the table. "They've never had that kind of range until today."

I nodded slowly. "She'll be back eventually. How many did we lose?"

"Three," Elarith answered. "And a fourth is damaged. That only leaves four northern towers in working order."

"Why did they stop?" Willow asked abruptly and everyone silenced.

"What do you mean?" Nyxiel, from the other end of the table.

"The Balor. Why did they stop?"

"They portaled away," Vaelith said. "I saw it."

"Yes," Willow responded. "But why?"

Silence. No, not just silence, a pall. Because we all knew, something didn't fit. They could've finished the towers. Could've done more damage—a lot more. And they didn't.

"Umbryss," Morvaine said. "We would've summoned him. Mother Darkness knows that."

I nodded faintly. It made sense. And yet...

There was a sharp ache between my eyes, like something just out of reach was trying to surface. Something had happened, something that had changed the calculus of the attack.

I straightened a little. "We can't wait for her to come back stronger. We need to fix those towers."

"That'll take months," Morvaine said. "And we don't have the karanite to do it."

"Lord Stiles," Willow said.

"House Silverdeep," Naerith clarified. "They have trolls that mine silver for them. They're experts. Better than the dwarves of the Light Fae if you ask me. The problem is, he'll never let them loose to come work for us. And we couldn't afford to cover his losses."

"What does he spend it on? There are twelve realms, including this one."

"Stiles trades with other primarchs for luxury goods for his people to keep them fat, dumb, and happy," Willow said. "He's probably the most loved ruler on the continent. Silverdeep is extremely peaceful."

"We'll have to disrupt that," I said flatly. "We need his trolls. And he needs to worry about his security."

"I'll send him an invite immediately," Naerith said. "I'll make sure Embereach and Thorn's Reach hear about it *after* he's visited."

I shook my head. "Do it in the morning. We need his cooperation; let's not wake him up in the middle of the night. And try to be thoughtful about it. We need him to show up under a pretense he'll believe."

"Yes, your grace," Naerith said.

"Vaelith, inventory the metallic karanite we've got left here," I added. "I want it counted and stacked in the forge by dawn. You need weapons, and I have a betrothal relic to make."

"Not necessary," Willow argued.

I ignored her. I had my reasons.

"On it," Vaelith said and stood. "It won't take long. There's not much left."

She stalked out to get to work.

"Morvaine," I said, tilting my head toward the sound of her

boots. "I need an updated reading on the wards. I want to know what held, what buckled, and what we thought was safe but isn't. I need to know every inch of how they work. Also, let's see if we can find a way to get a more precise estimate on how long the Veil will last. If Mother Darkness disappears, there's nothing between us and Embereach. I don't like that idea."

She hesitated, then asked quietly, "You want that tonight?"

"No." I shook my head. "She won't come back. Whatever she wanted, she got it. It'll be a while before she returns, so it can wait a couple of days. Besides, my brain is like tapioca right now."

And for a moment, the room was silent again—but not the same kind of silence as before.

"Does anyone have any other suggestions?" I asked, then hastily added, "I'm all ears."

No one spoke up.

"I should have helped," Willow muttered.

A sharp pulse of something—fear? embarrassment? Irritation, maybe?—flared under my ribs. I pushed it down. "I'm the Princess Regent of the Vermilion Court," I said, more firmly than I meant. "This is my responsibility."

She exhaled a harsh breath. "Being Princess Regent doesn't make you invincible."

"No, it doesn't, but you being here," I countered, voice low, "doesn't mean I'm going to let you get torn apart in a fight that's not yours."

Silence. She didn't seem angry, just worried.

"I can take care of myself, Cait," Willow murmured.

"I know." I swallowed. "But I'm not losing you. Not to this."

She didn't respond to that at first, and I wasn't even sure why I'd said it. But it was true. And it wasn't because of things I'd rather not examine. It was practicality. Runa would kill me if she died defending my home. At least, that's the reason I gave myself.

"Let's get you to bed," Willow said.

Willow and I stood, but Sithraine interrupted. "A word in private, if you don't mind, Your Grace."

I sighed, then gave Willow a light hug. "Wait for me in the hall, please."

She returned the hug and filed out with the others.

"What is it?" I asked, rubbing my aching forehead.

"You'll make a formidable Queen," she stated and then held up a hand to forestall my burgeoning protest. "I know you don't want it, but please consider it."

I drew in a long breath and blew it out. "You're right. I don't know how formidable I'd be, but Princess Regent implies an absent Queen. And that doesn't exist. But, let's make sure we have a realm to rule intact and some semblance of a court before we do anything about it."

"Very Good, your grace," Sithraine said and walked out.

Willow and I made our way back to the tower in silence.

I walked slowly, trailing my fingers along the walls to orient myself, letting the cool stone guide me. Willow held one arm, letting me lead the way.

At my quarters, I didn't argue. Didn't try to shut her out. She helped me undress—no awkwardness, just quiet care.

I made my way barefoot onto the balcony and took in the moist air, trying to clear my head. Rainwater still clung to the edges of everything. The tiles were slick with it. I knelt down and ran a finger on them. Something about it niggled at me, tugged at a loose thread in my head, but I couldn't pull on it to save my life.

Finally, I let it go. I was just a burnt end at the moment, but if I was honest, fear still clung to me.

"Why?" I whispered, a thousand different questions in that one word. *Why me? Why am I like this? Why do I love it so much? Why Willow?* And so on.

Mother Morrigan didn't answer. She never did.

Because it's what we are, Nastasia said from some secret well of grief.

That was another question. Why was my guiding conscience a violent Russian vampire these days? I simply had no idea.

"Come, Cait," Willow murmured, drawing me back inside.

She turned back the bed covers and helped me in. When I'd

settled, she slid in behind me, one arm draped lightly over my ribs, her breath slow and warm against the back of my neck.

I said nothing. I didn't want to be alone with the bitter aftertaste of the battle.

"It's not just about —" She started but cut herself off.

I wasn't sure what she was talking about, but I left it alone. I was too exhausted and my thoughts too leaden.

Moments later, I drifted off into an exhausted but blissfully uneventful sleep.

CHAPTER SEVENTEEN
WHAT MAKES A FAE SOUL

Willow was gone when I woke, which was good, because I had things to do and she was a… distraction.

Nyxiel guided me toward the eastern wing of the palace.

"Ms. Medlyn will likely come for you," Nyxiel said.

"I know," I said, feeling a mixture of anticipation and a whole lot of dread. Good Goddess, I'd never be able to explain this mess. And the kids… what would I do about them?

"And when she leaves?" Nyxiel asked. "Because she will leave when she sees the state of things."

I shook my head. "I won't let that happen. It wouldn't be safe for her. It's best to keep her here, until things are settled better."

Nyxiel slowed, drawing me to a halt. "That doesn't sound like you."

I tilted my head. "No, I suppose it doesn't. But I'm not human anymore. I can't think like one. I'm a queen, not a cop. That part of my life is gone. When I got here, all I wanted was to go home, but now… this place is full of possibilities. Liz will adjust. She always does. And Katie and Leah will love it."

"Elizabeth is a vampire, and so is Katie," Nyxiel said gently. "They can't remain here. Other courts will be in and out. Some primarchs would tear them to pieces just for breathing the same air."

"What if they weren't?" I asked as we walked again.

"Weren't what?"

"What if they weren't vampires anymore?"

"Weren't vampires?" Nyxiel sounded startled. "You can't strip a soul-bound curse out of someone. That's not how magic works."

"That's not technically true."

Her silence stretched, uneasy.

"Remake them? Like Maggie?" she asked at last. "But—"

The horror in her voice made no sense to me. It was logical. It would keep them safe, and then they'd fit in here. They'd want to stay. And besides, it was kind. It would be better.

"It would require me to channel the Morrigan," I said. "But only a little. I could do it. It would be safer for them. Better. A vampire's life is no life—hunting blood, avoiding sunlight, no food pleasure. Yes, they're strong and fast, but so are we."

Nyxiel went quiet, and not in an agreeable way.

"And you would do this without asking?" she eventually managed.

"Of course not," I said. "I can bargain for it. I'm sure there's something they want."

She didn't press further.

Good. The conversation was starting to grate, anyway. And the more I thought about it, the better the idea seemed. We could live here. All of us. Leah clearly had Fae blood, which meant Katie might too. Bringing it out would be just like with Maggie—minus the mental changes, obviously.

But Liz… I'd have to look. I didn't know what would happen if you put a human soul into a Fae body. It might require research. Or—

Another thought sparked that would be nice and clean.

"Nyxiel?"

"Yes?"

"What makes a Fae soul a Fae soul? Maggie only had a little, but I made it bloom. Could a soul be transformed completely —from scratch?"

She stopped dead. Her voice dropped, turning wary. "Why would you ask that?"

I shrugged. "No reason. Just curious."

"Well, Your Grace," She barked. "Stop being curious. That is a forbidden practice. One of the most forbidden. Manipulations of the soul, experimenting on it—it's an abomination. Do you understand me?"

I nodded. "Of course."

But she'd said forbidden, not impossible. Rules written by people who feared being outmatched weren't commandments. They were obstacles. Aurex had been right about one thing. If you have enough power, you can change the rules.

I'd ask Morvaine. She was less... rigid.

We finally reached the forge, where I dismissed Nyxiel and locked the door. This was private work, delicate work. Not for prying eyes, especially the religious kind.

Willow had been almost right—I was making armor. Decorative armor, but still.

A defensive vambrace.

You couldn't forge Karanite normally. It took magic. Precise magic. Even after last night, using my power wasn't difficult—just unsettling. Still, Obín had taught me well. I shaped the metal with careful will, smoothing it into perfect uniformity, coaxing it into the design I saw so clearly in my mind.

A black vambrace. It was perfect. The texture was hammered like ripples in night water. Flowers amid vines and leaves curled over it in soft blue relief. The clasps were two sets of delicate, reaching hands. I refused to give anyone—least of all Willow—something ugly or sloppy.

Once it was finished, I removed the spell book from my bag.

I'd spent hours combing the library for a binding spell fit for a political bride.

There were dozens. Many were outright curses, granting dominance over the other party. Gross.

But one stood out.

A softer one. Romantic, even.

It mirrored the spell Willow used on the necklace—but with a twist. It would return to her arm if somehow lost, but with Karanite as the focus, the vambrace would tell me precisely where she was, unlike her pendant. I'd know where, how far, and what direction. But this one did something even more:

when she felt strong emotions, I would feel a whisper of them. The stronger the emotion, the more present it would become in my thoughts.

I wasn't exactly sure why I chose it. It just seemed the easiest route. I wasn't in love with Willow. And the engagement was basically a hostage situation with jewelry. But I wasn't cruel. If we were going to be bound, I should at least be committed—probably to a mental institution. Still, knowing her emotions would help me keep her happy.

Keeping her happy would keep her close.

And keeping her close would keep her mine. She would be mine after all, and I needed to take care of her.

Eventually, I'd make one for Liz. That would solve things. Make them easier. Much more predictable and manageable.

Everything would make sense then.

Everything.

Late that night, I finally decided I had the ritual down. I inscribed the sigils on the floor and set the candles.

The casting was simple and clean. Magic flowed into the karanite like water, finding a groove and carrying with it a wisp of silvery light from my soul. When it was done, the metal pulsed faintly beneath my fingers, warm and perfect. It felt like a part of me.

I ended the spell with a final whisper, letting the circle dim and dissolve. Then I let out a relieved breath I hadn't realized I was holding and grabbed a towel to mop sweat from my forehead. For once, something had gone according to plan.

I carefully slipped the vambrace into a velvet bag that Morvaine had given me and returned to my room. I set the bag on my bedside table.

"Now, don't go telling on me," I murmured to the palace, feeling a little foolish, but she had already been through my things once, replacing my clothes, so I didn't feel like it was entirely unearned.

As I went to bed, the vambrace pulsed gently but blankly in my thoughts, soothing.

Everything would be okay.

The thought settled easily, and yet…

Somewhere in the back of my mind, a memory stirred. A dim, human thing. Me, in a cramped apartment, insisting that consent mattered even when it was inconvenient. Especially then.

I frowned, annoyed at myself. That woman had been tired. Naive. She'd believed rules existed for a reason.

Still, the unease lingered, like a word on the tip of my tongue that refused to be spoken.

CHAPTER EIGHTEEN
WHAT WE KEEP, WE CHANGE

"Is it safe to open a portal?" I asked. The winds through the open windows of the throne room all but swallowed my voice.

In my hand, the small box containing Willow's betrothal relic felt absurdly light for something capable of detonating my entire life.

"Yes," Sithraine said. "Now—again."

I exhaled sharply. "We've already done this six times."

"And we'll do it a seventh," she replied, palm out. "This has taken two months to arrange and we're doing it right."

I handed her the box. "Fine. I open the portal. I present myself as Lady Caitlin, Queen Regent of the Vermilion Court, bearing a gift for my betrothed. Then we wait."

"And when she arrives?"

"I ask her to accept this gift in honor of our betrothal." The words scraped the inside of my throat. Willow had used the same line to trap me. Perfect symmetry. Horrible symmetry.

"And then?" Sithraine prompted.

"I place the vambrace on her wrist," I muttered. "And swear the oath."

Sithraine gave a quiet, approving hum. "Good. Clean. Regal."

Regal. Right.

The dress helped—formal, suffocating, heavy with expectation. And slippers. Yay—slippers. Nothing says "future terror of the Vermilion Court" like footwear better suited to a seventh-grade choir recital. All I wanted were my boots. My real boots. The ones that could survive blood, mud, and bad decisions.

But no. Apparently, princesses glide.

Sithraine had painted my face into something "appropriately severe for Vermilion royalty." I didn't know what that meant, but from Vaelith's scandalized whistle earlier, it probably meant I looked terrifying.

I wished I felt terrifying.

I opened the portal with a smooth weave, imagining the way Umbryss had once seen Moonstone. Threads tightened, space bent. The tunnel in spacetime opened flawlessly.

"Beautiful work," Sithraine murmured. It didn't sound like flattery. That was concern wrapped in admiration. Did she think I was becoming too fluent with magic?

We stepped through. Rain-wet earth and wildflowers slapped me in the face. My slippers soaked instantly. Fantastic.

The guards approached. I straightened, every inch the princess I didn't feel like.

"I am Lady Caitlin," I announced, voice cold. "Queen Regent of the Vermilion Court. I bring a gift for my betrothed."

One guard fled. The rest relaxed.

"So far so good," I whispered.

"Here she comes," Vaelith said. Awe softened her voice. "And she looks… wow."

A pulse of nerves shot through me. I didn't know Willow's face—just her voice, her scent, her skin under my hands that night I regretted thinking about. I hated that I wanted to know more.

"Lady Caitlin?" Willow called, warmth tucked into my name. "Protocol?"

"Let's just do this," I muttered.

Willow let out an odd sigh I couldn't read. "Sure."

Sithraine placed the open box in my hands. I pulled out the vambrace—karanite shaped into vines, flowers, dark beauty. Mine, but also… hers.

"Please accept this gift in honor of our betrothal."

I pushed meaning into it like poison. It didn't matter why or how we'd gotten here. This oath would protect my family. That was what mattered.

Willow traced her fingers along the metal, breath catching. "It's beautiful. And... it's so very you."

Something tightened in my chest.

"I won't let it be said that the Vermilion Court treats its promises like afterthoughts—no matter how they were obtained."

Shit. That was rude. I felt the sting of it even as the words left me. *Well played, Cait.*

Willow went very still. Not a word. She simply offered her wrist.

My fingers brushed her skin as I fastened the clasps.

"With this vambrace," I said softly, "I promise myself to our union."

The magic sparked.

A warm ripple bloomed in my breast—hope, shyness, yearning so tender it almost hurt.

Willow's.

And instead of recoiling, I felt my breath catch.

It didn't feel invasive. It felt... right, like the latch of a door clicking closed, sealing two rooms into one.

Oh gods. That wasn't a feeling I had any business having.

Not hunger. Not lust. Something gentler. Something that wanted her near, wanted her safe, wanted her seen. Wanted... her.

Why?

I had no idea. I had Liz. I loved Liz.

But this feeling wasn't asking permission; it was demanding.

She said something then which didn't help at all. "Then let it be known that the Night Court treasures what it's given..." Her voice dropped to a whisper. "Especially when it never expected to be given anything at all."

The reply caught me off guard. There was no formal etiquette for her in this, except simply to say she accepted. She wasn't supposed to be gracious about it, damnit, or...

remorseful. Definitely not sweet. She was the devil Dark Fae daughter who'd trapped me into a horrible arrangement that blew up my life. That whispered acceptance, soft, vulnerable, reverent. It landed right beneath my sternum. It... hurt. It made me want to comfort her.

"Are you okay?" she asked.

I forced a smile she couldn't see. "Perfect."

And still, the lie tasted sweet.

She kissed my cheek. The warmth from her emotions spiked again, brushing against me like a hand stroking along my sternum. I wanted to lean into it.

No. No. No.

But wanting didn't stop anything.

I turned to Sithraine, and she handed me the invitation for the Potting of the Seeds thing.

"An invitation... to the Bloom Seating? How formal," Willow said, and I caught the edge of a smirk in her tone.

I wanted to say, *Yeah, whatever.* What came out was, "It's important to do this right."

She squeezed my hand, and a bout of warmth mixed with grief hit me—hers, sharp and deep. I nearly swayed. That vambrace might have been a mistake.

Inside, something foreign and yet very much me uncoiled, pleased, stretching into the space the bond had carved open in me.

"I'd like to see your home another time," I said before I knew I'd decided it.

"Perhaps," she whispered, and the hope in the words slid into my chest like a blade of light.

She walked away, but at the edge of my perception, I felt her look back. It tugged at me.

Hard.

The portal snapped shut.

"You handled that well," Sithraine said carefully.

I walked to the balcony, letting the cooler air hit my flushed cheeks. I wished for Boston summer sun. For normalcy. For something that didn't twist my insides into knots.

"She's more complicated than I expected," I whispered.

"How so?"

"She's catching feelings." I swallowed. "And I... felt it."

A long silence. "The vambrace?"

I nodded and sniffed, swallowing hard. "Yes."

"And you're pleased," Sithraine said quietly. Not a question. An observation.

Heat climbed up my neck. "I didn't say that."

"You didn't have to."

I bristled. "It's the enchantment. It's supposed to warn me if she's in danger, and it gives me... emotional bleed, too. That's all."

"That's not 'all,' Your Grace," Sithraine said gently. A little too gently. "You seem unsettled. What is it, exactly?"

"It felt natural," I said.

"Yes," she murmured, "and that's a problem?"

"Yes. No. I don't know. I can't tell anymore."

I pressed my palms to the railing, breath shaking.

"She can't take it off," I whispered, the realization hitting like ice water in my veins. I would feel her needs, her wants, her desires... and her hates. Forever.

What had I been thinking?

And yet, oddly, that cold feeling settled away into something warm as soon as I asked myself the question, like it was exactly as it should be. I'd been thinking that I needed her, and I needed to be as close to her as I could be, and the vambrace? It did that, didn't it?

"The betrothal enchantment?" Sithraine asked.

"Yes." My throat tightened. "I enchanted it to bond to her. The clasps won't open. I didn't tell her."

Sithraine shrugged, maddeningly serene. "Sounds like a perfect betrothal gift for a Dark Fae queen's consort."

"What?" My voice cracked on the word.

She didn't answer. She just stood there, waiting, patient in that infuriating way only someone ancient and smugly correct could manage.

"Sith?" I whispered. "What's happening to me?"

"You're thinking like what you are, not what you were taught to be." Again, that flat tone. But then it softened. "And clearly that bothers you."

I made a half turn, tilting an ear toward her. "Of course it does. When I became a vampire, everything was muted, but I was still me. This... this is something else entirely." My voice shook. "Yesterday, when I went to the forge, I thought absolutely nothing of figuring out how to transfigure a human soul into Faerie. Just to keep Liz with me if she showed up. And I accepted it, like it was a perfectly fine thing to do. That's not... me."

"Your Grace..." Her voice changed—older, deeper, the sound of someone who'd mothered a thousand generations and buried most of them. "Cait. Come sit with me."

We moved to a side couch, and she took my hand in both of hers.

"Fae do not love the way mortals do. We love with territory, with instinct, with claim. Those impulses have always slept inside you. Now they're waking because what's in your soul is now what you are."

"But... Liz," I whispered desperately. This felt worse than when The Morrigan clawed at my mind. At least then I could fight back, lose, maybe try again. This wasn't a battle. This was a coup. "What can I do?"

"Nothing," she said. "This is not an error. Your instincts are rearranging your morality. That is not corruption. It is inheritance."

My throat closed. Inheritance. Like a second crown I'd never agreed to wear and couldn't take off.

"What you love, you keep," she continued. "What you keep, you change. That is how our kind survives. This isn't a failing, Cait. It's the tide."

I blinked at her. "The... what?"

Sithraine's voice softened into something painfully gentle. "You're flowing toward your true shape. Your thoughts feel foreign because you've never lived in a body that allowed for them. Humans are so messy inside. But now... now your body has all the parts needed for you to be whole... to be what you are."

I stripped off my blindfold and folded it in my lap. "So...

puberty?"

She laughed, rich and startlingly genuine. "If you want to think of it that way. But really, your mind is settling into its correct course. Everything in you is shifting toward its natural center. It may feel disorienting, even frightening, but you're not meant to fight it." She paused for just a beat, then said, "You're meant to follow it—to see what you become when nothing in you is muffled."

"I'm scared. I could lose everything."

"No," she said softly. "You could lose Elizabeth. The children can still come. Here, a weekend is months. They'll adapt."

I put my head in my hands. That was it. And even knowing the fear, knowing the source, my mind still slid straight into the same awful orbit: keep Liz close, pull her in, change her, fold her into my world so deeply she could never slip out again. Not with her own will, not with fate, not with anything.

And I hated it. I hated how natural it felt.

The thought didn't feel borrowed.

It felt perfectly normal, satisfying even.

And it was maddening.

I lifted my head, throat tight. I needed one last truth, even if it ruined me. "Are we all like this?"

"Just the powerful ones," she said. And there was a hint of a smile in her voice—as if this, all of this unraveling inside me, was the surest sign that I finally belonged here.

CHAPTER NINETEEN
INVITATION EXTENDED, CONSEQUENCES PENDING

The next day, I spent my time with Vaelith in the training circle because that's all I wanted: to train. I wanted to forget about Willow and stop thinking about Liz and the kids. But I couldn't.

"Alright, Reagan," Vaelith barked. "What is it? I'm kicking your ass and you should be handing me mine."

"I can't stop thinking about Liz," I said flatly. "It's driving me nuts. And then there's Willow and it's like she's pulling me from inside my chest."

Vaelith laughed and needled me. "Oh, woe is me. Is the princess overwhelmed with dating options?"

"I'm serious," I grumped, dropping down on a bench. "Liz is stubborn. Amazingly stubborn. Yes, Willow stirs something unfamiliar and bright and unbearable in my chest. But that doesn't touch what I feel for Liz. It's not the same kind of wanting. It's not even in the same category."

"Are you sure?" Vaelith asked, and I could hear the sly grin in her voice.

"No," I muttered. "Not at all. This sucks."

"You're Faerie, Cait," she explained. "You've found your bond. It doesn't happen often, and usually it's cause for celebration, but…"

"Yeah," I said. "Not so much."

"Look," Vaelith said. "Liz isn't here. You can't leave. Until something changes, it's not a big deal. It's not like Willow's living here."

I shrugged. That was a fair point. I'd just have to avoid Willow as much as possible. Maybe this pull would fade.

Practice was much smoother after that, and I managed to pull a few tricks out of my magical ass that kept Vaelith on her toes. The workout made me hurt in all the right ways, and after a shower, I felt a million times better.

It was after dinner, as I was thinking about bed, that things turned... mildly pear-shaped.

I received a soft knock at my door. I'd already bid goodnight to Sithraine and the rest, so I was shocked when I opened the door to find Queen Runa standing there.

For a change, she gave me a polite, almost-bow and nod. How she'd just walked in, I didn't know, and I made a mental note to clarify that point with the twins.

"Your Majesty," I said respectfully and invited her in with a gesture.

She stepped across the threshold. "Your Grace."

Okay, so this is interesting. "What can I do for you?" I closed the door and gestured toward the sitting area, where she stepped in to relax.

I had one bottle of what Nyxiel had said was the 'good stuff,' so I dug it out and poured myself a glass.

"I've come to beg a favor," she said.

I almost fumbled my glass. "I'm sorry—what?"

My mind lurched, not because I was intimidated, but because I knew how loaded that phrasing was. Fae didn't beg. Primarchs definitely didn't beg. And they certainly didn't beg from me. It's not like I'd grovel for her.

"I said that I've come to ask for a favor." She leaned back in the chair, and I took a seat on the sofa opposite her, a plush thing that was fabulous to lounge in, but not great for a formal visit like this. I sank awkwardly into the cushions and had to pull my robe closed. "What can I do for the Night Court?"

"It's a personal favor," she said. "I'd like for you to invite my daughter to stay here."

I raised an eyebrow. "I'm sorry?"

She tilted her head and took another drink. "Are you having an issue with your hearing, Your Grace?"

"No, Your Majesty," I answered, ignoring the jab. "I'm just a little confused."

She took a breath. "My daughter lives in a small home in a remote portion of my realm. Because of my own... Because of a choice I made long ago, she cannot reside at the palace, nor is she offered protection. As a result, and given your upcoming nuptials, she is at risk."

I took a long sip of my wine, dragging out the moment. Honestly, it was like honey. She'd fucked up. "Don't you think this is something you should have considered before our betrothal?"

"Cait—may I call you Cait?"

"May I call you Runa?"

She chuckled. "If you like."

"Fine. Runa. You and your daughter played on my ignorance and engineered this. Now you come asking for a favor. I should be offended."

"And?" She prodded.

I didn't scowl, though I wanted to. What I needed to do was figure out how to get the most out of this. Of course, I'd bring Willow here. The calculus was simple. Liz would understand that, I was sure. But Runa didn't need to know any of that.

I sighed. "I can't imagine any good could come from having her here."

"The good is this. I will assign a platoon of my elite guard to operate here and provide security for you and your retinue."

I laughed. "That's even worse. In addition to having your daughter here under my protection, I'd have to host a potentially hostile force?"

"You misunderstand," Runa said. "I did not have anything to do with your... indiscretion with my daughter. I had no intention of offering her hand. She disgraced our house long ago. She was stripped of her title and name and exiled from court except under very strict circumstances."

"Then why did you?"

"That is not the important point."

That wasn't going to cut it. I wanted more information. "What could she have possibly done that would have warranted banishment?"

"No one in my court is permitted to speak of it. But... I suppose I'm not in my court right now."

I caught something in her tone, not regret so much as sadness, and I got the impression it was the sadness of a mother who had to choose the law over her child. I said nothing, though, simply waiting.

"During the late reign of Maura, my forces were pressed. I sent Willow and her sisters into hiding to preserve the line if something happened to me. They had strict orders to stay put. In the meantime, I sought to lure Maura and her forces into a poor position within my domain. One where we could set the terms of the engagement.

"However, I was unaware that my daughter had gone to the source, to Crann Bethad, which, as you know, is deep inside Vermilion Court territory. There, she sought to treat directly with The Morrigan."

I shook my head. "How did she even get there? That's hundreds of miles through enemy territory."

"Umbryss."

"Ah." *The guilty lizard wanted to fix his mistake.* "Okay."

"I don't know exactly what transpired at Crann Bethad, but several things followed. Kiran, my advisor? His daughter Iriani, Willow's lover, had gone with her. She died at some point, though how is still unclear. And given Willow's reticence to talk about it, I can only assume she feels responsible.

"Willow was blinded, as you know, and then captured. She

tried to barter knowledge for my life and the lives of my other daughters. She didn't know everything, but she knew enough. She was my successor, after all. The only saving grace was that I learned she'd gone before we engaged Maura and was able to shift my strategy—buy time and call for allies."

"She betrayed you," I whispered.

"She betrayed her people. Her intentions were—well, I don't know if pure is the right word—but they were born out of love. Foolish, really, but endearing. The result, though, was nearly catastrophic. In the end, we held out long enough for allies to arrive, and we won the day, but her brother Noem was killed as a direct result of rear-quarter fighting that should never have happened."

"I had no choice but to strip her of her name, her title, and exile her from court," Runa continued. "I used her blindness, her courting of The Morrigan, a perceived enemy, and her disobedience of my order as a public excuse. I did that rather than reveal the true betrayal. But whispers spread, anyway. The nobility demanded her head." She paused, her voice quiet. "As a compromise, I placed her in what we call The Stillness."

"I've read about it," I said. "In one of the older volumes in our library. It's a magical stasis—no decay, no dreams."

Runa gave a small nod. "No decay, but... dreams? There are dreams. And nightmares. She remained there until recently."

"She was asleep for all that time? It was what? Twenty thousand years?"

"Eighteen," Runa said.

I couldn't imagine the dreams and nightmares I would have. Just the idea made me shiver.

"The world moved on without her. Her name faded. She was lost to history. Almost everyone she knew, besides her family, had died in the meantime. When she woke. No one knew who she was. No one had known even where she'd been kept. No one remembered I even had another daughter." Runa did show a glimmer of real sorrow then, real hurt. "She begged me to put her back, or..." She paused and drew in a breath. "... end her life."

I leaned back, feeling the weight of my wine glass. It felt

heavier, like gravity was pulling on it a little harder—tugging something in my chest with it. Willow's story was a disaster, but gods, it was the exact kind of disaster I could see myself stumbling into.

Had stumbled into.

Different battleground, same damn intentions.

"That's... heartbreaking," I said finally.

"It was necessary," she replied.

Silence stretched thin between us, straining at the edges.

I'd won. I could feel it, the faint, quiet shift of the room, the negotiation turning my direction. It should have satisfied me. It did satisfy me.

But underneath that, something bright and hot twisted, the certainty of having Willow here—in the palace, in my reach. It made my pulse jump.

I swallowed it down. Business first. Instinct later. Or never, if I were smart.

"Alright," I said at last, setting the glass down. "But I need something from you."

"I'd expect no less."

"The karanite mines need upkeep, and I'm short-handed. I need twenty experienced miners—hard workers, no slackers. I don't care how you get them, and I won't mistreat them. And I'll need something formal. If you want her under our protection, I need documentation. Something Sithraine can work with."

Her voice tightened. "The men I can provide. A formal request would not be politically viable. This is the only request I'll make—privately."

Of course it was. No record. No paper trail. Just my word and hers. Everything would fall neatly on my shoulders if it went wrong.

And still, disturbingly, the thought of refusing her daughter's presence made my stomach twist like a hand closing.

"I'll need to speak with Sithraine," I said, already knowing it was pointless.

"I assumed as much." Runa set down her empty glass. "I'm

glad we reached an agreement. Otherwise, I couldn't accept that the engagement makes much sense."

And there it was. The carrot and the stick. Refuse, and she walks. She unbinds the Night Court from this shaky alliance, and I lose our only shield.

I had no choice.

"I'll give you my answer tomorrow," I said, jaw tight. "If there's nothing else…"

She rose. "Cait."

I looked up.

"She's still my daughter," Runa said, voice softening. "Whatever else she's done. I agreed to this because I already know what kind of person you are. And I trust that."

That made one of us. I didn't trust myself at all right now—not with my thoughts shifting under my feet, not with Willow tugging at me like a live wire—but that wasn't something I was going to confess to her.

I said, "I appreciate your confidence, Runa." And then, because my mouth hated me and my instincts were apparently learning to walk on their own: "I will, however, expect a separate and equal favor in return one day."

"It'll be something reasonable, I'm sure," she said and stepped onto the balcony. Then she turned back. "And Cait, take the soldiers. We're on a course that was set long ago. You're going to need the protection."

A moment later, a portal opened—and she was gone.

Within seconds of her departure, the wards flared to life.

The next morning, after a surprisingly brief conversation with Sithraine, who looked disturbingly proud of me, we extended the invitation for Willow—and only Willow—to join us at the Vermilion Palace under our protection. Such as it was.

It wasn't official. No formal papers. No diplomatic procession. Just a letter, sealed with my own initials, carried by one of Elarith's couriers. The language was carefully constructed—neutral, respectful, and devoid of sentiment.

But we all knew what it meant. We were taking her in. We were keeping her close. We were going to keep her safe.

Willow sent her response by raven, just as she'd done with

my invitation to the Midsummer festivities.

All it said was, "I accept your gracious invitation. Thank you. Willow."

No royal titles. No timeline. Nothing else.

Nothing... except the soft whiff of ember that accompanied my first intentional bargain, simple and irrevocable.

Sithraine remained quiet when I handed her the note. She just tucked it away with a slow nod. But I could feel her scrutiny of both the letter and me.

It wouldn't hit me until much later what I'd actually set in motion. Because I was already thinking like a Fae. And Fae don't see disasters.

We make them.

CHAPTER TWENTY
WHAT THE FLOWERS KNOW

It didn't take long—just one day and one more night. Willow appeared at the main gate, just a small suitcase in one hand. We all greeted her at the doorway, doing our best, given how few we were. It was sad, really. Willow. Alone. No entourage. And then there was her greeting party: us—seven members of a bereft house in a ruined kingdom. It seemed both fitting and yet… cruel.

As she stepped over the threshold, I caught it—something in the way she moved. A shortness to her steps. A hesitation in the sweep of her footfalls across the stone floor. Not fear. Something closer to being… unwanted and abandoned. I hated that it made me want to lean closer.

"You packed light," I said wryly, forcing a little warmth into my voice.

"That's me," Willow answered, her chuckle easy enough to fool anyone else. "Always the simple life."

I laughed with her. "Well, not anymore. Your quarters are one floor below the royal suite, next to mine. And tomorrow, you'll be fitted for appropriate clothing. Though I'll point out that the palace has interesting ideas about what might be appropriate for my court."

"I recall," Willow said. "I believe Nyxiel described your outfit at dinner as something akin to blind vengeance meets sex goddess."

I rolled my eyes. "Well, Nyxiel has a naughty mind."

"Yes," Willow affirmed, now even more amused. "Yes, she does."

"Now, now," Nyxiel warned lightheartedly.

"May I take your suitcase?" Vaelith asked.

"You may incinerate it if you like," Willow said tightly, handing off the bag. "Other than the seed packets, there's nothing in there that I'd actually want, but I wasn't sure if I'd need clothing."

Someone suppressed an amused snort, Nyxiel probably.

We crossed the main hall in a hush of footsteps. The vastness of the space stretched out around us, each step stirring up faint echoes on old stone and polished marble.

The staircase curved up before us, wide enough to let six men walk abreast without touching. The railings, a recent gift of the Hidden Servitor, were smooth under my hand. Willow's steps stayed close to mine, her free hand brushing the balustrade lightly as well. She followed the turns in steps. I couldn't hear her counting. I just… knew.

As we ascended, the scent of wildflowers and a hint of woodsmoke rose with us, clinging to the newly gilded walls and drifting up into the vaulted ceiling high above.

This was a place meant for thousands, not the handful of tattered souls we had left. Just empty grandeur. And yet, one more presence in the household, one more set of footsteps, made it easier to imagine laughter returning. Made it easier to believe the halls could bustle again.

"We have breakfast prepared," I said. "Nyxiel has made a full Irish breakfast with a little black pudding."

"Blood sausage," I said. "Delicious, especially when it's crisped just right."

"Okay," Willow said slowly. "Well, I'll try anything. When I was a child, my mother used to make kagha."

I tilted my head. "Kagha? Never heard of it. Something with meat, I assume."

"Organ meat," Willow said brightly. "Chopped, spiced, and cooked inside the selúin stomach."

I froze—and then grinned. I didn't know what a selúin was,

but I knew haggis when I heard it. "Haggis! You're describing haggis. It's a Scottish dish from Earth. And don't let anyone tell you it's not fucking delicious."

Willow laughed. "My sisters hated kagha. But I loved it growing up. There was something... comforting about it."

I took Willow's hand and gave it a quick squeeze. "A woman after my own heart," I said, one corner of my mouth turning up. "We might just get along after all."

"After your heart, am I? More likely your larder. I'm starving." The words were bone dry.

There was a smile in her tone, and for the first time, I really wished I could see it. It must have been dazzling.

We made our way to the dining hall, hand in hand. I told myself it was just comfort, just friendship. And if I didn't pull away, well—neither did she.

The next few days were hectic. There were court invitations, changes to my wardrobe... again, and Sithraine bringing Willow in and out to discuss who would need what.

I did my best to keep our interactions simple and perfunctory. Still, there were brushes, touches, a closeness that wouldn't quit. And it wasn't just here. I found myself with my hand on her shoulder or bumping against her with a smile when something seemed worthy of it. And Goddess, it felt good. It made my heart race, and a grin split my face.

I tried to shove it down, but... I just couldn't. I barely knew her. I didn't understand why this was happening. Maybe Willow was right. Maybe there was no stopping it. But I wasn't going to admit that it was beyond my control. Maybe I had the feelings, but I wouldn't act on them.

So, rather than risk running into her in the evenings, I simply took to walking the palace, getting to know the place, feeling the quiet. And patrolling. I made a few loops. Passed a few more Nerin who'd filtered in over the following few days. They bowed or nodded with the sort of deference that fit me like a second skin. I just tried—and failed—to look like someone who didn't think it was her birthright.

I wandered through a pair of doors I'd never seen, down on the first floor. The smell of fresh flowers and tilled soil immediately caught my nose. I reached out and found a wall on my right and a series of columns on my left—a cloister, wrapped around what sounded and smelled very much like a large open-air courtyard.

Then, voices. Off somewhere in the distance. I slowly made my way out into the yard, following a long line of trimmed bushes. I was sure I'd never been in this part of the palace before—not shocking given the palace was a half mile by three-quarters, rising eight floors. No wonder it seemed so empty.

I paused as I got closer to the voices.

"Morvaine's right, you two are threadcalled," Nyxiel said. "We all see it. You can resist it all you want, but it won't change a thing."

"Threadcalled? We're both Fae, sure, and that gives things a tug, but Threadcalled?" Willow said. "I didn't think you were the type to buy into that."

"Buy into it? Willow, it's just… it's Mother Shaddan's truth," Nyxiel said with a helpless little shrug. "Even Morvaine admits it's real, and she thinks half the Book of Ash and Thorns is one long joke. Ignore it if you want, but it'll only sting worse later. And you're not wrong. Elizabeth's going to take this hard. The whole thing is a mess."

"Exactly," Willow murmured. "What am I supposed to do? I'm not trying to hurt anyone. None of this was supposed to happen. A tiny part of me wishes she'd never made the trip."

I blinked. You didn't need a genius badge to figure out who "she" was.

"Please don't repeat that," Willow added quickly.

"Sure," Nyxiel said.

Too late. I let a faint smirk slip, not out of cruelty but because at least Willow's mood finally made sense. The vambrace only ever gave me broad strokes; it didn't explain why she felt the way she felt, just that she did. And the annoying part was how familiar that tug was getting. Threadcalling might've been "Fae superstition" last week, but this week it sat in my chest like a greedy little troll, wanting more and more. Pretending it didn't matter was starting to feel childish.

Sure, I could try to go back to normal: Liz, the kids, the house, the car. But the second I even pictured it, I could feel the lie in my teeth. I didn't want to choose. I wanted both of them tucked in close, warm, and comfy. And picturing that? I felt like the world finally clicked into its proper shape. Infuriating didn't even scratch the surface.

I exhaled, long and low, and just… let it be what it was. Fine. I wanted them both. I'd figure out the rest. Keeping two brilliant, complicated women happy? Difficult, not impossible. I had tools now. Magic. Bargains. Weird Fae instincts. A whole birthright full of inconvenient little advantages.

I could make it work.

Before I could stew in that further, their chatter broke off at the sound of scuffing feet and something that definitely resembled digging.

"Here, put it in there," Willow said. "Careful."

"I don't know how you've gotten it to grow so fast," Nyxiel said. "You must have a magic touch."

"Family secret," Willow replied evasively.

I raised an eyebrow. *What exactly were they doing?*

Deciding I was being rude, I continued toward them, only to trip over a root and tumble to the ground, landing with something hard, like a rock, digging into my shoulder.

"Ow, shit," I groaned. "That's gonna leave a mark."

"Cait?" Nyxiel called from somewhere ahead, followed by a patter of footsteps. "Here, let me help you up."

"Gotta mind the landscape," I muttered.

"What are you doing walking in the garden without help?" Nyxiel asked as she started brushing me off. "Are you okay?"

"The only casualty is my pride."

Willow laughed. "I've done it a million times, Cait. Your pride is safe."

I returned the laugh. "Yeah, I suppose so."

There was an awkward moment of silence, then Nyxiel broke it.

"Well, I'm going to go and take care of the dishes. I think between the two of you, you should be able to make it back without braining yourselves."

"I'll guide her out," Willow called, and Nyxiel padded off in another direction.

"Couldn't sleep again?" Willow asked.

"Again?"

"You're out walking the palace every night. I thought it was insomnia. Or are you just avoiding me?"

I didn't answer. Instead, taking advantage of the fact she was blind to my pinkening cheeks, I dropped into the dirt next to her and changed the subject. "So, what are we doing?"

"Planting Starblind Bells," she said with a hint of amusement. "They're my favorite."

"I'm not familiar," I said. "Sounds like a Fae flower."

"Native to Ebonmere. I had some bulbs from home that I brought with me. They're a soft blue and faintly translucent, kind of like little bell-shaped crystals half buried in moss. Here." She took my hand and carefully placed one of the bulbs into it. "Be gentle, they're fragile."

I nodded, pointedly ignoring the instant goosebumps the brush of her fingers brought to my skin.

The seed did indeed feel like glass and moss. It also had a hum to it, mid-pitched and very faint. I held it to my ear. "What is that?"

"That's the magic of them. They sing. They only bloom when someone speaks a secret truth near them. And when they do, they ring with that music for a time.

"The Common Fae of the Night Court plant them outside nurseries and near schools. They're supposed to teach the beauty of honesty. They are not typically kept in at Court, as you can imagine."

I snorted a laugh. "No, I suppose not. Though they'd be handy for interrogations."

"They wither when they hear pain," Willow offered. "So, not so much."

"Huh."

"Here, feel this." She took my other hand and drew it to the ground, to a small hole she'd dug. Her fingers were dirty and gritty, but they felt... nice. And so soft.

I swallowed down a momentary pang of longing and

cleared my throat. "Yeah."

"Now, gently place the bulb in, and I'll cover it."

"Where did you learn to garden?" I asked as I gingerly put the bulb into its resting place, and she scooped dirt over it.

"I picked it up over the last few years," she murmured. "To pass the time, really."

"What's your place like?" I asked.

"Lonely," was all she said. Then, "Here, watch the magic."

I felt the tug and observed. Threads of red sprang from her hands like webbing, spinning into the ground. It filled the little hole, growing brighter, the color shifting toward white. Then the smell of damp soil tickled my nose.

"Now we wait," she said.

I gave an incredulous snicker. "So, that's your big family secret? A simple growth spell?"

She bumped me, shoulder to shoulder. "Of course. It's not rocket science. And I'm not a patient woman. Besides, quickly growing a house full of plants can be helpful—if you know the right ones. Some for medicine. Some for beauty, though that's really for others. Some for their scents or textures; those are for me. And, occasionally, a few that are... um... helpful for self-defense if you know where to plant them and how."

I raised an eyebrow. "So, man-eating plants, then."

She giggled. "No, just Faerie Snare and other things to keep pests away or incapacitate interlopers. I do have some seeds for more lethal varieties, but they're back at the cottage. A few molds and spores, too, kept in a glass terrarium."

"And what do those do?"

"Depends on the mold or spore. Some of them are quite nasty, really. Eat you from the inside out. I keep those as a last resort."

"Sounds like ophiocordyceps."

"I'm not familiar with that one," Willow said. "What is it?"

"It's found in rainforests on Earth. It infects the brains of ants and other insects and then turns them into zombies, using them to spread to others before it consumes them from the inside."

She shivered against me. "That's terrifying. Not that we

don't have some home-grown varieties that are just as awful in some ways, but seriously? Fungus zombies?"

"They're just ants. It doesn't live inside people, we're too warm."

"Small favors," she muttered.

After a few minutes of easy silence, Willow said out of nowhere, "You're easy to be with, you know that?"

The compliment caught me off guard. "I'm just me," I said, feeling a flush run up my cheeks. "Or maybe it's because I'm all *Dark Fae*." I said that last in a goofy ghostly voice, and she giggled.

"Maybe. Tell me you don't feel it, too, though."

I knew what she meant. "I do." My voice was low and soft. I wanted to add that I just couldn't act on it, but I didn't.

Surprisingly, she didn't pursue it. Instead, she changed the subject. "You're different when you're like this. You seem more at peace."

I shrugged. "There's no pressure here. We're just planting flowers. It's not some performance. You seem more at ease yourself."

"Same. It's just us."

Simple words, but so loaded, and I could hear the desire beneath them and the loneliness.

"Do you believe in it? Threadcalling?" she asked.

I froze. Trying to decide what to say. I knew full well she didn't, but my mouth said, "Don't you?"

"No," she said flatly. "Fae are drawn together sometimes, but destiny? Please."

I took her hand, and before I could stop myself, I said, "Willow, it's more than that. I've felt it from the moment we met."

There was a long moment of silence between us. I could feel her so close, leaning in, her lips just a hair's breadth away.

Abruptly, our little corner of the garden began to fill with a soft sound. It wasn't music exactly, but a pleasant tinkling sound, like chimes.

She pulled back as she said, "And that's what they sound like."

I pressed my lips together, even as her breath filled my lungs. We stayed there, her hand resting on mine as the flowers around us sang. Then she guided my fingers to the petals. As I touched it, the tone changed slightly, becoming richer, more vibrant. The petal itself didn't feel like a plant... or glass. It was soft, almost like skin. And warm.

"They say that the petals feel different depending on the truth that they hear."

I nodded. "It's... it's amazing."

"Notice I didn't say the truth that was told."

"Ah." I got it. Supposedly, these flowers could hear the truth beneath the words. I didn't try to discern what it meant when they were warm and soft like this. Instead, I released the petal, though the music didn't return to the same middling tone, the fullness stayed.

"It's getting late," Willow said. Her voice was quiet and a little strained. "We should probably get going."

"We should do this again."

Why? Why did I say that? We should absolutely not do this again. Nothing good was going to come of it—just more confusion, more tangled feelings, and the spectacular emotional crash I could see coming from a mile away.

Willow packed up her things and, whether she'd memorized the pavers or was just more certain of her footing, she took my arm and guided us out. Literally, it was the blind leading the blind, except one of us wasn't second-guessing every step.

And as we left, another bloom erupted in song.

CHAPTER TWENTY-ONE
Not Innocent Anymore

The next morning, the palace finally admitted I needed to be able to fight on occasion. Laid out for me were a V-necked, wrapped tunic and thick, supple leggings made from some unfortunate creature I couldn't identify. And boots. Actual boots. No more slippers, which I took as a personal victory.

I told myself I had a plan today. Wake up early. Get dressed before anyone can ambush me with feelings. Definitely avoid the gardens. Drink a cup of coffee so hot it scorched yesterday out of existence. Then stroll into breakfast like a woman in total control of her life, someone doing her damned best not to hurt the woman she loves—again.

I didn't know where Elarith and Naerith were, off on some mission out west, but Sithraine was busy wrangling the twenty miners the Night Queen had loaned us, while the accompanying soldiers patrolled the halls like disciplined ghosts.

I, on the other hand, relied on avoidance, caffeine, and pretending I hadn't almost let Willow kiss me in a garden.

My big plan survived all the way until I reached the dining room, because of course, Willow was already there.

She leaned against the long table. Vaelith sat at the far end, her voice radiating the kind of regret usually reserved for diplomats and babysitters, which meant trouble. Or feelings. Both, really.

"It's bloody disgusting," Vaelith announced.

"It is not," Willow shot back. "Now, shush. It's a surprise."

Great. A surprise. Just what I needed.

"Hi," Willow said, that damned smile clear in her voice. "Come sit down. I have something for you."

I raised a brow, but didn't bother trying to stare her down—no one would win that contest. Instead, I stumbled my way to the table and slid into the nearest chair.

"Is it what smells so good?"

"I hope you have a strong stomach," Vaelith muttered.

Willow disappeared into the kitchen and returned with a plate, setting it in front of me with that careful elegance that made me irrationally nervous. I leaned forward, caught a whiff of something savory and rich, and tried not to inhale it like a starving wolf.

I forked up a bite and let the flavor speak for itself.

"Oh. Goddess." Another bite. Then a third. "What is this?"

"That's Kagha. Do you like it?"

I was five mouthfuls in before I remembered to breathe.

"It's fabulous."

Willow laughed—a soft sound, warm enough to make something in me go molten. "Kagha was my favorite. Everyone else hated it. But when my mother made it, it felt like home."

Home.

A word I wasn't ready for.

Not from her.

Not while Liz was back on Earth, still building a life for us both.

Still, a warm smile came unbidden to my lips. "It's delicious," I whispered.

"I knew you'd love it," Willow said, her voice quieter now. She slipped away again, the soft pad of her slippers vanishing into the kitchen. When she returned, the smell of fresh coffee announced her a second before she set a cup beside my plate. She poured another for herself and finally took the seat across from me.

Vaelith gave a theatrical sigh. "That's all you. I don't

understand how anyone can eat that."

"It's just organ meat," I said mid-chew, licking grease from the corner of my mouth. "In Ireland, Mameo used every part of the animal she could. That's what poor folks do. And while haggis is Scottish, the principle's the same. Waste nothing, flavor everything."

"It's revolting," Vaelith muttered, stabbing her fork onto her plate. "I'll stay with my eggs."

"Don't you mean bird embryos?" Willow said with a grin.

"Rude." Vaelith kept eating, dignity intact if not entirely defensible. Then she added, "Enjoy your selúin anus."

I laughed. She wasn't wrong. If Kagha was to Haggis what Willow claimed, then yeah—there was probably some unfortunate anatomy involved. I didn't care. It was delicious. It was warm. And for five whole minutes, I forgot that my life was a slow-motion train wreck.

"You get a day off, Your Grace," Sithraine said, her tone smooth and slick as freshly polished marble.

She crossed the room and headed straight for the kitchen. "We'll be prepping rooms for the Night Court envoys."

"Isn't it a little early for that?" Willow asked.

There was something off in her tone—just enough for me to clock it. A shift. A tremor, maybe? Then I felt a touch of anxiety through the vambrace.

"What is it?" I asked, setting down my fork.

Willow hesitated. "I just thought we had more time. It's been quiet. I've been enjoying the company. Once the court arrives, we'll be really busy."

That wasn't it. There was more. I suspected the idea of having the Court that spurned her here and suddenly prepping her wedding festivities wasn't appealing. I wasn't all that thrilled myself, given the circumstances.

"Oh, you do," Sithraine replied breezily, emerging with her own plate. "The delegation isn't due for three more days. Plenty of time for you two to gossip, plot, and corrupt each other further."

I snorted my coffee. "No one's corrupting anyone," I said defensively through a coughing fit.

Embarrassment, anger, possessiveness, desire, frustration—each emotion slammed through the vambrace in a messy blur. Willow's feelings.

Willow cleared her throat. "No. We're just chatting."

"Who made Kagha?" Sithraine asked as she sat, her plate landing lightly on the table.

"That would be our interloper," Vaelith said with a sniff. "She's single-handedly undermining Her Grace's palate."

Sithraine chuckled. "Thank you, Willow. That was kind of you."

There was a moment there—I felt just a flicker of pride on Willow's part.

"So…" Willow started, tone light. "Want to wander with me?"

Wander. With Willow. In a palace full of abandoned rooms and the ghosts of my ancestors. That sounded like a potential disaster waiting to happen. My gut screamed, "Absolutely not." But apparently my mouth was working freelance this morning, because it said, "Sure!"

"Great," she said brightly. "While we walk, you can tell me about how you got that brand on your chest."

I instinctively covered the spiral mark, fingers brushing the fabric where it peeked along my neckline. "You don't know?" I asked, surprised.

"No." Willow's voice was matter-of-fact. "All we know is that it was just there one day."

So, her mother didn't know everything. They'd never known about Skaja. About what I was. About who I'd been.

"You have the honor of meeting the only person ever born of one of the Three twice," Vaelith said, not looking up from her plate.

"Really," Willow said, her curiosity piqued. "How is that possible?"

"I'll tell you as we walk."

Breakfast settled into a lull after that.

The rest of the meal passed with idle chatter—mostly Willow and Sithraine volleying names back and forth: various court primaries and the social landmines they came with, who needed silk pillows, who demanded what kind of wine at what temperature, all the predictable politics of bored immortals.

I listened. I didn't contribute. My focus drifted—between the fading taste of kagha and the tightness in my chest that hadn't really gone away since Willow said, "I've been enjoying the company."

And the whole time, my fingertips kept brushing the edge of my brand like it was going to disappear if I rubbed hard enough.

We wandered the halls for a bit, each of us sharing bits of life, the occasional silly story. I talked about Zilyana—really talked about her—for the first time since I'd woken from my vampire coma. I'd told Liz, but it had just been a rundown, and maybe an admission of my feelings. But now, I let it all out —her smile, her figure, Goddess, her figure. Just her presence.

Zillyana had been a force all her own, and I shared with Willow the ache that had been with me since I'd woken from the curse-induced coma. And for the first time, it didn't hurt so much.

Willow just listened, adding in tidbits of her own experiences that mirrored mine, and asking a few questions. She understood how I'd been born twice, she knew the spell— well, of it anyway. What she hadn't known was the full extent of my family's power. No one had ever told her that Nemhain could snatch a soul after death.

"So," Willow said after a long following silence. "What's Liz like when she isn't doing her whole vampire thing?"

I barked a laugh. "She doesn't really *do* a vampire thing. Liz is… Liz. Level-headed. Kind. A little possessive."

"Possessive," Willow murmured. "That tracks." It wasn't a dig, just stating a fact. "But kind? I thought compassion was something the curse suppressed."

"It usually is," I said. "But she doesn't let it. I don't know how."

Willow nodded. "She's stronger than I expected, then. Fiercer, too."

I frowned. "You don't even know her."

"I don't need to," Willow replied. "You forget, my mother has eyes everywhere."

My breath caught.

"And," Willow added, quieter, "I've seen you. There's no question what she is to you."

The floor dipped under me. "Okay, so... that's why you're suddenly interested?"

"It isn't sudden." Willow angled her head toward me. "I'm trying to understand the shape of your heart."

"That's—" My voice cracked. "That's not how this works, Willow."

"It is for us," she said, gentle but unyielding. "Fae hearts beat fierce and free. They don't fit inside human rules. They don't turn the way humans expect them to. They don't apologize for wanting."

I stopped walking.

Willow kept going, her fingers brushing my arm to draw me with her. "You keep trying to pretend you're bound by human morality, Cait, and you're doing it very badly."

My breath stuttered. "I'm trying not to hurt Liz."

"That's not morality," Willow said softly. "That's love. That's choice. Those are yours. But pretending you don't feel what you feel?" She shook her head. "That's human shame talking. And it doesn't belong to you. Not anymore."

My stomach twisted. "Willow..."

Willow tugged me gently to a halt. "I told you I don't believe in threadcalling," she said, voice low. "That was a lie. Or... well, I don't want it to be true. I don't want to believe magic could make me feel differently." She huffed a humorless little breath. "But it's hard to argue with the way things are."

I swallowed. "Willow—"

"I'm not saying it's destiny," she rushed on. "I'm not saying it's fate or the universe or any of that nonsense. I'm just saying that whatever this thing is between us, it's real. And Liz is right in between, but I'm not trying to take her place."

"I know," I said softly. And I did. Goddess help me, I understood that. But Liz wouldn't.

She let out a slow breath. "Then stop pretending you can

resist it."

That hit like a pulse of heat up my spine. I didn't answer—not because she was wrong, but because she was right.

"I can't. Liz will leave," I said.

"Then she leaves. You can't control that." Willow bumped my shoulder gently. "You can't control her—as much as you might want to."

I didn't trust myself to speak, so I let the silence settle between us—thick, charged, frighteningly easy. I couldn't fall in love with her. I couldn't let myself.

You've fallen already, Nastasia's voice coiled through my thoughts like silk over a blade. *You really need to quit lying to yourself, Dorogaya.*

"Did you hear that?" I asked.

"Hear what?"

I shook my head. Maybe I really was losing it. "I just... I keep hearing Nastasia's voice."

"The dark-haired vampire?"

"Yeah. In my head. I feel like I'm going crazy."

I felt Willow shrug against my shoulder. "You bear the Morrigan. Maybe it's not your imagination."

That pulled me up short. "No," I said softly. "Ghosts don't exist." At least I hoped they didn't.

Nastasia should be on about her business in her next life, not lingering around me like some miserable wraith, watching but never involved. That sounded like hell to me.

"I suppose not," Willow said, but she didn't sound convinced.

We kept walking, and we passed through the ambassadorial wing. In the background, Morvaine and Sithraine were in a room nearby arguing about arrangements. Furniture scraped about in another room, moved by the Hidden Servitor, I was sure. We nodded to a pair of Runa's guards as they passed us on patrol.

"So, do you have any favorite things to do? Other hobbies?"

"Are you really interested? Or just making conversation?" Willow asked.

"Can't it be both?" I asked.

"I suppose," she said with a sigh. "Well, I like botany, which you know, though that's a new hobby. I love technical magic. I think you've probably realized that, too. The more sophisticated or innovative the spell, the more I'm interested. I think that's because it's one thing that I still have. I've always loved magic. I used to paint, but that's no longer an option. And I miss all the things I'll never see again. Honestly, I've been alone since I woke up, for the most part, so I haven't really figured out much of what still interests me."

"Yeah," I whispered. I understood that all too well. And I understood what she meant about magic. Like she said, it was something I could still do, even if it sometimes made me incredibly nervous.

We grew quiet for a while, and around midday, we found ourselves back at the tower lift. I stepped onto it. "Well, I think I could stand a nap."

Willow laughed and said simply, "Royal Conservatory." She said it like a joke, still, though, the bars started to rise.

I glanced at her. "What?"

Willow's grin was audible. "Let's see something we haven't."

"By see, you mean stumble around in the dark and fall over things," I replied wryly, an eyebrow cocked.

"Exactly. It'll be an adventure."

We rose slowly through the shaft, wind spiraling in cool breaths. The stone walls echoed with distant life—birdsong stolen from an open balcony we passed along the way. I tried to focus on that, anything but the pressure coiling in my chest.

The platform slowed. The rails retracted with a soft sliding sound.

I stepped off first, a little cautious.

Willow sniffed. "Smells like… polish? Something wooden. We're in the right place."

Arms out, I pushed into the room ahead of us. Along one wall, my fingers passed over cool varnish, then I felt the subtle tension of the strings beneath. Then more. A curved frame. A shape I knew better than my own face: a harp.

I plucked at the strings. It was slightly out of tune, but after a moment of fumbling around, I found a pouch on the floor next to it with the tools I needed.

After a few more minutes searching, I found a cushioned stool—with my shin, of course, because, well, fucking blind woman.

"There's a lot of stuff in here," Willow called from another part of the room. "I think I found something I know how to play."

I set to work tuning up the strings. "You just happened to pick the Royal Conservatory. Just on a whim?"

"Well, look at me. First time I pick a floor, and it's this."

I shook my head. "If this is fate, I'm a selúin's ass."

Willow chuckled. "Sometimes you are. So it could be."

"Uh-huh. Yeah, okay."

Ten minutes later, I sat upright, brushing my hands over the strings. The harp responded in soft tones and ghostly notes that reminded me of a dozen recitals and even a competition or two. At first, my plucking was a little tentative, like I was feeling an unknown face in the dark. But, after a few wrong notes and a muttered curse or two, the first bars of Over the Hills and Far Away by Gary Moore finally flowed out of me.

Willow made her way over and slid a chair next to me. "Stop. Let me find the key."

"Averai," I said, the term for the key of D among the Shaddani music scales.

I heard the gentle thunk of an instrument settling in her lap, followed by a soft hum of tensioned strings—rich, but not too bright. I reached over and felt across the instrument. It was a seven-string guitar, by the feel of it, or something very close. Her hand brushed mine for just a second, but I pulled it away.

I started again, and just did a quick play through until Willow caught the tune, and then I started once more—singing this time. Willow listened to the chorus and then joined in on the second round.

Her fingers flew over the strings. She was good, very good. Better with her instrument than I was with the harp. It was... beautiful.

I blushed slightly as my heart skipped.

When we'd finished, Willow insisted we go again. We'd had a few missteps, but she wanted to get it perfect.

It made me wonder when I'd stopped caring about things like that, when I'd really put aside my harp. I'd toyed with it semi-regularly over the years, but I'd stopped loving it. I didn't know why.

As we played, the music curled around the edges of my chest, soft and warm. It was magical, and there wasn't a bit of glamour in it—just Willow... and me. I knew I wasn't supposed to enjoy this. It was the whole reason I'd been avoiding her.

Every moment with her—how we met, the party, that damn garden, my room—it all wove itself into something I hadn't meant to start but couldn't pretend wasn't real. I knew what was growing between us. Not forbidden. Just... not something I could crack open.

The song was a tragedy—because, of course, it was. Celtic roots and all. A woman losing her secret love to betrayal, waiting years for him to return from prison. I hadn't meant to pick it. At least, I told myself that. But halfway through, I felt something in Willow unspool: that same longing. The vambrace made sure I knew. It was the quiet ache of someone who'd waited for far too long already. I felt the backwash of it in my own heart, my grief recognizing its reflection.

I should have stopped this, I knew.

I wasn't cheating. Not really. That was the line I kept repeating to myself. I wasn't touching her. I wasn't saying anything I couldn't take back. But the longer we played, the longer I listened to her voice next to mine, the more that excuse started to rot in my mouth.

Liz was at home, carrying the weight of the world. And I was here. Making music with someone else. Not flirting, not touching—but still intimate in a way that was harder to name and even harder to justify. And yet, we didn't stop.

We kept playing, song after song, each of us teaching each other one tune or another, from a few Irish tunes to a dismally sour thing concocted by some Night Court composer. We even played through one old Japanese tune I'd learned in middle school. I'd forgotten I'd even known it until just then.

Between us and the music, we buried our hurt for a while. For that short time, we weren't betrothed. She wasn't an outcast, and I wasn't "Her Grace." Just two women with the same wound, pressing melody after melody against it like bandages. Hoping it would scab over if we just kept playing.

And when we were done, Willow just stood, put the guitar away, and stalked clumsily out of the room in silence. Outside, I heard the sound of the lift bars rising and the platform moving away. I felt her turmoil. And something inside me said that this was so wrong.

It wasn't innocent, as much as I told myself otherwise. Not anymore.

And I'd let it happen anyway.

In the end, I'd been wrong. This wasn't like it had been with Nastasia.

Willow sounded like her, at first—all that talk about how we were alike, how she knew what I really was. But this? This was different.

There was a pull, yes, and it had urgency, like if I didn't hold on to her right now, she might vanish in a puff of smoke.

Nastasia had been dark. Irresistibly dark. Her kind of freedom—untethered, amoral—was seductive. But it swallowed me whole. I forgot there was any light left in me at all.

Willow didn't do that.

She was kind. Sweet, even. And that would've been fine—harmless—if not for the other thing. The thing I was loathe to admit.

I was falling for her.

It wasn't dramatic. No lightning bolt, no great declaration. Just flowers. Music. The way she touched my shoulder lingered a second too long. All of it chipped away at me until suddenly, she was in me—woven into my heart before I could stop it.

People talk about love like it's a choice. But it never is. We don't jump into it. We fall. We trip. We stumble. We do our damnedest to stay upright, and still it catches us.

This time, it was going to hurt.

Then again, maybe it would all work out. Maybe no one would end up shattered.

But as I returned the harp to its place of rest and my hand lingered on the frame, my thoughts circled around a single word: threadcalled.

CHAPTER TWENTY-TWO
DROPS OF... BLOOD?

Thoroughly irritated at myself for indulging these feelings about Willow, I decided a late ride with Umbryss would clear my head. I just needed to get away for a while, ride the sky, maybe dip a toe in the ocean. Anything to gird myself against the absolute annoyance I felt.

My boot slid on something slick at the doorway to Umbryss's lair, pulling me from my musings.

I froze.

That wasn't water. Nothing down here should be wet anyway. And I didn't smell the telltale hint of moisture or mold.

I crouched. A different odor hit me hard enough to sting the back of my throat. I caught the scent of acid and sulfur, like someone had boiled chlorinated water with a rotten egg. I gagged, drew both blades, and shifted my sight into the Weave.

The world snapped into threads.

And whatever was on the floor wasn't supposed to exist.

Drops... no, splatter, maybe. Viewed magically, they glowed faintly at the core, a sickly violet pulse wrapped in a few strained purple threads—the normal world trying to make sense of it—but the rest of the strands were jagged. Broken. Black. Little piles of ruptured magic like charred fiberglass, like someone had shattered a spell and let it rot.

Nothing Fae made that.

That was Mother Darkness, through and through. And looking at the drops of corrosive liquid, it had to be wounded.

Wevkrana—or something close. Maybe one had crawled off after the battle, half-dead and dazed. I didn't know.

My hands snapped to my blades. I reached out into the corridor, stretching my senses as far as they would reach. And felt nothing. No breath. No heartbeat. No scuttle of a mouse.

Just the quiet.

My pulse thudded once, hard.

Not from panic.

From instinct.

Predators get very still before they strike—or before they're hunted.

I slid forward, following the trail as it curved around the corner. The drops weren't drops anymore. They were smears, long strokes of ruined magic dragging along the stones like something had been pulled. Or dragged itself.

In the Weave, the black threads writhed, twisted, pulling themselves together like something... alive. This wasn't Wevkrana. I didn't know what this was. But the trail was headed right for the spiral stairs that led to the Veilstone.

Fuck.

I stepped as carefully as I could, suddenly thankful for the grace of the Fae. My soft footfalls didn't make so much as a peep.

"Ward this hallway," I whispered.

The palace wards flared to life at my command—violent red magic, flooding the corridor like a holiday fever dream. Walls. Floors. Supports. Every nail. Every fracture line. The whole place lit up in crystalline detail through the Weave.

And the trail was unmistakable: jagged black magic tearing through the glow like claw marks in flesh, leaving dead spots behind it.

I bolted like a wraith in the darkness, not making a sound, even at speed.

The Weave flowed around me—scarlet clarity and broken shadows—showing more damage. The whisper-faint sigils, etched at every junction against intruders, were nothing but bruised darkness.

Whatever had left this... it hadn't just moved through the hall. It had violated it. Bent the magic. Distorted it. Fed on it.

And the trail angled downward toward a spiral staircase—*the* spiral staircase. The one that led to the Veilstone and the beating heart of the palace below it.

My throat went tight.

It was ahead of me. And moving with purpose.

With some semblance of sight where I could see the terrain, I all but flew down the stairs to the next lower level, practically running down the curving wall.

I reached the bottom in seconds—and froze.

There, in front of me, was... something. It wasn't a hole in the Weave, though it looked like one at first. It was a space full of burnt, black magic. Magic that moved. Magic that twisted, reshaping, constantly reforming inside with no definite center or core. But the outline looked... Fae. It was shaped like a woman.

I didn't hesitate further. Swallowing down the rising nausea from the Veilstone, I launched forward, running, and leveled a strike at the thing as I passed.

I caught nothing but air.

The amorphous black thing simply split and opened around the sweep of my bóllom. Then it spun toward me, gobs of its viscous skin splattering against the wall, the floor, and my skin.

The droplet puckered against my knuckle as if taking a breath, then split open into threads finer than hair. They unfurled wetly, slithering over the back of my hand with an obscene delicacy. Each filament clung with a tiny suctioning pull, a series of soft, rapid tugs that made my nerves light up like they were being plucked, one by one.

"Oh, Goddess," I breathed. It was on me.

Panic lanced through me as I staggered back and my nisís clattered across the stones. I swiped at the thing with my sleeve, desperate, but it clung to my skin with a sickening tug.

The spindly black filaments of magic inside it coalesced,

knitting together into something needle-thin and hungry, rising to strike, to burrow in, to infect me.

I drew on the ambient magic. It surged under my ribs, ripping through my chest and firing down my arm. My muscles locked. A scream tore out of me, anger and agony tangled together.

"Get off!"

The tendrils tightened, burrowing, but the power inside me detonated. Purple lightning spidered from every pore and burned the thing to ash and vaporized the sleeve of my dress.

I gasped. It was gone.

"Shit, shit, shit." More droplets dotted the floor, thicker now and pulsing with life, leading into the chamber where the Veilstone hovered.

I swallowed hard, snatched up my nisís, and crept around the corner to peer inside.

The thing stood there, a tendril stretched toward the Veilstone. And through the Weave, I saw the remnant, the horror that lived inside that artifact, react: a black, oily consciousness pulsing beneath the surface, reaching back. Every instinct in me knew I couldn't let that thing get closer.

I sheathed my blades. If I couldn't stab it or slice it, I'd use something else. Even the monsters of Mother Darkness had cells. Cells could be crushed.

I lifted my hand and pulled the magic forward, shaping one of the simplest spells I'd learned. I jolted the thing upward and formed a perfect sphere around the creature. It hovered, trapped.

"Cait!" Vaelith's voice, then Willow's from the stairs.

I ignored them. I only needed a few seconds.

The sphere shrank to half its size. Inside, the thing screamed and folded in on itself. Smaller. Half again. Its next cry was a squeal, strangled off. Still, the protoplasm writhed.

I poured more power into the spell. I would not reach for her. I would do this on my own.

I screamed with the effort, with the fury burning through my ribs. "This is my home! These are my people! *I* am ruler here! *You* are nothing! I know you can hear me. I am going to kill you!"

The sphere collapsed impossibly small.

The creature burst like a tiny star.

Most of the shockwave sank into the spell, channeled into the Weave, but the rest slammed into me and threw me back.

My back hit the stone with a crack I felt more than heard. The world went white for a heartbeat, then dissolved into spinning shadows. Air punched out of my lungs. Everything inside me went slack and distant.

Voices blurred toward me. Footsteps. Power.

"Cait!" Willow's scream was the first thing that pierced the ringing in my skull.

Shoes skidded across the floor. Someone dropped to their knees beside me. My vision doubled, then tripled; Willow's presence flickered in and out.

"Don't move her, yet," Vaelith snapped. "Her spine—"

Fingers landed on my shoulder, magic crawled down through my back like ants under the skin.

I shifted—and gave a broken painful groan of agony. My back was broken.

I tried to suck in a shallow, painful breath. The room tilted and the Weave of the palace smeared into a red haze. My limbs didn't listen; my magic didn't either, guttering wildly under my skin.

"She's concussed," Vaelith said, voice high, shaking. A cool hand cupped my cheek to keep me still. "Her pupils are dilated—Cait, hey, hey, stay with me."

I blinked hard. Everything dragged. The words came out as a slur.

"I... I... 'm... f—fine."

"You are absolutely not fine," Willow muttered. Her hands were shaking too. "She shouldn't have been able to take that blast. Goddess—Cait, what were you thinking?"

I tried to answer, but I couldn't think really.

Vaelith pressed two fingers to the side of my neck. "Her pulse is stable."

"Cait," Willow said again, quieter now, right beside me. "Look at me, dearest. Can you hear me?"

"Tha' hurt," I whispered tiredly.

"Keep your eyes open," Vaelith said.

I managed a groan. Or maybe it was a curse. I couldn't tell.

"She needs healing now," Vaelith said. "Her spine may be fractured."

"I can do it," Willow said. "But not here."

"Hold on to her," Vaelith ordered.

The world tore sideways.

No warning. No grip. No breath.

One second, there were hands on me, heat against my shoulder, Willow's magic threading through my ribs. The next, everything collapsed into a smear of darkness and wind, like falling through a scream.

Cold swallowed me whole. The shadows dragged their claws along my skin as Vaelith pulled all three of us through, and my stomach lurched like it wanted to climb up my throat.

We slammed back into reality in the exact same pose—Willow with her hands braced on my sternum, Vaelith crouched with her arms still wrapped around us.

Except now the stone beneath me was different. Smooth. Warmed by spells. The air smelled like antiseptic herbs and bitter tea.

A low sound crawled out of my throat. Everything inside me throbbed in time with my pulse, each beat a stab of wrongness. My magic was a shredded thing, shivering under my skin. My spine felt like a cracked icicle.

"Easy," Willow murmured, her voice soft and close, like she was afraid I'd bolt. "You're in the infirmary. You're safe."

Safe. The word drifted through me without meaning.

Willow squeezed my hand—at least I thought she did. My fingers felt like they belonged to someone else. "Cait? Dearest, can you hear me?"

Cold. Why was it so cold?

I tried to speak, but my jaw wouldn't cooperate. All I managed was a faint, broken gasp.

I couldn't hold on to anything. Not the room. Not my body. Not the voices.

Just cold.

And the faint, distant thought that I'd done something very, very stupid.

The world folded in again, small and dark and mercifully quiet, and then just... nothing.

CHAPTER TWENTY-THREE
THREADCALLED

It was like slipping upward through tar, slow and in pieces. First came myself, or, well, the wreckage of myself. Everything hurt in one way or another, but my ribs and skull were leading the pack. My head felt like someone had parked a truck on it.

Then the world started knitting itself together around me. Presence. The room hummed with faint magic. I sensed someone on my right, sitting, tense. Vaelith. I was pretty sure.

Willow lay on her side, breathing shallowly. The magic in her flickered, like it had been burned down to the wick.

"What happened?" I whispered. My throat felt like scorched paper. I tried to sit up. That was stupid. Pain knifed through everything at once. "Ohh."

Vaelith's breath caught, and her chair scraped as she stood. "You scared the shit out of us."

"It wasn't that bad," I rasped.

"You're shitting me, right? You almost died," she said, and her voice wasn't angry. It was frayed with worry. "You're lucky Willow was here. You were—" She stopped. "What were you doing?"

I lifted a hand toward my face. My blindfold was missing. I snapped my eyes shut hard. "Don't look."

"At what?" Vaelith asked, genuinely confused. "Your eyes? I'm not mortal, Cait. Do you know where you are?"

I sniffed—antiseptic smell, herbs. I frowned. "The

infirmary?"

My throat burned. "Water."

She slipped away for a second and returned with a cup. Guided it to my lips. The first sip felt like grace.

"What were you doing?" Vaelith demanded again.

I swallowed hard. "Fusing atoms," I rasped. "Apparently."

"Don't." Her voice went sharp. "Don't make this a joke."

The humor died in my throat. "I'm trying not to panic," I admitted. I turned my head toward Willow. "Did I hurt her?"

"No, you didn't hurt her," Vaelith said. "She ran the edge of burnout to heal you. It's apparently a special gift of hers. But it was her choice."

It was nice of her to say, but I'd screwed up. I'd thought I was invincible. I'd been arrogant. I could have simply moved the thing—whatever it was—out of the chamber. Willow was run down to the nub. Vaelith had been terrified. And I could have vaporized the plateau.

I looked at Willow's sputtering magic again, and my heart felt like someone ran a dagger through it. I hadn't felt this way since Reese had taken Katie and Liz. "What *is* it with us?"

There was a rustle at the doorway. "You already know," Morvaine said, and her voice carried a sympathy that made it feel ten times worse. "You're threadcalled. You're a bonded pair."

I shook my head. That was a mistake. "Ow. What does that mean? I mean, really."

"It means your souls are tied by something greater than time," Morvaine explained, voice calm in an infuriating, academic way, as if Willow and I were a diagram on a chalkboard. "Threadcalling isn't biology, Your Grace. It's a bond of souls, documented long ago.

"Some are forged deliberately. Others happen under stress, ritual, or proximity to deep magic. We've even seen it in combat. Once formed, they persist. They echo. People change. The bond doesn't. It draws those two souls together— sometimes across worlds or multiple lives."

She nodded toward Willow. "Nyxiel was sure. I suspected. I became certain when Willow spent herself to save you."

"Wait," I said, my eyes wide. "Are you saying I did this?"

"Not necessarily," Morvaine answered. "It's hard to say when it happened, or which of you was responsible."

"But one of us started it."

Morvaine exhaled through her nose. "Yes. Just not either of you as you are now. Someone who wore your soul once. Or hers."

I opened my mouth, then closed it again.

No. Not that. Not her. I shoved it away.

I wasn't sure what to say. Threadcalled still sounded like some Fae bullshit for fated lovers, but... I felt it, real and alive. And it had gone so much further than just some physical urge. I'd fallen in love.

I wanted to take Willow *and* Liz right to me, hold them, mold them into little extensions I could keep close. That urge wasn't going anywhere and I didn't know how much control I actually had. It was maddening.

"There's nothing I can do?"

Morvaine shook her head. "No, Your Grace. It's the way we're made, I'm afraid. I hope it works out."

She sounded so calm about it.

I snorted. There was no world in which this... worked out.

CHAPTER TWENTY-FOUR
ASHES, FEATHERS, BONE, & FIRE

My body recovered some, my thoughts did not. They weren't turbulent, they just kept going round and round, and I found them landing on Willow: the feel of her flawless skin, her long black hair against my neck and back. The guilt that should have come over Liz and just wouldn't. I still loved her as much as I ever had, but Willow was in there with her, and I *should* feel something about that. But still, there was nothing. And I didn't hate it. It felt oddly more like me.

But then there was the thing, for lack of a better term. Blob? Ooze? Pudding? I had no idea what to call it. And we still didn't know how it had gotten in. The only thing I could imagine was that it had slipped in under the cover of the battle. But that was months ago. Was it just lurking around the palace all this time? It seemed impossible and… unpleasant, in the worst of ways.

A little later, limping slightly, I found my way to my balcony, where I closed myself off to my people-sense thing and stripped off my blindfold, letting it drape over the railing. The sudden release of tension felt like relaxing after squinting at small text all day.

I let the warm summer breeze roll over my skin and ruffle my sleep pants. At least the palace had stopped stitching me nightgowns. I'd never liked them. Probably never would.

"Beautiful night," Willow said, and I jolted in surprise. I'd almost forgotten that she was right next door and we had adjoining balconies, just a small balustrade between.

"Is it?" I asked absently, feeling a light coiling of grief over my lost vision.

"I think so. Listen. Do you hear them?"

I turned my head, tilting my ear out and away from the tower. It took a moment, and then I heard it. Laughing... children laughing, somewhere far below and incredibly faint.

"Night Pixies," I whispered, moving a little closer to her side. "The kids are playing. What is that song?" Down below, the little Faeries were singing a repetitive tune. It reminded me a little of *Ring around the Roses*.

"Just a kid's song," Willow said, her tone more relaxed and bright than it had been for a while. "It goes: Ashes, ashes, feathers, bone. Emberbearer finds the throne."

"What does it mean?"

"It's from an ancient poem, from the Book of Ash and Thorns:

> Fourfold soul in silver bound,
> Three in shadow, one in light.
> Walks the line and wears the crown,
> Day shall kneel and so shall Night.
>
> Touch the flame and do not burn,
> Speak no lie and betray no name.
> All who rule must first learn—
> Or feed the crown their pride and flame.
>
> Ashes, ashes, feathers, bone—
> Emberbearer finds the throne.

"As for what it means," she added with a shrug, "that's anyone's guess. It was written just a few years after The Sundering. The Book of Ash and Thorns is supposedly Mother Shaddan's final book of rules. Most of it is terribly vague and open to interpretation. It does, however, codify the requirements of Fae Bargains."

I frowned, a little confused. "Wait, that's written down somewhere? In a book? I thought it was just something everyone knew."

"It had to come from somewhere."

"Huh," I muttered. "I'd like to get a look at that book."

"Best of luck. There aren't many copies left. But if there's one anywhere, there's probably one here."

I nodded, and we grew quiet, returning to our vigil over the Night Pixies below. The children were now calling out to each other in some kind of Fae version of Marco Polo. And I snickered when I heard one of the children shout in protest, "Hey! Feet on the ground, Kara!"

"I wish I could go back to being that age," Willow said. "When I didn't have a care in the world. Maura hadn't reached our domain yet, and I'd never known a day without peace and wonder."

I nodded. "Yeah. My sister and I used to play in the surf on the ocean beneath the sun."

"What's it like?" Willow asked.

"What's what like?"

"The sun. I've never left Shaddan."

I blinked. "It's bright, and on Earth, it turns the sky a brilliant blue. And it's so warm... sometimes too warm... Adults... adult humans, I mean, they never really appreciate just how wondrous it is. I've died twice, you know. And still... it wasn't until I landed here that I really came to appreciate living."

"I can understand that. After... well, after, I was stuffed in the box. It was full of dreams and nightmares. It never seemed to end. And when my mother finally freed me, I wasn't sure for a long time if it wasn't just another dream. Sometimes, I'm still not. A lot of this—being here, you—it feels a little unreal... like glamour."

"It's not," I assured her, though I could appreciate that feeling. I'd had my close call with Fae glamour. The blurring of lines between what was real and what wasn't had made me question everything. I couldn't even imagine thousands of years of dreaming. "Do you remember them? Your dreams?"

There was a soft pop and a rush of air as Willow closed the distance between us: a glimmerstep.

I stumbled slightly, unprepared for it, and she grabbed my arm.

"Some of them," she said once I was steady. "But they're disjointed, and a lot of the early ones were about other people. I was hearing them die—sometimes watching them."

I nodded. "It's part of The Morrigan's domain. Death. When she finally left me, it was months, I guess, before I became aware of myself. Until then, I was in this never-ending spiral where I could see everything and…" I paused, squeezing my eyes against the memories. "And so many people at their last moments… their last breaths."

Her hand brushed my arm again and then followed it up, caressing my cheek. I thought to pull away, but I didn't. I should have, I knew. But it felt nice to be seen. Like Vaelith, Willow understood. She understood something different, but… it was another part of me and not a pleasant one.

"Does it still haunt you?" I asked. Somehow, just letting her comfort me like this didn't feel fair. She surely had needs, more than just… politics.

"Sometimes," she whispered, and then she leaned her head against mine, sliding an arm around my waist.

We stood there for a long moment, neither of us speaking, just taking in the night. Somewhere in the distance, I heard the massive wingbeats and a trumpeting roar as Umbryss took flight from his cave in the mountain behind us.

I laughed lightly. "One day, I want my kids to meet him."

"He loves children," Willow answered, a grin in her voice. "And not to eat, as it turns out, though he often threatens otherwise."

"That sounds like him," I said.

She was so close. And it felt electric. Part of me wanted to pull her around, fully into my arms.

I swallowed hard and cleared my throat, drifting away.

Willow shifted too—a soft, half-step to follow that died even as it landed.

She huffed a breath, low and awkward, and turned away

from me.

I opened my senses again and found her clutching the railing, fingers wrapped around the stone.

"So... uh... what are you reading?" she asked, voice a little too bright, a little too casual.

"What? Oh..." I'd forgotten that I had a book and my transcription rod in my left hand. "It's just a little book on outmaneuvering court politics."

"Not the one that Callie wrote?" she asked, suddenly showing intense interest.

"The very same," I replied. "She certainly has a pretty impressive view of herself."

"Yes, but it's actually a good book," Willow said.

"You've read it?"

"I have. Cover to cover. It's pretty ruthless stuff, though. Are you sure your upstanding mind can handle it?"

I gave a nervous laugh and fiddled with the transcription rod. "I'm not nearly as upstanding as I seem. I've been known to do some pretty evil shit on occasion."

"I doubt that," Willow said, a wry tone in her voice.

"You shouldn't."

I didn't elaborate. There was nothing but pain in those memories.

"I know you have a dark side," Willow said, her voice flat, but not quite emotionless. There was a hint of empathy there. "We all do. Sometimes it's hard to fight it, especially when times are tough." She paused for a beat. "In any event, let's not talk about that. Let's sit down and let the rod read Callie's expert advice, shall we? Maybe I can add context."

I shrugged. "Sure."

We made our way inside, and I all but threw myself onto the plush couch, grateful for something—anything—to hold onto that wasn't the look I was sure had been on Willow's face. But then, she sat down beside me, shoulder to shoulder, legs touching.

"Here, let me have that," she whispered and plucked the book from my hand along with the rod.

Again, the heat between us seemed to rise. Her knee

trembled against mine. Still, though, she opened the book and ran the rod over the table of contents. My mother's voice, or a fair approximation, began droning different section titles.

I turned toward her. "Willow… I…"

"Shh…" she whispered. "I know. I wish it were different." It sounded like a denial, but still she moved closer, her lips a hair's breadth from mine.

She paused there, close enough that I could feel her breath, giving me every possible chance to turn away.

I didn't.

I leaned that last fraction of an inch, and our mouths brushed—a soft, questioning, terrible, perfect mistake. The world went very still. For one heartbeat, I kissed her back, fingers curling in the fabric of her sleeve like I could anchor myself there. I wanted to stay there just like that, forever.

Mother of Waters, it was like kissing lightning. The hair on my neck rose. My chest fluttered like bees in a jar. I felt so… young.

And there wasn't a speck of guilt.

I needed her in a way that I'd never needed anyone.

My hand found the back of her neck, and I pressed harder.

But then, from nowhere… a memory. Liz holding me crumpled on a shower floor in the hospital after I'd returned from my first trip to Shaddan. I didn't know where it came from, or why now, but it turned something inside of me. Reminded me.

I tore myself away, heart hammering, breath ragged. And feeling so terribly lost.

"Stop," I blurted. "It can't be like this. I just… I can't."

She closed the book and set it down. "I'm not doing it on purpose." She stood, and I heard an audible swallow. Then she said, sounding almost hurt, "You're right. It shouldn't be like this. You're Faerie. Your heart is supposed to beat wild and free—not caged by human sensibilities. And you know what?" Her voice turned into something between anger and heartbreak. "It will. You can't stop it. It's what we are. You can only hide from that for so long."

With that, she turned and marched out to the balcony and

disappeared to the other side with another soft pop of collapsing air. The vambrace's charm flared inside me for an instant, not hurt, not longing, not eve desire, just... frustration.

After she was gone, I sat there for a long time.

A long time.

Just thinking and thinking, and trying to understand how this had happened.

A thousand years ago, she had said, you would have enjoyed trapping some poor, hapless human in a twisted bargain. It's in your nature.

And it was. Always had been. I was faerie, and she had no idea how wild my heart already was. I could feel it... rattling the cage.

About time you admitted it, Dorogaya. Nastasia's voice in my head.

"Oh shut up," I muttered and made my way to bed.

CHAPTER TWENTY-FIVE

My Court. My Rules. Your Funeral.

I sat painfully in the throne, my back still groaned at me, and my chest felt like an elephant had sat on it. Still, though, for someone who'd had her innards turned to mush two days ago, I wasn't in bad shape. All that was left from the attack two nights ago was soreness—and absolute boredom.

I wasn't even allowed a good book or my transcription rod.

No, this was a formal event, which apparently meant I had to sit perfectly still and look regal, like a taxidermied duchess. Sithraine had tried—*tried*—to stuff me into a miserable Edwardian death shroud of a gown. High collar, buttoned wrists, enough fabric to curtain a cathedral. One feel of it, though, and I'd threatened to burn it.

So we compromised. Which was to say: I lost slightly less. I was now wearing yet another bastard child of Dark Fae club wear and royal presentation garb that had become my life of late. The dress was tight, midnight-blue, and exposed my legs all the way up to my hips, more of a leotard with a waist-fastened train, really. At least the matching boots were only knee-high, and the tights felt nice.

I'd have preferred riding leathers, but those had been vetoed—on principle. At least I didn't look like some haunted Victorian monarch.

The swords were non-negotiable. After Mother Darkness's little intrusions, I'd decreed that everyone in my service went armed at all times, formal or not, so my nisís rode on my hip and the bóllom lay across my lap.

Now I sat forward on a red crystal throne to greet a dozen primarchs who I couldn't see and accept gifts from them I couldn't acknowledge. Above, a flock of crows had gathered in the arches loosing occasional croaks and caws. Sithraine had taken that as a good sign.

Me? I wasn't convinced.

This place was so… strange sometimes.

Sithraine had prepped me, but there was no way my mouth was going to stick to script. It never did. My chest was already tight and my adrenaline flowing like I was getting ready to do battle. It didn't help that the mother of the other bride was first, and that she had provided literally everything, including the Court Herald.

I tried to get comfortable as he called the first name on the list.

"Runa, Queen of the Night Court, Mother of Nightmares and Shadows…"

Sithraine shifted beside me. Mother of Shadows had been her title when she'd been Queen of the Nerin. For Runa to use it was an obvious insult, and one we couldn't return. And it really pissed me off. It was a shit move.

I didn't pay much attention to the rest of Runa's titles; they were way too dramatic for a woman who once hosted a masquerade where everyone had to dress as their ex. There were a fair number of Lady Shattermarks there, or so Willow had said.

I did, at least, straighten up.

Willow, bless her heart, was seated to my right on one of the thrones. Mine, technically. And if the Primarchs had thoughts about that—spoiler: they absolutely would—well, they could stuff it.

Runa entered, a blaze of living magic. Kiran and a small entourage trailed behind her like perfume and litigation.

"Willow," she purred, sweeping into the room with arms wide, "you remembered how to sit upright. I was beginning to worry about your spine."

I did my best to keep my features neutral, but I wanted to scowl. Willow deserved better.

"I figured I'd at least pretend I have one," Willow replied, deadpan.

Kiran cleared his throat disapprovingly. "This is meant to be a ceremonial occasion, Willow. You should—"

I tilted my head toward the voice and interrupted with the barest hint of acid. "In this court, Lord Kiran, women speak for themselves. Lady Willow is my intended and my counsel. You enjoy neither privilege."

Willow let out the tiniest, traitorous snort beside me.

"You've… redecorated," Runa noted, ignoring the back and forth. "And I see the seating chart is more flexible than tradition typically allows."

I offered her a tacit smile. "My court. My rules. Also, Lady Willow is my betrothed, so I expect her to receive full courtesy due a lady of the Vermilion Court. And you will address her as Your Grace."

"Of course," Runa said, not a hint I'd struck so much as a single nerve.

Runa and Kiran stepped aside as the doors parted again.

"Lord Stiles of Silverdeep," the Herald announced, and the short and stubby little beancounter entered. I still wondered at that. I hadn't known that we could get pudgy—apparently so.

I crooked a finger at Sithraine, who moved closer as Stiles approached.

"Where's Lady Shattermark?" I asked Sithraine. "I thought she was next."

"She did not show," Sithraine replied, her tone low and very grave. "We don't yet know why."

I nodded and turned my attention back to Stiles.

There were no theatrics with Stiles. He was all cold calculation. On his left stood his chief of staff, a troll woman named Ugganna, likewise stout, though her frame suggested more muscle than fat, and I wished I could see. I'd never met a troll, and I was seriously curious what they looked like. To his left was Karinna, his wife, formerly a commoner. She even curtsied, which was unnecessary but sweet.

The Fae had a tradition called the Journey of Gifts. Each Primarch offered something beautiful and expensive to the betrothed couple prior to the seating. Runa, as mother of the bride and the money behind this throne, at least for the moment, wasn't required to bring one, and I was grateful for that. After all, "gift" was a loose term. Mostly, they were assassination attempts in gilded boxes. Apparently, it wasn't required that they be non-lethal, just pretty.

Fun times.

Lord Stiles' gift was a beautifully appointed ledger of accounts requiring a payment to Stiles every time the owner said thank you. We hadn't accepted the gift at this point, so we were safe, but still, no one sane thanked the Fae for a gift... ever.

"Lord Stiles, your gift could only have come from Silverdeep," I said sweetly. "Its intentions were perfectly clear."

"May your reign be long and your.... accounts be forever balanced."

I suppressed a laugh and leaned to Willow. "There's a film about children being put into a blood sport that I need to let you listen to sometime. Stiles strikes me as someone who would appreciate it." Then to him, I said, "Your attendance is noted for the record, Lord Stiles."

He shifted slightly but then moved for the next entry, one I was far more interested in "seeing."

"Rhiannon," the Herald said simply. "The Hollow Moon, Queen of Duskwinter."

The doors parted again for a party of four. Rhiannon and her three daughters, no other entourage. I never understood her title, probably never would, other than it suggested cold and empty. And given the sudden tension in the room at her arrival, it was probably about right.

I leaned forward. "Queen Rhiannon," I said, my voice cool. "Your crystalline lily was... instructive. One petal broke, and it chose a rather ordinary memory of mine to display. I admit I expected something sharper." That was a lie. It had been a mortifying moment from my teen years, but I wasn't going to tell her that.

"Sometimes the Lily selects its own truths," Rhiannon responded. "We don't always approve of its priorities."

That was comforting. Not.

More courts followed one after another. Frankly, it was absolute boredom. I really wanted to nod off.

At one point, Willow patted my hand and hissed, "You're doing great."

"You're not in this dress," I countered. "The tights and the leotard are riding up my ass. I really wish the palace would pick something simpler."

"Maybe it likes your ass," Willow said cheekily, then added in a whisper, "I know I do."

I didn't laugh, but I couldn't escape the suddenly soft smile that graced my painted lips.

The associated gifts ranged from a crystal spider in a cage from Vermix of Skavreth to a vial of Waking Memory from Marielle, Queen of Eirinth.

Once they were settled, mostly to our right with Runa, the doors opened, and the real fun began.

"Lady Irexielle, Queen of Corvallen, Keeper of the Muse," I rolled my eyes behind my blindfold. Not strictly required, but it saved me from any serious offense caused by my tendency to express my—irritation? disappointment? disgust?—all over my face.

"Your Grace," Irexielle said formally.

"Lady Irexielle, your artistic works are legendary. I believe you have one of Lord Aurex that many consider... his best side." It was a life-size and, I'd been told, accurate nude. He was, by all accounts, not... impressive.

Irexielle gave a curt nod. "I'm working on one of you," she said, and there was an undercurrent of menace in her tone.

Again, I'd been warned.

"Then I trust your reputation for accuracy will hold," I replied, my voice low. "I'd hate to have to... correct the record."

She wouldn't humiliate me like she had Aurex. Nude? Fine. Out of proportion or somehow degrading? I'd throttle her myself.

"Welcome," I said, and inclined my head toward the seating on our left, where the more contentious courts gathered like a murder of crows. The cawing overhead had increased since they'd entered. Fitting. Maybe one of the birds would shit on Irexielle and I could have that moment captured. I'd title it "Monarch appropriately dressed."

Next was Roselle, Queen of Thorn's Reach. She entered with one of her personal assassins at her side, a member of the Sable Choir. I'd known she was coming, and I couldn't refuse, but Naerith and Elarith would be watching that one very closely the entire time.

I barely addressed her, turning to Sithraine. "Isn't she the one who brought the Gossip Bloom?"

Sithraine leaned down. "Yes, Your Grace, it requires your blood to keep it alive. Once fed, though, it'll say something awful about your parentage or family. I once watched as it destroyed a family when the bride found out about the rather odd proclivities of her betrothed and his father."

"So," I answered. "All the family kinks. Rude."

"Indeed, Your Grace," Sithraine said through her dagger smile.

I turned back to Roselle, schooling my expression into something that could almost pass for fondness.

"Roselle," I said, letting her name linger just a breath too long. "Your Gossip Bloom has been... enlightening. It's remarkable how eager it is to speak ill of its own roots." Then I paused. "Do find yourself a place. I'm sure the bloom will enjoy having you so close. Family always does."

I literally felt the scowl and rise of magic at the slight, but she didn't cause a scene. Not here. She'd save that for the Ball, and, I hoped, threaten my life, giving me leave to toss her out on her obnoxious ass.

Finally, I'd saved the best for last, made him wait almost an hour while I stretched pleasantries with the neutral houses: Aurex of Embereach. The asshole.

Aurex didn't wait to be announced. He pushed the doors aside and strode in as the Herald mentioned his name.

"Can it," he said flatly. "She knows who I am."

I nodded. And slid forward, re-crossing my legs as if poised to launch at him. "I do, Lord Aurex," I said. "Embereach's presence is noted."

Oh, and fuck you, you pompous, slave selling sleaze. I didn't say that part, but I so wanted to.

"I thought not to come at all," he said glibly. "The Vermilion Palace was once the pinnacle of our culture, but now it seems... tired," he feigned wiping dust from his fingers, "and drab."

I ignored the dig, just because I knew it would irritate him. Then I said something truly dangerous. "The gift of the Crown of Flameglass is... distinctive," I said. "Its terms are admirably clear. At some point, I imagine it will sit where it belongs."

"If it'll fit," he muttered. There was a round of gasps before he belatedly added, "Your Grace."

It wasn't a matter of fit. The Crown of Flameglass only stayed on the worthy. Everyone else... it burned to ash. The trick was, no one knew what made someone worthy.

I stood, left hand locking on my bóllom's scabbard, daring him to move. "At some point, we'll have to have a little contest. Maybe see who can actually wear it."

Sithraine moved up next to me.

"Blanched," Sithraine whispered. "And really pissed off."

"Perhaps one day, when the realm is calmer, we might resolve the matter properly," I said. "Let the crown decide which of us it judges worthy and which one is... less than."

I caught the groan of leather as his gloved hand tightened on his sword.

I cocked a hip and slid my right hand to the hilt of my sword. "Unless you'd like to settle the matter today."

My adrenaline spiked, and I took a step forward.

Pull it! Pull it now! Let's just see who'll survive.

There was no dais for the thrones; they sat flat on the floor. We could have it out here on the floor. Strangely, for someone whose life as a cop had been especially dedicated to de-escalation, I wanted violence: right here, right now.

"Your Grace," Sithraine warned in a soft hiss.

But Aurex didn't take the challenge, instead, he just said, "I'd love to see it on your head one day." And then, without a word, he turned his back on me and strode away.

There were more gasps and even a few comments of "how rude" from the other guests.

"Coward," I said.

He stopped then and turned his head, not quite looking back. "We shall see, Red Queen. We shall see." Then he stalked from the room.

Sithraine edged closer, her voice barely above the rustle of silk. "If he'd drawn, half the courts would have taken it as permission, Your Grace. It would have been a bloodbath."

"That would have simplified things," I said, my heart pounding, my blood seething, and my blind eyes still narrowed toward the doors.

Fae betrothal receptions were seriously fucked up affairs. I was still standing there, looking imperious—I was sure—when two names bellowed from the Herald that I had never in a million worlds expected.

"Lady Aoife, Younger Princess of the Vermilion Court, and her... uhh... plus one, Lady Medlyn of Terra Victa."

I forgot how to breathe.

CHAPTER TWENTY-SIX
What a Crown Costs

I did not, by any sane definition, *handle* seeing Aoife and Liz in the throne room. I survived it.

Protocol did most of the work: the herald announced them, I gave them the formal welcome in the Vermilion Queen voice, promised them a private audience "at a more suitable hour," and then let Vaelith and three different attendants whisk them away to be settled before any of us had the chance to scream or cry in front of half the courts. No scenes. No explanations. Just one more disaster postponed.

I decided, instead, to receive them in the only safe place I could think of: my sitting room. The royal apartments were quiet, and there was plenty of room. No prying eyes. Now all I needed to do was get my brain to get with the program. I paced the room in quiet circles as Willow tried to calm me down.

"I'm here," Willow said quietly as I made another circle.

She shouldn't be here. But I couldn't make myself send her away. As always, she was like some gravitational body, pulling me close.

I paced past her again, or tried to. She snagged my wrist with surprising strength and pulled me straight into her arms. Her hold was warm, and it steadied my nerves. It was also very much the last thing I needed.

"It'll be okay," she murmured into my hair.

My breath stuttered. My anxiety was clawing up one side of me while some darker instinct purred down the other at the contact.

There was a knock at the door.

"Come in," I said without thinking, and then cringed.

Shit.

The door opened before either of us could move.

"Your Grace," Vaelith announced gently, "your guests are here."

I didn't turn. I didn't need to.

I felt her before I heard the footsteps—Liz. I'd recognize Liz's presence in a crowd of a thousand. The energy in the room changed abruptly. The tension ratcheted.

Willow's arms stiffened around me, then fell away like a marionette with cut strings. She cleared her throat and stepped back, suddenly very interested in her boots.

I straightened, trying not to look like I'd just been canoodling with my *other* wife-to-be. Then I adjusted my posture and smoothed out my skirt—or train or whatever—as if that might erase the moment. At least my blindfold was in place.

There was a silence I could only describe as loaded.

"You know what?" Willow said, voice bright as can be. "Why don't I go find Morvaine and look at those ideas? It'll give you a chance to catch up." Then, she hesitated for a moment, and I could just feel her wanting to kiss me on the cheek. Thankfully, she did no such thing.

"Excuse me," she said as she slid past Liz and out the door.

"Cait?" Liz said, voice so calm it jangled my nerves.

"Liz. Where are the kids?"

"Getting settled. I wanted to see you for myself before I brought them in. A good thing, I guess."

She walked toward me with the precision of someone balancing a glass of water on her head. Controlled. Deadly calm. Absolutely furious beneath the surface.

And then she stopped right in front of me. Lifted a hand. Brushed her thumb along my cheekbone, delicately—almost reverently.

"Hm," she murmured. "Not dead. Not curled in a corner. Not... devoured."

She paused and looked me up and down.

"And wearing a dress that screams you've been making new friends."

I winced. "It's not—"

"No, no," she said, tone whisper soft and sweet as broken glass. "Don't explain. Let me guess. Court fashion? Cultural expectations? Political necessity?" She tilted her head. "Or... wait? Someone helped you pick it out."

This was not how any of this was supposed to go. "Liz, honestly, it's not..."

"What?" Liz snapped. "What it looks like? Because it looks like you just fell into someone's arms in the two weeks since you left. God, why did I even bother?"

"It's been over a year," I whispered.

"What?" Her voice cracked with disbelief. "I bloody well know time moves differently here. So what? Does that make it better?"

"She was comforting what's mine!" I snapped imperiously, feeling something cruel and dark curl in my chest, surging upward.

Liz froze and took a long step back. "What did you just say?"

"I—" My mouth went dry. My pulse crashed in my chest. "I didn't mean—"

But I had.

I absolutely had.

"What does that mean?" Liz asked. I could feel her eyes narrow. "Comforting what's yours."

I bristled at her tone—how dare she speak like that—but I forced it down. Or tried. Something else rose instead, smoother, almost practiced in ways I didn't remember learning.

"Liz," I murmured, soft as spider-silk. "Just my nervousness. There's nothing to be jealous of."

Silence.

I clasped my hands in front of me, folded small. A picture of

SHADOW VEIL

restraint, of vulnerability.

And yet—I studied her movements, her breathing, and her voice like I was taking notes.

Liz eased forward slightly. "What's happened to you?"

I moved toward her—just a halting half step. "I don't love her." The lie rolled right off my tongue, like silk, like I'd been born to it. "I love you." Another half step. "You have to believe me."

She moved a little closer, slow and cautious, like she thought I might bite. Her hand rose, hesitant, then cupped my cheek. "Your heart's beating." She leaned in, disbelieving. "And you're warm."

Inside, the Faerie curled up like a cat in sunlight—pleased, victorious. No contest. No struggle. Liz stepped right where it wanted... where *I* wanted.

"It was awful," I whispered. No need to pretend. The pain in my voice was real enough. "I was burning up from the inside. The curse... the Dark Gift... it was consuming me. And then I opened my eyes."

Tears spilled down my cheeks.

"I'm blind, Liz. Forever. It can't be fixed."

She pulled me closer, hands on my face. "Oh, Gods," she breathed.

I folded into her, arms around her. *Mine.*

Better than I could have done on my best day, Nastasia's voice whispered, cool and close.

Still, though, I was hyperaware of Liz—just by instinct, I could feel her confusion.

"Please, Liz," I said quietly, pulling away and dropping into the ridiculous couch. "Come sit. I'm sorry. There's... a lot."

Liz didn't move. She was still watching me, perfectly silent. And still standing by the chair, almost like I was a threat.

That stirred a warm and electric feeling low in my chest, foreign and weird.

I didn't want to scare her. I didn't. But the fact that she was wary meant she still cared. All I needed to do was nurture that, remind her that she was mine. She'd always be.

"Will you *please* come sit down?" I said to Liz, and she

finally came over and sat, but only on the edge.

"Cait," Liz said, her voice was deadly serious and… frightened. "Tell me. The truth. What happened to you?"

"Everything," I murmured, placing a hand on her thigh. "And nothing. I just… I've become what I was meant to be."

Liz was silent. It was hard, sitting there under what I knew was an intense scrutiny when I could see absolutely nothing and all I could sense was her basic presence, no face, no expression—no eyes. It was unnerving.

Finally, she said, "Is that why you're acting like I'm prey?"

"I'm not—" I started, but she cut me off.

"I'm three hundred years old, Cait. I know when I'm being worked. The small posture, the crocodile tears? You're stalking me, trying to manipulate me. And I can smell that… *woman* all over you. You might as well be covered in wildflowers."

"She was just hugging me, Liz. Of course, her scent is on me." I said. Why was I scrambling to justify myself?

"Who is she… really?" The way she said it could have sliced stone.

"We can't just have a moment together? I've been here for what felt like a lifetime, alone."

"Obviously not," she said.

I jerked at that. "You know what I mean."

"No, Cait, it still looks like you have a lover and you're just trying to gaslight me."

I scowled, then. I'd had enough. My voice turned cold as ice. "No, Elizabeth. We're just two predators in a room. I don't have time to gaslight you about court matters."

Silence. Long, protracted silence.

"Oh, gods," she gasped. "It's a betrothal!"

She stood, turning her back to me as the shock registered in her voice. "I just walked into a hornet's nest of political bullshit, and you're fucking engaged to that *woman*."

She spat the last word, and I had a gut instinct to defend Willow. Willow was mine, and she was off limits. I held up my hands, trying to stop this before it got any worse.

But Liz barreled on. "Why didn't you fucking warn me?"

I narrowed my eyes beneath the cloth, my own frustration

peeking out. "How, Liz?! There's not exactly cell signal here. And there was no one to send. I can't believe you actually made it here alive as it is."

My voice steadily rose. "And I can't leave! Ever!"

"What?" Just a whisper.

There it was. She still cared. This would be fine.

"I almost died, Liz. Look at me. I'm this way because... because it was the only way to save my life. My body was so twisted up with magic and *your* fucking curse! It was all killing me."

Still, all I felt was her backside.

"Look. At. Me!" I shouted, my voice bitter and angry.

She spun.

"Yes, I've changed. More than changed. Mother Morrigan *remade* me—is *still* remaking me. And that isn't my fault. And this life? My heritage? It keeps costing me. I keep walking into yet another fucking thing, and all I want to do is go home."

Tears started running down my face.

She wasn't really listening, though. She was thinking about our future—about the apartment, the kids, the quiet life we promised ourselves. And now, all she could see was a throne room, a wedding, and a crown. None of which I'd asked for.

I took a deep breath, pushing back the rage—that hint of chaos that had started to spill in. I didn't need to lose control. That wouldn't help me here. I needed calm. She just needed to understand. "Liz, please, there's more that you don't know."

"I'm sure there is," she interjected, and her voice was so full of hurt and pain that it gutted me. "But I can't hear it right now."

Still, she didn't move at first. She just shook her head.

"Damn it, Cait," she swore at me. "This isn't you."

She stalked out, and I startled slightly as the door slammed.

When she was gone, I didn't crumble. Instead, I assessed. She still cared. She still loved me. All I needed to do was keep her close, and it would be okay. I could fix it.

Vaelith had been bringing the kids to me, but immediately turned them around when she got to the floor, claiming she could "feel the tension from the hallway." Fair enough. Now here they came, returned like a pair of caffeinated tornadoes.

I blew out a breath and steeled myself. Liz's and my crap could wait.

"And then Vaelith showed me how to pivot without opening my guard too much and—" Katie stopped short when she saw me. "Oh. Finally. Are you and Auntie Liz done fighting?"

"Nice to see you too," I said, dry as dust but with a smile on my face and my arms open. They both rushed the bed.

"She doesn't mean it like that, mama," Leah offered, a bit softer, eyes bright with undimmed wonder.

I laughed. "I know. So, how was your playdate with the very large, very flammable giant death lizard?"

"Amazing," Leah breathed, collapsing back onto the bed and letting loose a sigh that could power a wind farm. "He's so big. And his voice rumbles like a hug."

She wasn't wrong. "He's just a big teddy bear," I whispered with a slight chuckle. "But don't tell him I said that."

Katie flopped into a chair with her usual teenage grace, which is to say: none. "He called Leah 'Snack-Size,' Mom. With a straight face."

I laughed. "He what?"

Leah giggled. "I think he likes me."

"I'm sure he does," I said, digging my fingers into her ticklish sides. "He's probably deciding which little tea cakes pair best with twelve-year-olds."

"He said he thought I was special!" Leah beamed.

Katie nodded. "Oh, you're special, alright. I can't believe you asked him about dental work."

"Hey, dental hygiene is important," Leah said. "And he has

huge teeth. And his breath smells like an old diesel engine."

I shook my head. I'd missed this. "And you?"

"Oh, Vaelith and I did some sword drills while Morvaine showed Leah where the wards are tuned. She's good, Mama. Even as fast as I am, I didn't land a single hit." She grinned. "Also, she gives serious 'I could kill you with a butterknife.' And she has the coolest eyes and an awesome smile. I like her."

"Uh-huh," I said. "Do tell?"

Katie suddenly turned quiet, and I nibbled my bottom lip. A few hours together, and somebody already had a crush.

"Oh! Morvaine gave me a crystal!" Leah added, digging something sparkly out of her pocket. "It has smoke inside and the outside shimmers like a pearl."

Katie rolled her eyes. "Pretty sure that's a soul stone, Leah."

"She said it's fine. It's not, like, my soul."

I blinked. "Okay, great. So, just part of someone else's eternal essence. Totally bedtime-appropriate."

In truth, it was just a burned-out chunk of Karanite, but I wasn't going to tell Leah that. Besides, she was smart. She'd figure it out on her own, especially if Morvaine continued tapping her as her little helper. The ward stone was in the heart of the palace—really the safest space.

They both ignored me, and I let out a slow breath. "Well. At least some of us had a good day."

"Did you do anything exciting?" Katie asked.

"Just the usual," I said. "Fancy reception, one man with way too much ego, and gifts I'm putting somewhere very high up."

Katie laughed. "Was that that Aurex guy we passed in the hallway? What an asshole."

"Katie!?" I barked.

"What? You say it all the time."

I hung my head—she wasn't wrong. I really needed to watch my language. Still though, she had a good read on Aurex.

"Mama?" Leah prodded quietly. "Um... I heard some people talking in the hallway. Are you getting married?"

I pressed my lips into a thin line. "Maybe we should talk

about this when Auntie Liz is around. It's really complicated."

"Wait, are you?" Katie asked. "Someone was talking about Lady Willow. Is that the woman we saw coming out of the door in the veil?"

"We're just friends," I said, deciding it was best just to tell them. "And it's a political marriage. Do you know what that is?"

"Like Catherine of Aragon and Henry VIII," Katie said. "Without the beheading, I hope."

I nodded. "Yes. It's to make sure I can keep you and Leah and Auntie Liz safe."

"What about Auntie Liz?" Katie asked. "Are you not getting married?"

"Okay, so…" I paused. "Like I said, Auntie Liz and I should talk to you about this together."

"You're not?" Leah asked, turning worried.

"I didn't say that," I said. "It's just complicated."

"Wait, isn't that illegal?" Katie asked.

"Alright, stop. I just said I'm not talking about it right now. Everything will be okay, and you have nothing to worry about. Auntie Liz and I will work it out."

"You promise?" Leah asked, her expression worried. She was flipping around the little karanite crystal in her hand.

I suppressed a sigh and chose my next words carefully. "I promise we're going to try."

Leah crawled over to me and tucked herself under my arm. "Okay. Mama, I did want to tell you that I'm glad we're here."

My throat caught a little. "Me too, sweetheart. Me too."

Katie snuggled in on the other side and kissed me on the cheek.

They hung out for a bit longer before I asked Leah to go tell Liz about her day. Then I gave Katie a bit of blood. She hated taking it, I hated pushing, but she was getting twitchy, and there was no sunrise here to knock her out. She'd need regular feedings until Sithraine figured out something—anything—useful.

Katie left after that, too, trailing behind her sister, and the room finally went still.

I sat there for a long moment, listening to the quiet pulse of the palace. Every nerve in me felt pulled thin, overstretched. Seeing them had helped. Seeing Liz had... not.

Either way, I'd hit my limit.

It was late—really late—and exhaustion dragged at me like a wet towel on cement. I pushed myself upright, feeling the weight of the day settle over my shoulders.

Enough. I had the Seating of the Bloom in two days, and I needed sleep before I did something even stupider.

CHAPTER TWENTY-SEVEN
PRETENDING

The next day was a blur of courtesies, security briefings, and thinly veiled threats. By the time I reached Liz's door, I'd run out of excuses.

Liz wasn't human-soft inside the way I used to be. She was a predator—sharp, perceptive, impossible to fool. She'd taste any lie I tried to give her. So if she was going to hear me at all, really hear me, it had to sound like the woman she used to know.

I wasn't that woman anymore. But I could try to shape myself into her for a little while.

Not to deceive her—but so she could hear my love through all the Faerie noise.

"Liz," I called after I'd knocked for the fifth time. "I know you're in there. Please open the door. I just want to talk."

Slowly, the door cracked.

"Fine," she said. "Talk."

"Can I come in?"

She clearly wasn't going to make this easy, but she did step back and open the door wider, inviting me in.

"I've never been in here," I said. "Can you help me to a chair?"

She didn't argue. She just took my upper arm and guided me carefully to a seat on another of the ridiculously plush couches, where I sank in like a teenager on a beanbag.

"These fucking sofas," I muttered.

Liz didn't wait; she just jumped right in. "I need to know. Are you in love with her?"

I cleared my throat, which had suddenly gone tight. Of course, I wasn't in love with her, not the way she meant, not like a human. That was a biological imperative.

What kind of question was that, anyway?

And how dare she—

No. No. That wasn't the old me. I needed to stick to what the old Cait would say.

"No." The lie again. And I was still shocked how easily it rolled out, and yet, it made me feel… dirty. Not because of the lie itself, just that I'd lied at all. It was strange. "It's just been… a mess. I landed in the court. I'm blind. I… she's just a friend."

I paused, trying to build the sentence in a shape she'd recognize.

"This body, it's not human. It looks mostly human, but… it's different. I've changed because of it." None of that was a lie. I was definitely a different person. Even I could see that.

"I'm listening." Her voice was flat and dispassionate.

I'd come too early. She needed to want this. I was going to have to beg otherwise, and I don't beg. I closed my eyes beneath the cloth and took a deep breath, pushing down that angry feeling. This was going to be a lot harder than I thought.

"I still love you. You're all I want," I said. My head was screaming at me now, because that last was an absolute lie. And while the lies rolled off my tongue easily enough, I was having a harder time with the aftermath. It was as if my brain just recoiled at the concept.

"Why didn't you come find me this morning? Why did you make me wait all day?"

"I thought you needed space," I said. Not quite the whole truth, and my brain seemed to accept that just fine.

"Faerie do not lie," my mother had told me once. "We prevaricate. It's easier." I finally understood what she'd meant.

I pressed on, though. I needed to be honest Cait—Cait-the-cop. "And it's not that I couldn't come. It's that the part of me that's changing… didn't see why I should. It wanted you to come to me. It wanted to be pursued."

"*It* didn't see why you should?" Liz asked.

"I'm not deflecting. I didn't want to come. I wanted you to come find me. I wanted you to want me. I wanted you to be so desperate for my love that you'd give me what I needed." I rubbed my forehead. "And that's not me. That's not who I've ever been."

There was a long moment of quiet, then, "No, Cait, that's not you at all."

A hot pulse of discomfort rolled through me. I quashed the rage that followed it.

"I don't know who I am anymore," I admitted. "Everything I've always been—pushy, stubborn, reckless, needy—it's still there, but now it's… bigger. Wilder. I love you with everything I am, but the thoughts that come with it are dark. I need to pull you close and keep you there where you're safe and mine alone."

She went quiet. Too quiet. The kind of quiet where choices start calcifying. I didn't rush. I didn't plead. I just waited, still as a grave marker. If I played it poorly or handled this wrong, I'd lose her.

Handled? Played? I shook my head. *Goddess, who am I?*

"You're not the woman I fell in love with," she said at last, and she wasn't wrong. I heard everything unsaid between the syllables: You're different. I don't recognize you. I don't know if I still love you.

"I am the woman who loves you, though," I whispered back. "I wish I could make you see—"

And then I stopped. Because the intent of those words slid sideways in my head, sharp and hungry. Make you see. Make you want to see. Make you change.

Old me would never. New me? Too easy. I swallowed it down.

"Liz," I said instead, gentle, nudging. "I'm trying. And I won't lie to you. I'm scared. I'm terrified. I did something the other day—"

A long breath. This was going to burn through everything I'd said so far, but if I were still Cait-the-cop, I would tell her. I had to tell her.

"I made an agreement with Runa, the Night Queen."

Another breath.

"She can't protect Willow legally. So I agreed to take her in here."

Liz vanished.

I blinked beneath my blindfold as if that might bring her back. But I just couldn't sense her anymore. The plant in the corner? Yes. Even Nyxiel at my door across the hall, knocking, though just barely. But Liz? She was just… gone.

I panicked.

"Liz?"

Nothing.

I stood and put my hands in front of me, stumbling forward. "Liz?!"

"I'm right here," she said.

Her voice came from a foot to my left—and I crashed back into myself all at once, breath tearing out of me. My senses caught her again, sudden and shocking, as if someone flipped a switch on a map and her marker lit up bright red.

It took several heart-pounding moments to understand what had happened: she hadn't moved. She hadn't spoken. She hadn't breathed. She'd simply stopped. She'd gone perfectly still. It had made her invisible to me.

I sagged back onto the couch, pulse racing like I'd sprinted up a mountain.

"You didn't even ask me?" she whispered. "You didn't even tell me?"

"What?"

Her breath shivered, barely there. "This agreement with Runa, bringing her here, you didn't even consider me at all, did you?"

I opened my mouth, already answering in the instinctive, cold logic of the Court: Why would I? It was a Bargain. Politics. A queen's duty. Nothing to do with—

"Of course not," I said automatically.

The silence that followed was enormous. Hollow. A cliff-edge emptiness where Liz had just reappeared.

Three whole seconds at least passed before the meaning finally slammed into me.

Shit.

The silence broke like a gunshot.

"You didn't even think of me."

It wasn't a question; it was a verdict. And I hated that she was right. I hated it almost as much as I hated that I still didn't see what the problem was. I should. I definitely should. Intellectually I knew, but emotionally? Nothing. I opened my mouth, but her voice cut through the air—low, lethal, trembling with rage she wasn't bothering to hide.

"You made a bargain with another Queen. You invited your little betrothed into our lives. You reshaped the future of this entire family. And you didn't even fucking think of me."

That last word wasn't human. It was a snarl pulled into a whisper.

I could feel her stepping closer. Her very presence expanded, a coiled, cold predatory pressure she had *never* aimed at me.

Until now.

"And you expect me to trust you?" she hissed. "You expect me to believe a single thing you say when you make life-changing deals with people who apparently want you dead and don't bother waiting until the woman who—" She stopped herself. Barely.

But the unfinished sentence hung there like a body from a noose.

She leaned in—so close I could feel the cool of her breath.

"You didn't forget me, Cait." Her voice dropped to a razor-thin whisper. "You *dismissed* me."

Something twisted in my chest. Hard.

Liz didn't relent. "I'm not your afterthought. I'm not your little mortal pet you get to inform when it's convenient."

Another half-step closer.

"And I'll never be the woman waiting outside your throne room while you make decisions that burn my life down."

She let that sink in. Savoring it. Letting it hurt.

Then—

"If you want trust? You'll have to earn it." Her ensuing, incredulous laugh landed like a blade flat against my ribs. "And you're nowhere near close."

Something in me snapped taut. Instinct—bright, sharp, ancestral—flared up my spine before thought even had a chance to catch up. A shield rose around me with a sound like cracking ice. I stood.

I'd never felt Liz turn predatory on me before. But I wasn't going to let her hurt me. I wasn't going to let her challenge me. Not here. Not in my own hall. This conversation was over. I wasn't going to beat myself bloody against something she clearly didn't want anymore.

I scowled—she didn't need to see it to feel it.

"This is *my* palace," I said, my voice low and seething. "*My* home."

I stripped away that ridiculous pretension of humanity, uncoiled—and struck. "And don't even think about storming out. You can't."

I felt her still.

"As of right now, the wards won't recognize you, or Leah, or Katie."

It was a threat and protection, all tangled together.

"Before you call it punishment," I pushed on, "understand this: I did it so you don't get ripped apart running off like a spoiled child whose toy broke. Or kidnapped by a primarch trying to make me kneel."

That landed.

"Get out!" she barked.

I felt her hand almost before she moved, trying to take my upper arm. It hit my shield with a flat, useless smack, like she'd grabbed a wall that hadn't been there a second ago.

"You don't order me to do anything," I hissed. "And don't you ever presume to lay your hands on my like that again—*ever*."

Then I turned and stalked out, magic wafting off me like smoke, and the door slammed behind me so hard the air in the corridor shook.

"Nyxiel!" I shouted. She was here just a minute ago.

"Yes, your grace," she said as she came hustling down the hallway. "I was just getting supplies for Willow's apartment downstairs."

"Downstairs?"

"Yes," Nyxiel said. "I naturally assumed with Ms. Medlyn here…"

"Don't assume," I barked, then took a deep breath. "My apologies. I'm just agitated. Please keep her apartment next to mine. And please ask Sithraine to come see me. I'll be in the throne room. We have a problem to discuss."

"Yes, Your Grace," Nyxiel said and hurried off.

I shook my head. I'd wanted her tucked in tight. Now I realized Liz and the kids needed to be as far away from us as possible.

As far away from me.

CHAPTER TWENTY-EIGHT
ALL OF THE ABOVE, ACTUALLY

The third floor of the Vermilion Palace was dominated at its center by the Grand Ballroom. It had no other name, nor did it need one. According to Vaelith, my escort for the ceremony, it sat against the northern wall, overlooking the main gates below. Covering over twenty-five thousand square feet and stretching upward to a height of over fifty feet, it was beyond massive. A barrel-vaulted ceiling of textured crystal seemed almost to hang, suspended and open to the sky above, supported by two massive colonnades on either side. With the restored veneers and artwork, it would have put even Versailles to shame.

For once, I was glad I couldn't be awestruck. I couldn't see the beauty, only feel the sheer weight of it—the echo of what it must have cost. The sweat. The blood. The lives spent raising something this grand. This was where we would host the Seating of the Bloom.

An affair, Nyxiel had called this. Insane was another word.

Row after row of carved pews lined the floor, all facing the rear of the palace where the great spire rose behind us—visible through the crystalline ceiling like a spear of blood-red glass. Fireflies glimmered in lazy spirals overhead, magical and strange.

A contingent of Night Pixies, their wings on full display, had arrived at my invitation, clad in sheer, iridescent finery that hid literally nothing. They'd claimed the growing forests near the plateau's edge as their new home, and I wanted them here —if only to ruffle feathers. Which they did.

Most of the high Fae in attendance gave them a wide berth, as if the Pixies might bite—or curse—or both. Which, to be fair, they might.

Of Willow, I had neither sensed nor heard a peep. But that, apparently, wasn't unusual. We weren't supposed to see each other before the ceremony. I'd tried to use our mutual blindness as an excuse to stop by her apartment and say hello, but Kiran had rebuffed both attempts.

Vaelith, at my side, wore full Vermilion military livery, blood-red, crisp, and severe. Aoife had reluctantly agreed to escort Willow when the time came, walking her to the raised dais at the far end of the ballroom. We hadn't talked much. There just hadn't been time. But she, at least, had some understanding of what was happening to me—better than I did, apparently. So, for the moment, she was staying out of my shit with Liz.

The gown Sithraine had chosen for me was heavy— shadow-dyed velvet layered with veils of sheer black that whispered little crypt-born secrets, all hushed and impossible to make out. It fell to the floor, though the hem never touched the marble. Magic apparently saw to that. Long sleeves spilled past my wrists, open at the ends, the inner lining streaked with deep crimson—a nod to my court and maybe the blood this was going to cost me.

Silver thread glimmered like spider silk across the bodice in twisting vinework, curling toward the triple-moon sigil of the Vermilion Court stitched faintly down my spine—only visible in flickers of moonlight through the crystalline ceiling. The high collar framed my neck like a blade's edge. Of course, the triple-raven of the House of the Morrigan was embroidered at the hem.

My hair had been braided back tightly and crowned properly with the silver-and-karanite I always wore. If I were honest, it suddenly felt very, very real.

No booties or slippers for this. My feet were bare, dusted in crimson pigment that stained the marble beneath each step. A sign of humility or something—I didn't quite catch that bit. More like the footsteps of pestilence, but it made every step feel deliberate and ritualistic. The whole thing said something like, "I am the heir of war and death, and I clean up well, so worship me, or don't. I'm still going to terrify you—just very politely."

The ceremony itself wouldn't be at all what I'd expected, either.

There would be no vows of love or declarations of fealty. Instead, Willow and I would each affirm the union of our Houses—then choose, independently, one of four flowers placed before us. Then, if we selected different flowers, we would be permitted to confer for a moment and decide on which bloom we wished to select. The Seat, as it was called, was a large font of water sculpted by artisans of the offering house. In this case, the Night Court. Once the bloom was seated and we offered our final confirmation of the vow, the water would become soil, and if we were lucky, the bloom would root. If not, well, that supposedly didn't bode well.

The trick was this. Neither Willow nor I knew what the other would select. And many engagements, arranged or otherwise, had stalled right here, coming apart when the couple-to-be couldn't agree on which flower to select. Occasionally, wars had started.

I had something else in mind, though, where that wouldn't be a problem. At least, I didn't think.

More importantly, it wasn't at all forbidden by any rules of the ceremony. Probably because no one was crazy enough to try it, but if we pulled it off, they'd be talking about it for eons to come.

"What's that look?" Vaelith asked as we waited in the wings.

"What look?"

"Remember the other day when you used that stumble spell on me?"

"Yes," I nodded, a smug smile playing on my lips.

"You had the same look then."

"Hey, you issued the challenge. You said combat magic like that was too slow to cast mid-fight."

And yeah, normally? She was right. A standard snare took a few seconds. You had to weave the threads into something like a rope. Too much fuss. I skipped the craftwork. Just slammed a chunk of semi-solid magic right at her feet for half a second. Same result. She ate floor.

"Yes, and I was wrong. But you're avoiding the question."

I chuckled lightly. "No, I'm not. You asked about that stumble spell."

"No, I asked about the smug look on your face."

"There's no smug look," I whispered out of the side of my mouth as the commencement music started.

Vaelith snorted. "Fine. Just don't trip yourself out there, Your Grace."

"I'll try not to," I whispered, and we began our slow syncopated progression toward the central dais.

"How does she look?" I murmured softly. Willow had to be in view by now.

"Like a rabbit in a trap," Vaelith hissed back. "But, absolutely gorgeous. Her hair is in a long single braid down her back, and she's wearing the most expensive and chic Seating gown I have ever seen." Then she added softly. "I'd marry her."

"Please do," I whispered quietly. I opened my senses as far as I could, but, as expected, no Liz. I wasn't disappointed. I didn't blame her for not coming. She could be somewhere in the back, watching, but I doubted it.

"Would you be upset if I asked your sister out? She's built like she could carry me and my bad decisions without breaking a sweat."

"You're straight," I murmured.

"Oh, yeah," Vaelith said with a chuckle. "Still though…"

I bit my lip to keep from laughing. We were way too close to the altar, and more importantly, Queen Runa, who was officiating this ceremony.

Stepping up onto the raised dais, I felt the anxiety practically banging in Willow's chest. I had no idea what she was worried about. The ceremony was really simple, even if the assembled primarchs and their entourages made this insane. For that matter, I should have been the one freaking out. After all, this was where we would probably end up putting a match to my future with Liz.

"Are you okay?" I whispered when we were finally face to face.

Willow cleared her throat, demurely. "Perfectly," she said.

My response was skeptical, to say the least. "Uh-huh."

The Night Queen raised her hands. And began to recite the opening of the ceremony. "In the presence of Court and Kin, under moons that watch but never wane, we bear witness to a bond not lightly given."

"That's for sure," Aoife muttered. Willow almost barked a laugh but turned it into a cough.

I had to imagine the withering glare that Runa shot my sister before she continued. "One bloom for strength, one for cunning. One for eternity and one for fearlessness. Let these roots entwine not just in soil but in spirit. Let the chosen bloom that grows between you mark the shape of what you will become.

"For in a bloom, there is beauty, and in a bloom, there is rot. Let neither one take root without the other's knowing. Speak now your commitment—not as a promise, but as an offering. Not as surrender, but as intention.

And may what is planted here today grow wild and true, or never grow at all."

Willow and I spoke then as one:

"We come before our assembled guests and the Queen of the Night Court to offer each other not just allegiance but admission. We admit mystery. We admit danger. We admit desire. We offer thorn with bloom, shadow with flame, silence with vow. Let what grows between us not be tamed—only tended. This is no binding of love, but of will. Of shared purpose. Of chosen peril. We do not ask for ease. We ask for strength. And in front of gods, and the Fae of Night, and those who whisper behind their fangs, we declare: Yes. We will be joined."

We each took a sip of Faerie wine—Willow first, then me.

It arrived cool at the lips, carrying the hush of damp earth and crushed berries before the taste even landed. On the tongue, it unfolded as dark fruit and soft smoke, then something greener and wilder, like leaves torn by hand. The finish hummed with faint sweetness and metal, a tingle that lingered long after the swallow. For a moment, I wondered when I'd developed the sommelier palate.

Once we'd each drunk, Runa took the cup, her fingers brushing mine as she set it aside.

"You may now make known your personal intentions," the Queen intoned.

This was, apparently, the second trickiest part of the whole thing. Dark Fae vows of commitment were... different. You couldn't just promise your heart—you had to guard it with your teeth. It had taken me all night to construct one with the appropriate amount of promise and yet menacing. What was a Dark Fae engagement vow without a threat? Inappropriate, as it turned out.

I was the accepting party, so I went first.

"I give you my strength, not as a gift, but as a weapon you must choose to wield wisely.

If you use it to harm what I protect—my children, my family—

know that I will take it back,

and leave nothing behind but ash."

I felt a trickle of honestly warm feelings from Willow. I bit my lip to avoid laughing. Mother of Waters, she actually thought my vow was sweet.

And then she spoke.

"And I offer you my loyalty, not because I was told to, but because I chose to.

Betray that, and you will lose more than just a crown.

You'll lose the one soul in this court who would have loved you without conditions."

I swallowed hard. Was she professing her love? She wasn't supposed to do that, not here—and definitely not now. But... she was. A few soft murmurs of disapproval drifted from the pews.

I reached over and squeezed her hand, and whispered a quiet, "Don't listen to them. I love you, too."

Surprise, warmth, affection, and gratitude, it all sang through the bracer.

I pressed down the butterflies that rose saying that. I'd done it. I'd crossed that line... the one I shouldn't have. But I had to. She needed it. And it wasn't a lie. My head even agreed.

Runa spoke again. "You may each select a bloom to represent your union. Speak your choice aloud, and place it in the sacred vessel."

Four flowers lay next to us in shallow carved basins, each cradled in a ring of softly glowing mist. I could feel the magic in them—distinct, strange, and alive.

The whisperthorn was hungry. Sharp and bloodthirsty, its thorned vines curled malevolently, seeking flesh from which to drink.

The local nightshade was pretty and delicate in appearance, but it held hidden spores full of deadly poison that popped if not handled gently. Of all, this one was the most immediately lethal.

The Shaddani moonflower pulsed gently with a soothing warmth, full of longing and a promise the couple would never be able to keep—namely, forever.

And the glowing nightwither—my personal favorite— shone in blue. Not metaphorically. It glowed genuinely, luminously blue. Its tendrils twitched faintly, reaching toward my fingers. Even in our Goddess-born blindness, we could still *feel* its hypnotic pull, wanting to lull us into deathly stillness while it slowly burrowed into our flesh and consumed us from the inside out.

All of them were beautiful. All of them were dangerous—

except, strictly speaking, the moonflower.

I stepped forward first, hearing quiet murmurs swell behind me like a tide. Everyone was waiting to see what I'd choose, what statement I would make. Or try to, given I wasn't alone in this. We were, after all, supposed to select one bloom to represent our union.

I let my hand drift over the basins, then turned to Willow. "All of them."

The silence that followed could have swallowed the stars.

"I—I beg your pardon, Your Grace?" The Night Queen managed.

I ignored her, speaking to Willow. "Each of these represents something expected, something symbolic in a marriage. Strength. Cunning. Eternity. Fearlessness. And frankly, I don't see how you get through a marriage like this—especially one like this—without all four."

Stillness. Then a breath. Not from me—from Willow. I could feel her thinking, turning it over in her mind. And then, slowly, she stepped up beside me.

"Bold," she murmured in my ear, just loud enough for me to hear. "Possibly idiotic. You do realize that, don't you?"

"And yet…" I coaxed with a wild, reckless smirk.

It had never been done and likely never would again. Of course, we might both die in the attempt as well.

It was a calculated risk. As long as we didn't touch the nightshade stamen, we'd be okay, and no one had bled out from the whisperthorn in at least a hundred years. However, it did occur to me that it might have been that long since anyone last selected it.

She took a breath and reached first, taking the nightshade gently from deep beneath its roots, lifting it gingerly from the basin. I suppressed a laugh as literally everyone held their breath. We didn't. We were too close. If the nightshade cut loose, we were both dead.

I lifted the whisperthorn, which, predictably, bit into my right arm with its thorns and swiped a leaf edge at my wrist before it began to drink greedily at my blood.

"Faithless liar," it whispered immediately.

Willow picked up the moonflower. Its roots slithered around her fingers and reached for mine as I lifted the nightwither. We then turned toward each other and closed the distance, our hands, wrapped in writhing roots and vines, joining between us.

"Heartsick pretender," the whisperthorn murmured as it bit into Willow's hand. She didn't so much as flinch, but I felt the shame that cascaded through her, if only briefly.

Abruptly, my head buzzed, and my balance faltered.

I staggered.

Everyone gasped.

Runa backed away.

Aoife made to move toward us, but Vaelith crossed the space and stopped her, pushing her back with a hissed, "No. They have to do this themselves."

The flowers tilted dangerously, plucking another terrified gasp from the guests.

"Mama!" Leah called out, frightened.

I was falling.

It was the whisperthorn. It was drinking too fast, and the nightwither's tendrils had dug into the artery at my wrist.

Swallowing hard, my thoughts turning leaden, I tried to remember... which one was the nightshade.

Where was it?

But the pulse of the nightwither dug further into my head, and I was already woozy with blood loss.

I just wanted to rest... to sleep.

Willow's hands splayed beneath the flowers. Somehow, she managed to balance the nightshade and moonflower in one hand and use the other to tear some of the whisperthorn painfully from my forearm.

My head cleared a little with the pain. Blood spattered the platform at my feet.

"Up," she hissed. "I have it, but if you fall, we die."

I gave a quick nod, suddenly realizing I was down on one knee, my arms lifted like a supplicant begging for forgiveness.

Wobbling a little drunkenly, I drew up to stand, following Willow's pull.

I set the nightwither in the basin. The whisperthorn dug more of its thorns back into my arm.

As swiftly as we dared, we placed the remaining three blossoms into the sculpted stone vessel together. Someone in the crowd squeaked as Willow shook her arm loose of the whisperthorn, brushing the nightshade.

Finally, they were down.

Blood flowed from my left wrist where the nightwither had been dug in.

I sighed in relief and gripped the edge of the basin.

"We commit," we said together.

The vessel shimmered—light that I could only see as a flare of magic emanated from the water in quick, rippling waves—and then, impossibly, the vines of the four plants began to twine together as the water turned to rich, dark soil. No resistance. No chaos. They braided like they'd been waiting for each other.

Magic blew through the chamber and twined about Willow and me. We both gasped for a second, feeling an unshakable bond snap into place between us. The feeling settled into a background awareness of her existence. I could feel her living essence inside me.

There was a sound behind me—a choked gasp or a stifled swear from Runa. Possibly both.

"The sacred vessel accepts your offering," the Night Queen said, voice cracking ever so slightly. "The union is… sealed."

Vaelith, off to my left, let out a long breath through her nose like she was trying not to laugh.

Somewhere over Willow's shoulder, Nyxiel muttered, "Well. That's going to cause a stir."

There was soft, slow clapping then. It took me just a moment to realize it was Aoife.

I blinked.

The applause spread to the pews.

Willow grasped my arm and squeezed, trying to staunch the blood flow.

And then, everyone was standing. Katie whistled from the front row. I even heard Leah's laughter. The entire room was applauding us. Ten minutes ago, we'd been two of the most reviled people in the room, and now they were cheering.

Willow leaned over and kissed me lightly on the cheek.

"To the infirmary with you," she whispered. "Let's get you stitched up."

Vaelith, Aoife, and Willow helped me down from the platform and out through the back doors of the ballroom.

I passed out somewhere along the way to the infirmary.

CHAPTER TWENTY-NINE
WHERE WAR WEARS HEELS

The Grand Ballroom had been transformed into a pageant of silk and lace, according to Morvaine—an ocean of high collars, long trains, and jeweled sleeves that screamed pedigree and posture. Dozens of lords and ladies glided beneath chandeliers like they were performing synchronized smugness.

And then there was me. I didn't just enter. I arrived. One bootstep at a time.

The train of my dress whispered across the stone as I passed under the arch. The midnight fabric clung to my body like a shadow, slit high to bare my legs. The bodice—if you could call it that—plunged dangerously low, every curve sculpted and bound in black lace and thorn-patterned brocade. It felt like armor.

The blindfold was violet silk, tight across my eyes, the color of dusk before the stars awaken. I'd tied it myself. No pins. No glamour. Just a promise: *I can't let you see them, but by the Goddess, they are watching every last one of you.*

My arms were bare except for dark blue cuffs at the wrists. I needed a place for my handkerchief, after all—and the punch dagger. A short line of stitches peeked from beneath the left one.

And then there were the boots. Thigh-high, matte black, embroidered in stardust silver vines and buckled like I'd just left a war.

I wore no gloves. No proper cloak. No house colors. Just the betrothal necklace, set with a single blood-red gem, my valtárí brand on full display, and the crown, braided in my hair.

A scandal indeed against the high-necked, and, I thought, ridiculously conservative outfits worn traditionally by the primarchs. Like that first dinner with Willow, I was showing a lot of skin—a lot of skin. But then, the whole point was... causing a scandal.

There was silence as I walked in. One of those perfect, surgical silences where even the string quartet forgot what it was doing. I let it stretch. Let them all look because they weren't just staring at a scandal. They were staring at a Primarch.

The silence broke in a din of murmured comments. Mostly appalled.

I didn't care. Let them talk. Let them hiss and whisper and pretend to be outraged. I'd just made one thing absolutely clear: This wasn't their court. It was mine.

I caught the thrum of something from Willow, surprise, and... well... something that made me blush slightly. I donned a crooked smile and followed that feeling until I found her.

Liz, I knew, wasn't here. Sithraine said she was in her room, still... debating. I didn't blame her. I had to be here. She didn't.

"Holy shit, Cait," Willow whispered as she took my arm on the far side of the room. "Aoife told me what you're wearing, and I know Morvaine said you were going to make an entrance, but—damn."

"Jaysus, Mary, and Uncle Joseph, Sis," Aoife said, followed by a low whistle. "Didn't know you had that in the wardrobe. Or the spine. I guess you decided to stop pretending to be the quiet one."

"It's my house," I said. "I'll dress how I like. Besides, Aoife, it's *always* the quiet ones. You know that."

That's my girl, Nastasia's voice echoed. *You look more and more like me every day.*

"Maybe," I whispered under my breath with an evil smirk.

I'd given up trying to banish the voice. And honestly, given recent events, I felt like I needed her presence, illusory as it was.

Willow laughed, warm and close. "Well, at least you don't look like you're about to conquer the place—by the sword, I mean." Her fingers drifted low on my thigh, feeling the leather. "Those boots, though…"

"They'll be all the rage next season," I murmured.

Willow leaned forward and whispered in my ear. "How are you feeling?"

I nodded into her. "I'm okay. Morvaine stitched me up. And the blood loss seems to have fixed itself."

"You're Faerie, Cait," Willow said, as if that was supposed to explain it to me. "In any event, my mother approves."

"Of my clothes or our crazy Seating?"

"Both, I'd say," Willow replied.

"How can you tell?" As far as I knew, Willow was just as bat-shit blind as I was.

"Because she was honestly complimentary of our absolute nerve, and even after your entrance, she's still standing over there talking to Lord Stiles of Silverdeep, acting as if nothing's amiss."

"Silverdeep, Northeast of your mother's patch, right? The one with the trolls."

"They do have other things," Willow said primly. "They have silver mines and a fair number of farms."

"And trolls," I whispered, deadpan.

Willow giggled. "Shall we go meet him? He keeps staring at you like I don't own you for the evening."

I laughed with her. "Sure. Let's see what he wants."

Aoife snorted. "That'll be my cue to go find what's her name? The Hollow Moon?"

"Watch it," I whispered to her. "She's probably about thirty thousand years too old for you. And she's not our friend."

"Not yet," Aoife said with a chuckle and wandered off.

"Lord Stiles. Mother," Willow greeted as we approached. "Lovely party."

"Yes, I half expected the palace to be run down," Stiles stammered, a little awestruck. By the decor or my dress, I wasn't sure, given that the angle of his head suggested he was looking right at my cleavage. "It's like nothing ever happened in here."

One of Runa's servants came by and offered us wine. I accepted a glass for myself and one for Willow.

"It didn't always look like this," I said, glancing around. "Six months ago, this place was half ruin, half architectural cry for help, half decorator's nightmare." I took a sip. "It was a mess. But she's coming around."

"That's three halves," Stiles chuckled.

"It was that bad, Lord Stiles," I answered with a laugh.

"Impressive seating," Lord Stiles said. "I don't think I've ever seen the like. And selecting the moonflower? That was daring."

"The moonflower?" I prodded. "I'd have thought the excessive blood and the way we almost died would have been the spectacular bit."

"Oh, most impressive." He paused. "Even the moon's shadow will fade, but we will find each other again. Always."

I coughed. Something suddenly felt very wrong. Willow leaned in and whispered in my ear, barely loud enough for even my ears. "You didn't know?"

"Know what?" I whispered back, trying to keep my smile plastered.

"Yeah... uh... so we probably need to talk," she said evasively. "But not here."

I had no fucking idea what they were on about, but it didn't sound good. Forever? What forever? Sithraine hadn't said anything about a forever flower. The moonflower symbolized that, sure, but magical forever? No one had said a gods be damned word about it.

Thoroughly distressed, but with nothing I could do about it, I decided to change the subject. "So, tell me, Lord Stiles, how are the trolls? Still marauding the farms?"

I heard Queen Runa spit-take into her glass. Willow squeezed my upper arm, but I could feel her trying desperately to suppress her laugh.

"Under control for the moment," he said sourly. "They used to be so docile, but lately... I don't know what they're worked up about. It's not like anything's changed."

I knew. Elarith's spies had reported that the trolls of Silverdeep were tired of the mine conditions. I'd ordered the twins to work toward arranging for the trolls to join us and mine karanite. First, though, they had to create a problem for Silverdeep and keep him occupied. If any of the six unaligned lords were going to go to war, they needed his food and money. With him busy and unable to function effectively, it would slow them down. I'd suspected that Naerith and Elarith could foment a rebellion like a pair of Green Berets. I was glad to see I was right.

While we talked and Lord Stiles complained about his trolls, I noticed a sudden hush as it fell over the room. Heads were turning. I didn't need to look; there wasn't any point, but still, I turned my head toward the entrance. Liz was standing there, her back straight and her chin up. She had been born into aristocracy, and she'd been alive for three hundred years in a world that moved a hell of a lot faster and more brutally than this one in many ways. And she was a vampire. No one had a damn thing on her.

"What's she wearing?" I whispered to Runa.

"Virginal white gown with red trim that looks like blood trails. Spectacular heels, too. Bold." Runa hissed.

Willow took my wine glass and goaded me forward with a gentle shove. "Stop stalling and go."

I hesitated, only for a second, then moved across the floor with as much grace and style as I could manage. Everyone watched me, and no one said a word.

"I'd say you look lovely, but I have to imagine it," I said as I stepped up. "I'm glad you came."

"Wouldn't miss it," she replied and took my upper arm. There was no edge to her words, but neither were they warm. I laid my hand over hers to find she was wearing her engagement ring. "Now, introduce me to your other fiancée." She didn't quite spit out the word other, but only just.

I drew her across the floor, doing my best to ignore the unpleasant murmurs: abomination, soul stealer, blood fiend, and several others. If I could hear the closer ones, Liz certainly heard all of them. Liz just kept walking without a word.

This should be fun, Nastasia whispered in my head.

"Shut up," I muttered under my breath.

"I've heard worse," Liz said.

Clearly, she thought I meant the assembled guests and their bad manners. I didn't correct her.

"Lady Willow," Liz cooed as we stepped up to her and her mother. Lord Stiles had moved elsewhere, apparently. "It's lovely to meet you. I'd say that Cait's told me so much about you, but honestly, she hasn't really had the chance."

Liz's hand left my arm as she held it out, and Willow took it.

So far, so good. No one had been murdered in the first ten seconds.

"Lady Medlyn," Willow's tone was more formal but still friendly. "It's an honor. This is my mother, Her Majesty, Runa, Queen of the Night Court."

Liz didn't bow or curtsy. Instead, she offered her hand. Runa was too much of a lady not to take it, but I suspected she wasn't thrilled at this turn of events.

"I understand we have you to thank for these festivities," Liz said with a cold, cruel smile that I could hear.

Ooh, blood in the water, already, Nas commented. *I think I misjudged Liz.*

I took a long drink of my wine. This could go so wrong in so many ways—right here.

"Hardly," Runa replied. "The serving staff is mine, but the rest was all Her Grace's doing."

"Her Grace," Liz mused, her tone thoroughly acerbic. "That'll take some getting used to. Living in something this palatial again wasn't what we'd planned for, but I suppose we can make it work."

I threw back my wine and swapped the glass from a passing waiter. I couldn't speak. Fuck. What would I even say? At least the wine was keeping me warm. The banter certainly wasn't. I'd never seen Liz like this, so... ruthless. It was fucking sexy as hell—and maybe just a little terrifying.

"I guess we'll have to," Willow broke in, all rich decorum. "It wasn't part of my plans either. But then there was Cait."

"And Her Highness," Liz said, and I could almost feel her smile turn predatory. "I do want to thank you both for looking out for us like this—politically, I mean."

"Well, I'm not sure you needed much looking out for yourself," Runa said, and there was something in her voice I hadn't heard once yet, not even with her daughter: respect. Something about Liz had impressed Runa. Not that she wasn't impressive, but Runa was rarely struck by anyone, at least as far as Willow had said.

Liz nodded, and I felt her relax. Her hand returned to my arm. "This party really needs more... something. Honestly, when I was younger, I always found formal balls so... dreary. Not much has changed."

"Perhaps I can encourage a little more life," Runa said, and then she slipped away.

I just stood there, dumbfounded. I'd expected... Well, I didn't know what I'd expected. Fireworks maybe? Claws and fangs? A good gutting? But this was a side of Liz I'd never seen. And Runa seemed genuinely to like her. I should have been taking notes.

Moments later, the music lifted from quiet background to a soft waltz, and Liz said, "Care to dance?"

I stammered. "Uh... If you want."

"I was speaking to Lady Willow," Liz said, and the tone could have coated me in frost.

Willow coughed but then recovered. "Me? Certainly, I'd love to." She handed me her wine glass, and she and Liz glided away, leaving me quietly sidelined.

It took me a moment to figure out what just happened.

Of course, she asked Willow. That was the whole point. I wasn't the one being challenged—I was the prize. It started to piss me off, but then, I stopped for a moment and considered. Liz was sizing Willow up, and probably vice versa. And that comment about having Runa to thank for this. Damn. My girl was a pro, assuming she was still my girl.

Still, though, I was okay not being at the center of this for a second, and it gave me time to think as I put the empty flutes on a passing tray.

Of course, Lord Wonderful crept up on me then, trailing his trademark scent of scorched ozone and sulfur.

"Lovely party," Aurex hummed, watching the dance floor. "And I thought, when you walked in, that no one could steal the show from you. My mistake."

I gave a dry, humorless laugh. "Yes, well, no matter how terrific you think you are, there's always someone better."

"Indeed." I could feel the scowl in that one word, and it was so satisfying.

"So, come here to threaten me?" I asked. "I saw you talking to Roselle over there. Making sly deals under my roof?"

"Just a discussion, and as for threats, I don't threaten. No, Red Queen, I mean to kill you," he said, a warm, honey-laden smile coloring his tone.

"In my own court? That'll be a trick. You can try, of course, but I don't think you'd like the outcome." My hand slid to the punch dagger tucked into my left cuff. "I'm not a pushover."

"Perhaps not, but I wouldn't soil my hands to do it myself. You truck with monsters."

"That's rich," I hissed. "The reputation of your rulership precedes you, as does your bloodline. If I were you, I'd be careful who you call a monster. She's not part of my court, you know, just under my protection."

"I don't see much around to protect you," Aurex said.

With careful smoothness, I slid the punch dagger from my left cuff. Then I slipped my hand behind his back and pressed it to his spine. "Let's not get ahead of ourselves. That's a cold iron blade, Ifrit-boy, and it will slip between your vertebrae like butter. After that, they'll be calling you Lord Crutch. Understand?"

He nodded slowly, not moving. I could feel the heat coming off him in waves. It was almost too much.

"This is my house, my people. Harm any of them, and I'll burn your realm to ash. Make no mistake, I can do it." It would kill me, almost certainly, but he didn't need to know that. "Or worse yet, I will pick up Mother Darkness and happily drop her into your domain." Now, that was an idea, not a great one, for a host of reasons. Most notably, the veil wouldn't reach that far, but it made an awesome threat, and it did get his attention. The part fire elemental's bearing suddenly went a little stiff.

"Lords have gone to war for less," he growled. "And aren't we invited guests? We're under your protection as well."

Nice try. I knew the rules. Sithraine had schooled me well—very well. "You threatened me personally, Lord Aurex. You have forfeited my protection." I pressed the blade a little harder. "Do we have an understanding?"

He nodded.

I palmed the punch dagger and slid it back into my cuff before walking away.

I'd sounded confident, and I'd been cool as a cucumber in the moment, but my hands were in fists to hide their trembling. Up to now, it had all been mess—feelings, politics, shadows in the corner. But Aurex? He wasn't subtle. He'd said it out loud.

And just like that, war had a face.

CHAPTER THIRTY

WE'RE ALL WEARING KNIVES TONIGHT

I found Sithraine lurking in one corner of the room, quietly observing everything. I had a second glass of wine in my hand, but I hadn't taken a sip yet. It was more prop at the moment. Several people had commented to me on Liz and Willow, who were still dancing, now enjoying a very slow song. I didn't feel any tugs of strong emotion from Willow, and I'd even heard her laugh a few times. All of which made me extremely uncomfortable.

"How was your chat with Aurex?" Sithraine asked, almost absently, her head swiveling across the crowd.

"Short. We threatened to kill each other."

"I'll assume he started it," Sithraine said.

I nodded. "Then I threatened to kill him and move Mother Darkness into his realm."

"Nicely done," Sithraine chuckled. "You've certainly found your steel again, Your Grace."

"I guess," I responded, turning my attention to the dance floor. "What on Earth could they be talking about?"

"You, Your Grace, what else?" Sithraine said calmly. "Would you like me to slip in and find out?"

"No," I said. "It's time."

"I do not envy you this moment, but if you don't do it, someone will eventually kill her. And your duty is to your court."

There it was. The bargain I'd struck. The responsibility I'd agreed to that I hated with every last shred of whatever heart I had left.

I sighed. This was going to hurt like hell.

"Point taken," I said, depositing my wine glass into Sithraine's fingers.

Then I stalked toward the slowly waltzing couple.

"Lady Willow? Do you mind if I cut in?"

"Of course," Willow murmured and then just sauntered off.

"I'm—"

"Don't speak," Liz ordered quietly. "Just dance."

I zipped my lip and pressed to her. Surprisingly, she rested her hands on my hips and then pulled me in. I thought for a moment she would just crush me right there and get it over with, but she didn't. We danced like that for a bit until I eventually rested my head against her shoulder. The scent of dragon's blood filled my nose, and I just melted. Goddess, she smelled so good.

"She's nice," Liz whispered. "Not quite what I expected."

I didn't lift my head. "Can we not… talk about her?"

"We'll have to eventually," Liz said. There was no edge in her voice, no venom. Just her, and I wanted this to last, at least for a minute.

"I know, but… I missed you. Like I said, for you, it's been a couple of weeks. For me…" I paused, drifting with the music. "I just want to be right here."

"The song will end soon," Liz said.

I shushed her. "Please, Liz."

She nodded against me. "Okay."

And for the next minute or so, we just moved. I could feel the eyes of every primarch on us, watching. measuring. Calculating what her presence by my side meant. What it might cost them. What it might cost me.

And several of them… I was sure… had already added her name to their mental hit list.

Willow was chatting with a few people, guests from her court, I thought, though I couldn't tell, honestly. She was just on the edge of my awareness. It was interesting, though, how, like Liz, I could spot her in the crowded room among everyone else.

Afterwards, we found a quiet corner to sit and talk.

"She loves you," Liz said, scooting her chair next to mine so that our shoulders brushed. "Or at least she thinks she might."

"I know," I said. Through the bracer, a single feeling kept finding its way to me: sympathy. Willow knew. She knew what was coming. Sithraine had told her.

There was a long moment of pause, then Liz asked, "Why did you sleep with her?" Apparently, Sithraine had spoken to Liz, too. "I won't say you constantly cheat," Liz went on, "but your heart flitters like a butterfly."

My voice rose. "What do you really want me to say? That I feel guilty? Why would I? When you feed, you get off on it. It's not sex, but only by degree, and we both know it. I'm okay with that. It's in your nature."

"So you're saying it's not in your nature to be faithful?" she asked. Again, she didn't sound angry or even hurt. And honestly, I had no idea where this conversation was going, but we had to have it.

"Was it ever?" My heart skipped a beat. Goddess, I was throwing our relationship right onto the bonfire. "I'm a Fae Queen, Elizabeth." I was standing now. "It's mine to know my heart and my needs."

It has to be done, Dorogaya. Nastasia again, currently the least helpful part of my brain.

A heavy sigh escaped my lips. Liz and the kids needed to leave before they got hurt. I'd already crossed so many human lines with her, anyway—Fae lines, even. There was no fixing this.

And for her and the kids, there was only one way out.

Sithraine was right.

"Cait —" she started, but I held up a hand.

"I'm not her anymore. I'm not human... anymore. I never really was, you know that." My voice started to break, and I reeled my emotions in, swallowing them into some black pit inside. I couldn't be weak. Not here, not now.

I wasn't that person anymore. That door was shut, locked,

with a deadbolt and a prayer.

"The wards will be open to you in two days. I can't have you publicly shunning me like I'm the bitch of the week."

"Excuse me?"

I was so, so glad to be blind right then. I didn't need an excuse not to look at her. Because what I had to do next would destroy us. It had to be loud. It had to be public. Everyone had to believe it, especially Liz. And because I was a Queen of the Dark Fae, it had to be cruel. Or no one would buy it.

I stood.

I turned to face her.

Then I placed my hands on my cocked hips.

"The real truth is that I do love Willow. I've been in love with her for months. I've been clinging to a life that was never mine. And, honestly, at this point I've had enough of trying to twist myself into an acceptable shape for you."

Liz sat there in stunned silence.

"What? Cat finally got your tongue? Nothing to say? No shots to take at me? Good." I raised my voice slightly. "That's just perfect because loving a blood fiend isn't conducive to a functioning court, and I *need* a functioning court. I will give you forty-eight hours to pack your shit and get out of my palace. Shaddan is no place for humans or blood fiends." I almost cracked… almost.

"Cait… what are you doing?" Liz whispered, voice hardly there—like someone who just watched a door slam on every single plan she'd ever laid.

"Does your condition make you deaf?" I demanded, heat flaming my cheeks, burning away the last of my humanity, and my hope. To everyone else, it would be read as rage. But… it was all too human shame. "I said, get—the fuck—out! Before I decide what price your presence now costs."

Liz stood, lifted her chin, and turned on her heel, but not before one final shot. She said, "You didn't just lose me. You lost the life you swore you wanted."

The dagger that pierced my heart was so sharp I barely felt it slide in. It was only a beat later that the pain tore through me, white-hot and total. My throat tried to close around a sob;

I forced out a quiet cough instead, like I could clear the words from my lungs.

I turned to face the rest of the guests, though I already knew everyone was watching. "Well?" I barked, waving sharply. "Go on. Show's over."

Silk rustled. Voices rose again, carefully casual. No one came to comfort me. No one dared. The Vermilion Queen had spoken, and they'd just watched her gut her own life and smile through it.

My insides were still twisting around Liz's words when Sithraine's presence cut through the noise.

"Well done, Your Grace," she murmured at my shoulder.

"Do you think any of them bought it?" I whispered glumly. My voice didn't even sound like mine. It sounded hollow and barely scraped out.

"They all did," Sithraine said. "Even Elizabeth."

I nodded, crumbling on the inside. But I didn't dare show it. "Good," I said softly.

It wasn't. It wasn't good at all; it was a horrible thing that had just ripped away a piece of me.

I turned on my heel and stalked from the ballroom, pulse hammering in my ears. Down the corridor, left, right. Not to my apartments. I couldn't go there yet. I had duties, still. And there was no way I would come back—not with her scent in the air and the ghosts of my kids' laughter hanging in the air.

The little washroom off the gallery was empty. Good.

"Ward this door except for me and mine," I whispered, fingers brushing the frame. "And no sound."

A hum filled the air for just a second, and the sounds of the party only a few doors away dropped to nothing. No music. No laughter. Just the roar of my own heartbeat.

Now that I was encased in silence, my knees gave out.

I slid down the wall next to one of the marble sinks and hit the floor hard enough to jar my teeth. The tiles were cold under my bare thighs; the dress had ridden up, but I couldn't be bothered to fix it. My hands came up of their own accord, covering my face as the first sob ripped free.

Then another.

Then too many to count.

I folded in on myself, shaking, choking on air. Every image came barrelling through at once: Liz asleep on my chest back home. Katie treating the Traulsen like a blood vending machine. Leah's drawings. Grocery lists. Coffee and a cannoli just when I needed it so much. The tiny, fragile life I'd wanted so badly I'd been willing to bleed for it.

Gone. I'd just set it on fire in front of every immortal in Shaddan and called it protection.

"I'm sorry," I croaked into my palms, though I wasn't sure who I was apologizing to. Liz. The kids. Myself. Mother Morrigan. All of them. None of them.

The spiral came vicious and fast. I couldn't leave. Liz and the children couldn't stay. They would never be safe if anyone believed for an instant that they mattered to me. Every face in that ballroom had looked at Liz and seen a lever.

And Liz... Liz would never play the quiet, obedient queen-consort while I turned into this—this creature. And there was no way she could keep the secret. It would bleed out somewhere. I just couldn't take that chance.

"I had to," I whispered, rocking once, twice, trying to breathe around the shards in my chest. "I had to."

It didn't help.

I thought of her voice, flat and stunned: *You lost the life you swore you wanted.*

She was right. I had. I'd taken that life in both hands and snapped its neck so the courts couldn't do it first. I'd chosen the crown, chosen the goddamn throne room over Sunday mornings and school runs and her cold feet under my legs on the couch.

This was my one moment to come apart. There wouldn't be any more. Queens didn't get second breakdowns. Tomorrow, this room would smell like soap and nothing, and I'd have to pretend this never happened.

I pressed my forehead to my knees and let one last, broken sound escape me, low and raw and ugly.

And when Willow found me moments later, I was grateful.

She was all I had left.

She sat right next to me and pulled me into her arms, shushing me as I sobbed.

"What have I done? What have I become?" I whispered.

"You did what you had to do," Willow answered. "You can't abdicate. You're just too powerful. They'll just kill you. You can't run. There's nowhere to go. You did the only thing you could. You freed them from this."

"But we're not supposed to hurt like this," I mumbled. "Are we?"

"It's worse for us," Willow said. "Humans can compartmentalize their desires—push them into tight little spaces, and eventually they fade. Us? We are born of desire. Our need to keep things in their proper order and place becomes an obsession. And our need for amusement and control is voracious. When things slip away, or our idle passions are unquenched, it burns like fire."

And that was it. I burned inside—burned to ash.

Only a few minutes later, makeup magically fixed, I slipped back to the ballroom with Willow. We wore smiles so polished they could've sliced marble. Mine felt glued on. Hers... I didn't even know anymore. The second the doors closed behind us, the applause and harp music muffled into something distant and irrelevant.

Inside, though?

It was just ash and hollow space. Like the biggest piece of me had been scooped out and replaced with duty and spite.

The Vermilion Palace was enormous, but somehow I felt like I was really the only one standing in it. A queen with no court. A palace with more echo than heartbeat. A life that still moved, still functioned, still was seen... and yet utterly vacant.

Sithraine intercepted me before I could exhale, murmuring logistics into my ear while Willow drifted away toward her tower room like smoke. I wanted to follow, but queens don't wander after their heartbreak. They perform.

I straightened. Smiled. Let the mask drop into place.

Then I made the rounds as the primarchs made their way to the freshly repaired forecourt: a bow here, a graceful nod there. False gratitude that tasted like chalk.

My fangs showed every time I smiled. I didn't bother hiding them. Let them think I was feral. Let them all wonder what I'd become. It was petty, but vaguely satisfying.

I gave empty thanks for attending, politely, dutifully, the way Primarchs do.

Except for Calerithon.

Calerithon got a smile sharp enough to peel paint. He knew what he'd tried with that little "gift," an Oath Pearl. Acceptance would have made me tantamount to his slave. He should have known what price it would cost him later if I found out. He and I were going to have a moment at some point.

I didn't need to say a word.

By then, I was running on fumes—anger and exhaustion braided together, holding me upright. My lungs felt tight. My heartbeat felt like a broken drum. And the worst part? If Liz had stopped for one second, if she'd looked at me, really looked, she would have understood why I had to push her away.

Wouldn't she?

Probably not. She'd wanted peace, a quiet life, soft mornings, and safety. Human normalcy with children and love.

She deserved that. She did. But that was never going to be with me. We'd just never known it until now.

By the time the last primarch left, the mask was cracking. And when the doors finally shut behind them, I headed back toward my room—bone-tired, furious at everything, and trying not to think about the fact that I had no one left to fall apart with.

CHAPTER THIRTY-ONE
The Night Cait Reagan Truly Died

I slammed the door to my apartment, rattling the hinges and whatever paintings flanked it. I didn't even mourn my sight at that moment. The darkness suited my mood just fine. I wanted to lose it. To throw a tantrum, to split the tower in two, but I was just too tired.

I took a breath of the night air, hearing the beasts below. Some of them sounded familiar, owls and other nightbirds, and some sounded strange. They were all so far away, down on the plateau—and yet their cries carried all the way up here. The gentle sounds were grounding and with another breath, I felt my heartbeat slow. My anger turned sullen and dark.

My fingers found the crown in my hair. I slipped the braids apart and managed to pull it loose—carefully. I still wanted to throw it across the room, or off the balcony, but I might hit someone down below. And besides, Sithraine would just pull out another one, probably heavier.

The boots came next. Thigh-high, stitched tight, every buckle feeling less like a statement now and more something ridiculous and petty. I sat on the edge of the bed and peeled them off one at a time, my movements slow and mechanical, leaving behind angry lines from the leather. The ritualistic effort kept my hands from shaking.

In the closet, I stripped out of my clothes, placed the crown on its little velvet rest, and tossed the boots in the corner.

Naked and alone, I felt my way back out to the balcony. The wind blew a little cooler than it had earlier, and thunder rumbled far away, bringing with it the scent of distant rain.

I must have been preoccupied, because it was still a few moments, basking in the night breeze and feeling it crawl across me, before I realized I wasn't alone.

She was already there.

Willow stood with her hands braced lightly on the balustrade, head tilted up toward the slowly turning sky. The way she always did. Listening to the wind, the creatures calling from the forests far below, and, tonight, the distant sounds of departing entourages, peeling away from the wreckage of my life.

She didn't speak, and neither did I, but I made my way to the railing between us. I didn't bother to duck back inside or cover myself. What could she see? For all she knew, I walked around nude most of the time.

"For what it's worth, I'm sorry," Willow said at last.

I said nothing. What was I supposed to say? Thank you? It's fine?

It wasn't fine.

Eventually, words ground their way up. "Do you believe in fate?"

"Like being threadcalled?" Willow asked.

"No. Bigger than that. Like real fate. Like you're born and this is your lot and, surprise, you're going to do it whether you want to or not. That kind of fate."

"Oh." Willow exhaled. "You mean destiny. Of course I do. We don't choose much, if anything, in this life. It's all an illusion. Less real than Faerie glamour."

The corner of my mouth twitched, a wry little smile full of misery. "No. I don't think we do."

I leaned against the wall, a finger trailing over the rail between us. It was blessedly cool under my hand.

"It's a mess," I muttered. "I thought maybe…" I trailed off.

I thought what? That a vampire who needs sunrise and sunset could live here, in a realm that never sees either? That she'd survive when half the room had already put her name on their to-do list for murder? That my kids would be happy in this crypt of a palace?

"I should never have come," I whispered. And what I didn't say was: Maybe I should've just died back home. It would've hurt less.

There was a soft pop, a little rush of displaced air, and Willow glimmerstepped the distance between us, slipping through the railing and through me like neither was more than mist.

I was a little jealous.

She turned me gently and cupped my cheeks. "Then you'd be dead," she said. "Snuffed out entirely."

I touched her wrists, feeling her pulse beneath my fingers. "Then it wouldn't hurt so much."

"No," Willow agreed quietly. "But then I would never have met you. And this little time we've had together would never have happened."

Her thumbs brushed my cheekbones. "This place is so broken right now. My mother's said it a thousand times—we're not supposed to be like this, at each other's throats. She's not even sure when it started. Before the Red Queen, for sure."

"She sounds like Nyxiel," I said.

Willow huffed a soft chuckle. "Nyxiel, the last priestess of Ash and Thorn. She'll never give up. The last true believer."

"Have you ever read it?" I asked.

"Almost no one reads it all," Willow said. "How many of the Christians of your world read their Bible? And of those that do, how many really think about what's in it? How many don't just cherry-pick what they want to believe and cast aside the rest?"

I snorted. "Most do that last bit. I'm not sure how many even manage the first part, given how screwed up their world is." Their… world, not mine.

"Exactly." Her fingers laced with mine. "Maybe you should read the book of Ash and Thorn, Cait. It might help."

Then she tugged my hand, guiding me toward the door. "Come."

We fumbled a bit, but made our way through my room to

253

the bed.

"Sit with me," she whispered.

I dropped down beside her, my eyes pointed somewhere around where my feet might be.

"We're bonded forever," she said. "Maybe we always have been. I don't know much about any past lives my soul might've had." She gave a soft laugh and bumped my shoulder. "Who knows? Maybe I was a musclebound, curvy Gray Elf in a previous life. The timeframe might even fit."

I gave a thin, exhausted huff that almost passed for a laugh. "You joke, but sometimes I feel..." I paused, uncertain and feeling a little foolish for even thinking it.

"Feel what?" she asked, squeezing my hand.

I shrugged. "Nothing. Nevermind."

"I can't fix it," she said. "I can't fix what you did tonight. Or what it cost you."

That landed like a stone.

"But," she went on, voice quieter, "I can make the hurt go away for a while. All you have to do is let it happen."

I tilted my head toward her. "Please."

"Just... relax," she breathed.

Something soft brushed the edge of my thoughts. Not a shove. Not an outright taking. More like someone drawing a curtain. My memory of Liz and the kids went... foggy. Not gone. Just softer. Blurred at the edges, like it all happened months ago instead of hours.

Maybe I should've pulled back, or maybe told her to stop.

But I didn't. I couldn't. It hurt too much, and I didn't want to feel it anymore—any of it.

So, I let the numbness in.

I turned my face toward hers, and from nowhere, her lips found mine. That same relentless need surged in my chest, and this time it was unassailable, powerful. It was like a kiss full of lightning.

I didn't fight it. I didn't want to. I wanted to give in and let myself have... something.

She pushed me back onto the bed.

I didn't resist. I should have felt guilt flood in, cold and punishing. I should have thought of Liz and the girls and the life I'd wanted to claw back, piece by piece, if I had to.

But guilt didn't come.

Nothing human did.

Her hands roamed across my skin, and then her mouth found mine again.

And that's when it happened.

Something inside me cracked—cleanly, quietly, like a bone that had been weak and waiting to break.

My breath hitched. Heat flashed through me. And in that flash, I felt it. A part of me—small, human, and painfully earnest—went silent. Snuffed out like a candle in a storm.

In its place rose something older. Wilder. Something aflame. Something that had always been mine.

My heart slammed against my ribs, not from fear but from a pulse of fierce, reckless freedom. A hungry exhale. A claim. The truth of what I was rising in my chest like fire through dry grass.

Not human. Not vampire. Faerie—dark, royal, and ruinous.

For one breath, one impossible instant, I felt utterly alive.

A queen taking her last step toward her throne.

Willow's tongue along inside of my thigh lit me with a longing I'd never felt before.

I lay there, my breath coming more labored as her soft palms slipped up my calves, over my knees, and pushed my legs apart.

"Yes," I whispered, just a breath.

She took me, then. So gentle and soft. Like the mouth of an angel, and I just melted into it.

Her fingers slid up my belly and found mine, brushing lightly before she laced them together, and then she brought my knuckles to her lips. A kiss, feather-soft, as if I might break. My breath hitched. She was being careful—so careful—but there was so much heat under it. Barely contained. I could feel it, the fire burning between us. It wasn't just lust.

It was love, real and thick and feral.

I moaned with desire and frustration as she lifted.

"Move back," she whispered, and I crawled further up onto

the bed. She once said to let her surrender to me, but that wasn't what was happening—not at all.

I was surrendering to my nature, my new nature. And there was no more Cait. No Skaja. No Weyna. I didn't know who I was... not anymore. Or more, not yet.

There was a shush of fabric as Willow stood and slid away her long, soft gown. My hands rose to meet her when she returned to the bed, lying across my body, pressing her mouth to mine in a desperate kiss. I bit into her lip, claiming just a drop of blood.

Fingertips ran over my skin, slow as sin, reverent and hungry all at once. She explored by touch the way I was learning to survive—by feel alone. But where my hands had searched for solidity in darkness, hers searched for wonder. And she found it, somehow, in me. I could feel it.

"You're perfect," she whispered, and even that sounded predatory. "And I love you."

And I grinned at the satisfaction of her need, her want. One day, soon, I would own all of her. I wanted it.

But for now, I was too lost. I didn't want to think. I didn't want to feel. I wanted her, and whatever pleasures would let me drift away.

I couldn't form words. My heart was pounding, my body aching with need. I reached for her, sliding my hands over the hard lines of muscle and the softness beneath. Her skin was warm. Alive. She groaned softly at my touch, and I felt the sound like a vibration in my chest.

She kissed me again—rougher this time, like she couldn't help herself—and I pressed into her, my hands tangled in her hair, my body arching toward hers, desperate for more.

And for the first time in weeks, I wasn't thinking. Not about Liz. Not about guilt. Not about pain or fire or... Earth. Earth... not home. This was my home now.

"I'm here," I whispered finally, needing her to know it. "All of me."

"I know," she breathed and then shifted to hover over me, her breath warm against my throat. "You're perfect like this," she said, voice hoarse. "Open. Needy. Mine."

She said it like a prayer, like a benediction—and then she sank down, kissing a line between my breasts before dragging her tongue in slow circles around my nipple. I moaned, arching. Her mouth was everywhere, hands spreading me apart, opening me wider. She kissed my inner thigh, then up, then—

"Oh Goddess," I gasped.

Her mouth latched onto my clit, tongue flicking in practiced strokes that made my toes curl. She didn't stop—just kept pushing me, teasing, devouring. One finger slid inside me, and then another. Curling. Drawing circles against that perfect spot. I was soaked, and she groaned against me like she was drinking it in.

It melted through me, softening everything and sending my thoughts asunder. I cried out, shuddering as my climax hit like a wave, soaking Willow's mouth with a gasp so loud it echoed off the walls.

I barely came down before I was flipped over, Willow sliding beneath me.

I didn't hesitate.

I straddled her, bracing one hand on the headboard as her mouth found me. She was relentless, tongue stabbing deep, licking in wide, slow circles, then suckling me until I was panting, jerking, begging.

She grabbed my hand, guiding it back between her thighs. I found her slick and hot, and the moan she gave when I slipped two fingers inside her went straight to my core.

I came again—harder this time—my thighs clenching around Willow's head. She didn't stop. Didn't even slow down. I rode her face through the aftershocks, crying out as I slid my fingers in and out, thrusting until I was soaked all over again.

Then I turned on Willow.

She was already panting, her legs spread for me without a word. I moved between her thighs, tasting the sweetness of her. It didn't take long. She was already so worked up. She came with a scream—tight and fierce—her body seizing as I took her apart piece by piece.

Her climax was a thing of art—arching, shaking, wrung from her like a song. She gripped my hair and cried out my name until she had nothing left.

We collapsed after that. Tangled, sticky, breathless.

But we didn't stop. We couldn't have if we'd tried. It was a drive, a need. Predatory and compulsive... and emptying.

We made love off and on for hours, until neither of us could think. There was only heat, need, and the soft murmurs whispered between bodies slick with sweat and release.

Somewhere in that mess of limbs and moans and tenderness, I realized something: we weren't just making love. I was becoming something new. And with Willow, this was something darkly sacred.

Something both glorious and fell—and completely mine.

When we were finally spent, we didn't fall asleep. Willow didn't speak. She planted a kiss on me, and left with only one last comment.

"This is what you are. The hurt will return soon. I'm sorry I couldn't do more."

I rolled over and ran a sharp nail across my pillow. I felt no remorse, but still, I dreaded what was to come. And I wished that I had asked Willow to stay.

And then in my head, her voice spoke unbidden.

You were always this. It's why I wanted you.

"Nas," I whispered. "I don't know what *this* is."

There was no answer.

CHAPTER THIRTY-TWO
THE SABLE CHOIR

Sleep usually came easy after sex, but tonight... I was stuck. Confused. Uncertain.

Willow had been right; the pain crawled its way back into my chest. And it burned me. I wanted to forget again, but I couldn't. I needed to feel this. I needed to understand it. Because that burn wasn't guilt. No, this was loss. Keen and dark and angry.

It was grief. And it would pass quickly, but I still had to feel it.

I lay curled up on my side, Jabba thoroughly comfortable stretched across my hip. Docked with the mothership, Leah called it. But still I couldn't sleep.

I thought about going down to the infirmary for something, but nothing Morvaine had worked quite right since I went blind. No light meant my brain had no idea when to shut up.

Jabba perked up, hissed, and shot off the bed into the corner.

"Hey," I cooed. "What is it, buddy?"

I thought maybe Fiona, Aoife's purple lemur thing, had gotten into my room. Jabba didn't like him—at all. But as soon as I sat up...

I felt them—two people, outside on my balcony, creeping along. My bóllom and nisís were leaning against the far nightstand. I didn't wait. Launching across the bed, I rolled off to my knees and grabbed them. Then I came up.

"Liz!" I shouted. "Willow! Assassins!"

The figures charged in, and gods, they were fast. I dropped a chunk of semi-solid magic at the corner of the bed, and the first one tripped, tumbling into the wall.

I ran by, stabbing him as I did so, but his compatriot was there, swiping down.

I dove, hearing more than feeling the blade cut through a lock of my hair as I collided with a chair.

The door burst open, and Liz was there. She blasted forward, knocking my assailant across the room. In a split second, she was on top of them, the blade sinking in.

"Oh, God! The kids!" she exclaimed.

"Go!" I barked as I regained my feet, and she was gone towards the stairs. I would have just slowed her down.

Instead, I ran to Willow's room. "Willow? Willow?" No answer.

If there'd been a fight in here, I'd have expected the smell of blood or the foul scents of death, but there was nothing. I stepped out and checked the balcony, but I didn't stumble over any bodies, so it was clear.

A loud bang and a rumble sounded from upstairs. These idiots had gone after Aoife. Big mistake.

Then, a spike of icy fear slammed into me—and it wasn't mine.

The vambrace!

Willow!

From the terror in her thoughts, she was in the fight of her life—in the girl's room.

With no time, and them a level below, all I had to go on was instinct—and panic. There was no time to measure distance, no time to think. Her fear was pounding in my chest like a second heartbeat. Liz. Willow. The kids. They were going to die, I could feel it.

I ran for the edge. Didn't hesitate. Didn't breathe. I jumped.

One… two… Glimmerstep.

The world shifted. And I slammed straight into cold stone.

CRACK.

My ribs lit up with pain as the railing caught me just under the arms. My sword tumbled away into the darkness below. I hadn't missed the floor entirely, but I damn sure hadn't stuck the landing.

The fabric of my shirt tore as I slid over the edge. I scrabbled at the stone—hands slick, everything slick, sweat or blood or water, who knew. I hung there, gasping.

Four hundred feet of empty air yawned below me.

I hauled myself up with a snarl, elbows screaming, shoulders on fire, bare feet scrabbling for traction. My muscles burned, and I dragged my ass back over the edge. And then—

Something snapped inside me—like a pause in the world.

I felt them. All of them.

Willow, standing between two assassins and Liz, her shield half-formed and barely up.

Liz, crouched low, curled over two small bodies.

The children. *My children.*

Six attackers in the room.

Too many. Too fast. Too damn close.

That was all it took.

One heartbeat. One realization.

Why the fuck do I keep fighting like a human? Cait Reagan died the day I woke in the Queen's Glass. I was the Vermilion Queen—the Red Queen.

Willow's shield shattered with the sound of exploding glass, as a blade punched clean through her magic like it was paper. She screamed.

I stepped across the balcony to the door.

"Hey! Assholes!" I shouted, my voice shaking the tower, then turning deadly low. "You want the Queen? You get the Queen."

I pulled on the magic, not just mine—*hers*—The Morrigan's. And it wasn't uncontrolled and chaotic. I finally understood why I hadn't been able to control it, why she had been eating me alive. I'd been fighting like a fucking child. Begging for a handout rather than demanding the power.

Not anymore.

I gave a vicious smile full of fangs and and bloodlust.

With a flick of my wrist, the two assassins in front of me just blasted apart in a shower of ash.

The other four charged toward me. I spoke a single syllable and sent streams of lightning at the two closest to me. Thunder cracked like a gunshot, and their bodies just caved in around the impacts as they simply vanished from my senses—dead. A second syllable and the other two hit the back wall with a crack and fell to the floor. Neither dead—but they soon would be.

Liz was looking at me. I didn't need to see her face to know the horror that was there.

Which, honestly, was too bad.

This was me. This was who I was.

"Leah? Katie?" I said, my voice deadly calm. "Are you alright?"

"We're okay," Katie said, shocked and trembling.

"Willow?"

No answer. I could sense her, but all I felt through the vambrace was fear... fear and pain.

"Willow?" My voice turned to a shriek. "Willow?!"

I all but tumbled down on top of her, feeling over her body. She groaned. I felt hot blood on my hands as I reached her abdomen.

What I saw in the Weave terrified me. "Oh, Goddess," I breathed. "Liz, get Morvaine."

The magic in her body was disrupted, severed. A foul blackness spread out from the wound and into the surrounding tissue, up through her blood vessels, along her nerves. The blood-red threads in her skin were fraying apart even as blood gushed from her abdomen.

"Move," Liz said, roughly shoving me aside. She scooped up Willow and took off at a run.

I reached out, fumbling around until I found the girls and pulled them to me.

"Ow, Mama, you're squeezing too hard," Leah said, sounding much more composed than either Katie or me. "Are they all gone?"

"I think so," I said.

"Mama, too tight," Leah grunted, and I loosened my grip.

"I'm so sorry. I'm so sorry." It was all I could say.

I sat there for a minute, holding them. This had been so close.

"I got one," Katie muttered, finally. "But there were too many. And how were they so fast?"

"I don't know, baby," I said. "I don't know."

"Is Willow going to be okay?" Leah asked through trembling lips.

Tears rushed over my lashes. "I hope so."

Please let her be okay.

Outside the infirmary, Kate, Leah, and I waited with Aoife, who was none too pleased with me. Morvaine had been doing more repairs on the wards when the attack had happened, which was why they'd been down, which was a discussion we'd have very soon.

My whole body felt heavy, like a sack of sand. The adrenaline of combat had worn off almost as soon as it was over, and I was running on fumes. But I had to know. The vambrace wasn't giving me anything.

Sithraine finally joined us a few minutes later. "Probably Thorn's Reach," she said. "But there are no markings, no way to prove it."

"Do we have to?" I growled. "It had to be them. The Sable Choir. They were fast, Sith. Vampire fast."

"They've been magically altered, and the cursed weapons are typical of the Choir, but without proof, we can't do anything."

"Yes, we can," I growled. "I can end her!"

"No," Sithraine said. "You can't just go in blazing fire, Your Grace. There are rules, and we're in a precarious situation. If we're wrong, hell, even if we're right, there's not enough evidence. Roselle will claim we attacked unprovoked, and that will be the end of it. The rest of the Primarchs will side with her and Embereach. You're living down a reputation, remember?"

My shoulders slumped. I felt so gods-be-damned helpless. "So, what? We just let it happen?"

"No," Sithraine said. "We'll respond, but it can't be an overt attack. We have to be careful. I've heard some rumblings recently, and I have an idea."

"What idea?"

Before she could answer, the door to the infirmary opened. Liz stepped into the doorway, leaning tiredly against the frame.

"Willow?" I asked, extricating myself from the girls.

Liz nodded. "I'm pretty sure she'll make it."

I stepped over to her. "Thank you."

Liz crossed her arms. I couldn't see her eyes boring into me, but I could feel them. "You don't need to thank me," Liz said. "I'm a doctor."

I shook my head. The copper tang of blood filled my nose, and through the Weave, I could see the black stains of the cursed blades still lingering on her.

"Are you going to be okay?"

She nodded again. "Physically? Yes. They're just cuts, and they're healing. A little slower than normal, but faster than shadowsteel wounds. Morvaine says it's some kind of disruption spell. It's not really effective on Katie and me. Thank God for small favors."

Her hand trembled, and I went to take it, but she jerked away.

"Are you sure you're okay?" I asked.

"You killed them…" Her voice was raw.

My brows knitted. "Of course I did. That's nothing new. They threatened my family. It's not like you've never seen that side of me before."

"No, Cait," Liz said, shaking her head. "This wasn't that. You destroyed them in the blink of an eye."

"Oh." The word came from my lips, but it was weirdly disconnected, like I was just acknowledging a spoken truth, not surprised at all. I pursed my lips, looking for the right way to say what needed to be said, but whatever old Cait might have said? It wouldn't come.

Instead, I just said. "The Vermilion Court is mine to protect. And you four are my family. You're mine to protect. I've been acting like a child, fighting with one hand tied behind my back when I have more power at my disposal than half the Primarchs of Shaddan put together. This was what I was meant to be."

"We can't stay here," Liz whispered. "It's not safe for us."

"I'll make it safe," I said flatly, reaching for her. "No one will hurt you or Willow ever again."

Liz flinched—just a half-step back. Her arm slipped out of reach like she'd touched something too hot.

That tiny recoil hurt more than any accusation she could have thrown at me.

"Do you hear yourself?" she whispered. "I don't even know who you are anymore."

"She's right," Katie said, still sitting there stroking Leah's hair. "You're different. You're one of *them*."

I blinked at that, and my gut clenched. "What?"

"Maybe monsters can live here, but we can't. Leah's not built for this place, none of us are. It's always dark. There's no sun. And these people, they don't care."

I swallowed and knelt. "But... Katie, honey, it's my job to keep you safe."

"Keep us safe? You're the reason we're in danger!" Katie shouted, lifting Leah off and standing to get in my face. "If you cared, you'd let all this go and come home."

"It's not that simple," I said. "I have responsibilities and... "

"And you're a Queen now, and we're nothing. We're just... leverage. I thought you loved us."

"I do!" I called as she stormed down the hallway, but she just kept going.

"What... what's going on?" Leah asked.

"We're leaving," Liz said. "I'm taking you and Katie home."

Leah grabbed my arm. "No! We just got here. I'm not going. I like it here. Morvaine was showing me how to work the

265

wards."

I knelt down. "Leah, I promise I'll fix this. But Auntie Liz is right. You have to go home before anything else happens."

Roselle had to know that her plan failed by now.

"I'm not leaving!" Leah cried and took off down the hall. Liz chased after.

"Well done, Sis," Aoife said as she peeled herself off the wall.

I glared at her from beneath my blindfold. "This isn't my fault."

"It never is," she said. "You need to figure out how to get that monkey off your back and go home to your family... while you still have one." Then she just marched away after the others.

"Aoife!" I called before she'd gone more than a few steps. "I need you to keep them safe. Get them someplace the other primarchs can't get to them. I'll straighten things out here, and then we'll try to... figure it out."

There was no figuring it out, but I needed them safe.

Aoife nodded and turned on her heel.

I watched her round the corner, then turned. "Sithraine?"

"Yes, Your Grace."

"Have Vaelith guard my family. Have Elarith and Runa's Queensguard scour the palace in case there are any more. I want the rest of the Nerin in the War Room in thirty minutes. We have some things to discuss."

My heart told me to pull them in, lock them in a room, keep them close, fight like hell to make this work right here. But that was a fool's errand, and the Vermilion Queen wasn't a fool... not anymore.

CHAPTER THIRTY-THREE
THE SECOND ATTEMPT

I needed to change. I was covered in blood. Vaelith and a host of Runa's Queensguard had taken the kids back upstairs into Aoife's room, which had been swiftly cleaned and repaired.

I made my way to the eighth floor via the closest stairs. Something niggled at my senses. A feeling of movement.

I paused.

The servitor? It didn't feel like the servitor. It felt like—

I didn't have time to finish that thought as something dropped on me like a weighted blanket, covering me in a leathery, writhing mass that flowed like water. Tentacular protrusions slid around me. My arms and legs were bound instantly, that horrid black goo cinching tight, cold and alive. At least it wasn't trying to infect me this time, but I couldn't move.

Then it slid over my mouth and nose.

A sour, chemical rot flooded my senses as it sealed down.

Panic clawed up my throat.

Fuck no. I'm not going out like some cornered bitch.

Then I felt it.

A ripple of magic. A twist in the weave.

It's a portal, Dorogaya, Nastasia told me in my thoughts. *I think you should stop that.*

Horror sliced through me, sharp as piano wire. This wasn't an assassination.

It was a gods be damned kidnapping.

"Fuck you," I growled into the smothering void. The sound was barely a vibration in my own skull.

I forced myself still. Queens don't thrash. Queens don't beg. They strike.

I reached outward, tearing into Mother Morrigan's magic, dragging at it, feeling her very being seep into me, threading into my essence like cold needles. That mingling of thought. That awful closeness. I grabbed hold anyway and spun a spell without gesture, without breath, nothing but will and fury. A single tear in reality, straight across the portal she was trying to open.

The rift buckled. Collapsed.

The thing shrieked.

Heat gathered over my skin, raw magic burning in the microscopic space where the creature's body met mine. My clothes crisped away in an instant. The goo constricting my arms flaked to ash. The creature screamed again, a metallic howl scraping the inside edges of my skull.

Still, I pressed. Harder.

Around my face. Around my mouth.

Mine, not yours.

The leathery cover recoiled, peeling back just enough for air to punch into my lungs in a ragged gasp.

"I told you," I hissed, stepping free of the writhing mass. "I'm not yours."

I spoke the next words like a verdict passed in old Shaddani: "In the fires of the ancient world... you burn."

The spell detonated.

Heat roared outward in a sphere, so hot I could practically feel the color of it.

Pressure slammed into me, a brutal shockwave that ripped stone apart.

Blocks tore free, hurtling upward—I heard them punch through the ceiling, the crack of stone, the scream of shattering slate.

Air followed, a hungry gust pulling upward through the newborn hole.

Rain punched down in cold sheets, hissing across my skin, turning the cooling stone around me into steaming grit.

When the echoes died, I stood alone in the wreckage, naked and soot-covered, but otherwise untouched. My breath shook in my chest.

And beneath my skin… she stirred.

Mother Morrigan.

Just there—closer than she had ever been. Her presence was warm, simmering, coiled like a second heartbeat. Not devouring me this time. Not using me.

Becoming me.

Or maybe I was becoming her.

But the rush of addiction I'd always felt wasn't there. No frenzy. No spiral of power. My head was clearer than it had ever been.

I laughed—a sharp, breathless, wild thing, filled with shock, adrenaline, and the aftertaste of power. Mother Morrigan's voice braided through my own, low and ancient, too close to be separate.

Mother Morrigan laughed with me.

The two sounds were almost the same.

"Your Grace!" Vaelith called, rounding the corner.

"You're a little late," I said, voice flat. "Lock down the palace. Do all the Nerin have their shadowsteel blades?"

"Yes, Your Grace," Vaelith said.

"Good. Carry them at all times."

I tilted my face into the rain streaking down from the hole I'd blown in the tower. Cold drops fell onto my face—straight through the wards.

And that was the moment it clicked. Liquid, it wasn't magic or force or a body that could be stopped by a barrier built for weapons and spells. It flowed. It had flowed when it hit me. Spread across me. Compressed itself solid only after it found its mark.

The wards blocked anything solid.

But rainfall? A thousand tiny separate droplets? The wards let that through so the gardens wouldn't die and the cisterns wouldn't run dry.

That's what the first attack had stopped so abruptly. I'd shown her the way. I'd brought a storm to put out the fires on the plateau.

Mother Darkness had watched the rain fall into this palace, the one thing the wards didn't reject.

And she'd built herself a creature that could fall the same way—little bits of itself split apart until it was through. It was ingenious.

And terrifying.

Even Faerie Queens were terrified from time to time. And two attempts in one night were more than enough to do it.

Vaelith hadn't gone two steps to execute my orders before the wards shuddered under an impact so hard it shook the entire palace.

CHAPTER THIRTY-FOUR
NOT HER

The armor came when the walls rocked.

Shadow slid over my skin and resolved into leather, seamless and familiar, the weight of my weapons appearing and settling precisely where they should. The Defender's leathers. Badb's armor. Right on time.

I flexed my hands once, the creak of the leather was reassuring—comfortable. The nisís rode easily at my hip. The magic answered without resistance. Good. Whatever was coming, I could meet it like this.

The palace shook again, harder this time. Somewhere below, stone groaned and wards screamed as they absorbed another blow.

I drew a slow breath and let everything else fall away. Fear. Wonder. The useless question of whether I was ready. I'd crossed that line already. This wasn't about me anymore.

Everyone in this palace was under my protection.

"Get Leah to the ward chamber," I ordered. "Now."

Vaelith nodded and vanished instantly from my senses. I followed the wall to the grand staircase and down to the entrance.

Aoife. Sithraine. Naerith. Liz was standing too close to the front for my liking. And beyond them, Runa's Queensguard in clean lines, their captain at the fore. Andelyn. Young for a High Fae.

"You're not required to be here," I told her. "You came to protect us from other Fae, not my family's monster."

"We failed, Your Grace," Andelyn said without flinching. "Our people failed to protect you from the Sable Choir." A thin, humorless smile. "Besides, if we're being honest, our asses are hitched to yours."

"Okay then," I said. "Then you'll hold the second line behind the Nerin."

My gaze flicked to Liz. Just long enough.

"Back to your quarters," I said. "And stay there."

I didn't wait for a reply. I didn't check to see if she moved. If she hesitated, someone else would handle it. If she didn't, she'd be alive later and angry with me.

Aoife inhaled sharply. "Cait, you're blind."

I lifted a hand.

The room went silent so fast it was almost a physical thing.

"This is my palace," I said, voice low, precise. "This is my realm. If you're here, you fight. If you don't want to, leave now. I won't stop you."

No one moved.

The palace shuddered again, deep and violent. Dust shook up from the floor and down from the ceiling as the impact rolled through the structure.

"What the hell is that?" someone whispered.

"Balor," Sithraine said. "She's trying to bring down the wards."

Aoife turned toward me. "Can she do that?"

"Yes," I said. "The wards weren't built with Balor in mind."

Another tremor rippled through the floor.

Vaelith and Elarith joined us a moment later.

"Apparently, she sent everything," Elarith said. "They're holding back the ground forces while the Balor pound the wards. Morvaine's extended them around the defensive towers until the Balor are in range."

"Then we'll get them in range," I said, then turned to Vaelith. "Where's Leah?"

"Getting a crash course in battle tuning wards," Vaelith said. There was no humor in her tone.

I waved an arm, and the main door opened inward. The world beyond was black for me, nothing. If the creatures were there, they were too far away.

"Fucking hell," Aoife whispered.

"Vaelith?" I prompted.

"Four Balor at the ridge, maybe a half-mile out—too far for the towers to reach yet. Too many wevkrana and emisai to count."

"Let the Queensguard take the wevkrana. Focus on the emisai. Any Pteraket or Koşant?"

"No," Vaelith reported. "Not that we can see, at least not yet."

I shifted my perception, layering the flow of the Weave over what I could already sense. The black silhouettes of the enemy appeared briefly, then sharpened—just enough to make them worse. The threads of magic were thick, tangled, and shifting like smoke underwater. The more I focused, the more it felt like trying to make out faces on a static-filled television. It hurt more than it helped.

Still, I got enough.

The force arrayed against us was massive. Hundreds of twisted figures moved with purpose, half-hidden in the haze of magic.

And then I saw them: the Balor. Hulking shapes—taller than the rest, harder to parse—and glowing. A deep, baleful red aura shimmered around them. They were shielded.

One flared briefly and violently in a burst of bruised purple magic. The impact hit. The palace shuddered. And the flash was like a nova going off in my skull. I yanked myself out of the Weave, clutching my head, before it could scramble my brain any worse.

"That sucked," I muttered. "Vaelith, the defense of the forecourt is yours. I'm taking to the sky." I turned to Sithraine. "Take me to Umbryss."

She grabbed me, and the biting cold slapped at my face before I landed on the bone-strewn floor of his lair.

"Get on," he rumbled.

Sithraine helped me strap into the battle harness and shoved a bow and a fat quiver of arrows into my hands.

"Karanite tipped," she said.

I nodded. Apparently, I was now a blind archer riding a dragon. Sure. Why not? It must be Tuesday.

Underneath the sarcasm, I was just praying nothing else went wrong. Somewhere deep in the back of my mind, I knew —I couldn't take another hit.

Not today.

Umbryss and I launched from the cavern and high into the sky. We swooped around. I pressed a hand into one of the hollows, surveilling the battle through his eyes. Aoife was casting magic down from the main entrance into the ruins, carving great furrows through the approaching lines of wevkrana. The emisai loped behind them.

Katie was in the field, and my breath hitched. She darted around, sowing chaos among the emisai. She carried Badb's dagger, rescued by Liz from the Charles no doubt. Everywhere she went, the glowing dagger slashed, and the monsters crumbled to ash. The enemy couldn't even touch her. She was so swift, like some avenging angel of death, with absolutely no fear at all.

"Be careful, baby," I prayed. "Please."

The rest were in a line, waiting for the crush of the first wave.

Before we were in range of the Balor, Umbryss soared further upward into the low clouds overhead. I lost vision and stood, shifting my perception to the Weave again.

"Do you think you can push one of those Balor into range?"

Umbryss didn't answer; he just dropped into a steep dive. I leaned back hard in the harness, barely keeping my feet. Then he reared up, and I dropped into the saddle.

The dragon slammed all four feet into one of the Balor from

behind, sending it tumbling off the ridge into the city ruins. The four defense towers swiveled and opened fire, pelting the wallowing Balor with bursts of raw magic. Seconds later, the massive beast crumbled into ash.

I flung my hands out, barely managing a brittle shield between Umbryss and the remaining three—just as one fired. The shield exploded on impact, but it absorbed the worst of it. Umbryss flapped backward and up, dodging a second blast with a graceless roll.

"Well, that got their attention," he said dryly as a third blast sailed past his wing.

"Good," I muttered. "Evade. Every shot they take at us isn't one at the palace."

Mist slapped my face as another shot missed by inches—but we were back in the cloud layer now, high and hard to hit.

"Any other ideas?" I called, racking my brain.

"Cait, could you get the monster off my back please?" Umbryss shouted.

I turned—and swore. A Koşant had a spiked arm driven into Umbryss's scales, and a ptereket was peeling away, its four insectile wings buzzing furiously.

Good. Fine. Just two more problems.

I reached for the Weave with the same cold certainty I'd had in the tower. A flick of my hand. A thought that snapped like thunder.

Ash.

Nothing.

Not even resistance. Not even that familiar give of reality before it broke. The Weave slid off them like oil on glass, my power skidding wide and useless.

For a heartbeat, I just stared into the dark, stunned by the absence.

"Shit," I muttered.

The Koşant wrenched harder, yanking at the scales. The ptereket's wings screamed as it banked away.

Fine.

If they wouldn't burn, I'd kill them the old-fashioned way.

I drew, fired. Three shots in rapid succession.

The first slammed into the ptereket's back, dropping it mid-flight. The second went wide. The third—blessedly—hit the Koşant dead in its sensory socket. It sagged, dead weight, the spiked arm still embedded in Umbryss.

"Get it off," he snarled. "It's coated in poison!"

I couldn't see it anymore—it was dead, and dead things didn't register in my senses.

"Fuck it," I muttered. "Climb!"

I popped the restraints just as Umbryss surged upward.

I dropped like an arrow, legs first, hoping—praying—this would work. A solid thud reverberated up my spine as I landed hard on the Koşant, jarring it loose and taking the poisonous talon with it. Unfortunately, that also meant I was now tumbling off the dragon's back.

Focus, Cait. Focus. You have all the magic you could ever need. You can do this.

I closed my eyes and pulled hard on the Weave. I didn't know if I could still do it, and for one agonizing heartbeat, I was sure I was going to go splat like a bug on a windshield. And then—

Wings exploded from my back, catching the air. Not the ravens wings I expected, insectile wings—dragonfly wings. I leveled out on instinct, hovering, dazed but alive.

Umbryss flared at the edge of my senses, diving, and I drove toward him, catching the saddle and scrambling into place and letting the wings ghost away.

"Now that's what I'm talking about!" I shouted, grabbing the harness. It took a few seconds, but I got it locked back into place.

"Well done," Umbryss said.

"Will you be okay?" I asked, heart still hammering as we dropped into a steep dive.

"Eventually," he said. "But we're not done."

We circled wide, sweeping around through the chaos. Through the blazing weave of magic, I saw the three remaining Balor below. The palace wards were down.

Shit.

I fired at each of the Balor. The karanite-tipped arrows

punched through the shielding, leaving fat gaping holes in their wake.

"There!" I shouted. "Now!"

Umbryss pulled up hard and skimmed low over them, unleashing a stream of fire. Their shields flared—flickered—then snapped and vanished. One by one, the Balor collapsed, their forms crumbling into ruin. But not before one got a shot off—a clean one—straight through Umbryss' left wing.

We went down.

The only thing that saved me from being flattened was pure instinct—I popped the restraints again and threw up another weak shield as we plummeted. Even so, I was launched, tumbling through the air, until I crashed into the sandy pumice along the lower slopes of Nochtanmore's rise.

I staggered to my feet, every part of me screaming in pain.

"Umbryss! Umbryss!" I ran forward, arms out. I could sense him—thank the Goddess, he was alive—but he wasn't moving. The weight of him. The impact? He had to be hurt badly. "Please answer me!"

Tears pricked at the corners of my eyes. He was silent. "Umbryss, please!" I shouted in desperation. "Answer me."

"I'm fine," he grunted finally, pushing himself upright on all fours. "My wing is wrecked, though. I won't be flying again for some weeks."

"So it'll heal?" I asked, almost breathless.

"Yes, Cait," he said gently. "It'll heal."

He bumped his snout into me, nearly knocking me over, but I threw my arms around him anyway. I caught the edge of his lip and got a mouthful of gasoline-scented saliva for my trouble.

I didn't care. He was okay.

"What's the situation?"

"I'm not dead," he huffed. "But there's still half an army out there."

He never finished.

Pain tore through my skull like a hooked blade, bright and sudden, and for a fraction of a second, I wasn't on the hillside at all. I was inside something smaller. Softer. Terrified.

Leah.

The pure animal horror of a child in danger, the kind that slid past my thoughts and went straight to my heart.

And then fear. Her fear. Hot and breathless. A trapped, scrambling thing with nowhere to go.

My stomach dropped out. My hands went cold. The world tilted.

"No," I said, and it came out as an inhuman growl. Then, lower, like a vow: "Not her."

The terror tried to bloom, to drag me under, to make me see all the ways this could end. I crushed it flat. I couldn't afford it. Not for one moment.

My magic surged and the air split open with a crack like breaking bone. A portal yawned wide to the forecourt, spilling light and smoke and the copper-stink of blood.

"Burn them to ash," I told Umbryss. "And watch out for Katie."

Then I stepped through and ran.

"Ward the halls," I snapped. I didn't slow. I didn't turn.

The wards flared in answer, thin and unstable, just enough magic to keep me upright as I tore down the corridor. The palace screamed around me, magic tearing at itself, but all of it blurred into noise.

Not my daughter.

Please, I thought, and hated myself for it. It was my job to keep her safe.

The stairwell to the Veilstone felt impossibly far. I hit the steps at a dead run, missed one, nearly pitched forward, caught myself on the wall, and kept going, boots skidding, breath burning in my chest.

Too slow. I was too slow.

I hit the bottom hard, stumbled, swore, and rounded the corner—

—and there it was.

The Veilstone chamber.

The reason for all of it.

The creature stood between me and the crystal, its feminine shape roiling and unfinished, one arm full of shredded magic raised, palm out. The other held Leah.

"Stop," it said, voice wrong and layered. "Move any further, and I'll kill her."

My heart hammered so hard it stole my breath.

"Leah," I gasped.

She was half-swallowed by the thing's shifting mass, her arms pinned to her sides by a ropey vine of the stuff.

Morvaine lay crumpled nearby, shaking.

The world narrowed to one point.

To Leah.

"No." The word came out as a snarl. I didn't think. I didn't negotiate. I didn't breathe.

I drove my power forward in a single, vicious line, everything I had knotted tight into one killing shot.

For one bright instant, it was perfect. Clean. I had it. She'd be safe.

The blast tore from my hand with a high, singing crackle.

The creature blurred and tore away through a hole in the world.

A portal.

Mama! I didn't hear it. I felt it in my head and beneath my ribs.

Then she was gone.

My magic didn't stop. It couldn't. I'd already loosed it.

The beam hit the Veilstone.

The powerful wailing that followed ripped through my head like a tangle of barbed wire, like glass dragged across my skull. The crystal spiderwebbed with cracks, fractures racing through it in an instant.

And then it shattered.

Fragments fell in slow, terrible silence. The remnant inside spilled out, a tumble of twisted, grotesque magic. It bled across the floor in ribbons of smoke before it thinned and vanished.

For a heartbeat, I couldn't move.

Couldn't swallow.

"No," I whispered, and it broke into something uglier. "No. No."

My hands were shaking. My chest hurt like I'd been gutted.

"Shit," I choked.
I'd lost her.

CHAPTER THIRTY-FIVE

GODDESSES DESIGN. MOTHERS CHOOSE

"This is your fault," Liz accused.

Her words cut into me like knives. For her, it was rage. For me, it was truth. I'd fucked up. I'd kept them here too long. I'd believed I could make them safe.

I didn't stop walking. I couldn't. If I stopped, I'd have to feel it. I'd have to admit what my heart already knew, what my mouth had been refusing to shape into words since the moment the Veilstone went dark and Leah's presence winked out of my perception.

I'm no better than the Finchers. Just more polite.

Mama! That last telepathic scream of terror echoed in my head, and I almost stumbled—almost. I wanted to flinch, and crumble, and falter. But Leah was leverage. I was the target.

"Yes," I said, my voice glass smooth. "And it's mine to fix."

My hands found the lift. Liz stepped onto it before I could speak.

"Royal Apartments," I commanded.

My fingers found the wall before the lift had fully stopped. And I moved with a purpose. Like my heart wasn't in pieces and I wasn't trembling through my whole body.

Liz moved in front of me anyway. A wall of heat and blood and fury. The way you can feel a storm before it breaks.

"No," she barked. "You're not going without me."

A year ago, that tone would have stopped me. It would

have brought me up short and snapped me back into being human. Wife. Partner. Someone who asked instead of commanded. I would have relented. I would have let her lead. I would have been a willing partner in this.

Now it just hit the crown.

I tilted my head slightly, as if listening to her was a courtesy I could afford.

"You don't get to tell me how to save her," I said, and my voice didn't waver. "And where I'm going…"

I stepped forward. Just a fraction.

"…you can't follow."

There it was. The worst part. Not the cruelty. Not the command.

The distance.

Liz made a sound that wasn't quite a laugh and wasn't quite a sob. It scuffed at the air… and died in her throat.

"Cait," she said, lower now. "Don't do this. Don't shut me out like I'm —"

I threw up a hand, cutting her off. I couldn't hear the next part. Like I'm disposable. Like I'm leverage. Like I'm one more thing you're willing to burn to keep the rest of the world warm.

If I let her finish that sentence, I would break. I'd let myself drag her into danger, just like I had Nastasia. I wasn't willing to burn her. Or Katie. Or any of them. Leah was in danger. It was my fault. And no one else was going to die because I thought I could save everyone I cared about.

Empathy had been something I'd been losing by leaps and bounds for months, and now it roared back—because of Leah. And I wouldn't let that empathy make me do something stupid, like take Liz to a place where she'd surely get killed.

If I broke, Leah would be consumed, or… or worse.

I turned into my apartment with barely a touch. The door. The cold edge of the too-deep sofa. The left-hand bookshelves.

Fourth shelf down.

My fingers slid along the spines, not reading titles, just counting textures. Smooth vellum. Worn leather. Embossing. The little nick in the wood where I'd chipped it in an angry fit.

There.

The small box sat nestled behind a row of histories. It wasn't a secret, just placed so no one would accidentally open it.

The box of awful.

My hand closed around it, and for a second, my stomach lurched—just like the Veilstone chamber.

I knelt to the floor and opened it.

Even before my fingers touched the pendant, the air changed. It felt closer, and colder, and angrier.

The medallion felt wrong in my palm. Cold, yes, but more than that. Expectant. It knew somehow. It was filled with a mockery of life, like all of Mother Darkness's creations.

Liz sucked in a sharp breath.

"What is that?" she whispered, and the horror in her voice made the words heavier than any scream.

I'd wondered, distantly, if it would look different to her, inside Shaddan. If Mother Darkness would recognize her own hook and let it show.

Apparently so.

"Kim's medallion," I said. My mouth went dry around the name. "This was how she stayed ahead of us. This was how she coordinated everything she did. The Liberty hotel, the attack on Boston. All of it. She used it to speak directly to Mother Darkness."

Silence. The kind that happens right before someone tries to stop you and realizes they might not be able to.

"What?" Liz's voice came out thin, stunned. And then the comprehension landed in that one syllable like a door slamming shut. "You can't."

I didn't answer. I didn't reassure her. I didn't explain, *I'm doing this for Leah, I'm doing this because I have to, I'm doing this because I don't deserve to live if I don't bring her back.*

I couldn't afford to make it human. Leah needed the Queen. Leah needed Katie's monster.

I lifted the chain over my head.

The metal brushed my throat and my skin went tight, every instinct in me screaming wrong wrong wrong.

Liz moved, fast. I felt her reach for my wrist.

I moved faster. Just a thought. And her hand smacked against a simple shield.

"Cait stop," she wailed.

I settled the medallion against my sternum.

It hit my skin like a brand.

And I still didn't turn toward Liz.

Because if I did, if I turned my face toward her voice and felt her grief up close, I might hesitate.

And hesitation was how Leah would die.

The room vanished. I still felt it, under my legs and in every breath. Liz's pounding became an echo of sound, heard through water.

"And there you are," Mother Darkness said in my head. Her voice still had that horrid hiss it always did, but less... harsh. Speaking instead of screaming. "You made it so easy. You're so predictable. A creature of habitual grief and guilt."

"I want her back," I answered, every bit the Fae Queen. "Now."

"An exchange then?"

"An exchange. Her for me."

"Alone."

"No," I said. "I will bring one. To ensure her safety once I'm gone."

"Fair terms," she said. "You will exchange yourself for the girl. You will let me take you. You will be drawn inside for me to devour."

I smirked. "I will enter. But devour? Only if you can."

"No."

"Then no deal," I said. It was a bluff. If she refused, I'd cave. But I gambled. I gambled that I was too tempting for her to pass up. And the stick was very real. "I'll come to destroy you instead in vengeance."

There was a long silence. "I accept those terms."

"The girl will be released into the custody of the one I bring and never pursued by you again."

"Yes."

"You will release her as soon as I have arrived at the bed of Lindon Danu."

"Yes."

I let out a long exhalation. Settling into the inevitability of this moment.

"Cait!" Willow's voice. "Stop."

A spell hammered the shield.

It shattered.

"The bargain is struck," I said with absolute finality and slumped.

A peal of thunder rolled over the palace as Liz snatched the amulet off of my neck.

It was already crumbling to dust.

And I was bound by Mother Shaddan. Her thunder was my only warning.

"Cait," Willow whispered. "What have you done?"

"I traded myself for Leah." I still sounded like I was in control.

"I'm going with you," Liz said.

I hoisted myself up and lifted my chin, brushing the dust and dirt off my leathers. "No, I already told you. You can't. You'd be no help. I can only take one. Willow, you're coming. Once the trade is done, you will portal Leah here and get them all home."

Willow took a step back, but then she said, with all decorum, "Yes, Your Grace."

"What?" Liz said, and I heard everything in that one word. You're sidelining me when our daughter's in danger. You don't trust me. You believe in her. You choose her.

The bargain was struck. The consequences plain.

I had been made to be perfect for purpose.

I chose my child.

CHAPTER THIRTY-SIX
WHATEVER IT COSTS

The portal snapped shut as Willow and I stepped through. We stood at the lower edge of the miles-wide crater that was once the lake of Lindon Danu. The fog was gone.

I expected to see a horde of her creatures here—thousands of wevkrana skittering across the broken earth, emisai sliding through pools of their own filth, koşant prowling the perimeter like death given form. But there was nothing. Not a sound. Not a single one of Mother Darkness's monsters appeared in my sense of the Weave.

She'd sent everything. We'd destroyed everything.

It had been her Hail Mary, and it had worked.

Here I was.

Through the Weave, Mother Darkness resolved into something my mind struggled to process. Something I hadn't known the last time I was here. Her shape wasn't random. It was... home.

The Vermilion Palace.

Or rather, a grotesque approximation of it. The proportions were wrong, stretched, and warped. Crystalline spires bent where they should have stood straight. Archways gaped like screaming mouths. The elegant symmetry of the Vermilion Court had been translated into something hungry, something that tried to shape itself in beauty and had failed.

It was Drusera's memory, twisted by years of neglect and

hollowed out by loneliness.

The palace-creature no longer moved. It rested neatly on the ground, fully covering the broken branch of Crann Bethad, the Tree of Life, the source of our ambient magic. Atop the central spire—two hundred feet of nightmare crystal—still rested the two enormous black spheres, dormant.

And at the very apex, seated on the flat platform, sat the same figure, though the great obsidian mirror reflected nothing.

Avra.

I wondered if she was still in there, alive and aware, or if her mind had been consumed.

The former God-Empress of Oşen looked almost peaceful, meditative, as if communing with the monster beneath her. Behind her, that octagonal black lay empty, not a single image presented itself on the surface. Mother Darkness really had spent all that she had in this last desperate gamble.

"What are we going to do when you're gone?" Willow asked, her voice sounding small.

I tore my attention from that horrible parody of the Vermilion Palace. "I've already set down succession," I told her, surprised that my voice came out so calm. "If I don't come back, the Vermilion Court passes to you along with all obligations, treaties, and bargains."

"Cait…" she whispered, but I held up a hand.

I sniffed. "I know."

Everything inside me screamed at me not to do this. Let Leah go. But I couldn't. I wouldn't. She was my baby. I'd die for her.

"If I don't come out, tell Liz that I love her, and I'm so sorry for everything."

"You won't," Willow said flatly, and there was no comfort in her honesty. "She's going to take you."

"I know."

"Please don't go," she said.

I took her shoulders. "Willow. I love you. But Leah is more important to me than you are."

She took a long breath and hugged me close. "That's as it

should be," she whispered.

This was it. Everything I'd done in my life—every fight, every sacrifice, every impossible choice—came down to one simple decision: me for the life of my child.

The mockery of the palace pulsed once, as if in acknowledgment, and I felt that terrible voice beginning to press against my mind like an ice pick finding purchase.

Cáitlín. I've been waiting for you.

I squared my shoulders, and we began our descent into the crater.

It didn't take long—maybe ten minutes to cross the distance that separated us from the base of that obscene palace-creature.

Ahead, just in front of what would have been the palace gates, stood the liquid monster, one arm holding Leah tightly to her.

Through the Weave, I could see Leah clearly, her body a cerulean glow. She trembled. The terror radiated off her in waves as she drew in shallow, panicked breaths. And there, on her forearm, a spot of wrongness that made my blood run cold: a mote of black, a point of infection that pulsed with Mother Darkness's corruption. It was small, barely more than a pinprick in the tapestry of her life force, but it was spreading. Tendrils of shadow crept outward like roots seeking purchase, claiming her inch by inch.

My daughter. My child. Marked like livestock.

"Remove it," I barked at the creature standing beside her, wearing my shape like a moving statue carved of oil and latex. It was a beast, moving with my mannerisms, smiling with my mouth.

"No," the creature said, and even its voice was mine—my cadence, my inflection, stripped of warmth and filled with malicious amusement. "That wasn't part of our deal. You said her for you. That's all."

Rage flared hot in my chest, but I swallowed it down. There was no room for anger here, no space for negotiation. I'd walked into this with my eyes open—metaphorically speaking —and I'd known the terms.

"When you get her back, go to Morvaine." I felt Willow tense beside me, felt her begin to understand. "There's a book in the Library—Metamorphosis of the Nascent Soul. She'll know where it is, and you'll know what to do."

The infection couldn't claim her then. Couldn't corrupt what had been transformed beyond its reach. It was a violation of everything I wanted for Leah—her choice, her humanity, her normal life. But it was also her only chance at surviving the poison Mother Darkness had planted in her flesh.

Willow's hand found mine for just a moment, squeezed once. Understanding. Acceptance. Forgiveness for what I was asking her to do.

"Fine then," I called out, my voice carrying across the broken ground. "How do you want to do this?"

The oil-and-latex version of me gave Leah a push that sent her stumbling forward on shaking legs.

"Walk, child," the creature said, its tone almost gentle, almost kind.

Leah took one step. Then another. Her eyes found mine across the distance, and even without seeing her face, I felt the weight of her gaze—the betrayal, the terror, the desperate hope that somehow this wasn't really happening.

I held her gaze through the Weave, let her see me standing there, and willed her to understand: *I'm sorry. I'm so sorry. But you're going to live. Whatever it costs me, you're going to live.*

She took another trembling step toward me.

Toward freedom.

Toward a life she didn't know she was about to inherit—one measured not in decades but in millennia, written in magic and starlight and pointed ears.

I walked forward.

Each step felt like wading through water, like the universe was giving me one last chance to reconsider, to turn back, to choose differently. But there wasn't another choice. There had never been another choice. And Mother Morrigan was silent. I took that silence for her assent.

Perfect for purpose. Maybe this was what I was supposed to do. I honestly had no idea.

I did this for you, Nastasia said.

"Yes, you did," I whispered.

The difference is, Dorogaya, you can still fight.

"Will you be with me?" I asked.

Until the end or until you free me, she said.

When Leah and I reached each other in that dead space between freedom and captivity, I paused. Through the Weave, I drank in every detail of her—the rapid flutter of her pulse, the warmth of her living presence, the beautiful, terrifying fragility of her mortality.

"Go with Willow," I said, and my voice cracked like glass under pressure. "I'll be along shortly. I need to deal with this. She'll get that stuff off your arm, too, okay?"

Leah threw her arms around me, and the contact was everything—warm and solid and real in a way that made my chest constrict with the weight of what I was about to lose. "Please don't go."

The words slid into my heart like an icepick.

"I made a bargain, Leah. You know I have to, don't you?"

She nodded into my shoulder, and I felt the dampness of her tears against my neck. "I know. Faerie bargains should never be broken."

Smart girl. My brilliant, beautiful girl.

"No," I agreed softly, running a hand through her hair one last time, memorizing the texture, the way it caught on my fingers. "And especially not one made by a Queen. But you're going to be my Faerie princess, okay?" I pulled back just enough to tilt her face up, wishing desperately that I could see her expression with my own eyes instead of through the abstract poetry of the Weave. "And then we'll be together."

"You promise?"

The question broke something in me. A promise. She wanted a promise—the most binding thing a Fae could give. And I couldn't. I couldn't lie to her, not now, not when these might be our last words.

I sniffed, fighting back the tears that burned behind my ruined eyes. "I promise I'll try."

It was the best I could offer. The most honest thing I'd ever said.

"Okay," she whispered, accepting it with a grace that made me wonder when my little girl had become so brave. Then, almost so quietly I nearly missed it even with my supernatural hearing, she added, "She has her own soulstone. It's where the wardstone would be."

The words hit me like lightning.

A soulstone. Mother Darkness had a soulstone—the crystalline heart that housed Drusera's immortal essence, the actual core of the goddess who'd been imprisoned and torn apart. Mother Darkness wasn't the entity itself. She was an appendage, a husk of severed emotion made physical and grown like a cancer around Drusera's soul. All that rage and betrayal and hurt, given form and purpose, wrapped around the one thing that truly mattered.

Drusera's words from a long-ago dream: *Find the crystal within the crystal.*

Holy shit.

The soulstone was the prize. The center. The source.

Leah had just told me where it was: where the wards would be. In the center. In the heart of that twisted mockery of the Vermilion Palace.

She'd given me a weapon. My daughter, terrified and marked and barely holding herself together, had given me the one piece of information that might—might—give me a fighting chance.

"Okay, honey," I said, my voice steadier now, purpose crystallizing in my chest like ice. "Go with Willow. I'll be with you as soon as I can."

I peeled her arms from around me, and it was like tearing off my own skin. Every instinct screamed to hold on, to run, to grab her and Willow and tear open a portal to anywhere else.

But I didn't. I couldn't.

Leah nodded, and I felt her turn, felt her footsteps carrying her back toward Willow, back toward safety.

I didn't move. I just watched her go—a bright, beautiful presence growing smaller with each step, the infection on her arm a dark smudge that would soon be burned away by transformation and magic.

She reached Willow, and I saw them embrace, saw Willow's hand come up to cradle the back of Leah's head in a gesture so tender it made my throat close.

Then Mother Darkness struck.

Long tendrils—thick as my arms, slick and horrid—snaked out from the creature behind me with horrifying speed. They wrapped around my arms and legs before I could even think to struggle, lifting me off my feet with the casual ease of a child picking up a doll. The world blurred as I was drawn backward with frightening velocity, pulled toward that pulsing palace-creature that wore my home's face like a death mask.

The last thing I saw through the Weave was Willow opening a portal—a tear in reality that blazed with bruised purple light and the promise of home. Leah stumbled through it, Willow's arm around her shoulders, and then they were gone.

The portal snapped shut.

Leah was safe.

And I was already being swallowed by Mother Darkness, dragged into the crystalline depths of her body, into the twisted halls of my own palace rendered in nightmare architecture.

Thank you, baby girl. Thank you for being brave enough to look.

The tendrils tightened, and the creature that wore my face leaned close enough that I could feel the wrongness radiating off it like heat.

"Welcome home, Cáitlín," it whispered with my voice. "Let me show you what I've made for you."

And then there was only the sick purple-blue-black glow of Mother Darkness's interior, and the sensation of being pulled deeper, deeper, deeper into her vast and ancient heart.

CHAPTER THIRTY-SEVEN
A Pantomime of Glory

The movement ceased, and I found myself lying on a perfectly smooth surface.

For a long moment, I just breathed. In and out. In and out. My heart hammered against my ribs, and my head spun with vertigo from the violent journey through Mother Darkness's body. I'd expected to be thrown around like a rag doll, carved up by crystalline edges, destroyed in some casual, thoughtless way. But my landing had been perfectly gentle, almost tender —like being set down by a careful parent.

I was still alive.

That realization sent a chill through me that had nothing to do with temperature.

Slowly, I pushed myself up from the floor, my palms flat against the surface. Through the Weave, everything around me glowed with that sick purple-blue-black luminescence—the floor, the walls, the vaulted ceiling above. I could make out shape and structure but not fine details. Still, even in the Weave, the architecture resolved itself perfectly. My breath caught in my throat.

Mother of Waters.

I stood in the reception chamber of the Vermilion Palace. Or rather, I stood in a poor copy of it—a reflection seen through warped glass and faulty memory.

The proportions were subtly wrong, like a photograph

stretched or compressed. The ceiling soared too high in some places, pressed too low in others. The throne sat where it should, but it appeared featureless, a blank sculpture with only one seat instead of the triple throne that Willow and I shared. The graceful columns that should have framed the space were present but thick and clumsy, like a child had tried to draw them from description alone.

The room itself lacked the grandeur of even that small part of my home. This was just a hollow, misshapen memory—cold and empty and wrong in ways that made my skin crawl. It was the uncanny valley made architecture, familiar enough to recognize but alien enough to chill my blood and make me want to run.

"Well?" my voice said from the throne. "What do you think?"

I turned slowly, unwilling to give the creature the satisfaction of a startled reaction, and in the Weave, I watched that same black substance rise from inside the throne, oozing up like tar from a split seam in the world. It climbed, gathered, and shaped itself into my form with disturbing fluidity. The figure settled cross-legged on the seat, mimicking my preferred posture with mocking precision.

The magic of it was impressive, I had to admit. Unlike the palace around us, when viewed as raw magic, this thing had definition. Every surface was exact, as if the Weave itself had been forced to render it in cruel, intimate detail: my face, my hair, the set of my shoulders. But that precision only made the truth louder. There was nothing behind it. Hollow. A shell with no weight of life, no inner rhythm, no mess of organs or breath. Just surface pulled tight over emptiness, like a doll animated by the vast intelligence buried in these crystalline walls.

A puppet for something that had never known how to be real.

To my right, I felt something else—a presence that was not exactly physical, hovering just out of view like heat shimmer on summer pavement. Familiar. Beloved. Something I'd been sure was just an element of my grief, but I knew now was real.

"Nastasia?" I whispered, barely daring to hope.

To the end, she answered, her voice warm with affection and dark humor. *But let's not try to let that happen, dah?*

Relief flooded through me so intense it was almost painful. She was here. Not gone. Not lost. Still fighting.

"Oh, yes," the creature on the throne said, and hearing my own voice drip with false sympathy made my stomach turn. "Shame what happened to Nastasia. Her death was... well... your fault, now wasn't it?"

What a pompous bitch, Nas laughed in my mind. *You're definitely related.*

Funny, I thought back and even smirked. "No. Nastasia made her own choice. She died heroically." I kept my eyes on the false-Cait, letting steel creep into my voice. "The only tragedy was that she didn't understand what she was facing."

You can say that again, Nastasia added unhelpfully. *You know that hurt, right? Like a lot. Let me tell you, a knife in the chest? Oof.*

You've become quite the chatterbox, I replied, warmth and exasperation mixing in my thoughts.

I'm finally fully awake. By the way, the sex with Willow was so hot.

Heat flooded my face. *Well, shut up. I'm trying to figure out what to do here.*

Sorry. You just noodle for a bit. I'll watch.

Yeah, you do that. I dragged my attention back to the creature wearing my skin. "So, here we are. Finally. I figured you'd just do whatever it is you want to do and be done with it—not monologue like some B-movie villain."

"But I want to savor this, sister," she said, and the word sister came out with genuine warmth that made my skin crawl. "I am also a Queen of the Fae, after all."

The claim hit me like a slap.

I snorted before I could stop myself, the sound harsh and disbelieving in the empty chamber. Like hell she was. "Oh, really? Do tell."

The false-Cait leaned forward, and for a moment, the expression was so perfectly mine—eager, earnest, desperately wanting to be understood—that I felt something twist in my chest. "I'm the oldest. Therefore, I'm the next in line for the Vermilion Throne."

I stared at the thing on the throne, and beneath my anger, beneath my fear, I felt something unexpected: pity.

She really believed it. This creature made of severed emotion and crystallized rage, this appendage wrapped around a lost soul—she genuinely thought she was alive. Thought she was Drusera. Thought she had a claim to my throne, my home, my life.

It was sad, in the way that broken things always are.

But I wasn't going to brook any challenge to my authority. The Vermilion Seat was mine. Earned. Fought for. Bled for. Died for.

"You have to have a soul to be considered for that position," I said quietly, letting each word fall like a sharp-edged rock. "You don't qualify."

"But I do have a soul." The creature's voice rose, defensive now. The palace rumbled. "What I need is a body."

"No." I shook my head, and I let all the sorrow I felt color my voice. Let her hear it. Let her understand what she was. "What you are is a tragedy. A creature that doesn't know what it is. You're not my sister." I paused, making sure she was listening, making sure this landed. "You're just what remains of her mind when all the rest is gone. You're the anger, the hurt, the betrayal. The parts Badb cut away so Drusera could survive her imprisonment."

For a heartbeat, the false-Cait's facade flickered—the smooth surface rippling like disturbed water. I saw something beneath it, something vast and ancient and furious.

Then she moved.

One moment she was on the throne, the next her hands were around my throat, and I was airborne. My back slammed into the crystal wall with bone-jarring force, and my head cracked against the surface hard enough that stars exploded in my thoughts.

"I am Drusera!" she growled, and the voice was no longer mine—it was layered, multiple, the sound of a thousand throats screaming in unison. "I am all that she ever was!"

Her fingers dug into my throat, and I couldn't breathe, couldn't speak. I just stared into my own face twisted with rage and saw the truth written there: she believed it. She believed it. And that belief was the most dangerous thing about her.

I waited, because I wouldn't waste my first hit until I knew where it would matter. She wanted me living, after all.

As suddenly as the violence had come, it ended. The creature dropped me, and I crumpled against the wall, gasping for air. She stepped back and made a show of brushing imaginary dust off herself—my mannerisms, my gestures, rendered obscene by the casual violence that had preceded them.

Was that how people saw me?

No, Dorogaya, she's insane, Nas said, her voice tight with concern.

Ya think? I thought back, fighting to stay conscious as black spots bloomed in my vision.

"Now," she said sweetly, as if nothing had happened, "no more of that talk."

My throat ached, and I could feel bruises already forming. But I pushed myself upright, refusing to stay down, refusing to show weakness.

"Let's walk," the creature said and held out a hand—my hand, offering comfort with fingers that had just tried to crush my windpipe.

I didn't take it. "Sorry if I don't trust you," I said, voice hoarse, "but kidnapping my daughter and all."

Something flickered across the pantomime face—disappointment?—but she turned away, moving toward one of the distorted archways.

She led me through the "palace," such as it was, and with each step, the horror of it deepened.

Nothing was truly misshapen, just... wrong. Fundamentally, unsettlingly wrong.

Hallways stretched either too long or too short, their perspectives broken and dreamlike. In places, shards of crystal hung from the ceiling like frozen rain, or protruded from the floor at odd angles, or grew from corners where walls met in geometries that shouldn't exist. It really was like a child's memory—distorted by time and imperfect understanding, reconstructed from fragments and feeling rather than facts.

But there were places where the details were perfect.

We passed through what should have been a sitting room, and the proportions were flawless, every measurement exact. The placement of the windows—though they showed nothing but swirling purple-black void—matched my memory down to the inch.

Then we reached the commons that should have held the garden, and I stopped breathing.

The space was perfect. Not almost perfect—perfect. The columns were exactly right, their spacing and height, and the delicate carved details all precisely as they existed in my true home.

This thing had studied this garden. Watched it. Memorized it.

Because this was where Willow and I had planted flowers together. Where we'd laughed and gotten dirt under our fingernails and almost kissed between the flowers. Where we'd built something beautiful in a world that so often demanded ugliness.

And Mother Darkness had watched somehow, perhaps through the creature that had infiltrated the palace, the one I'd eventually crushed.

The garden itself was filled with knife-edged crystals that jutted from the floor like a field of frozen blades. Each one, flooded with magic, was shaped loosely like a flower—here a rose, there a lily, scattered tulips, daffodils, and honeysuckle, even the starblind bells—rendered in razor-sharp geometry. Beautiful and deadly, a garden that would cut a person to ribbons if they tried to walk through it.

Here sat perfect metaphor for what this creature had made: something that looked like love but was only capable of harm.

I stood at the edge of that crystalline garden, and I understood with terrible clarity exactly how closely Mother Darkness had been watching.

How much she wanted it for herself.

How much she wanted to be me.

"Beautiful, isn't it?" the false-Cait said beside me, and she sounded genuinely proud. "I remember everything, you see. Every moment. Every choice." She turned to me, and in the Weave, I saw her smile—my smile, worn like a trophy. "I know you better than you know yourself, sister. Because I am you. Just older. Wiser. Stronger."

No, I thought, staring at the crystal flowers. *You're not me. You're what I could have become if I'd let the anger win. If I'd let the hurt turn me into nothing but rage.*

I was Fae, and that came with its own brand of casual violence and dangerous desires—the predatory grace, the swift retribution, the ancient hungers and instincts. But it wasn't this. It wasn't rage curdled into purpose. It wasn't hurt crystallized into an entire existence.

I could lose and survive without demanding vengeance. I could be hurt and still choose mercy. I could hold anger without letting it consume everything I was. And I could still show my children all too human love, even if Liz and Willow sparked something else.

Mother Darkness was what I'd become if every single day were me standing over Holley, watching the terror bloom in his eyes as he died of fright. If I'd let that one moment of savage satisfaction—that dark, primal vindication when the man who'd violated me finally paid the price—define everything that came after. If I'd turned that feeling into a religion, worshipped it, built a temple to it in my soul... and never left.

And suddenly, I understood what I had to do.

"Show me the rest," I said quietly. "Show me everything you've made."

CHAPTER THIRTY-EIGHT
A Tug of War

And so, she did. She gave me a grand tour.

There was no elevator—no practical consideration for movement through space like a real building would require. Instead, she simply grabbed me around the waist and carried me, launching upward through the distorted tower with dizzying speed. We rose through the twisted architecture, past crystalline corridors and warped chambers, until we reached the top of the central tower.

There we stopped.

I expected a throne room—some grand but twisted vision of my own seat of power. But there was nothing here except an open platform exposed to the starry sky above, and in the center, before that massive octagonal mirror of obsidian, sat the figure I'd seen from the crater's edge.

Avra.

The God-Empress of Oşen, motionless as a statue.

"Here," false-Cait said, her voice soft with something that might have been pride. "See through her eyes."

Before I could ask what she meant, an oily hand covered my eyes, and the world lurched.

I reeled, vertigo slamming into me like a physical blow, and nearly fell. But false-Cait's arm wrapped around my waist, holding me upright with surprising gentleness as my consciousness suddenly split, fractured, expanded into something it was never meant to be.

Vision, sharp and clear, filled my head.

Avra stared blankly into the black mirror, and her face reflected back perfectly in that polished obsidian surface. And she was... beautiful. Heartbreakingly beautiful. Upswept ears like mine, elegant and pointed. Grey and black irises—storm clouds shot through with shadow—stared back from a narrow face with delicate features: a refined nose, regal cheekbones, a mouth that had probably once smiled easily. Her skin glimmered with that same iridescent sheen as the other Kyliri I'd met, Umbrá and... Aoife.

But her eyes were empty. Hollow. A puppet's eyes, glassy and distant.

No one was home.

"Is she alive?" I asked, my voice barely more than a whisper.

"Oh, yes," false-Cait replied with casual cruelty, as if discussing the weather. "I have her in thrall. Her mind is cornered in her own head, pushed back into the smallest, darkest part of her consciousness. I'm simply using her to see. To watch. To touch your world through her connection to it."

Bile rose in my throat. I wanted to vomit, to scream, to tear this creature apart with my bare hands.

It was an abomination.

Change someone? I wasn't above that—I'd done it, would do it again if necessary. Alter their soul even? Yes. I could do that too. I'd done it to Maggie. Transform them into something new, something Other? I'd just asked Willow to do exactly that to Leah.

But this? Trapping someone for years inside their own head, forcing them to watch as their body was used like a puppet, as their power was turned against others? Making them a prisoner in their own flesh with no hope of escape, no respite, just endless, crushing awareness of their violation?

That was torture of a kind I couldn't fathom. A cruelty so profound it made my worst sins look like mercy.

"Let her go," I said, fighting to keep my voice steady. "You won't need her. You have me now."

False-Cait gave an imperious laugh—my laugh, but empty of anything resembling humor. "Absolutely not. She's mine. She gave herself to me to change a world, and now she pays the price we agreed on. Forever."

My blood ran cold. "A Fae bargain?" I asked, though I already knew the answer.

"Indeed," false-Cait said, and I could hear the satisfaction in her voice. "She belongs to me. Body, mind, and soul. And no one can touch her. No one can break our contract. She is mine until the stars go dark and the universe ends."

I thought of the bargain I'd made with this creature. Of how specific and short-lived I'd been with the wording, making sure the bargain was to deliver, nothing else.

Avra had made no such provisions.

She'd been desperate, trying to save the other slaves and the women of Oşen, and she'd bargained with something she didn't understand. Something that wore a kind face and spoke with a kind voice but wasn't kind at all.

"Be careful," I said quietly, letting a note of warning creep into my tone. "That kind of obsession can be painful later. When you realize that owning something isn't the same as having it love you back."

If the words registered at all, she didn't show it. Her face remained impassive, unreadable.

She turned away from Avra's frozen form and grabbed me again, carrying me back down through the crystalline depths of her palace-body, descending into whatever fresh horror she had prepared below.

Behind us, Avra continued to stare into the black mirror, seeing everything and able to change nothing, trapped in an eternity of helpless witness.

I'll come back for you, I promised silently, though I had no idea how I'd keep that promise.

We returned to the mock reception chamber, and false-Cait glided back to the throne with eerie grace, settling into the seat as if she'd never left.

"So, Mother Darkness," I said, keeping my voice casual, conversational.

The chamber rumbled—a deep, visceral vibration that came from the walls themselves, from the crystalline structure that surrounded us. The creature stood abruptly, and when it spoke, the voice wasn't mine anymore. It was layered, resonant, booming from a thousand throats at once.

"Don't call me that," it thundered, and I felt the words in my bones. "I am not the mother of anything. I am Drusera! And you will address me as such."

I held my ground, though every instinct screamed to take a step back. "So... Drusera," I said, emphasizing the name with just enough edge to let her know I was humoring her, buying time while my mind raced through possibilities, escape routes, anything that might get me out of this alive. "Tell me. How does one go about taking a body? I mean, I'm kind of in here." I tapped my temple. "And I'm pretty sure I'm not going to just let you push my thoughts into a corner like you did to Avra."

She sat again, the rage draining from the room as quickly as it had come, and that creepy imitation of my smile crawled across her face—slow, predatory, knowing.

"Oh, you'll give your body to me," she purred. "Freely."

I raised an eyebrow, letting skepticism drip from both syllables. "Will I?"

"You will," she said with absolute certainty, leaning forward like she was sharing a delicious secret. "Because if you don't, I will hunt them relentlessly. Leah may be off limits, but Elizabeth. Katie. Willow." She paused, savoring each name like a fine wine. "Anyone else who loves you. Anyone who knows you. I'll peel them apart slowly, make them beg for death, and you'll watch it all through Avra's eyes until there's nothing left of your world but ash and screaming."

Ice flooded my veins, but I pushed down on the absolute dread that threatened to choke me. Kept my face neutral. Kept breathing.

"I see," I said carefully. "But if you take my body and inhabit it, won't that make you vulnerable? And I think Mother Morrigan..."

"Mother Morrigan!" it shrieked, cutting me off mid-sentence. The false-Cait's face contorted with rage and something else—fear. "She's a beast. A monster of the primordial chaos. She has no power here. She can't touch me in this place!"

The words hung in the air, and suddenly, I understood.

I was thunderstruck by the revelation, by the sheer impossibility of what she'd just admitted.

She didn't know.

She had no idea that I carried Mother Morrigan. That the mantle had passed to me. That her greatest fear was already sitting in this room, wearing my skin.

Don't, Dorogaya, Nastasia said urgently, her presence pressing against my consciousness like a hand on my shoulder. *You'll lose yourself. The power will consume you.*

Sorry, Nas. No choice.

I pulled on the power—not gently, not carefully, but with both hands and all my will. I ripped it up from the depths where it lived, let it flood through every cell of my body until I burned with it, until I was it.

"I'm yours," I whispered, and the words sealed it.

I allowed her to fully invest herself, just as I had in Boston. I let her pour into me like water seeking its level, and it was like swallowing a star, like containing the sun inside my ribcage. I thought I'd be nothing in this moment—that she would overwhelm everything I was, drown me in her vastness, erase Cait Reagan like a bad line in an old drawing.

But it was quite the opposite.

She and I became one.

For a brief, beautiful moment, I became aware of things that simply couldn't be—shouldn't be—things that would break a mortal mind like glass under a hammer.

Other worlds spinning in the void like soap bubbles. Every death on Earth, past and present and yet to come, spilled out before me like a tapestry. Every last moment. Every last breath. Every flatlined monitor or peaceful end in dreams or horrid conclusion in violence. I saw them all, felt them all, knew them all with terrible intimacy.

And it didn't break me.

Every spell, every bit of magic, every possible permutation

of the Weave became mine to command. I held the fundamental forces of creation in my mind like a child holds building blocks, understanding how they fit together, how they could be taken apart and reassembled into new configurations.

I was infinite.

And I gritted my teeth, because it fucking hurt. I couldn't contain this for long.

"What are you doing?" false-Cait said, and for the first time, I heard genuine panic in that stolen voice. "Stop! Stop!"

She launched herself at me. I lashed out, encasing it in magic with a gesture.

"You can stay right there, thanks," I said pleasantly. It wouldn't last, I knew. Eventually, she'd throw everything at me. And that wouldn't be something I could just hand-wave away.

Mother Darkness shook with rage, the entire palace-creature convulsing around me, tilting the floor at impossible angles as she tried to throw me off balance, to make me stumble, to assert any kind of control.

I simply hovered above it, rising into the air with no more effort than breathing. I hung there for a moment, feet dangling, hands on my hips—completely unbothered by her tantrum.

I looked around, really looked, with the vision of a goddess. And what I saw?

Rubbish.

Without her attention, without her magic focused to make it seem grander than it was, the palace was just… sad. The walls sparkled dully with mismatched magic, spells layered on top of each other with no coherent design. What could have been a beautiful thing—what should have been beautiful—looked drab and thrown-together, like a child's art project made from scavenged materials. Cracks spidered across the crystalline walls in delicate fracture patterns. The throne was actually split in two, held together by nothing but a desperately spun bit of the Weave.

"Sad, sister," I said softly, and that word—sister—carried such a different meaning now. Not mockery. Not anger. Just profound, aching sorrow for what she could have been and wasn't.

Through my expanded awareness, I traced the lines of power that stretched downward through the walls, through the floor, deeper into the body of Mother Darkness herself. They pulsed like arteries, feeding her, sustaining her, connecting her to the soulstone at her core. And beyond to Crann Bethad.

That would be a problem.

This was going to be a tug of war, and I didn't actually know if I could win. My power now came from Mother Shaddan herself, but Mother Darkness's came from the World Tree. We were two sides of the same coin, drawing from similar, nearly infinite wells.

It should have terrified me, but all I felt was oddly... annoyed.

As if reading my mind, tentacles lashed out from the walls —thick, muscular things of crystallized shadow that moved with serpentine intelligence. They snatched at me, wrapping around my arms, my legs, my throat, pulling me down toward the floor with crushing strength.

I struggled. I burned them—called up fire and lightning and noxious chemical flames that ate through matter like acid. Tentacles blackened and fell away, crumbling to ash.

But for every one I destroyed, three more appeared. They erupted from the walls, the floor, the ceiling, an endless tide of grasping appendages that pulled and tore and squeezed. I couldn't keep up. Couldn't burn them fast enough. The more I destroyed, the faster they regenerated.

I pursed my lips in irritation. I wasn't worried. I just felt weirdly put-out considering I was currently being crushed to death by an eldritch horror. "All the fucking power in the world, and I'm still going to lose?"

One or two, I could handle easily. This was overwhelming.

"NO!" Mother Darkness bellowed, and the sound was agony—pure, primal, world-ending rage.

The false-Cait simply evaporated like morning mist, the black substance dissolving into nothing. The tentacles around me burned away in an instant, consumed by my fire when no more took their place.

Another bellow that nearly deafened me, shaking the palace-creature from foundation to apex. "She's mine!"

But the rage wasn't directed at me.

It was directed outward at something beyond these walls. Something outside had captured her attention and pulled her focus away from me for just a moment.

Something had distracted her.

I let my consciousness simply expand, as if it had been a power I'd always had. Two sets of instincts settled into place, and the world arranged itself accordingly.

Outside, Aoife had snatched Avra from her perch on the platform. She was trying... to help. I didn't have to wonder how she knew. Off in the distance, through that same... knowing, for lack of a better word, I found Liz and Willow at the edge of the crater.

Thanks to my children? Family? Lovers? I wasn't sure of the right word. They'd bought me a few minutes. Maybe less. But it would be enough.

Finish this, Dorogaya, Nastasia urged, her presence bright and fierce in my head.

"Too fucking right, Nas," I answered, grinning despite everything—despite the pain, the irritation, and the impossible odds. "Too fucking right."

CHAPTER THIRTY-NINE
JUST EXHALE AND STEP

I floated out of the reception hall and made the first right, following the mental map of my own palace overlaid on this broken mockery. I reached the place where the opening should be—the archway that led to the spiral stairs descending into the heart of the Vermilion Palace.

It simply wasn't there.

Just smooth, unbroken crystal wall, glowing with that sickly purple-blue light.

I scowled in frustration, pressing my hand against the surface as if I could will an entry into existence. "It should be right here."

"Maybe it is," Nastasia said.

And this time her voice wasn't in my head. It came from over my shoulder—clear, sharp, perfectly real.

I spun. "Nas?"

Hovering beside me, translucent and ghostly but there—actually, impossibly there—was Nastasia Volkova. Her form shimmered like heat haze, edges blurring into the air around her, but her face was as I remembered it: sharp cheekbones, knowing eyes, that smirk that said she knew something you didn't.

"So," I said, throat tight with emotion. "Not alive?"

She shook her head, and even that small movement had an ethereal quality to it, like watching someone underwater. "No. Not yet. But maybe you'll fix that." She gestured at herself—at the ghostly outline of her body. "I'm inside you. When I died, you grabbed my soul and all that I was. Snatched me right out of death's hands."

Just like my mother had done.

I actually could snatch a soul from death itself.

The realization sent a shiver through me, the power and the responsibility.

"Yeah, sorry about that," I said, not sure if I was apologizing for saving her or for the circumstances that had made it necessary.

"Well, it's no picnic, being stuck in your head with no way to do anything," Nastasia said dryly. "Months of it. Watching everything, experiencing everything, but unable to speak, unable to touch, unable to do. But then again." She spread her translucent hands, examining them with clinical interest. "I'm still in one piece. So I can't complain—yet."

I grinned. I couldn't help it. The sheer absurdity of it— floating in the belly of an eldritch horror, having a casual conversation with my dead girlfriend's ghost while the entire structure shook with rage around us.

And then I laughed. A real laugh, born of relief and joy and the simple fact that Nas was here, still Nas, still snarky and brilliant and herself.

I tried to hug her, reaching out instinctively, but my arms just passed right through her form like smoke. The sensation was strange—cold but not cold, present but absent, there but not there.

"I love you," I said, meaning it with every fiber of my being.

"I know," she answered, and that smirk deepened. Then she pointed at the blank wall where the stairs should be. "And that wall isn't a wall."

I nodded, understanding immediately. A thin growth of karanite. Something meant to keep intruders out—or prisoners in.

And I also understood that if I went through it, Mother

Morrigan would be forced out of me. Not a terrible thing given that my body would likely fail in minutes.

There was nothing for it.

I gathered my will and glimmerstepped.

It was like wrenching myself through a straw.

The Morrigan's presence—that vast, cosmic power that had filled me moments before—drew back in a long, thin strand, stretched to its limit. The connection attenuated, grew gossamer-thin, but held—barely. The colossal power I'd had just a second before felt sucked away like water down a drain, and a void appeared in my chest—empty, aching, wrong. I landed unevenly on stone steps and nearly tumbled forward.

I caught myself against the wall, breathing hard. Colossal cosmic power, sure, but karanite was karanite; it sucked away magic.

My entire body hurt. Every muscle ached. Every nerve sang with pain. Now I knew what it felt like to be pushed through cheesecloth: supremely unpleasant.

"Nas?" I whispered, suddenly terrified that I'd lost her in the transition.

I'm still here, she answered, and her voice was back in my head where it belonged—warm, present, and alive in the only way she could be. *My soul is hitched to yours, I think. Wherever you go, I go.*

The palace-thing shook again—a massive, convulsive tremor that sent me staggering down the stairs, one hand on the wall for balance. Whatever was happening outside, Mother Darkness was not happy about it.

There was no landing where the Veilstone would be in my palace, which made sense. It hadn't existed when Drusera had been alive—that was an addition, Morvaine's ward, our protection.

I continued downward, taking the spiral stairs as fast as I dared while the structure trembled around me. I picked out little details around me: cracks spreading across the walls, chunks of crystal breaking loose and tumbling past me, the groan of stressed architecture that had never been meant to move this much.

Finally, I reached the level where the wardstone would be—should be—in my own palace.

The space was completely encrusted with razor-sharp crystals.

They jutted from every surface like a forest of blades—some as thin as needles, others as thick as my arm, all of them gleaming with that purple-black oozing magic and sharp enough to slice through flesh and bone without resistance. It was a killing field, a trap, a final defense against anyone who might reach this far.

I pushed my way through anyway, feeling the crystals catch on my clothing, tear through fabric, and cut at my exposed skin. Pain bloomed across my arms, my face, my shoulders—dozens of small cuts that bled freely. But I could see it through the forest of death: right where the wardstone would have been, anchored in the exact same spot.

A crystal, glowing deep crimson like a beating heart. Roughly as long as my forearm. The size of an American football.

Drusera's soulstone.

The palace shook again—harder this time, violent enough that I heard something crack in the superstructure. There was a great shuddering boom that rattled my teeth, and I lost my balance, pinwheeling forward. I almost tumbled directly onto the lethal crystalline spikes that would have impaled me like a pincushion.

As it was, I caught myself with my hand, and a blade-sharp edge sliced my palm open from thumb to wrist. I hissed in pain, blood welling hot and fast, but I didn't stop. Couldn't stop.

I reached Drusera's soulstone, wrapping my bleeding hand around its smooth, warm surface, and focused my perception of the Weave to understand what I was seeing.

Oh.

Oh!

Mother Darkness grew because Drusera's soulstone funneled the magic of Crann Bethad—the World Tree, the source of all Fae magic, the wellspring of our creation. The soulstone acted like a tap, drawing infinite power from the source and feeding it into the appendage that had grown around it. As long as the stone remained anchored here, Mother Darkness would continue to exist, continue to grow, continue to spread.

Remove the stone, sever the connection.

I took a breath, steadying myself.

"Nas, are you ready to go?"

I was ready when I stabbed your aunt, she shot back with characteristic bluntness. *Quit dawdling, Cait.*

I took hold of the soulstone with both hands despite the agony in my sliced palm, wrapping my fingers around it, feeling its warmth pulse against my skin like a second heartbeat.

Tendrils sprung from the walls—thick, desperate things that wrapped around my waist, my legs, trying to pull me away, trying to pry my hands loose.

"No! You can't! You're mine!" Mother Darkness roared, and the sound was apocalyptic—the death scream of something vast and ancient realizing it was about to end.

Then the most pitiable cry that twisted my insides. "Please," she begged. "Don't"

My ears rang with the sound, pain spiking through my skull.

One... two... three... I counted mentally, centering myself, finding that still point of calm at my core.

Then I blew out a breath and glimmerstepped.

There was a great cracking sound—like a mountain splitting in half—and the musical tinkling of a million shards as Drusera's soulstone tore loose from its base. Tendrils snapped like broken cables, whipping through the air. The entire palace screamed.

At first, there was just the edge of the Ma—that liminal space between worlds where glimmerstep took me, that grey nowhere that existed outside normal reality. But then I dove deeper, Drusera's crystalline coffin still clutched in my arms, pushing through the Ma with everything I had—through the walls of Mother Darkness's palatial body.

The instantaneous nature of the step turned slower and slower as I lost momentum, as the weight of passing through all that karanite dragged at me like an anchor. The step that should have taken no time at all stretched out, became long, became a journey instead of a transition.

The faded edges of the impregnable palace walls flashed past—quickly at first, but not fast enough. I could feel Mother Darkness reaching for me, feel her rage and desperation clawing at the edges of my consciousness. Mother Morrigan let me loose as I slipped from Shaddan; her grip peeled away.

And then we were out.

But I didn't return. Didn't snap back to the Vermilion Palace or the crater or anywhere familiar.

I just… stopped.

Hanging in the grey void of the Ma, Drusera's soulstone clutched to my chest, with nowhere left to go.

I was trapped…

…in the Ma.

And there were things here.

I wasn't alone.

CHAPTER FORTY

HER RING

I wasn't sure how long I floated there, my body curled around the soulstone like a child clutching a treasured toy. There was no sense of time in this place—no heartbeat to mark the seconds, no breath to measure the minutes. Only my own thoughts, spiraling endlessly in the grey nothing.

Honestly, I didn't want to leave.

I could feel things moving around me—massive, incomprehensible things that existed in the spaces between spaces. Entities that drank little Fae Queens like soda pop and crushed the can without a second thought. Leviathans of the void that made Mother Darkness look like a child's nightmare.

And I... I couldn't bring myself to care.

They would investigate like circling sharks, nibbling and pulling at my existence. Once they tasted it, they would circle back and strike.

I would be gone. Drusera would be gone—finally, mercifully released from her crystalline prison. Willow could inherit the realm and do what she wanted with it, rule it better than I ever had. Liz and the kids would be safe. The bargain would be broken by my absence, rendered void by my death.

And this place was warm. And quiet.

No monsters clawing at the gates. No people depending on me, looking to me for answers I didn't have. No expectations pressing down on my shoulders like stones. No more fighting.

No more losing people I loved. No more being afraid.

Just... peace.

Something brushed against me—hungry and curious—sending my weightless form drifting in the void, floating from nowhere to nowhere else. The space between worlds, where nothing truly existed, and everything was possible.

A mote appeared in the distance.

Small and scented of wildflowers—impossible in this place without smell, without sensation, and yet there nonetheless. And I could see it in the infinite black, a pinprick of light where no light should exist. I shouldn't have been able to. I knew that on some fundamental level. But still, it was there: a little star that shone like a beacon, floating toward me through the grey.

I held Drusera's soulstone in my hands like the precious cargo it was and just watched, transfixed.

The star grew a little, spreading outward, petals unfurling. An opening. A doorway. A way back.

Beyond was noise and tumult and feelings and horrors—life in all its chaotic, painful glory.

And love.

There was love there. So much love it blazed like the sun. It drowned out everything else—the fear, the pain, the exhaustion. Just pure, incandescent love reaching through the void, searching, calling.

The Faerie in me—that cold, logical part that had made impossible choices and survived impossible odds—refused. Pulled back. I wanted the quiet, the peace, the ending.

But a tiny part that was so simple and still human despite everything that had changed? It watched in fascination. What would it be? What would that mote become?

Something slipped through the gap—pushing through from the other side with desperate determination, wriggling and seeking.

Fingers. Five of them. A hand, reaching into the void, palm up, fingers spread wide in invitation.

And on one of those fingers, sparkling in the light that wasn't light, catching reflections that couldn't exist: a diamond ring.

Liz!

My heart clenched—an organ that shouldn't even be beating in this place, but somehow still ached with recognition.

Don't do it, I told myself firmly. *This is warm and quiet and an ending. That is pain. That is loss. That is watching everyone you love grow old and die while you remain. That is making choices that will haunt you for eternity. That is being afraid every single day that you won't be enough, that you'll fail them, that you'll lose them.*

That is life. And life hurts.

Reach, Nastasia whispered quietly. *Reach, Cait. Don't let love go. Ever.* A pause, heavy with meaning, but with no regret. *I didn't.*

The words hit me like a physical blow.

Nas, who'd held onto love even when it cost her everything. Who'd died protecting the woman she loved. Who'd chosen pain and self-sacrifice over life because some things—some people—were worth bleeding for. Because she thought I deserved to live.

I deserve to live. I deserve love.

I closed my eyes, feeling tears slide down my cheeks and float away.

I opened my eyes, and Liz's hand was still there, still reaching, still waiting with infinite patience for me to decide.

"Reach, god damn it!" Liz shouted from what seemed like an interminable distance.

I'm sorry, I thought to the quiet, to the peace, to the ending I'd almost embraced. *But I can't. Not yet. Not while there are still people who need me. Not while she's still reaching. Not while there's still love.*

…and I reached back.

My fingers found hers in the grey nothing—solid, real, and warm. And the moment we touched, something in the void screamed. Light exploded around me, searing and brilliant, and I felt myself being pulled, dragged back through the doorway toward noise and chaos and beautiful, terrible life.

And Liz—my Liz, my love, my home—pulled me through.

Back to the world.

Back to the pain.

Back to her.

Power flooded through me as Mother Morrigan regained her hold—snapping back into place like a rubber band, but more tenuous, like it had been before I'd offered myself to her fully. The cosmic awareness, the infinite knowledge, the ability to command the Weave itself—all of it diminished. Still immense. Still dangerous. But no longer everything.

I landed in Liz's arms.

The impact drove the breath from my lungs, and for a moment, I just lay there, stunned, clutching Drusera's soulstone to my chest while Liz held me like she'd never let go.

"How... how did you find me?" I asked, my voice cracking with a million swirling emotions that crashed over me in waves: anger at being pulled back, despondency at what I'd almost chosen, love so fierce it hurt, hope that felt empty but wouldn't leave, and others I couldn't even name.

"I didn't," Liz said softly, and her voice carried so much tenderness it made my chest ache. She glanced up. "Willow did. She just opened a rift so I could grab you."

My heart stuttered in my chest.

"How?" I asked, still trying to process what had happened, how she'd reached me in that grey nowhere between worlds. "The necklace?" I reached up instinctively, feeling its weight still resting against my sternum.

Willow knelt down next to us and ran a hand through my hair. Her face wasn't quite pointed toward mine.

"The Moonflower," she said simply, as if that explained everything. As if it were the most obvious thing in the world. "It bonds us forever. I just followed that bond." Her fingers tightened slightly in my hair, possessive and yet tender.

"I helped," Aoife interjected, her voice carrying a note of pride and exhaustion. "I'm sorry you weren't here to see my heroics. But I'm not sure what to do with her." She pointed at a figure on the ground next to her, crumpled and still.

Avra.

The God-Empress of Oşen lay unconscious, covered in dirt

and soot like she'd been dragged through a warzone. Her dress—that iridescent white that had seemed so pristine atop Mother Darkness—was torn and filthy, no longer white at all. She breathed shallowly, her chest rising and falling with disturbing irregularity.

Free. Finally free after decades of imprisonment in her own body.

But at what cost?

"It's too much," Liz said suddenly, and her voice broke. I looked up and saw tears glistening in her eyes—anger and sorrow and exhaustion written across her face. "I won't do this anymore."

The words crushed my chest.

I placed a hand on hers, feeling the coolness of her skin, the solidity of her presence. "I know. Just… Just… "

My heart felt like it was being torn out. My ribs squeezed the air from my lungs, making it hard to breathe, hard to think. Don't go. Please don't go. I need you.

But I couldn't say it. Wouldn't say it. She deserved better than all this.

"I'm taking the children home," she whispered, and the finality in her voice was absolute. "And you're a fucking liar."

I blinked, thrown by the sudden shift. "About what this time?"

She snorted—a sharp, bitter sound that was almost a laugh. "That performance at the ball. Bloodfiend? Honestly, Cait." She shook her head. "I almost believed you, until you said that. You'd never say that in a million years. Bloody stupid."

Damn it. She'd seen right through it.

Of course she had.

I sighed. "I just don't want you hurt. And they will hurt you. The Fae don't forgive, Liz. They don't forget. If they think you're close to me, if they think they can use you to get to me —"

"They won't," she interrupted firmly, steel in her voice now. "Because we're leaving. And no one will know. And maybe one day, in a year, or a hundred, or a thousand, you'll figure it out. You'll find us." She paused, and her expression softened just slightly. "And maybe, if you're lucky, I'll listen to whatever explanation you've come up with."

Willow frowned but said nothing, and I loved her for it—for giving us this moment, for not interfering in something that wasn't hers to interfere with.

"I love you, Liz," I said softly, meaning it with every fiber of my being. "I'm just not who I was. I'm sorry."

She raised an eyebrow, and for a moment, I saw a flash of the woman I'd married—sharp, intelligent, unwilling to accept bullshit. "You're different in so many ways, but you're wrong about that. You're exactly who you've always been." She gestured off toward Mother Darkness. "You just threw yourself away to save someone you love—someone I love. I just wish it were enough. Or that it was over." Her voice cracked. "But it's not. And we can't be a part of it anymore. The kids can't be a part of it anymore."

I nodded morosely, feeling the truth of her words settle into my bones. She was right. I'd put them through enough—Leah's kidnapping, the Fae manipulations, the way I'd treated her, the constant fear, the endless danger. And there seemed to be no end in sight. The primarchs wouldn't stop. The threats wouldn't stop. And I couldn't guarantee their safety, not really, not while I wore the crown. And I still couldn't leave.

She helped me up, and I stood on shaking legs, still clutching Drusera's soulstone.

I wanted to say something—anything—that would make this better, that would ease the pain of this ending. But words failed me. So instead, I just hugged Liz, pulling her close and breathing in the familiar scent of her: Dragon's Blood,

"I'm so sorry," I whispered into her hair. For everything. For not being enough. For choosing this life. For loving you and still letting you go.

"I know," she said, and she hugged me back—fiercely, desperately, like she was trying to memorize the feeling. Then she pulled away, and the moment ended.

I looked down at the soulstone in my hands and sighed. I had no idea what to do with her.

I looked at Liz. "Now what?"

"Now we go back to the palace. You save Leah, and I take the kids home."

"But—" I started.

"I didn't have time," Willow cut in, guilt coloring her voice. "When I felt you slipping away, I had to choose. Get you back or save Leah." Her jaw tightened. "She's okay for the moment. The infection hasn't spread further. But even with Mother Darkness gone, she won't survive long. A few days at most, I think."

"Gone?" I looked north from where we stood, across the empty bed of what had once been the lake of Lindon Danu.

In the Weave, all that remained of Mother Darkness was a crumbling mass of magic—the palace-creature collapsing in on itself like a dying star. No movement. No life. No rage.

Just ruins.

The appendage had died when I'd severed it from its source. Without Drusera's soulstone to anchor it, to feed it power from Crann Bethadh, it had simply... ended.

"Nas?" I whispered, suddenly afraid that I'd lost her too in the chaos. "Are you still here?"

Unfortunately, she answered dryly, and I could hear the smirk in her mental voice. *You're not getting rid of me that easily.*

Relief flooded through me so intense it made my knees weak.

At least I hadn't lost everyone.

At least I still had Nas. And Willow.

At least I still had a chance to save Leah.

"Alright," I said, straightening my shoulders and feeling the weight of the crown—invisible but ever-present—settle back onto my head. "Let's go home."

CHAPTER FORTY-ONE
LEAH'S BLOOMING

I found Leah in the infirmary, and the sight of her stopped me cold.

Her breath came shallow and ragged, each inhalation a struggle. The pinprick of blackness that had marked her arm when I'd last seen her had grown into a malignant mass that covered most of her forearm now, spreading like ink through water. Dark tendrils crept up past her elbow, reaching toward her shoulder with inexorable hunger. And it was wrong, even for Mother Darkness. Without her to guide it, it was just a consuming, mindless growth.

She was dying.

Katie sat by her side, holding Leah's uninfected hand with desperate gentleness, as if afraid that gripping too hard might shatter her sister like glass.

When Katie looked up at me, the accusation that had lived in her eyes since the ball was gone—burned away by something more immediate, more visceral. The pain and fear for her sister was all that remained, raw and naked and pleading.

She launched out of the chair and threw her arms around me with bruising force, her face pressed into my shoulder. "Can you save her?"

The question hung in the air, heavy with hope, but I could hear the terror beneath that I might say no.

I nodded, wrapping one arm around Katie and holding her close. "Yes. But she'll be different."

"I don't care," Katie said immediately, fiercely, her voice muffled against my shirt. "I don't care if she's different. I don't care what you have to do. Just save her."

Liz stood by the door, arms crossed, watching with an unreadable expression. She didn't comment, didn't object, and I thought maybe—maybe—she understood what I was going to do. What transformation I was about to work on her daughter. Our daughter.

I didn't wait for permission anyway. Didn't ask. This was happening.

I gently pushed Katie aside, guiding her back to stand with Liz, and turned my full attention to Leah.

I drew deep into the power of Mother Morrigan—pulling it up from that well within me that connected to death itself, to endings and transformations and the fundamental forces that unmade and remade existence.

She started to slip in again, immediately. Two sets of instincts aligned, and my hands knew what my mind hadn't learned. I felt her pushing toward my soul, pressing against the boundaries of who I was, wanting to merge, to become indistinguishable from me. The presence was hungry, patient, inevitable.

I drew in a deep breath, steadying myself for the invasion.

There would be a price for this. I could feel it already—the weight of it settling into my bones, the subtle shift as Mother Morrigan's hold grew tighter. But I would pay it. Whatever it cost, however much of myself I lost in the process, Leah was worth it.

I reached down into her very substance—past skin and muscle and bone, down to the fundamental architecture of her soul—and began to unweave. Carefully, delicately, like picking apart a tapestry thread by thread, I found what I was looking for. It was there like I knew it would be. That mote of Dark Fae magic that had always lived inside her.

It was small. Barely more than a spark. A seed that had never been allowed to germinate.

I fed it.

Poured power into that tiny mote until it swelled, until it caught fire with possibility, and let it bloom forth into all it could be—all it should be. I coaxed it outward like encouraging a flower to open, watching as it spread through her soul like roots seeking purchase, like vines climbing toward sunlight. In one instant her soul was a flicker... and then it was a star, burning brightly.

Leah struggled on the bed, her body arching, and a whimper escaped her lips—small, pained, frighteningly young. But she didn't wake. Good. I hoped desperately that she wouldn't remember this—wouldn't retain the memory of being unmade and remade, of dying and being reborn.

Some transformations were too profound to witness from the inside. That, I knew.

I felt Mother Morrigan more fiercely now. Yes, it would definitely cost me. But it didn't matter.

Nothing mattered except the girl dying on this table.

Slowly, methodically, as one hand unspun Leah's form—dissolving the infection along with everything else, breaking her down to component parts—I took what remained and remade it.

Pale skin, smooth and unblemished. Brown hair with hints of auburn that caught nonexistent light, too lustrous to be human. Pretty gray eyes that would see the world differently now, would perceive magic and the fundamental weave of reality. Upswept ears—subtle, elegant, undeniably Fae. And organs that were... different.

Her soul, once the process started, bloomed like blue and purple starlight—still uniquely her, but very different. Her body spun itself back together with the life of Shaddan woven through every cell, the Vermilion pulse of the world.

Until finally—finally—she took in a deep breath.

A real breath.

"Mama?" she croaked.

The word was soft, confused, still half-dreaming.

I reached and touched her face. She felt the same on the outside at least, still recognizably Leah, still the girl I'd raised and loved and fought to protect. But through the Weave, I could see what she'd become: something other, something eternal, something that would outlive empires and watch civilizations rise and fall.

High Fae.

My daughter. My Faerie princess. Just like I'd promised her.

I kissed her forehead, feeling the warmth of her skin, the steady pulse of her heartbeat—a little slower now, more measured, perhaps the rhythm of immortality.

"Yes, baby girl," I answered, voice rough with emotion.

"I'm hungry," she whispered, and the simple, mundane complaint after everything we'd been through—after I'd literally rewritten her existence—was so perfectly, wonderfully normal that something broke loose in my chest.

I laughed. A real laugh, born of relief and joy and the sheer absurdity of it all. "You can have whatever you want."

Behind me, I heard Katie's sob of relief, felt Liz's presence shift as tension drained from the room.

Leah was safe. Changed. Transformed. But safe.

And I had just bound myself more tightly to Mother Morrigan, had felt her sink deeper into my soul with every thread I'd rewoven, every cell I'd transformed.

The price was coming due.

But as I held my little girl, I couldn't bring myself to regret it.

Not even a little bit.

EPILOGUE

I stood in the doorway, watching Liz close her suitcase and pile Jabba into his carrier. Liz wasn't unkind. She didn't rail or complain or say much of anything, really. She just packed quietly while I stood by, the silent observer.

Part of me wanted to slam shut the wards and tell her she couldn't leave. But I didn't. I wouldn't. Somewhere inside me, I'd found something still human. Leah had dredged it from wherever it had been hiding, and I wasn't going to let it go now.

Maybe it was just a remnant, but it was an ember, and I'd try to blow on it the best I could. I'd try to remember who I was and hope.

"I'm ready," Liz said, turning to me, suitcase in one hand, Jabba in the other.

I nodded. I couldn't speak past the lump in my throat.

We made our way to the lift and then down to the eastern side of the palace and to the Carriage House on the first floor.

Aoife was there with the kids. No one else. No one could see me send them off. Sithraine had made sure that everyone in the palace believed me. Willow was likewise absent, giving me space.

"I don't want to go mama," Leah said through her tears. "I want to stay with you."

"I know," I whispered as I knelt down to her, feeling my own eyes water.

"What if the other kids pick on me?" She rubbed absently at one pointed ear.

The corner of my mouth tilted up. "Ignore them," I said. Though part of me really wanted to tell her to use the spellbook I'd secreted into her suitcase. She needed to learn. And there wasn't anything in there that was too predatory. "Besides, you're the daughter of the Queen of the Vermilion Court. I think you'll be Queen of the school in no time. Just remember…"

"I know," she muttered. "Don't make any promises to anyone. Especially open-ended ones."

I grinned and pulled off my blindfold. "You can look at them now."

Her hand touched my face, and her finger slid under my eye across the blackened section of flesh. It was still mostly numb and I could barely feel it.

"When you're done being Queen, will you come home?" she asked.

I shifted my focus to Liz and then turned my face toward her, asking, not demanding.

"Maybe when Mama gets things sorted here, she can come back, and we can see if we can make things better," Liz said.

"I'll come back," I told Leah.

She gave me a tart grin and sniffed. "You promise?"

"When I'm done being Queen, I'll come back. I promise," I said.

The taste of embers and night-blooming jasmine filled my nose and mouth.

"Is that what it feels like?" Leah asked.

I nodded. "Yup. You're first Fae bargain. Now you promise you won't make any more?"

She nodded. "I promise I'll try."

I snorted a laugh. "Very good."

Katie wrapped me in a tight hug as soon as I stood upright. "I'm sorry, Mama. I know it's not your fault."

"It's not about fault," I told her. "It's about responsibility. And sometimes, for Faeries, it's just as hard as it is for you. We get hungry, too. But like you, I have to keep that instinct in check, you know?"

"I know," she answered.

Then Liz stepped over to us. "Why don't you two go wait in the car with Auntie Aoife?"

"She's still not talking to me?" I asked.

"She'll get over it," Liz said.

"And you?"

"I'll make you a deal," she said.

"Dangerous statement," I answered with a wan smile.

"You fix things here. You get this," she waved her hand in that 'you're whole deal' kind of way, "under control, and then you come back to Boston. Get your cannoli and coffee, and then come to the house, and we'll talk. That's all I can promise."

I nodded. "I'll finish what was started. Who knows, Mother Morrigan might let me go."

She snorted. "You're still Faerie, Cait. That's what you need to get a handle on."

"Yeah," I whispered.

There was an awkward moment where I didn't know what to do. I wanted to hug her, but I didn't dare. I hadn't earned that right. I'd done just the opposite. But then, she wrapped her arms around me and sniffed hard.

"Thank you," she whispered. "For bringing her home."

I nodded into her shoulder and squeezed her close. *Mine*, my thoughts said, but I pushed that feeling down. She wasn't mine. If I wanted that claim, I'd have to earn it. And as she'd pointed out, I was very far away from that.

Then she got in the car, and they pulled away.

I closed the carriage house doors and stood there for a long moment, listening to the echoes fade. Then I turned back toward the palace and the work I still had to do.

Back in the throne room, I watched as Night Pixies, on loan from their Queen, Selene, hung banners from the highest points. I chuckled as the crows squawked and cawed and the pixies shooed them away. But the mirth didn't last.

They were celebrating the coronation of a Queen who had just watched her family leave.

"She's gone then?" Sithraine said next to me.

"Yes," I answered morosely. "They left."

"Good," Sithraine said. "Shaddan is no place for humans, except the foolish or desperate."

I snorted. "No, I guess it isn't."

"It wasn't the power," I told her.

"What wasn't?"

"The reason I was so cruel and controlling. It was fear. I had these feelings and needs I didn't understand. And… they scared me, Sith. They still do."

"You'll learn balance eventually," she said. "You have to learn what you are first, then you can learn to temper it. Willow, the Night Queen, even me. We all had Fae childhoods. We learned over time how to quiet our darker natures when necessary. You… you simply haven't had the benefit of those years."

"No," I whispered. "It's not that. I know better than to let my instincts control me. I blew it. It wasn't the Morrigan, or even my nature. It was me. I let my darkness win. I did the same when I was a vampire. I let myself become a terror."

"Then you have much to think about," she said. "Why don't we take some tea and let these lovely ladies work?"

I nodded and followed her out.

Two days later, I was crowned.

The gathering was small, appropriate for a bereft house and a ruined court. Still, there were bright spots. The Night Queen attended and managed civility with Willow. Willow stayed at my side once the crown settled. And the Night Pixies were, improbably, fun.

It wasn't until after that things turned darker.

At midnight, four couriers arrived demanding entrance.

I received them in the throne room, as a Queen now, and they delivered their messages.

Irexielle. Aurex. Calerithon of the Azure Vow. Roselle.

All had declared war on the Vermilion Court, the Night Queen, and Morari.

Perfect for purpose.

We'd soon see if that was true.

Cait Reagan Will Return

In

FLAMEGLASS CROWN

ABOUT THE AUTHOR

Aoibh Wood lives in New England with her wife and their wonderful orange Tabby, who may or may not resemble an intergalactic gangster of some notoriety. She enjoys writing, playing guitar, and the occasional game or two.

From the world of Cait Reagan comes a new series

The Remi Shaw Adventures (Coming 2026)

A Demon's Kiss (Book 1)
Remi Shaw investigates the crimes Boston's preternatural unit ignores. When a missing lover brings vampire Valerie Cross through her door, Remi plunges into a demon conspiracy that could end the world. Somewhere between the lies and the blood is Vivian Locke, a seductive demon crime boss Remi wants badly enough to risk damnation.

THE SENATOR'S WIDOW

BUT I'M NOT A SUPERVILLAIN!!